HIGHLAND ROMANCE

"What if Richard already found the brooch, or Sir Leslie? Papa will be an absolute terror. He'll *insist* that I marry them. Him. Whomever." She covered her face, feeling ill. "This is a disaster."

A moment later, Kade gently pulled her hands away and gathered them to his chest. His gaze was tender and more than slightly amused.

"If you dare to laugh, Kade Kendrick, I swear I will throw you out the window."

"I wouldn't dream of it, sweetheart. But you know as well as I do that your father cannot make you marry anyone."

"No, but he and Mamma would pester me endlessly. And *everyone* will be talking about it, and *everyone* will be pressuring me to uphold the family honor. Either way, my life will be ruined."

He shook his head. "I won't allow that to happen."

"Kade, you don't understand. This is going to be—"

He let go of her hands and tipped up her chin. Then he lowered his head and . . .

Kissed her.

Every thought scattered to the four winds, and she felt like she was falling—falling *up* and into him . . .

Books by Vanessa Kelly

MASTERING THE MARQUESS
SEX AND THE SINGLE EARL
MY FAVORITE COUNTESS
HIS MISTLETOE BRIDE

The Renegade Royals
SECRETS FOR SEDUCING A ROYAL BODYGUARD
CONFESSIONS OF A ROYAL BRIDEGROOM
HOW TO PLAN A WEDDING FOR A ROYAL SPY
HOW TO MARRY A ROYAL HIGHLANDER

The Improper Princesses
MY FAIR PRINCESS
THREE WEEKS WITH A PRINCESS
THE HIGHLANDER'S PRINCESS BRIDE

Clan Kendrick
THE HIGHLANDER WHO PROTECTED ME
THE HIGHLANDER'S CHRISTMAS BRIDE
THE HIGHLANDER'S ENGLISH BRIDE
THE HIGHLANDER'S IRISH BRIDE
THE HIGHLANDER'S HOLIDAY WIFE
THE HIGHLANDER'S KILTED BRIDE

Anthologies
AN INVITATION TO SIN
(with Jo Beverley, Sally MacKenzie, and Kaitlin O'Riley)

Published by Kensington Publishing Corp.

The Highlander's Kilted Bride

Clan Kendrick

VANESSA KELLY

ZEBRA BOOKS
Kensington Publishing Corp.
www.kensingtonbooks.com

ZEBRA BOOKS are published by

Kensington Publishing Corp.
119 West 40th Street
New York, NY 10018

All Kensington titles, imprints, and distributed lines are available at special quantity discounts for bulk purchases for sales promotion, premiums, fund-raising, and educational or institutional use.

Special book excerpts or customized printings can also be created to fit specific needs. For details, write or phone the office of the Kensington Sales Manager: Kensington Publishing Corp., 119 West 40th Street, New York, NY 10018. Attn. Sales Department. Phone: 1-800-221-2647.

Zebra and the Z logo Reg. U.S. Pat. & TM Off.

First printing: September 2023
ISBN-13: 978-1-4201-5455-9
ISBN-13: 978-1-4201-5456-6 (eBook)

10 9 8 7 6 5 4 3 2 1

Printed in the United States of America

PROLOGUE

Inveraray Castle
Summer, 1814

When an eagle cried overhead, Kade Kendrick glanced up from his book. The magnificent bird drifted, held aloft by the invisible eddies of the summer breeze off Loch Fyne. The scent of roses and lilacs filled the air, along with the crispness of recently mown grass. The gardens behind the castle shimmered with color in the bright summer sunlight. The lovely afternoon had beckoned Kade to slip away to read, and he'd found the perfect place in a secluded nook under a stand of oak trees.

After the incessant fog and drizzle of the last three days that had confined most of the guests to the castle, the sunshine was a welcoming gift. In Kade's experience, clan gatherings were loud and rambunctious affairs, best held outdoors. At this one, Campbells had been cooped up with MacDonalds, Kendricks, and other bits and bobs of clan families invited to the Duke of Argyll's gathering.

Not everyone got along, as last night's argument between Kade's grandfather and Lord Kinloch had demonstrated. Grandda was a MacDonald, as was the wife of Lord Kinloch. But that kinship tie hadn't stopped them from brangling at earsplitting volumes. The argument had been about some fusty old battle and the role of Clan MacDonald. Grandda had taken offense over some minor detail and had ended up challenging Lord Kinloch to a duel. The Duke of Argyll, along with Kade's oldest brother, Nick, had been forced to intervene. The combatants had been separated and had then received a stern lecture from the duke, resulting in an uneasy peace.

The peace hadn't lasted. Two hours later, the twins—Kade's older brothers—had accidentally set a small out-building on fire when they'd tried to produce homemade fireworks. Poor Nick had rather blown his top over that one, especially after Grandda had defended the twins. Even the duke's patience had run out, and the twins and Grandda had been banished to their bedrooms for the rest of the evening.

Kade loved his family, and they usually made him laugh with their antics. But this time it was all rather embarrassing.

He returned his attention to his book. At least *he* wouldn't cause Nick any trouble. Still, his brother worried about him all the time. Everybody worried about him, mainly because he was sick so much, which sent everyone into a tizzy. Fortunately, he was so much better these last few months, which was the only reason Nick had let him come to the clan gathering.

Now Kade wished he'd stayed home at Castle Kinglas, where he could have studied in quiet and practiced his music. But Grandda had thought it would be a grand treat for him to spend time with the clans instead of holing himself up in the castle's quiet schoolroom with a bunch of *moldy old books*, as his grandfather called them.

"Ye might learn somethin' aboot being a proper Highlander, laddie," Grandda had said. "Instead of pokin' about on that piano and playing ditties by all those bloody *Sassenachs* and foreigners."

When Kade had pointed out that he was studying the

great Mozart, Grandda had scoffed that Germans were as bad as *Sassenachs*. He'd also waved off Kade's attempt to explain that Mozart had been born in Salzburg, not Germany.

"Clan gatherings are stupid," Kade muttered as he refocused on his book.

He started to slip once more into the history of music as the peace of the garden settled around him. But then quick footsteps scrunched on the gravel path. Someone was coming his way—probably a maid sent to tell him to come inside and get ready for dinner. Or maybe it was just another guest out for a stroll in the gardens.

He hoped if he kept his head stuck firmly in his book, the guest would leave him alone.

"There you are," said a girlish voice. "I've been looking *everywhere* for you."

Resigned, he looked up to see little Charlotte Stewart standing a few feet away, fists propped on her kilted hips. The daughter of Lord and Lady Kinloch actually wasn't that little, since at eleven she was only two years younger than Kade.

Charlotte, something of a scrapper, was not like any girl he'd ever met. She wore kilts, for one thing, and never seemed to care about her appearance. Today, she had on a short jacket over her kilt and a pair of scuffed riding boots on her feet. Her shiny gold hair was pulled back in a messy knot, and there was a smudge of dirt on her jacket. She'd probably been out riding—or maybe mucking about in the stables. Charlotte loved horses and had even gone riding with the twins. Kade's brothers had said she was a regular corker, taking every hedge without a smidge of doubt or fear.

She also drove her mother mad with her boyish ways, and Lady Kinloch seemed to deliver scolds to Charlotte on a regular basis.

"Why were you looking for me?" he asked.

Charlotte plopped down beside him on the wrought iron bench. "Because I wanted to talk to you. Why are you hiding out here? What if you fell down and hurt yourself? No one would be able to find you. Except for me, of course. I always find what I'm looking for."

That was another thing about Charlotte. She liked to talk. He didn't really mind. Sometimes he thought she was a bit lonely, even though she was always tumbling from one adventure to the next.

"I'm hardly likely to fall while just sitting on a bench," he replied. "I'm not *that* clumsy."

"Of course you're not clumsy. It's just that . . ." She trailed off.

Kade stifled a sigh. "It's just that I'm rather sickly? I know everyone worries about me, but I'm quite well. Really."

"Of course you are," she stoutly said. "It's just, well, you know. People worry over the stupidest things."

In his case, worrying wasn't so stupid. He'd almost died from fever when he was younger and had been sickly ever since. He did think he was getting better, though. At least he hoped so.

"I know my family worries about me," he admitted. "I hate it."

She scrunched up her nose in sympathy. "It's because they love you, of course. So that's not such a bad thing, is it? I think it's rather nice, to tell you the truth. No one ever worries about me."

"That's because you're indomitable."

Charlotte looked puzzled. "I don't know what that means."

"It means you're fearless."

She seemed to ponder that as she absently plucked a piece of straw off her sleeve. "That's nice, too, I suppose."

They both fell silent as a pair of songbirds flitted in the branches of the oak tree above, warbling a cheerful song.

"Why aren't you out playing or riding with the others?" he finally asked.

"The Campbell boys, you mean? Because they're boring."

"You've been knocking about with them since you got here, though."

"It's better than being cooped up inside that gloomy castle. I'd rather be out in the rain than have to listen to Mamma scold all day."

Kade grinned. "She does scold a lot, doesn't she?"

She comically crossed her eyes. "Rather. Which is also boring."

"I'm quite boring, too, Charlotte. All I do is sit and read books, and you like to . . ." He waved a vague hand. "Do things."

"Please call me Charlie. Everyone else does. Except for Mamma and Melissa, my little sister."

He tilted his head to study her. "I heard some of the boys call you Charlie. I thought it was a joke."

"My father started calling me that long ago, and it just stuck. He wanted a boy but got me instead."

Kade frowned. "That's odd. You do have a brother, don't you?"

"Johnny didn't come along for several years after me and Melissa. Anyway, the name doesn't bother me, since I don't much like girl things. It's more fun to be with Papa. He even lets me go with him when he visits his tenant farmers and such. And I like spending time in the stables, learning everything I can about horses. They're fun."

"The Campbell boys seem like more fun than me," he carefully said.

She emphatically shook her head. "No, they're very dull compared to you. You're smart and you're nice. I'm not sure that Richard and Andrew are really very nice."

Kade felt a warm glow in the center of his chest. Not that her praise really mattered, of course. Once the gathering was over, he had no idea when he might see her again. But if only for a few days it was nice to have a friend, someone other than one of his brothers or the Kinglas servants, who watched over him with an eagle eye.

Charlotte wasn't the sort to make a fuss, and he found that refreshing.

Kade smiled at her. "Thank you. And I agree that Andrew Campbell doesn't seem very nice." Andrew was the oldest brother. "Richard seems all right, though."

She shrugged. "I suppose. But he's . . ."

"Boring?"

Charlie flashed a smirk and then leaned over and tapped the open pages of his book. "What are you reading?"

"It's a history about opera. I found it in the duke's library, and he was kind enough to let me borrow it. It's a bit dry, I'm afraid. I'm not sure you'd find it very interesting."

He had found it so interesting that he'd stayed up half the night reading it. But he doubted Charlie would be able to sit quietly to discuss the differences between Handel and Gluck. She was so restless and full of energy that Kade could almost imagine lightning shooting from her fingertips.

She twisted sideways to face him, and her chestnut brown eyes fastened earnestly on his face. The first time he'd met Charlie, he'd been struck by the color of her eyes because they were such an unexpected contrast with her golden hair.

"I think I would, though," she replied. "I love music, but I really only know the old Highland reels and jigs. Mamma never plays anymore—she says married ladies never do—and Melissa wants to learn the harp." She rolled her eyes. "I think the harp is stupid. Only girls want to play the harp, because then boys will think they're like angels or something dumb like that. But it's not nearly as nice as the piano or the fiddle, if you ask me."

He smiled at her artless chatter. "I have to agree with you, because I play both the piano and the violin."

"I know. I heard you playing the fiddle in the east drawing room the other day. You're so good. I wish I could play something that well." She screwed up her mouth for a moment, as if pondering. "Yes, the fiddle. I'd quite like to play that."

"If you want to play the violin, er, fiddle, why don't you?" he asked.

"Girls don't usually play the fiddle, do they?" she replied in a dubious tone.

He smiled. "You don't seem like someone who would be put off by such a thing. Is there anyone in your village who could teach you?"

She sat up straight, her gaze brightening with eagerness. "Yes, actually. Our vicar plays the fiddle, and he's very good, too."

"So ask him to give you lessons."

Charlie seemed to deflate a bit. "Mamma wouldn't like it. She doesn't want me doing anything girls aren't supposed to do."

Kade grimaced in sympathy. Despite her rough-and-tumble exterior, Charlie was terribly sweet. And he'd bet a bob that she actually *was* lonely, stuck between two worlds.

"Then why don't you ask your father? I bet he'd say yes."

She waggled a hand. "It depends on how much he wants to avoid annoying Mamma."

"Nick didn't want me to play the piano, at least not at first. He thought it would wear me out. But I knew it would make me better, so I just kept asking until he finally gave in. So maybe you should keep asking your father until he finally says yes."

She studied him, her head cocking in that funny little tilt he was beginning to recognize. For some reason, it made him want to smile.

"And did it make you better?"

He nodded. "When I play, I forget about being sick, and I always feel better afterward."

Charlie flashed him a cheeky grin. "Then I will ask Papa, although I won't tell him it was you who suggested it. He's still mad at your grandfather, so—"

Loud, scuffling footsteps interrupted her. They both looked up to see the Campbell brothers pelting toward them, kicking up gravel from the path in their wake.

Kade mentally groaned. While he didn't mind Richard, Andrew was a different story. Although only a year older than Kade, he was half a head taller and very athletic. He excelled at sports and seemed to dominate most of the games the boys played.

And he was a bully.

"Oh, thunderbolts," Charlie muttered.

"There you are," breathlessly exclaimed Richard as the brothers skidded to a halt in front of them. "We've been looking for you. Don't you want to go riding with us? It's a sunny day, so for once we won't get all muddy."

His big brother shoved him. "Charlie doesn't mind mud. She's a regular goer." He fixed his gaze on her. "You don't mind, do you?"

"No," she replied. "Although I don't know why you had to shove Richard to make that point."

Andrew shrugged. "Because he was whining."

"I was not," Richard said as he rubbed his arm. "And you didn't have to shove me so hard. That hurt."

"Baby," Andrew sneered.

"I'll go riding with you, Richard," Charlie said, pointedly ignoring Andrew. "I'll meet you in the stables in a half hour. I want to finish talking to Kade first."

Andrew snorted. "What's there to talk about with him, besides books or that stupid piano he's always playing? That's so boring."

Charlie's narrow shoulders lifted in a casual shrug. "He's not what's boring me at the moment."

Kade bit the inside of his cheek to keep from laughing.

Andrew glared at her for a moment and then shifted his gaze to Kade. A nasty smirk spread over his features.

"Or we could go listen to Kade's grandfather while he bangs on about some stupid battle. It would be boring, but he's such a fusty old quiz that a fellow can't help but laugh. Everyone does, you know. Laugh at him, I mean. Really, how do you all put up with him?"

Anger flared in Kade's chest. Andrew was trying to bait him, but he refused to fall into that trap.

"My brothers and I love and respect our grandfather," he calmly replied. "After my mother died, he helped raise us, especially me. Besides, he knows a lot about Scottish and clan history, and that's important."

Andrew snorted. "Clan history is only good for old coots stuck in the past. Nobody cares about that anymore."

"I wouldn't let the duke hear you say something so stupid," Charlie put in. "After all, he is the chief of Clan Campbell, and you're a Campbell."

"She's right, Andy," Richard said. "Papa said we have to show the proper respect to the duke, remember?"

Andrew gave his brother another shove. "Who asked you, anyway?"

Richard glared at him but was clearly unwilling to stand up to his bully of a brother. Not for the first time, Kade sent up a prayer of thanks for *his* brothers. Some of them might be rambunctious, but they all had the kindest of hearts.

Andrew switched his attention back to Charlie. "Well, are you coming riding, or not? If you don't come right now it'll be too late. We have to be back in time to change for dinner."

"I don't," Charlie replied. "I'm still too young to have dinner with the adults, remember?"

"I wish I was," Kade wryly said. "They're awfully long affairs. I'd much rather have dinner with you and the other children."

"That's because you're an idiot," Andrew contemptuously said.

Charlie jabbed a finger at him. "That's an incredibly mean thing to say."

"Who cares?" Andrew replied. "It's just stupid Kade. All he does is sit around and read books." Then he grabbed Charlie's arm and hauled her to her feet. "Now come along before it gets too late."

"Let go," Charlie snapped as she tried to yank her arm from his grip.

"No," Andrew replied as he began to try to drag her away.

But Charlie dug in her heels. She was a slip of a thing, but she was stronger than she looked. Still, seeing that bully trying to force her made Kade's insides twist with fury.

If there was one thing a Kendrick hated more than anything, it was a bully.

He put aside his book and jumped to his feet. "Let her go, Andrew. Charlie will come if she wants to, not when you demand it."

"And I suppose you're going to make me, are you?" Andrew sneered.

Kade took Charlie's free hand, and she threaded her fingers through his, holding tight.

"If I have to, yes, I will," Kade replied.

The big bully snorted—much like a pig—but then let Charlie go.

Kade nodded. "Thank you—"

Instantly, Andrew came at him and shoved him hard in the chest. Kade went flying onto the wrought iron bench, banging his hip on the edge. Though pain shot through his body, he refused to cry out.

Even worse than the pain was the stunned look on Charlie's face.

"I say, Andy," exclaimed Richard. "No need to hurt the poor fellow. He's not very well, you know."

"I'm fine," Kade gritted out as he struggled to right himself.

"Here, let me help you," Charlie said, offering him a supporting arm.

Kade felt a humiliating heat flare into his face. Being shoved was bad enough, but did she think he was so weak that he needed her help to get to his feet?

He shook his head and stood. Nobody pushed a Kendrick around and got away with it. Kade knew that one should never back down from a bully, no matter the consequences.

He stepped into Andrew's path and narrowed his gaze on his stupid, smirking face. He tried to put ice into his expression, like he'd seen Nick do a thousand times to bounders and fools. Nick was famous for intimidating people with his cold, calm stare, and Kade hoped he'd inherited that talent.

Amazingly, Andrew blinked, as if genuinely taken aback. He peered at Kade, seeming unsure what to do. For a delirious moment, Kade thought he might actually apologize.

Then the big bully let out an ugly laugh. "Bugger you, Kendrick. And get out of my way before I knock your stupid block off."

"No, bugger you," Charlie retorted.

Quick as a flash, she threw a sharp punch that caught Andrew right on the nose. The boy let out a muffled shriek and staggered back as he clapped a hand over his face.

"You hit me," he exclaimed.

Charlie grimaced a bit and shook out her hand. "And I'll do it again if you don't leave us alone."

Then she turned to Richard, who was gaping at her.

"Richard, please take your brother back to the house. His nose is bleeding."

Blood leaked out from between Andrew's fingers as he cradled his nose. The rest of his face was almost as red, mottled with fury, as he glared at Charlie.

"How d . . . dare you hit me!" he blustered.

She shrugged. "You deserved it."

The boy took a step forward, but Richard finally intervened.

"Stop it," he snapped, grabbing Andrew's arm. "You've caused enough trouble for one day. Let's just get back to the house before you bleed all over yourself."

As Richard dragged him away, Andrew threw an angry glance over his shoulder.

"I'll get you for this," he yelled at Charlie.

"I doubt it," she called back. Then she turned to Kade, a concerned expression on her elfin features. "Are you all right?"

He stared at her for a moment. "I'm fine. Are you?"

"My hand's a little sore. I'll ice it when we get to the house."

Kade let out a disbelieving laugh. "Really?"

Charlie rolled her eyes. "He's not the first boy I've hit, and he probably won't be the last." Then she looked vaguely alarmed. "You don't mind, do you? Did you want to hit him first?"

"I did, rather, but I suspect you're better at it than I am."

"I've probably had more practice."

Then she plunked back down on the bench and picked up the book. "Now, where were we? You were going to tell me about your book." She glanced at the page. "Gluck. He wrote some famous operas, didn't he? I've never heard an opera. I'd quite like to, one day."

Kade sank down next to her, letting her sweet, girlish

voice flow over him. He should be embarrassed that he hadn't acted quickly enough to defend himself, forcing her to step in. But he wasn't. Charlie obviously didn't see him as either weak or an invalid, unable to stand up to a bully. She simply saw him as . . . a friend.

And that was splendid.

CHAPTER 1

Castle Kinglas, Scotland
July 1828

Kade sighed as he met the Earl of Arnprior's flinty gaze.
A verbal trouncing from big brother was in the offing, and
he had only himself to blame, since he was the idiot who'd
got himself stabbed in the first place.

Nick stood behind his imposing desk in the equally imposing library of Kinglas. He continued to glower at Kade, seated
opposite him in one of the leather club chairs.

"Was it really necessary for you to sleep with a Russian
spy in order to complete your mission?" his brother demanded.
"Good God, lad. What were you thinking to put yourself in
harm's way like that?"

Lad.

Though Kade was twenty-seven and had been touring
the Continent by himself for years, to Nick and the rest of the
Kendricks he would always be the baby of the family who
needed more protection than the rest.

He pretended to ponder the question. "Hmm, let me see.
Oh, right. I was thinking that I needed to get close to Marina
to complete the mission mandated by the British Crown."

Royal, lounging in the chair next to him, smirked. "*Very* close, apparently."

Kade flashed his other brother a dirty look. Royal had been holding in laughter as Kade patiently explained to Nick the reasons for his sudden return home this morning. He *had* been hoping for at least one day of rest, but Nick had immediately marched him off to the library for the requisite interrogation and resulting lecture.

The Kendrick brothers were used to lectures from Nick, all having required course corrections over the years. All but Kade. He'd never been called onto the proverbial carpet in front of Nick's desk or had to escape out a window to avoid a thundering scold. He'd always been the perfect Kendrick, the one who never raised a ruckus.

"I thought you were on my side," Kade said to Royal.

"I'm always on your side, even when you do something stupid, which is admittedly very rare in your case." Royal placed a hand on his chest and looked soulful. "Oh, how times have changed. Now our wee lad is seducing opera singers and Russian spies."

"The opera singer was also the Russian spy," Kade retorted. "Besides, this was for king and country, and it was a necessary part of my job."

"And look how well it turned out," Nick sardonically said. "As for this spy business, which none of us even knew about until a few days ago, we will discuss that in a minute. What I want to know is how you could decide to take on such a dangerous mission without help from us? What if you'd been seriously injured, or even—"

Killed.

Nick clamped his lips shut, clearly distressed. That had Kade squirming with guilt. Life had been good for the Kendrick men for many years. Grand marriages to lovely lasses, lots of bairns, and thriving businesses to keep them all busy. True, there was the occasional kidnapping or smuggling ring to deal with, but for the most part they'd all been blessed.

But further back in the past, their lives had often been tragic and hard, leaving emotional wounds on all of them, but especially on Nick. Yet Kade hadn't been thinking of any of that when he'd agreed two years ago to take on the occasional intelligence mission for the Crown. He'd seen it only as an exciting diversion from the intensity of his life as a musician and concert pianist.

A wave of weariness suddenly swamped him. The last few weeks had been taxing. His mission had ended with a narrow escape from Paris, a grim dash to the coast, a rough crossing to Edinburgh, and then a long carriage ride to Kinglas.

He grimaced in apology to Nick. "I'm sorry I worried you. It's nothing more than a scratch, I promise."

Kade wasn't about to admit that it was only by the greatest of luck that he'd been able to roll out of the way quickly enough to avoid a knife penetrating in between the ribs. As it was, the blade had skittered down his back, saving him from a devastating injury.

While seducing Marina had not been the soundest of plans, he'd been convinced that her notebook was hidden in the bedroom of her lavish hotel suite. That notebook contained the names of some very important men she was blackmailing on Russia's behalf, including two high-ranking British officials. Acquiring it had been a high priority.

Meeting Marina hadn't been a problem, since both she and Kade were performing at the Paris Opera. The enchanting soprano had seemed eager to spend time with him, but somewhere along the way she'd deduced his plan. So while he was busy convincing himself that his seduction was progressing well—not to mention pleasurably—Marina had been planning his demise.

"It was more than a scratch, according to Aden," Nick

replied. "And his letter clearly stated that you were lucky to escape without additional injury."

Aden St. George was Chief of Intelligence at the Home Office. He was also half brother to Nick's wife, which made him family and thus less likely to withhold details when writing to Nick.

Kade shifted in his chair to ease the pressure on his still-healing wound. "It really wasn't that bad. Fortunately, Marina was unable to pursue me, because she was . . ."

"Naked?" Royal sardonically finished for him.

Kade sighed. "I had only taken off my shirt, so good for me. I easily made my escape."

He had no intention of revealing that Marina had also pulled a pistol from her nightstand and got off a shot as he pelted out of the room, boots and shirt in hand. He could only hope Aden had left that detail out of his letter.

Nick finally sank down into his chair. "Good God, what a bloody mess."

"Yes, the blood quite ruined my best shirt," Kade joked, trying to lighten the mood.

Nick scowled at him, while Royal simply shook his head with disapproval.

"Look," Kade protested, "the mission was vital. Besides, Marina is a talented and well-regarded soprano. I thought she was simply passing along useful information to her government. How was I to know she would leap on me like a deranged assassin?"

"Aye, and let that be a lesson to ye," Angus suddenly piped in. "No good can come of larkin' about with Frenchies, and an opera singer to boot. What were ye thinkin', lad, to be tricked by such a one as that?"

Their grandfather had been uncharacteristically quiet throughout the entire discussion—so much so that Kade had forgotten he was in the room.

Angus was settled near the fireplace in his favorite wingback

chair, looking predictably disreputable in his scuffed boots
and tatty old kilt. With his wrinkled features and puffball
white hair, he was beginning to resemble a Highland version
of Methuselah, benignly smoking his pipe.

But Grandda's blue gaze still held a sharpness that belied
his age. He'd insisted on coming along for the interrogation.
Ever since Kade was a wee lad, Grandda had watched over
him like a she-wolf with a lone pup, and he obviously had no
intention of relinquishing the post now.

"Marina is Russian, not French," Kade said. "And she
tricked me because she is a very good spy."

"Fah." Angus stood and started to drag his chair over to
the desk, scattering ashes from his pipe in his wake.

Kade jumped up, wincing at the pull to his healing wound.
"Grandda, let me get that for you."

"I dinna need ye treatin' me like I'm an invalid. That
would be ye, and I'll nae have ye hurtin' yerself more than ye
already are." Angus thumped his chair down beside him.
"Anyway, Russian, French, they're all the same, and not for
ye to be larkin' aboot with."

"I was *not* larking."

"Still, one does not expect an acclaimed pianist to engage
in nefarious doings. And that's especially true when that
pianist is a Kendrick," Nick said.

"I'm hardly the first spy in this family," Kade pointed out.
"And may I remind you that *I'm* the victim. Marina stabbed
me, not the other way around."

Angus puffed vigorously on his pipe, sending smoke billowing over Kade. "Like I said, that's what ye get for larkin'
aboot with French opera singers."

Argh.

Kade waved a hand in front of his face. "I'm supposed to
be recuperating, not getting asphyxiated."

Angus ignored his protest. "I canna think that Vicky will

be best pleased to hear of this. Yer her favorite, ye ken, and still her wee innocent laddie."

Victoria, Countess of Arnprior, was Kade's former governess, and had arrived in his life when both his physical and emotional states had been precarious. She'd quickly become more than a teacher, loving and protecting him with a fierce loyalty. The day she'd gone from governess to Nick's wife had been joyful for all of them, but she and Kade had always held a special bond.

Now Kade did not relish the prospect of facing his sister-in-law. Vicky had been down in the village this morning and so had missed his arrival.

"I'm actually her favorite, ye ken," Nick dryly said. "But your point is well taken, Grandda. Victoria does not need to know the specific details of this unfortunate affair."

Royal waggled his eyebrows. "Emphasis on 'affair.'"

"You're a tremendous help," Kade sarcastically replied.

"And she will hear nothing salacious," Nick sternly ordered. "Victoria is distressed enough by the fact that you received a near-fatal wound under somewhat murky circumstances."

Kade waved a dismissive hand. "The wound was only mildly infected. Braden took care of it as soon as I returned to Edinburgh."

Unfortunately, his minor infection had grown worse during his travels to Scotland. His brother—a ruthlessly efficient physician—had cleaned the wound and poured noxious potions down Kade's throat, all while delivering stern lectures on the idiocy of musicians pretending to be spies. Kade was closer to Braden than anyone in the world, but he'd been more than a little relieved when he'd finally been released from his brother's care.

"Braden wrote that you suffered several days of fever," Nick said.

Kade shrugged. "I'm perfectly fine now, so no harm done."

Nick shook his head. "You cannot blame us for feeling anxious, Kade. You and fevers have never had a good history."

"Aye, that," Royal quietly added. "We'd never recover if we lost you, lad."

And there it was, the Kendrick specialty. Anxiety and love combined to tremendous effect, producing the maximum guilt in the intended recipient.

"I haven't been sick in years," Kade replied. "And, again, can we please keep explanations as brief as possible for Vicky?"

Nick gave a brisk nod of approval. "Victoria doesn't need to know the sordid details, especially in her delicate condition."

Kade perked up. "Vicky's with child again? That's splendid news, Nick. Congratulations to you both."

His brother finally cracked a smile. "Thank you. But she needs calm and rest, Kade, not hair-raising tales of your adventures."

Angus waved his pipe, spilling ash onto the carpet. "Och, Vicky is as strong as an ox. There's nae need to fuss, lad."

"Still," Nick replied, "I will not have Victoria upset by this ridiculous—"

"Victoria already knows everything, including Kade's adventures with opera singers," said a stern voice from behind them.

Oh, hell.

Kade rose and turned around. His sister-in-law stood in the doorway, still garbed in her pelisse and bonnet, looking moments away from marching up and boxing his ears. But despite her thunderous scowl, he couldn't help smiling.

"Hullo, you," he said. "I hear congratulations are in order. The other bairns must be delighted to know another brother or sister is on the way."

Her mouth twitched. "I suspect that a degree of bribery

might be necessary to soothe little Kyle's feelings. He's grown quite used to being the baby."

"You'll wrap him around your finger, just like every other male in the family," Kade joked.

She pointed at him. "Do not think you can distract me, Kade Kendrick. I am *most* annoyed with you."

Nick went to meet her. "You can give Kade a splendid scold later, sweetheart. But first get out of this drafty doorway. I don't want you catching a chill."

She allowed Nick to steer her to one of the chairs in front of his desk. "Nicholas, it's the middle of July."

"Then we don't need you getting overheated," replied her overprotective husband.

"Give us a hug, lass," Kade said, holding out his arms.

She gingerly put her arms around him. "Are you sure you're all right? From what Braden said, your wound was terribly infected."

"My fault. It was raining that night, and I slipped on some cobblestones, landing arse down in a nice, dirty puddle."

Flat on his back and still without his shirt on, he could have added. It had hurt like the devil, but that had been the least of his concerns at the time. Not getting shot had been top of the list.

"By the way," he said as he and Vicky sat down, "how did you find out about the opera singer? Aden promised me he wouldn't tell you about that part of the, er . . . situation."

"Vivien wrote to me."

"Of course she did," Kade said with a sigh.

Vivien was married to Aden St. George. When it came to Kade's family, there were no secrets, at least not for long.

Nick looked apologetic. "I'm sorry I didn't tell you, sweetheart, but I didn't wish to worry you."

She rolled her eyes. "Did you really think I wouldn't find out? I *always* know when something is wrong with one of you."

"That's true," Angus said. "Our *Sassenach* lassie has a nose for trouble."

"It comes from my years of dealing with Kendricks," she replied. "That, however, is not my primary concern at the moment. Kade is. I cannot be happy about any of this."

Kade took his sister-in-law's hand and met her worried gaze. "I truly didn't mean to worry you." He glanced at Nick. "Any of you."

His brother nodded. "I know, lad, but worry we do."

Kade widened his eyes in mock surprise. "Really? I hadn't noticed. But from now on, my focus will be entirely on my music career. My spying days are over."

"Splendid," Nick said. "You have a concerto to complete, and a special commission from the king is nothing to be sneezed at."

Of that he was well aware, as the blasted thing was giving him fits. For some reason, the music wasn't coming as easily as it usually did.

"And Braden is certain your injury won't affect your ability to play in the future?" Vicky asked.

Kade nodded. "It's just a matter of time and proper rest. I should be able to return to a full concert schedule by mid-autumn."

"Then no long hours of practice, Kade. I know you, and I will lock up the music room if I have to."

"Yes, Mother," he dryly replied.

"Dreadful boy. But as Nicholas said, you can use this period of rest to work on your concerto. Kinglas is the perfect quiet environment. No one will bother you in the least."

Actually, they would *all* bother him. His family would fuss and twitter over him like a bunch of nervous hens and drive him batty within the week.

"Although I hope you won't be bored," Vicky added. "Your life is so glamorous that we must seem like a fusty lot in comparison."

"Touring isn't all that exciting. Mostly it's just work and spending too much time in carriages, jostling over bad roads."

Vicky flashed him a teasing smile. "Vivien said you're very popular, and that half the ladies in Europe are in love with you."

Kade waggled a hand. "Probably no more than a third."

"Kade Kendrick, I was joking!"

He laughed. "As was I. And I obviously need to have a little chat with Vivien. She's telling too many tales out of school."

Vicky patted his hand. "You've always been the sweetest and best-behaved Kendrick, so I'm sure those reports are exaggerated."

"Kade would nae do anything to embarrass the family," Angus said, stoutly defending his grandson. "But he is getting on in years. I think it's time for the lad to settle down. Meet a nice lassie and get married."

"Excellent idea, Grandda," Nick said with approval.

"I am *not* getting on in years," said Kade. "And I'm too busy to settle down."

"You only think that because you've not yet met the right girl," Nick replied. "And speaking of that . . ." He directed a meaningful look at his wife.

Vicky smiled at Kade. "Now that you're back home, dear, we thought it might be fun to throw a ball in your honor. There are some delightful young ladies in the neighborhood. The Davenport sisters, for instance."

Alarm crawled up Kade's spine. "Thank you, but I'm really not interested in socializing. Concerto to write, you know."

"Aye, the Davenport lassies," Angus chimed in. "Those two would give ye a run for yer money. Their da's rich as Midas, too."

Nick flashed Kade an encouraging smile. "The Davenport

girls are both quite lovely. I'm sure they'd be thrilled to spend time with you."

Kade began to envision a horrifying round of social occasions, all designed to push him into the arms of a Kendrick-approved young woman.

Trying not to look completely appalled, he cast Royal an imploring look. His brother wiped a hand over his mouth, as if to smother a laugh, but responded with his usual loyalty.

"Rather than dragging the poor lad to a dreary round of social events," Royal said, "what about a stay at Cairndow? Fresh air, the mountains, the peace of the countryside, that's what Kade needs. Not a pack of silly girls twittering after him."

"In case you failed to notice," Nick said, "Kinglas *is* the country. Besides, I would never drag Kade anywhere. I would simply suggest a few outings he might enjoy."

"You would absolutely drag me," Kade replied, shaking his head.

"Cairndow is the back of beyond compared to Kinglas," Royal said. "It's so remote that sometimes even I get lost."

Victoria scoffed. "Now you're being silly. Cairndow is only a day's ride north of Kinglas, if that. Although it is very quiet."

Cairndow was the small but tidy estate that Royal's wife, Ainsley, had inherited from her great-aunt. It was a rather old-fashioned place but still comfortable and welcoming. And unlike the rest of his relatives, Ainsley didn't give a damn about matchmaking. At Cairndow, Kade knew he would be left alone to work on his concerto.

"It sounds perfect," he said gratefully to Royal.

Nick frowned. "But you just got here, Kade. Wouldn't you like to spend more time with us?"

"Yes, of course, but—"

"Ainsley's not expecting me home until the end of the week," Royal cut in. "You can have a few days to visit with

Kade, and then I'll take him back to Cairndow for a proper rest."

"Well, if you're sure," Victoria dubiously said to Kade.

"I'm absolutely sure," he replied. "I've got to get working on that concerto, Vicky. Don't want to disappoint the old man, you know."

The *old man* was the king of England, Vicky's natural father.

She blinked a few times. "You're perfectly right. It would indeed be dreadful to disappoint him."

"Appalling, really."

"Then it's all settled," Royal said. "Cairndow it is."

Nick eyed Kade for a few moments, as if trying to decide whether to argue, but then shrugged. "I suppose it's for the best. We can throw a ball for you on your return, before you head to Glasgow. You can meet the Davenport girls then."

Or never.

"Absolutely," Kade said.

Angus stowed his pipe inside his vest and shoved himself to his feet. "Then I'd best be lookin' over my medicinals and whatnot. We dinna want to be caught with our trews down in the back of beyond."

Kade frowned. "Grandda, what are you talking about?"

"I'm going to Cairndow, too, of course. Someone has to look after ye."

"Thank you, but I am perfectly capable of looking after myself. There's no need for you to fuss over me."

"And we do have doctors in Cairndow," Royal said.

Angus scoffed. "Fah. I'll be takin' over our Kade's doctorin' from now on. I know all of ye better than I know myself, and I'll nae have our lad goin' off without me, as delicate as he is."

Kade stared down at his wizened grandfather, who barely reached his shoulder. "Grandda, I did not escape Paris just to have you kill me with your disgusting concoctions."

"None of yer fussin', son," Angus said in an indulgent tone. "Yer family kens what's best, especially me."

Vicky nodded. "That's true. You do need your rest, Kade. I think you should let Angus look at that shoulder, and then you can have a nice little nap. Doesn't that sound perfect?"

Angus rubbed his hands. "Aye, that's the ticket. I'll get my doctorin' things and meet you and Kade upstairs in the lad's bedroom. Our Braden did his best, nae doubt, but the old ways are still the best ways." He patted Kade on the shoulder. "Not to worry, lad. We'll get ye back on yer feet in no time."

"I'm *already* on my feet," Kade protested.

Royal grimaced. "And no one needs your medicinal concoctions, Grandda. Seriously."

Angus jabbed a gnarled finger at Royal's nose. "Ho, nae sass from ye, laddie boy. There's nae point in takin' chances, what with Kade's delicate constitution. He'll nae be relapsin' on my watch."

"Or mine," Vicky firmly stated.

Kade mentally sighed. Suddenly, Paris didn't look that bad anymore.

CHAPTER 2

As their carriage passed by the last straggle of cottages, a spectacular vista opened before them. Loch Leven, with its bright, sparkling waters, provided a stark contrast to the craggy peaks rising up from the opposite shore.

"That's the last of Glencoe," Kade said. "Just a few more miles to Ballachulish and then we're almost there."

Ainsley looked up from her periodical. "Thank goodness, because I've had quite enough of climbing up one blasted hill after another. Not to mention teetering along ridgelines or waiting for the carriage to tip over into some dreadful bog."

"Agreed," Kade replied with a smile. "I thought that switchback on the Black Mount was going to be the end of us."

She shuddered. "God, don't remind me."

Royal, seated next to Ainsley, patted her knee. "You must admit that the views were spectacular."

Their daughter, Tira, expelled a dramatic sigh. "Rannoch Moor looked really spooky. Too bad nobody but me wanted to stop there and look for ghosts."

"I would have stopped," Kade said to the twelve-year-old snuggled between him and Angus. "But your mamma put her foot down."

"I beg your pardon for not wishing my daughter—or you,

for that matter—to go falling into a possibly haunted bog, never to be seen again," Ainsley sarcastically replied.

Tira rolled her eyes with all the drama of her youth. "Mamma, I would never be so silly as to fall into a bog. And even if I did, Papa would rescue me."

Royal leaned across and tapped his daughter's nose. "You may be certain of that. I'm not sure I could save Uncle Kade, though. He's so big he'd sink straight to the bottom, never to be seen again."

"You'd rescue me," said Kade. "Otherwise I'd come back and haunt you."

"Tormenting me with your renditions of gloomy sonatas by gloomy composers, no doubt."

"Or maybe I'd take up the bagpipes and drive you completely insane."

"We already have Grandda for that," Royal joked.

Angus jabbed his grandson in the knee. "Don't be daft. I play the bagpipes almost as well as Kade plays that piano of his. Have ye forgotten the recital we gave at Kinglas last Christmas?"

"I don't think anyone has forgotten that particular performance," Kade wryly replied.

Although Angus was possibly the worst player of the pipes in Scotland, the old fellow remained convinced he was a virtuoso.

Royal heaved a sigh. "My hearing will never be the same."

"Philistines, the lot of ye," Angus grumped.

"I still think it's sad that we didn't get to look for ghosts on the moor," Tira said with a child's dogged determination. "We don't have any ghosts in Cairndow, or even at Kinglas. Which is so boring."

"Maybe Laroch Manor has a ghost or two," Kade said. "We can have a little hunt for ghosties and ghoulies, if you like."

Tira twisted on the seat, regarding him with hopeful

expectation in her big blue eyes. "Do you think so, Uncle Kade? That would be so much fun."

"From what your mother tells me, the original house is ancient. Bound to be a ghoulie or two about the place."

"If it's ghosts ye want," said Angus, "we should go to Glencoe and pay our respects. I'm sure the puir souls of yer murdered kin would be that comforted by a visit."

"Grandda, this is a festive occasion we're attending, remember?" Royal said. "Tramping about the site of a massacre would hardly put us in the proper mood for a family wedding."

"It's not as if Kade and I had any say about goin' to this bloody weddin'," Angus indignantly replied. "Ainsley wouldn't leave us alone aboot it. And with our Kade in such a fragile state, ye ken."

Ainsley looked apologetic. "I'm sorry, Grandda, but Lady Kinloch was very insistent that you both come. She is your cousin, after all. Besides, I think it'll be fun."

Kade had been as reluctant as his grandfather to attend the wedding of Melissa Stewart, daughter of Lord and Lady Kinloch. But with typical insouciance, Ainsley had simply informed Kade that Lady Kinloch and Melissa had begged for him to perform at the grand reception following the ceremony. Ainsley, unfortunately, had also promised the ladies that he would be happy to do so.

"You did what?" Kade had exclaimed, flabbergasted that she hadn't discussed it with him first. "But Grandda and I only arrived in Cairndow a few days ago. I need to work."

"You've been here for a week, and working the entire time. Besides, everyone at Laroch Manor is *very* excited at the prospect of your performance," she'd replied. "You certainly will not wish to disappoint them."

She'd then sailed out of the room, leaving his objections hanging in midair.

Now Angus snorted. "Lord Kinloch is about as much fun as

a barrel of manky oysters. How Elspeth—a true MacDonald—
could have agreed to marry him is beyond my ken."

"What's wrong with Lord Kinloch?" Tira asked.

"He's nae proper respect for the past, lassie. Besides, he
consorts with unsavory folk."

"That's a bit much, Grandda," Kade said. "He's a lord of
Parliament, as well as holding an old and distinguished title."

"He's very wealthy, too," Ainsley added. "The Stewarts
made a substantial fortune from the slate quarries around
Glencoe."

"I ken what I ken about the man," Angus said. "Besides,
all this draggin' Kade aboot the countryside canna be good
for him. Look at the poor lad. He's positively whey-faced."

"Grandda, I'm fine," Kade said. "You needn't worry
about me."

"I promised Nick—that would be our *laird*," Angus said
with unnecessary emphasis, "that I would look after ye. And
I always do as my laird commands."

"We all know who the laird is," Royal dryly commented.
"And actually you hardly ever do what Nick wants you to
do, so why start now?"

Angus pointed a bony finger at Royal. "None of your sass,
laddie boy."

"Giving you sass is *my* job," Ainsley said, winking at the
old fellow. "Everybody knows that."

"Aye, but yer a *Sassenach*, so ye canna help yerself. But
ye'll nae distract me from the subject at hand, which is our
Kade's health. I'll nae be lettin' Elspeth or anyone else run
the lad ragged. He should be recuperatin', not prancing
around like a trained monkey for a bunch of Stewarts."

"No one would dare make me prance, Grandda," Kade
said. "Not with you to protect me."

"Aye, that," Angus stoutly replied.

"I'm sure we'll all have a wonderful time and Kade will
get plenty of rest," Ainsley said.

Tira made a face. "I wish my brothers could have come with us, though. I miss them."

"I know, darling," Ainsley said. "But Royal Junior would hate all the fuss, and Georgie's much too young. Besides, we're terribly squeezed as it is. Kendrick men tend to take up a lot of room."

"I would have happily ceded my place to my nephews," Kade wryly said.

"Don't you like spending time with us, Uncle Kade?" Tira asked, sounding a trifle anxious. "It's been ever so long since you've come to visit."

Angus heaved a dramatic sigh. "Sad state of affairs when a Highlander has nae time for his kith and kin."

Kade ignored his grandfather, but he couldn't ignore the twinge of guilt over his niece's innocent question.

When he wrapped an arm around her narrow shoulders, Tira snuggled against him with a happy little sigh. Grandda was right. He had been neglecting his family, and that was a capital sin in Clan Kendrick.

"Of course I want to be with you, Tira. But back at Cairndow, with your brothers. Not at some godforsaken manor in the middle of nowhere, performing for strangers."

"Kade, you're a concert pianist," Royal said. "You're always performing for strangers."

"Yes, and that's part of the problem."

As much as he loved his career, he was less enamored with the growing lack of privacy that his life entailed, as well as the absurd enthusiasm his presence sometimes provoked. Kade had never sought fame. What he sought was the music. Of course, he'd had many wonderful opportunities to play in some of the greatest concert halls in Europe, accompanied by splendid musicians. Sometimes, though, it felt a bit much, as if his life and the music were being lost under the demands of his increasing renown.

Ainsley tilted her head, looking quizzical. "Kade?"

He smiled. "It's perfectly fine, really." He gave his niece a little squeeze. "And I'll have Tira to protect me from over-enthusiastic fans."

"I'll not let anyone bother you, Uncle Kade, even silly young ladies."

Royal winked at his daughter. "That will be very helpful. Your uncle is swearing off young ladies for the present."

"I hope there's a decent piano at Laroch Manor," Kade said, shifting the subject to safer ground. "Wedding or not, I will need to work on my concerto."

"I'm sure there is," Ainsley replied. "By all accounts, it's a splendid house, and Lady Kinloch has very high standards."

Kade waggled a hand. "Glencoe isn't exactly on the beaten path, but I'll take your word for it."

Angus visibly bristled. "Glencoe may not be yer high and mighty Paris or London, but there are few places more important to a Highlander, especially to a MacDonald. As ye well ken, it was the site of the worst act of—"

"You've been to Laroch Manor, haven't you, Grandda?" Royal interrupted, trying to forestall another foray into grisly tales of massacres.

"Er, well, it's been years, ye ken," he replied.

"Lady Kinloch mentioned in one of her letters that you attended a clan gathering only a few years after her wedding," Ainsley said. "That must have been quite a festive affair."

Angus scratched his chin, suddenly looking uncomfortable. "I dinna remember much about that, to tell ye the truth."

Kade exchanged glances with Royal and Ainsley, while Tira twisted around to stare at the old fellow.

"You're telling a fib, Grandda," Tira said.

"I never tell fibs, especially to bairns," Angus protested.

Royal snorted. "You tell them on a daily basis. What are you hiding from us?"

Angus clamped his mouth shut.

"Whatever it is," Ainsley said, "we'll find out soon enough. I do believe we're going through Ballachulish, and Laroch Manor is only about fifteen minutes outside the village, along the river. In fact, I believe we're already making the turn onto the road that leads to the manor. Lady Kinloch said it was just past the village church."

Kade peered out the window. "There's the church on the left. Not much to the place, is there?"

"Apparently, there are more shops and a public house if one travels farther along the main road."

"I do hope we can visit the shops in the village, Mamma," Tira said.

As the others chatted about plans for their stay, Kade let his attention drift to the surrounding countryside. The carriage was now bowling along beside a bucolic glen filled with heather and wildflowers. Hedges partly lined the road, interspersed with holly bushes and the occasional stand of trees.

In the distance, he could see the sparkle of swift water cutting through the glen— River Laroch, for which their host's manor was named. It was a peaceful scene, a quiet tableau of country charm set against the granite ridges and craggy summits that brooded over Loch Leven.

Suddenly, a horse and rider burst out from a stand of birches. The rider, a boyish figure crouched over the neck of an impressively big animal, galloped through the glen parallel to their carriage. The rider was wearing a kilt, which whipped around—

Kade practically pressed his nose against the window glass, trying to get a better look. Aye, the rider was a young woman, her long blonde hair streaming back from beneath her cap.

"Good God," he said.

"What's up, lad?" Royal asked.

"Look there, by the river. There's a rider."

Royal glanced out the window and did a double take. "Is that a girl?"

"Yes."

"Girls have been known to ride horses from time to time," Ainsley said with a hint of sarcasm.

Kade tracked horse and rider. She'd drawn slightly past them and was now cutting across the field at an angle, toward the road.

"True," he replied. "But this one is astride, in a kilt."

"Now, that I must see," Angus exclaimed, wobbling to his feet and practically falling into Kade's lap.

Royal clamped a hand on his grandfather's shoulder. "Don't fall, Angus."

"Fah." He tried to elbow Kade aside. "Where's the lassie?"

"Sorry, Grandda. She just disappeared behind that stand of trees up ahead."

"Drat," said Tira, who'd also been trying to get a glimpse over Kade's shoulder. "I wish I'd seen her. Are you sure it was a girl? What fun to be able to ride a horse that way."

"But you're a splendid sidesaddle rider, pet," her mother said. "You've never once fallen off a horse in all the years you've been riding."

"That's because I'm careful. And just think how much faster I could go if I was riding astride."

"Well, perhaps you can try it sometime when we're back at Cairndow," Ainsley replied. "But only with your father and certainly not in a kilt."

"I think a kilt would be dashing," Tira said. "Don't you, Papa?"

Royal smiled. "Very dashing, if a trifle scandalous."

"Who cares about that?" The girl heaved a sigh. "I wish I'd seen her, though."

After helping his grandfather get seated, Kade smiled at his niece. "Sorry, lass. She was out of sight in less than a minute."

Angus patted Tira's hand. "We might see her again. We're deep in the Highlands now, lassie. Things can get a wee bit strange up here."

"Very true," said Royal. "I remember when—"

A sudden jolt knocked them all off-balance. Royal grabbed Ainsley, while Kade clamped onto Tira. When the carriage jerked to a halt, Angus slid to the floor with a muffled yelp.

Kade plopped Tira down on the seat and reached for his grandfather, bracing himself against the rocking carriage. "Are you all right, Grandda?"

"Aye," the old fellow said as Kade hauled him up. "Dinna worry yerself, son."

"You hit the floor rather hard," Ainsley said in a worried tone.

"Just a wee thump on my arse." Then he shoved his hat out of his eyes. "But why in blazes is yer coachman sendin' us all akilter like that?"

"Perhaps we broke a wheel," Ainsley suggested.

Raised voices could be heard from outside, mostly from the coachman. Royal frowned and began to reach for the door handle, but the door opened to reveal Billy, their groom.

"Are ye all well, sir?" he asked. "We gave ye quite the jolt, but it couldna be helped, I'm afraid."

"We're fine. What happened?"

"Ye'd best come see for yerself, sir. Mr. Brown's about ready to pop his cork."

"So we can hear," Kade dryly said.

While Royal climbed down to the road, Angus peered out the window on the other side of the carriage. "Well, now, that's somethin' to see," their grandfather said with a chuckle.

"What?" Kade asked.

"Ye best come down, sir," Billy said to Kade, a bit urgently.

Kade stepped out of the carriage. Brown, their coachman, out of sight on the other side, was clearly directing his ire at another person. Royal had already gone around to join him, but Kade stopped to take a quick glance at the horses. They were annoyed, snorting and stomping a bit, but they seemed unharmed.

"You'll thoroughly check the horses?" he said to Billy.

"Aye, sir."

Ainsley poked her head out. "Kade, please help us down."

He turned back and helped her down, then took Tira in his arms and gently plopped her onto the road.

"Grandda?"

Angus waved him away. "I'm fine. Go help yer brother. He's trying to keep Brown from killing yon lassie."

Kade strode to the other side of the carriage and then pulled up short. The young rider stood a bit off to the side, the reins of a magnificent white stallion in one hand, her other hand up in a gesture of apology. Her golden hair flowed from under her tweed cap, then down her back in a wind-whipped tangle.

He glanced down at Tira, now standing by his side. "It looks like you'll get to meet our mystery woman after all."

CHAPTER 3

Charlie couldn't blame the coachman for tearing a strip from her backside. Only by the grace of God and Frost's excellent temperament had they managed to avoid disaster. Having her horse take that leap over the hedge had been a colossal mistake, and Charlie wanted to bash herself over the head for it.

And now, on top of everything else, *he* would have to be the one to witness her humiliation—in front of his family, no less.

Don't be a ninny.

Charlie pulled her attention from the man standing with the little girl back to the Kendricks' coachman, who was still delivering a blistering tirade. Once more, she tried to interrupt his rapid-fire flow of words.

"Truly, I am *most* sorry," she said. "This was all my fault, and I can only hope that no one inside the carriage was harmed."

"We're all fine. You needn't worry about that," said the kind man who'd come to her rescue.

He was Royal Kendrick, she assumed, because she knew very well who the other man was, even though the difference between the frail boy she'd known and the brawny man who now watched her with a faintly amused expression was nothing short of extraordinary. It was Kade's cobalt blue eyes and his resemblance to Lord Arnprior that allowed her to recognize him.

Charlie had no expectation that he would know who she was and almost wished he wouldn't. Of all the ways she'd dreamed of meeting Kade Kendrick again, this was surely not it.

"It's a blessing and a miracle that no one's come to harm, Mr. Kendrick," the coachman said. "But I canna say the same for my poor horses. At least not yet."

"I think they're fine," said Kade. "Billy is giving them a good check."

Charlie dredged up a smile for the coachman, her jaw so tight she almost expected her cheeks to crack.

"You handled your team expertly, sir," she said. "I was most impressed."

"No thanks to you," he snapped.

"You've made your point, Brown," Royal said in a firm tone. Then he frowned at Charlie. "And how are you, miss? I hope you didn't injure yourself in any way, or that fine animal of yours."

Charlie glanced over her shoulder at her horse, who was standing placidly and hardly even flicking his tail. It took a great deal to disturb Frost's composure, which was why she'd been able to bring him so quickly under control after her jump into the road. She'd been on a shortcut back to the house that she'd taken dozens of times without any mishaps. But she'd been so lost in her thoughts that she'd not even heard the sound of the carriage coming around the bend in the road.

"I'm perfectly well, sir," she answered Royal. "And Frost would let me know if there was anything wrong with him."

"He's a foine-lookin' beastie," said the old fellow who'd strolled up to join Royal. "Good as gold, from the looks of it."

Charlie remembered Angus MacDonald, grandfather and family patriarch. He'd been a regular pip to her, even though she'd been a rough-and-tumble little girl. Mr. MacDonald had actually *seen* her, something most adults had failed to do at that time in her life—unless they wanted to deliver scolds for her bad manners.

She smiled at him. "Yes, he's an excellent fellow. It's mostly due to him that I didn't come to harm."

By now, the groom was inspecting the two horses on this side of the carriage.

"Well, Billy?" asked Royal. "What's the verdict?"

The groom straightened up with a relieved smile. "No damage that I can see, sir, and they're not causing any fuss when I touch 'em. I'll take a better look when we get to Laroch Manor."

"Thank God." Charlie felt a bit dizzy with relief. If her carelessness had caused any harm, she would have never forgiven herself.

"Well, no harm done," said Royal in a good-humored voice to the coachman. "You and Billy can return to your places. We'll be off momentarily."

Grumbling, and with one last dirty look at Charlie, Brown climbed up to his seat while the groom disappeared around the carriage.

"Truly, I cannot tell you how sorry I am," she said to Royal. "It was most careless of me to not hear or see you on the road."

"Please stop apologizing, Miss Stewart," said the lovely woman who'd been standing with Kade and the little girl. "I'm Ainsley Kendrick, by the way, which I suspect you already know."

Charlie mentally sighed. Clearly, her mother had given Ainsley a detailed description that had allowed her to easily identify the black sheep of the family by her behavior and dress.

She bobbed an awkward curtsy because, well, one didn't generally give curtsies in a kilt. "We've been expecting you,

Mrs. Kendrick. I'm very happy to make your acquaintance at last."

Ainsley flashed a smile full of warmth and humor. "It's a pleasure to meet you, my dear, even under such unconventional circumstances."

"I'm rather well-known for those, I'm afraid," Charlie ruefully replied.

"Then we should get along splendidly. Allow me to introduce my family. This is my husband, Royal Kendrick."

"We met when I was a child," she replied. "It's a pleasure to see you again, sir."

Royal gave her a courtly bow, as if they weren't standing in the middle of a dusty lane with her looking like a madwoman.

"For me as well, Miss Stewart. I look forward to renewing our acquaintance."

Charlie mentally steeled herself to face Kade, who was now regarding her with a perplexed frown, as if trying to figure out who she was.

"And you're Mr. Kade Kendrick," she said. "I met you, too, although I'm sure you don't remember me."

She remembered, though. All these years, and she'd not forgotten one little thing about him.

Too bad for you, Charlie.

Kade stared at Miss Stewart, trying to remember who the hell she was. She regarded him with a bit of defiance and more than a bit of embarrassment. Though she'd stopped apologizing and had quickly collected herself, her high cheekbones were still glowing pink, and her narrow shoulders were hitched up in a defensive posture. Despite her embarrassment, her gaze held steady, as if willing him to recollect how he knew her.

He couldn't help but notice her striking eyes—an unusual,

velvety brown that stood in contrast to her golden hair, fair brows, and delicate complexion that held a touch of sun-kissed bronze. She was a slender lass and not particularly tall, but was obviously athletic, else she wouldn't have been able to handle the enormous stallion that stood at her shoulder.

She was a collection of contrasts, both intriguing and slightly bizarre, a fey sprite that rode like a warrior and dressed like a Highland lad. Somewhere in the back of his brain there was a wisp of a memory.

Her full mouth curled up in a rueful smile. "It seems you do not remember."

He began to feel like an idiot. "I'm afraid not, and shame on me. I'm assuming we were very young when we met."

"I believe you were thirteen at the time," Royal dryly said.

Kade frowned. "Really?"

Angus elbowed him. "Jinglebrains. Ye spent a fair amount of time with Miss Stewart, too." He smiled at the young woman. "But I remember ye, and I'd never met such a bonny little lass. A ray of sunshine, ye were."

Miss Stewart's rueful smile turned into a grin that was decidedly sunny. All at once, she seemed like the kind of girl who would always surprise, turning one's life upside down without even trying.

That little wisp in his brain began to take shape.

"That's very kind, Mr. MacDonald," she said. "Although I'm not sure my mother would agree."

"Och, yer dear ma was always a bit of a stickler. I reckon she's starched up about yer kilt-wearing and such?"

"Poor Mamma would faint dead away if she saw me right now," she said. "At the moment, I must seem like something out of Walter Scott's nightmares."

Blunt and full of surprises.

Kade snapped his fingers. "Of course! You're Charlie Stewart. We met at that clan gathering at Inveraray Castle. You're the girl who . . ."

"Hit Andrew Campbell?" She crinkled her up-tilted, quite adorable nose.

"At least ye remember her nickname," Angus said.

"I also remember Miss Stewart popping Andrew's cork," Kade replied.

"You might also recall that I got in a lot of trouble for doing that," she said with a slight smile. "Andrews's father raised an unholy fuss."

It was all coming back to him now, in all its hideous, hilarious glory.

"He earned that punch," Kade replied. "And believe me, I was very impressed. Also jealous that you made such a good job of it when I wasn't able to."

Her eyes opened wide. "You were jealous of me?"

"Absolutely. It was quite the facer, especially since Andrew was older and bigger than both of us."

"Thank you, but please don't convey your admiration to my mother. She has yet to recover from the incident."

"You really punched a boy?" Tira piped up in a wondering voice.

Charlie smiled at her. "It was quite naughty of me."

"Sometimes I wish I could punch my little brother when he gets irritating, which he does a lot," Tira said.

"I have a little brother, and he, too, can be quite irritating," Charlie responded with perfect gravity. "I put up with it, though, because I do love him."

Tira breathed out an exasperated sigh. "I love my brother, too."

"Allow me to introduce my daughter, Miss Tira Kendrick," Ainsley said in an amused tone. "Who is apparently rather bloodthirsty when it comes to her brother."

"I do love him, Mamma, but you must admit he can be very annoying."

"All men are annoying at times, my love," her mother

replied. "They can't help themselves, so we simply put up with it."

Angus wagged a finger at her. "Ho, *Sassenach*, none of yer sass."

"And it *was* very bad of me to hit Mr. Campbell," Charlie said to Tira. "He still hasn't forgiven me."

"The Campbell boys were always a pair of ninnies, just like their da," said Angus. "The entire lot of them are nothin' but poltroons and traitors."

"Why traitors, Grandda?" Tira asked.

"Because they attacked the MacDonald Clan at Glencoe," he replied in a dark tone. "Our folk wanted nothin' but peace, but they got slaughtered instead."

Tira's big blue eyes rounded with shock. "Then I'm very glad Miss Stewart punched that Campbell boy. I wish I could punch all those Campbells, too."

Angus patted her shoulder. "That's my brave lassie. Mayhap we can make a wee visit to Glencoe to honor our fallen ancestors once this wedding nonsense is out of the way."

"'This wedding nonsense' is the point of our trip," Ainsley said. "Besides, I'm sure we won't be stumbling across traitorous Campbells at Laroch Manor. According to Lady Kinloch, most of the guests are MacDonalds and Stewarts, along with some local families."

"Er, for the most part," Charlie replied, sounding oddly vague. "But I've kept both you and your horses standing long enough. And besides, I must get home and change. Mamma will have a positive fit if I show up for your arrival dressed like this."

She gathered up her animal's reins, preparing to mount.

Angus elbowed Kade again. "Give the lassie a leg up."

"That's all right," the girl hastily responded. "I can manage."

"It's no trouble at all, Miss Stewart," Kade said, walking over to help her.

"Oh, uh, thank you. And call me Charlie. Everyone else does. Except for my mother and sister. They don't go in for nicknames. And you aren't obliged to call me that, of course. It's just that you did when we were children."

"I'll call you whatever you wish," he said.

She'd been an unusual and talkative child. Clearly, she'd grown into an unusual woman, too, although he suspected she was rambling a bit because she was nervous.

Her brown-velvet gaze tracked over his features. She grimaced slightly, as if she could read his thoughts.

"Shall we?" he said, flashing his most charming smile.

"Yes. Thank you," she replied in a clipped tone.

Charlie slipped her booted foot onto his cupped hands, and he boosted her into the saddle. Her kilt rode up above her knee, partly exposing her leg. And quite a nice leg it was—slender, with creamy skin that looked as smooth as satin.

A moment later, she flicked her kilt down over her knee and settled herself. Kade stepped back, castigating himself for being a moron.

Charlie gathered her wealth of hair in one hand and flipped it back over her shoulder before flashing a quick smile at the group.

"I'll see you all at the house," she said. "It's only a few minutes past the next bend. You'll see the gatehouse, so you can't miss it. And," she added with a slight grimace, "would it be awful if I asked you not to mention our meeting? Mamma would be mortified to know I was acting like a Highland hooligan again."

Kade smiled at her turn of phrase. "My family is well used to Highland hooligans. Your secret is safe with us."

Once again, her gaze swept over him. "You're not a hooligan, though. You never were."

He blinked, but before he could respond she clicked her tongue and sent the white stallion trotting into the lane. Once clear of the carriage, the horse quickened to a gallop.

Golden hair streaming out behind her like sunlight, Charlie disappeared around the bend, and the beat of hooves faded into the distance.

Royal shook his head. "What an extraordinary encounter."

"What an extraordinary girl," Ainsley said in a musing tone. "I had no idea."

"Hardly a girl," Kade pointed out. "She's only a few years younger than I am."

"Aye, she's a woman grown," Angus said. "And a foine one at that."

"If a bit eccentric," Kade replied. "Even for the Highlands."

"Yer just so used to city ways that ye dinna ken a keeper when ye see one."

Kade shot his grandfather a startled glance. "What's that supposed to mean?"

"I think she's a pip," Tira interjected.

"And I think it's time to be on our way," Royal said. "Brown has been glaring daggers at us."

He waved them all into the carriage, and they were on their way.

Less than ten minutes on, they came to the gatehouse marking the estate. The carriage turned in between the scrolled wrought iron gates and bowled up a paved lane lined by stands of oaks and elm trees. Beyond the trees were healthy meadowland and pastures, dotted with primroses and heather. It was a peaceful, bucolic scene set against the stark peaks of Loch Leven.

"Quite a good estate Kinloch has here," Kade noted.

"Aye, the old bugger has deep pockets," Angus grumbled. "I'll give him that, but not much else."

"I'm sure the entire family is charming," Ainsley said. "My aunt always thought highly of Lord Kinloch, and I've very much enjoyed Lady Kinloch's letters. And they are family on both sides," she pointedly added. "On mine as well as yours, Grandda. As you've told me on numerous occasions, family is everything."

"Depends on the family," he retorted.

Kade had a feeling that whatever was chafing the old fellow would surface sooner rather than later, despite their best efforts to keep him under control.

"Miss Stewart will be something of a challenge, though," Royal said to Ainsley. "You have your work cut out for you, my love."

"I'll sort it out. She seems like a charming girl underneath her outrageous exterior."

Kade lifted an eyebrow at his sister-in-law. "Sorry, what are you going to sort out?"

"Lady Kinloch asked Ainsley to help Miss Stewart. Give her some instruction, as it were," Royal said with a vague wave of the hand.

Kade knew every intonation of his brother's voice, and Royal's tone of bland innocence was decidedly *not* innocent.

"Instruction in what?" he asked.

"Something along the lines of how to comport herself like a proper lady," Royal said. "Ainsley's going to work her feminine magic on Miss Stewart."

"I'm simply going to give her a few pointers on things like dress and how best to behave in company," Ainsley explained. "Apparently, Miss Stewart is quite shy."

Kade stared at her. "She's the opposite of shy, as our little encounter surely illustrated. And I now fully recall that she was a hooligan as a child, much to her mother's dismay."

Although a charming hooligan, he had to admit.

Tira twisted sideways to look at him. "She's why we've come several days before the wedding, Uncle Kade. So Mamma can tutor Miss Stewart." She beamed up at him. "I'm going to be Mamma's assistant, which will be very fun."

"And I'm sure you'll make a splendid assistant, sweetheart." Then Kade turned his gaze to Ainsley. "I thought the blasted wedding was happening in a few days and then we'd be back to Cairndow. So please tell me, just how many days are we going to be stuck up here?"

"The wedding is in six days," Ainsley replied. "That way I'll have plenty of time to help Miss Stewart prepare for the festivities." She looked at her husband. "Did you not tell Kade about this, my love? I felt sure that you had."

"I thought *you* told him." Royal shrugged his shoulders. "Sorry for the mix-up, Kade. These things happen, you know."

"All too frequently," Kade said. "And from what we just saw of Miss Stewart's behavior, a week hardly seems like enough time to accomplish your task."

"Just be grateful Lady Kinloch didn't ask us to stay for a month," Ainsley said in a soothing tone. "We'll only be here for ten days or so, I'm sure."

"What fun," he dryly replied.

"I like Miss Stewart. I think she's quite jolly," Tira said.

"The lass has spirit." Angus reached around and jabbed Kade in the knee. "And she's got a fortune that's more than jolly. Kinloch's daughters will have grand dowries. They're true Highlanders, too. A fellow would count himself lucky to nab one of them. And one fellow in particular, if ye ken what I'm sayin'."

"Not this again," Kade said. "May I point out that I am here to work, not take part in ridiculous matchmaking schemes?"

His grandfather gave an insouciant wave. "Nothin' ridiculous about it. Girls are always fallin' all over ye, and I imagine Miss Charlie will be nae different. Ye'll hardly have to do a thing."

"While I appreciate the vote of confidence, I imagine Miss Stewart would be horrified by your assessment," Kade replied. "In any case, I would be grateful if you kept your deranged plans to yourself."

His grandfather jabbed a gnarly forefinger at him. "Now, see here, laddie—"

"We're here," Ainsley interrupted. "We can discuss Kade's marital prospects another time."

"I don't have any marital prospects, nor do I wish for them."

"Not yet ye don't," Angus put in.

"Enough," Ainsley ordered. "I will not have either of you embarrassing us in front of Lord Kinloch and his family."

Kade put up his hands. "What the hell did I do?"

"Language, dear boy. There is a child present," she replied.

Kade sighed. They hadn't even set foot in the house and the situation was already descending into perdition. "Sorry, Tira."

She patted his knee. "It's all right, Uncle Kade. Sometimes the way Grandda behaves makes Papa say swear words, too."

Royal choked.

By now, the carriage had come to a halt in front of the house and Billy was letting down the step. Kade handed Ainsley and Tira down and then reached for Angus.

"Grandda, behave yourself," he murmured as he helped him down.

Angus grumbled something unintelligible. Ignoring him, Kade turned to examine Laroch Manor.

Looming over them was a classic six-story tower house, centuries old and bookended with two medieval-looking turrets. Although a plain stone porch sheltered the front door, its stark appearance was softened by large clay pots of flourishing rosebushes and greenery on either side of the entrance.

Two wings in the Jacobean style stretched out on both sides of the tower in an elegant sprawl, with a crenellated roofline adding a fine embellishment. At the far end of one wing stood a fanciful two-story tower topped with a sloping slate roof that gave that part of the building a fairy-tale-like appearance. Dozens of windows gleamed brightly in the sun, and neatly trimmed bushes and smoothly cut lawns encircled the house. Laroch Manor exuded old-fashioned, quiet charm, with not a blade of grass or pebble of gravel out of place.

He'd half expected a drafty old castle, because that was often the case this far north. Since he'd grown up in one, he knew how challenging it was to keep antique buildings from falling to pieces. Laroch Manor, however, was the opposite of shabby.

The front door opened and a group of servants bustled forth, followed by what were obviously Lord Kinloch, Lady Kinloch, a pretty young lady, and a callow youth sporting a thin mustache.

Charlie was noticeably absent.

Lord Kinloch, a tall, portly man in his fifties, booted and garbed in country tweeds, advanced toward them with a welcoming smile.

"So, here be the Kendricks," he exclaimed in a bluff, brogue-tinged voice. "Welcome, welcome. I'm Lord Kinloch, and this is my good wife and two of my children. Your maid and the baggage coach arrived an hour ago, and we've already got your rooms set up nice and tidy. You'll be able to have a good rest before dinner."

Royal bowed and then handed Ainsley forward. "Thank you for your generous hospitality, Lord Kinloch. Let me introduce my wife, Lady Ainsley Kendrick."

Ainsley dropped a graceful curtsy. "It's a pleasure to finally meet you in person, Lord Kinloch. My late aunt always spoke of you with great affection."

Lord Kinloch heartily pumped Ainsley's hand. "No need to stand on ceremony, my dear. We're all family here, and we're exceedingly grateful you could join us for Melissa's grand affair." He winked at her. "And help us with our little problem."

Ainsley offered a winning smile. "I'm happy to help you and Lady Kinloch in any way I can."

Lady Kinloch stepped forward to join her husband, offering Ainsley a languid hand in greeting.

"My dear," she said in a soft voice, exchanging air kisses with Ainsley, "it is positively delightful to meet you in person. I've so enjoyed our correspondence."

Lady Kinloch was a slight woman, with delicate features and pale silver hair coiffed in the latest style. Her green silk gown sported fashionably large sleeves and was trimmed with abundant lace. Looking like she'd just stepped out the pages of a ladies' magazine, she was a marked contrast to her bluff, genial husband.

"Allow me to present my daughter Melissa," Lady Kinloch said.

The bride-to-be had been hanging back with her brother and darting surreptitious glances at Kade, but now hurried forward to join them. A dainty young woman who took after her mother, Melissa was nothing like her sister, and not as beautiful in his eyes. Charlie, despite her wild hair and dust-covered attire, was vibrant and captivating.

Not that it mattered whether Charlie was captivating or not.

Melissa murmured her greetings, dropping a pretty curtsy, then darted a glance at Kade and batted her eyelashes.

Good Lord.

"And you're Mr. Kade Kendrick," she said in a pretty, lilting voice. "Sir, thank you *so much* for coming and agreeing to perform for the guests. Mamma and I are greatly in your debt."

Kade gave her a slight bow. "It's my pleasure, Miss Stewart."

"Ah, the great Kade Kendrick," said Lord Kinloch. "My

wife and daughter have been able to speak of nothing else."
He winked at Kade. "Good thing my little girl here is about
to get riveted, else she'd be making a play for you, lad."

Lady Kinloch looked pained. "Really, my dear, you
mustn't say such nonsense. You'll embarrass poor Mr.
Kendrick."

"Just a bit of a jest, my love," he replied. "We're all family
here."

"And speaking of family," Royal said, tactfully interven-
ing, "allow me to introduce my daughter and my grandfather." He glanced over his shoulder and frowned. "Where
are they?"

Holding Tira's hand, Angus strolled around from the other
side of the carriage. "We were just lookin' for Tira's book. It
slipped down between the cushions." He eyed Lord Kinloch,
who was staring at Angus with an expression of abject horror.
"Ho, Kinloch. Yer lookin' a wee bit whey-faced. Had a bit of
manky fish for luncheon, did ye?"

"What the devil is *he* doing here?" yelped Kinloch,
pointing at Angus. He whipped around to glare at his wife.
"Elspeth, please tell me you did not invite this man. I specif-
ically told you not to."

"You did nothing of the sort," Lady Kinloch calmly
replied. "Mr. MacDonald is my cousin, after all. What else
was I to do when Lady Ainsley informed me that he was
staying with them?"

"You could have told the blasted fool to remain in Cairndow," her husband thundered. "Better yet, you could have
told him to throw himself off the nearest cliff and spare us
the affliction of his presence."

Lady Kinloch did not reply, simply looking pained again.
Kade suspected it was her habitual expression.

"I say, Papa," said the young man who'd been hovering in
the back. "No need to make such a fuss. I'm sure Mamma
knows what she's about."

Kinloch wheeled on him. "You know nothing of the matter,

Johnny. MacDonald is trouble, and I insist you stay well away from him."

The young man flushed but wisely held his tongue.

"Och, Kinloch, ye'll be givin' yerself an apoplectic fit," Angus said in an indulgent tone. "Yer not as young as ye used to be, dinna forget. And from the looks of ye, I wouldn't be surprised if ye've got the gout, too."

"Angus, enough," Kade sternly said.

Kinloch, struck dumb for a moment, now recovered his voice, and at full volume. "Not as young as I used to be. Why, you old—"

"Henry Stewart, you will cease your blustering right now," Lady Kinloch said in a surprisingly steely voice. "What will the Kendricks think of us, not to mention the servants?"

"I don't give a tinker's damn what anyone thinks of us," Kinloch retorted.

Angus made a show of covering Tira's ears. "Not around the bairns, ye ken."

Tira, who was clearly lapping up every ridiculous moment, immediately removed his hands.

Kinloch drew himself up to his considerable height. "I will not be party to this outrageous scene for one moment longer. Elspeth, you will keep MacDonald under control and out of my way or I will be forced to take drastic action."

"Yes, dear," his wife replied in a long-suffering voice.

After throwing one more death glare at Angus, who was rounding his eyes with faux innocence, Kinloch stormed into the house.

Lady Kinloch sighed. "Melissa, you'd best go find your sister. She's the only one who can calm your father down when he gets in one of his tempers."

Melissa also sighed but went off as requested.

"Angus, I am quite ashamed of you," Ainsley said.

The old reprobate simply shrugged.

"I apologize for my husband's behavior," said Lady Kinloch. "I'm afraid he was surprised by my cousin's appearance."

"Decided not to tell him I was comin', did ye?" Angus asked.

She gave a wry smile. "It seemed best not to set him off any sooner than necessary. And although it is splendid to see you, Angus, I must ask you to refrain from needling poor Henry. You know how he feels about you."

"Och, I'll be on my best behavior," Angus said. "Word of a MacDonald."

"If that was an example of your best behavior, God help us all," Kade said.

"Fah," Angus replied.

"Angus, why don't you go in and get Tira settled," Royal suggested. "We'll be up shortly to help."

Lady Kinloch flashed him a grateful smile. "Yes, one of the footmen will bring you up. We've prepared a lovely room for your daughter on the nursery floor."

"Let's get to it, lass," Angus said, taking Tira's hand and then following one of the footmen into the house.

After flashing another apologetic smile at Kade and Royal, Lady Kinloch ushered Ainsley in as well.

"Well, that was fun," Royal said to Kade. "If I'd known how Lord Kinloch felt about Angus, I would have left him at Cairndow."

"Do you have any idea why they so obviously hate each other?" Kade asked.

"I think I do," Kinloch's son interjected. "I'm John Henry, by the way, but you can call me Johnny. It's a pleasure to meet you and your family."

"Not so far, I suspect," Kade wryly replied. "But let's hope things improve."

Johnny, who looked to be in his early twenties, flashed a

grin. Like Melissa, he bore a greater resemblance to his mother than his father and seemed rather shy.

"So, lad," Royal said. "What can you tell us about the enmity between your esteemed father and my not-so-esteemed grandfather? I thought it was to be pistols at dawn for a moment there."

"It has to do with the Massacre of Glencoe," Johnny explained. "They had a fight about it a long time ago. According to Mamma, Angus called my father a scaly-toed traitor."

Royal snorted. "That sounds exactly like Grandda."

"But the MacDonald and Stewart clans have always been allies," Kade said. "The Stewarts had nothing to do with Glencoe anyway. And let's not forget it happened well over one hundred years ago."

"It's because of the Campbells," Johnny replied. "They were responsible for the massacre of the MacDonalds at Glencoe, and I suppose your grandfather still holds it against them."

Royal shook his head. "That still makes no sense, even for Angus. Campbells and MacDonalds have gotten along for years. There have even been marriages between various branches of the families. I distinctly remember all of us, including Angus, going to one such wedding when we were children."

"Since when was making sense a requirement for our grandfather?" Kade glanced at Johnny. "Where do the Stewarts fit into this bizarre scenario?"

"My father told Mr. MacDonald that it was silly to hang on to old feuds, that the Campbells were now good friends, and that the clans had better things to do than argue about ancient history."

Kade sighed. "That would do it. Angus is very devoted to clan history, or at least his version of it."

"According to Mamma," Johnny said, "your grandfather

demanded my father renounce his ties to the Campbells and swear allegiance to the old ties between the Stewart and MacDonald clans. Papa told him to get stuffed."

Royal covered his mouth, trying not to laugh.

"Apparently, there was quite a set-to," Johnny added. "Lord Arnprior had to forcefully intervene, although I'm not really sure what Mamma meant by that."

"I am," Kade dryly replied.

He had little doubt that poor Nick had been forced to cart Angus off bodily.

"How long ago was this?" Royal asked.

Johnny screwed up his face, thinking. "Maybe eighteen years ago? They've hated each other ever since. I'm surprised that Mamma invited Mr. MacDonald, though she's always been fond of him. I suppose she thinks it's time he and Papa lay down their arms."

"This so-called feud is completely ridiculous," Kade said. "Even for Angus."

"Welcome back to the Highlands, laddie," Royal replied. "Where old grudges never die."

"We'll just have to make the best of it," Kade said. "Keeping Grandda under control will be the usual challenge, but as long as there are no Campbells about, we should be able to manage it."

"You eternal optimist," Royal sardonically commented.

Johnny grimaced apologetically. "But there's going to be at least one Campbell here for the wedding. And he's coming early, just like you."

"Do you know which Campbell we're talking about?" Kade asked.

"Richard, the younger brother of Andrew."

Royal laughed. "Andrew. That would be the lad who your other sister, er, schooled in good manners?"

"You mean punched. Believe me, I've heard that story, too," Johnny replied.

"I take it that Richard Campbell is a special friend of the family, if he's coming early?" Kade asked.

"I'd say so. He wants to marry Charlie, and he's coming especially to ask Papa for her hand."

CHAPTER 4

Charlie sat on her bed, working up the courage to get dressed for dinner. After almost sending the Kendricks into a ditch, she'd acted like a complete ninny in front of them.

She was quite certain that Kade Kendrick had thought her one. While he'd been terribly polite, more than once she'd seen an expression of barely suppressed incredulity on his handsome features. At first, he hadn't even remembered who she was. When he did finally remember, it was because of that humiliating episode with Andrew Campbell.

If the Andrew incident was his only memory of her, she found that very sad. She had so many memories of Kade from that long-ago trip, stored up over the years like precious treasures. He'd given her so much. He'd given her the gift of music.

Until she met Kade, she'd mightily resisted attempting to learn the feminine accomplishments, like painting or playing the pianoforte. As to the latter, her old governess had pronounced her tone-deaf, telling Mamma the situation was hopeless.

Then that fateful day had occurred—the first time Charlie heard Kade play his violin.

All the other children had been romping about the grounds of Inveraray Castle. Charlie had been dashing down the hall to join the boys in a game of cricket. But then she'd heard the notes of a violin drifting out through the half-closed door of the music room, and she'd stopped dead in her tracks. The gently mournful music seemed to her full of a great longing, and it touched something deep inside her. It had wended its way into her heart and opened a hidden door.

Forgetting all about the cricket, she'd snuck into the room and crouched down behind a chair to listen. Kade had been standing by the fireplace, his black locks tumbling over his forehead as he played. His body moved with the instrument in an intense, captivating display of youthful talent and emotion.

Charlie had met Kade the day before and had thought him a sweet boy with a kind face and lovely blue eyes. But he was also painfully thin and obviously unwell, and she'd felt sorry for him because he couldn't participate in riding or other romps about the estate.

Once she'd heard him play, she never felt sorry for him again. He became the most interesting person Charlie had ever met in her young life, and she'd spent the rest of her visit dogging his steps. Though Kade had no doubt thought her an awful pest, he'd never treated her with anything but courtesy. Instead he'd talked to her about music, and had even showed her how to hold a violin and draw the bow across its strings.

The day she'd first picked up a violin had, thanks to him, changed her life forever.

But after today's disastrous encounter with the Kendricks, she doubted Kade would want to spend even a minute in her company. Given the kind of man he'd become—polished and sophisticated—he likely expected something quite different from young ladies.

Hoydens, she suspected, were not it.

Besides, she had nothing in common with him but a love of music. She was a girl of the Highlands, while he spent his time in cities like Paris, London, and Rome. Charlie had spent years following his career, gleaning every bit of information she could from the papers, ladies' magazines, and her mother's correspondence with Lady Ainsley and various other Kendricks. Kade Kendrick was a meteor blazing across the night sky. Handsome, talented, and charming, he'd no doubt met legions of beautiful women who would leave a country bumpkin like Charlie in the dust.

It was no wonder he hadn't remembered her.

Charlie sighed and stared down at her stocking feet, wiggling her toes.

"Well, old girl, you'd best get yourself dressed and down for dinner," she said to herself. "Otherwise Mamma will skin you alive."

As it was, she was already in trouble for not returning to the house in time to greet the Kendricks. Mamma had taken one look at Charlie and ordered her not to set a foot downstairs until she could present herself in proper form.

Unfortunately, presenting herself in proper form had always been a challenge.

She got up and crossed to her dressing table. Taking up her brush, she began working through her tangled hair. Susan, the maid she shared with her sister, would be along to help her dress, but Charlie preferred to do her own hair, braiding and wrapping it in a simple crown style. Poor Susan also thought she was hopeless and spent endless amounts of time trying to bring her up to snuff by sticking silly beads and feathers into the braid.

She'd just finished when a quiet knock sounded on the door.

"Come in, Susan," she called out.

To Charlie's surprise, a very fashionably coiffed head peeked around the door.

"Not Susan," Ainsley Kendrick said. "I thought to have a quick chat with you before dinner, if it's not too much of a bother."

Charlie jumped to her feet. "Not at all. Please come in."

Ainsley closed the door. "I ran into your maid out in the hall and told her that I would help you finish dressing."

Charlie eyed the lovely young matron, fashionably garbed in a periwinkle blue gown with enormous sleeves and wide skirts and trimmed with spectacular Brussels lace. Ainsley also managed to carry off her elaborate coiffure, feathers and all, without looking like she'd been attacked by a flock of extremely annoyed peacocks.

"Really?" Then she winced, realizing how rude that sounded. "Sorry, I didn't mean it to come out like that. It's just that—"

"That I look completely overdressed for a quiet country dinner with family?" Ainsley humorously replied. "Very true, but I thought it would impress your mother."

"She'll be impressed. Even I'm impressed, and as you have obviously realized, I'm not exactly one for the latest fashions."

Ainsley waved her back down. "Nonsense. You're a lovely young woman, and you clearly have your own sense of style. One that is quite striking, I might add."

"'Highland hoyden,' Mamma calls it," Charlie ruefully said. "I'm afraid you have your work cut out for you, Lady Ainsley."

"It's Ainsley, my dear. I very much intend for us to become good friends."

"Ah, thank you."

Argh.

Was she going to spend the next two weeks sounding like a booby every time a Kendrick crossed her path?

Ainsley inspected Charlie's coiffure. "I like what you've done to your hair. It's elegant."

Charlie raised her eyebrows. "Really? You're not just being nice, are you?"

"You'll find that I'm considered the not-nice Kendrick,

although I do share that title with Angus. We always speak our minds."

"Who's the nice Kendrick?"

"That would be Kade, although I suspect you already know that."

Annoyingly, Charlie found herself blushing.

Stop thinking about him.

"So, you don't think I need to do anything different with my hair?" she asked.

Ainsley cocked her head. "No, why would you?"

"Mamma thinks it's old-fashioned and plain." She turned on the stool and gazed up at Ainsley. "Unlike yours, which is very au courant."

"Very ridiculous, if you ask me." Ainsley plopped down on the bed, managing to look graceful as she did so. "Whoever came up with these absurd styles should be smothered in pomade and staked out in the hot sun."

"Don't let my mother hear you say that. She's depending on you to bring me up to scratch. It's an impossible task, I'm afraid."

"That's because you don't wish to be brought up to scratch." Ainsley tilted her head. "Why is that?"

Charlie carefully retied the bow on her wrapper, wondering just how much she could—

"You're wondering just how much you can trust me, aren't you?" asked Ainsley.

She sighed. "So you're a mind reader, too."

Ainsley grinned. "No, I'm just that good."

Charlie couldn't help smiling back. Ainsley's wry self-confidence was very appealing and reassuring. Other than the chance to meet Kade, she'd been dreading this week and what Ainsley would expect of her.

Ainsley leaned forward, neatly folding her hands on her knees. "I do mean us to be good friends, Charlotte, and I have no desire to make your life difficult in any way. The opposite, in fact. I'd like to help you."

Charlie frowned. "But why? What I want is definitely not what Mamma wants."

"Let's start there. What is it that you want?"

Ainsley had dodged Charlie's question, but she decided to let it go, for now. "For starters, I'd like you to call me Charlie, at least when we're alone."

"Done. Now, back to my original question. Why are you so resistant to your mother's plans? She said you were at loggerheads over the issue."

Charlie waved a hand in front of herself. "Now that you've met me, surely you understand why my mother wishes to change me. Highland hoyden, remember?"

"It's perfectly reasonable why you would balk at your mother's attempt to remake you. You are clearly your own person and wish to remain that way. Am I correct?"

"Yes, but I don't think I'm going to have much choice in the matter." Charlie sighed. "While Papa has always de-fended what he calls my 'little eccentricities,' Mamma's truly got her teeth into it this time. And Melissa's been kicking up a fuss. She's terrified I'm going to embarrass her at the wedding."

"And are you?" Ainsley asked in a gentle tone.

"I don't think so. Well," Charlie amended, "I hope not, anyway. I'm not averse to wearing a nice dress now and again, and Susan can certainly pummel me into style. So that's not really the problem."

"Then what is the problem?"

"I haven't a clue how to act like a proper young lady. I'm dreadful at dancing, for one thing. Except for sword dancing," she added, "a talent which is unhelpful at a wedding. My governess tried mightily to teach me, but I was a failure in every respect, especially with the waltz."

In part, she suspected, that was because her partner had been Melissa, who excelled at all the feminine arts.

Ainsley smiled. "I'm sure we can manage to address that issue. I'm an excellent dancer, as is Kade. I will dragoon him into service."

The hideous image of Kade witnessing her female ineptitude induced a surge of panic.

"What? No!" Charlie winced at the screechy note in her voice. "What I mean to say is that's not necessary. I'm sure Mr. Kendrick will be busy with his music. Or something."

God, she sounded like an idiot.

Ainsley simply smiled. "Kade will be happy to help. He's very sweet that way. But it's not just about the wedding, is it? There's something else that's causing you to resist your mother's plans."

Charlie rubbed her nose, feeling awkward. "Well, it's rather silly, if you must know the truth."

"Once you've spent a bit of time with my family, you'll see that we excel at silly. Angus is simply the tip of the iceberg in that respect. There's no need to be embarrassed, and you may rely on me to keep any confidences you wish to share."

"Mamma will quiz you, though. She'll want reports."

Ainsley mimicked locking her lips and tossing the key over her shoulder.

Well, why not tell her?

It had been ages since Charlie had been able to confide in anyone. For years, Johnny had been her confidant and friend, but in the last months they'd somehow grown apart. Or, rather, Johnny had pulled away from her. It was a troubling development that left Charlie feeling more isolated than ever.

"Did Mamma happen to mention Richard Campbell in her letters, or did she just say I needed sprucing up for Melissa's wedding?"

"She mentioned a potential suitor but gave no details. Her request was more a general expression of the need to help you acquire a little polish."

"I expect Mamma put it rather more bluntly than that," Charlie wryly replied.

Ainsley smiled. "A trifle, perhaps. So, who is Richard Campbell, and why is he a problem?"

"Because he's my potential betrothed. Ever since Melissa got engaged to Colin MacMillan, Mamma has been seized with the idea that I'm turning into a fusty old spinster. And it is true that I'm perilously close to being on the shelf. The very thought of that fills Mamma with horror."

Ainsley rolled her eyes. "Nonsense. You're a lovely young woman who has plenty of time to meet a nice man and fall in love—if that's what you truly desire."

Charlie could imagine one man she could fall in love with. But even under torture, she wouldn't share that with Ainsley.

"I've never really thought about getting married," she said. "And neither of my parents seemed to care whether I did or not. In fact, Papa always said that he hoped I wouldn't go running off with some silly fellow, and that he would miss me very much if I did."

"That's rather unusual. Most fathers are keen to marry off their daughters."

"I'm Papa's favorite, you see. It's because I'm the oldest, and also because Johnny came along so much later. Papa always wanted a son, but he had to make due with me for quite a long time."

"I'm sure he dotes on you for your own sake," Ainsley said in a gentle tone.

"It truly didn't bother me, because I loved being with Papa. I wanted to be just like him, so I did all the things he did and liked all the things he liked." She couldn't hold back a rueful smile. "He's the one who nicknamed me Charlie, much to my mother's dismay."

"It suits you, though," Ainsley said.

"Melissa says it's because I'm more boy than girl."

Ainsley frowned. "That's rather mean. One need not trick

oneself out in the latest styles or simper about like a ninny to be a woman, and a lovely one at that." She pointed at Charlie. "Which you are, and don't let anyone tell you otherwise."

"Thank you," Charlie replied, suddenly feeling rather shy. "You know, Melissa isn't truly being mean. The poor thing is terrified I'll do something dreadful at her wedding, like slurp my soup or inadvertently insult one of the guests. Neither is entirely outside the realm of possibility, I'm afraid."

Ainsley laughed. "I feel certain that you will not slurp your soup. And as someone who excels at insulting people— often intentionally—you'll receive no lectures from me on that score."

Charlie grinned. "I knew I would like you."

"I hope so, because I am squarely on your side. And speaking of that, why isn't your father standing up for you?"

"I think it's partly because of Johnny. He and my father were never very close." Charlie grimaced. "In fact, Papa used to joke that I was more of a son to him than Johnny was."

"That was not so wise."

"I told Papa that more than once, and he would just say he was joking. But I know it hurt Johnny, so I would spend as much time with him as I could, teaching him all the things Papa taught me." She sighed. "Unfortunately, while he liked to ride, Johnny was never much interested in hunting or fishing, or learning how to manage an estate."

Ainsley shook her head. "A capital crime to a Highlander."

"It got worse when he went off to university. He doesn't seem at all interested in the estate or anything to do with Papa's business."

"What is Johnny interested in?"

"Spending money and getting into trouble."

"So your mother's solution to these various problems is to marry you off? I'm not sure I follow the logic."

"Mamma thinks I've upset the natural order, and that once I'm gone Johnny will settle down and start taking his responsibilities more seriously." Charlie shrugged. "To be fair, I don't think she's entirely wrong."

"So your mother's view has prevailed."

"I think Mamma has simply worn my father down. And he is worried about Johnny. We all are."

"Now, tell me about Richard Campbell, and why you don't wish to marry him." A surprisingly hard expression transformed Ainsley's features. "Is he a bad man? Has he tried to importune you in any way?"

Charlie blinked, surprised by the intensity in her voice. "Believe me, if he tried to importune me, he would swiftly come to regret it. I am well able to defend myself."

More than one boy had tried to take liberties when she was younger, assuming her unconventional behavior meant she would be open to them. She'd soon learned to protect herself by employing a swift uppercut to the jaw or a knee to the privates. In fairly short order, the local lads, as well as those boys whose families came to visit, learned to leave her alone.

Ainsley visibly relaxed. "I'm relieved to hear it. Then, what is wrong with Mr. Campbell?"

"He's boring and suffers from a terminal lack of imagination." Charlie shrugged. "Other than that, not much, I suppose. Most girls would probably think him quite the catch, since he comes from a good family and has a very respectable income."

"But you're not most girls."

"No. Besides, Richard is very old-fashioned and disapproving of my behavior. We're entirely incompatible. I'd probably run the poor fellow through with a dirk before we reached our first anniversary."

Ainsley laughed. "Then why in heaven's name did your parents pick him?"

"Papa and Sir Hugh—Richard's father—have been fast friends since they were boys, and both of them wish to see us settled. Mamma likes Richard precisely because he is so old-fashioned and staid. She seems to think he'll bring me into line."

Ainsley shook her head. "It won't work."

"No, indeed."

"That being the case, what is your plan to manage this situation?"

Charlie rubbed her cheek. "Well, I was hoping to resist your efforts to make me over. I would mostly go on as I am, with the occasional tweak here and there."

"I see. Anything else?"

"I thought I'd wear my kilt as much as possible and perhaps organize a cricket game with the lads from the village. I also thought to make a point of drinking whisky in front of Richard. He would think it appalling for a young lady to imbibe strong beverages."

"I sense a hitch in these plans, though."

Charlie sighed. "I don't actually think they'll work. My dowry is rather stupendous. Most men will put up with quite a lot if the marriage settlements are substantial enough."

"Some man are indeed avaricious that way," Ainsley replied in a serious tone. "But there are those who are not. Kendricks, for one, don't give a damn about things like that."

"Richard does, though. Not that I intend to cave, you understand, but I suspect Mamma and Melissa will drive you batty with their deranged plans to sell me off. Melissa's already on the verge of hysterics over all the wedding folderol." She crinkled her nose. "It's too ridiculous."

"I'm certain I can handle both Lady Kinloch and Melissa."

"All right, but what will we do, then?"

"We will spruce you up just enough to appease your mamma, while also giving you room to maneuver around dreary old Richard."

Charlie expelled a frustrated breath. "I'm afraid that sounds rather complicated, to be honest."

"Yes, I'll need to think on it more. But I'll come up with something, never fear."

She'd been thinking, too, just in case annoyances like cricket games in kilts and the occasional belt of whisky failed to put Richard off. She needed an alternate plan that would make it clear marriage was entirely off the table—a plan that would work not only with Richard but with her parents, as well.

Ainsley glanced at the bracket clock on the fireplace mantel and came to her feet. "Goodness, look at the time. We'd best get you dressed or we'll be late for dinner."

After retrieving the dress hanging on the door of the wardrobe, Ainsley helped Charlie into it. The dress was a struggle, as always. Charlie hated the huge, puffy sleeves and even bigger skirts, but Mamma insisted she have a few fashionable gowns for visits with guests. Frilly gowns were wasted on her, since she invariably crushed her skirts or caught her trim on the doorknobs. On one memorable occasion, she'd set the lace of her sleeve on fire when she got too close to a branch of candles. Thankfully, no one had seen that except a sweet but terribly ancient uncle who didn't quite register that she'd all but gone up in smoke.

"This is a very pretty gown," Ainsley said as she moved behind her to fasten the buttons.

Charlie critically inspected the green silk gown, with its low-cut shoulders and trim-fitting bodice. "It's not a patch on yours, though. I look like an old spinster by comparison."

Not that she had any objection to spinsters. Unless something revolutionary was to occur, she expected to spend the rest of her life as one.

"You don't need frills and furbelows," Ainsley said. "You're perfectly lovely without them."

"You're very kind."

"I never lie about things as important as one's dress. That being the case, I will deliver my first lesson. You must recognize your own sense of style and stick with it. Whether you know it or not, you do have one."

Charlie closed one eye as she studied herself in the mirror. "I do?"

"Yes, a simple and elegant one."

She opened both eyes wide. "I can believe simple, but elegant? No one's ever said that before."

"Then the young men in this district must all be chuckle-headed morons."

Charlie smiled. "Not really, but most of them know I'd probably box their ears if they tried to flirt with me."

"It's not really flirting if the compliment is sincere."

"I suppose." Flirting was another feminine skill that eluded her.

"So," Ainsley said as she finished buttoning the gown. "You and Kade knew each other as children. That was quite an interesting revelation. Were you good friends?"

Charlie tugged at her neckline, oddly disconcerted by the change in topic.

"I certainly considered him a friend. But we were quite young, you know, and it was only that one time at Inveraray." She mustered a smile. "I'm sure he thought I was a terrible pest."

"I'm sure he thought you were charming."

"I was certainly something, though I don't think it was charming."

Ainsley gently turned Charlie around by the shoulders. "Don't tug on your neckline, dear. I'm sure that Kade appreciated you standing up for him. Although he's always had a great deal of courage, he needed protecting back then. I think it's splendid you stood up to a bully."

"Girls aren't supposed to be champions—or go around hitting boys, either."

"Sometimes that is exactly what they are supposed to be and do."

Charlie raised an eyebrow. "I'm beginning to think you're as unconventional as I am."

"I do my best, but let's get back to Kade. Even though you only met once, you obviously got to know each other quite well."

"So well that he forgot me," Charlie dryly replied.

"But you didn't forget him."

"No, I never could." Then she froze, aghast at what she'd just blurted out and what it revealed about her.

Ainsley, however, simply continued to fix her bodice and then puff out her sleeves to their full puffiness.

"Our Kade is quite unforgettable." The young woman took a step back and critically inspected Charlie. "There, you look lovely. That leads me to suspect that Richard Campbell is interested in something else besides your money, dear."

"Oh, God." Charlie sighed. "I hope not."

If Richard actually liked her as a woman, that would make the situation much more difficult.

"Now, you're not to worry," Ainsley said. "No one will force you to marry Richard or anyone else. We simply need to come up with a plan to scare him off."

Charlie snapped her fingers "I know. I can run his carriage off the road, too. That should do it."

"That seems like an awful lot of trouble, dear. Perhaps you'd best shoot him and get it over with."

Charlie spluttered out a laugh. "Don't let Mamma hear you say that. Richard is a great favorite of hers. But a few days in his company and I swear you'll want to shoot him, too."

"Then before we get arrested for murder, we'd best send him off with all speed. When does he arrive, by the way?"

"The day after tomorrow."

A prospect she regarded with as much enthusiasm as a tooth extraction.

"Then we'll leave that problem for now." Ainsley fluffed the skirts of her own gown and took a quick glance in the mirror. "I believe we're both now in prime twig. Shall we go down and join the others?"

"It's been much more fun chatting with you, but I suppose we must."

Mamma would likely still be annoyed with her, and then there was Kade. The prospect of facing him again after behaving like a twit made her stomach curl.

Ainsley hooked her arm through Charlie's. "There's nothing to worry about, dear girl. I will handle your mamma *and* come up with a plan to manage the hapless Richard. Trust me, the poor man won't know what hit him."

"Just as long as it's not me doing the hitting," Charlie said as her new friend towed her to the door. "Mamma would skin me alive."

CHAPTER 5

Kade frowned at the notation he'd just made on the sheet of music and then crossed it out. Closing his eyes, he tried to hear the right notes in his head, imagining how they would sound in a concert hall. The music usually came as easily as breathing, so much a part of him that he didn't need to think much at all.

Today he was struggling again. And when he did finally grasp the sounds, transferring the notes to the page and then to the piano, it came out . . . well, not wrong, precisely. But definitely boring.

He opened his eyes and scowled at the keyboard, as if the instrument had somehow betrayed him. Ever since he was fifteen, composing had served as an outlet for all the emotion he'd always locked up tight in his heart. He loved creating unique music that reflected not only his heart but also his experience of life.

Now he had to wonder if he'd stretched himself a little too thin. He'd been writing and performing shorter pieces for the piano and violin for several years, but this was to be an entire concerto with a full orchestra, and for the king, no less. Kade was beginning to think he'd suffered a momentary loss of sanity when he'd agreed to the request, given his concert schedule *and* the fact that he'd been running around Europe acting like the great, bloody spy.

"Great, bloody idiot," he muttered as he rotated his shoulder, trying to stretch it.

The wound was mostly healed but his muscles still felt stiff, especially when he played the violin. Well, at least he was no longer spying, which freed up time to write his concerto. Too bad all that extra time had failed to free up his creativity, too. He'd fallen out of practice, both mentally and physically, and had only himself to blame.

He began again, determined not to get up until he finished the variation he'd been working on since breakfast. Laroch Manor had everything he needed to accomplish the task. The excellent music room was in a quiet part of the house overlooking the gardens, and Lady Kinloch had made it clear that it was set aside exclusively for his use. Kade was grateful for the refuge. Since their arrival two days ago, he'd spent most of his time right here.

Even Angus had mostly left him alone, but for the occasional effort to force some noxious *healing* potion down his throat.

Putting aside his distracting thoughts, he focused all his attention on the musical worksheet.

Later, when the longcase clock chimed out the hour, Kade glanced up, surprised by how far the afternoon had advanced. Thankfully, he'd finally made progress on the variation. With a few more hours of work, he might even finish the blasted thing before he had to dress for dinner.

As he got up to fetch a glass of water from the sideboard, the door opened and Charlie hurried into the room. When she spotted him, her eyes widened and she stumbled, though she quickly recovered her balance.

"Sorry," she said, sounding a bit breathless. "I didn't hear music, so I thought you were finished for the day."

Ah, so she *had* been avoiding him. Kade had suspected as

much. Since their arrival, she'd barely exchanged two words with him, all but hiding behind Ainsley or Lord Kinloch when they gathered in the evenings.

He smiled to put her at ease. "There's nothing to apologize for, Miss Stewart. This is your house. I am merely an interloper."

"No, you're the guest of honor," she said. "Mamma has put us under strict orders to leave you alone so you can practice for the recital after the wedding."

Kade frowned. "A recital? It was my understanding that I was simply to play a few songs in the drawing room after the service and before the formal ball got underway."

Charlie made a little grimace. "Oh, dear. I'm sorry to say that Mamma has other plans for you, Mr. Kendrick. She'll probably have you playing an entire concert by the time the wedding rolls around."

"That might be a bit hard to pull off without an orchestra," he joked.

"My mother has full confidence in your abilities." She swept him a flourishing, comical bow. "After all, you're the great Kade Kendrick, toast of the Continent."

Kade rounded his eyes in mock alarm. "Please tell me that Lady Kinloch does not describe me in those terms."

Her lovely chestnut brown eyes twinkled with amusement. "Come to think of it, she might have put something similar on the wedding invitations."

When he laughed, her mouth quirked up in a fey little smile. "My mother is also under the impression that you're composing something special just for the wedding. I assume she's mistaken about that."

"It's the first I'm hearing about it," he wryly replied. "That being the case, I'd best start planning my escape."

"You can't do that. Melissa would take to her bed with hysterics, and Mamma would throw herself off one of the turrets. Honestly, I don't know which would be worse."

"The second, I would imagine?"

"You've obviously never seen Melissa in hysterics." Charlie gave him a mischievous smile. "I know. You could just play something by a lesser-known composer and tell Mamma that you wrote it for the wedding. In fact, you could probably play Mozart and my family wouldn't know the difference. They're not exactly musical."

"I will certainly take that under consideration," he said, amused by her comical observations. "But I do have a few original pieces I can dredge up. My thanks for the warning, since I'll now have time to work on them."

They gazed at each other for a few seconds, and then her lighthearted mood seemed to evaporate. As she glanced at the sheets of music spread out on top of the piano, he sensed again that she was uncomfortable in his presence.

"That's very kind of you, sir, but I'll cease pestering you now, since you are obviously much engaged."

Kade took a step forward, holding up a hand. "Please, there's no need to leave. I'm finished for the day."

He wasn't, but he found he'd much rather talk to her than return to his work.

Charlie hesitated. "Are you sure? I don't want to disturb you."

"I am absolutely sure."

At the moment, she was considerably more interesting than his blasted concerto, and certainly more enjoyable to look at. Charlie Stewart was a very pretty girl, with big brown eyes, a charming, uptilted nose, and a honeyed complexion that spoke of time outdoors. The average town miss would recoil in horror at the thought of exposing herself to that much sun, but clearly Charlie would never be a town miss. When not in a kilt or riding habit, it seemed she wore simply cut gowns that lacked the ridiculous extravagances of the current fashions.

And Charlie's quirky wit was just as appealing as her lovely face.

"Well, I was simply going to, um, fetch a book that I think I left on a table here," she said.

Kade suspected she was trying to find an excuse to avoid him again. Suddenly, he greatly disliked the idea of her feeling uncomfortable in his presence.

"Miss Stewart, I hope you're not embarrassed because of our initial meeting. I assure you, there's no need."

She gave a slight grimace. "Tell that to my mother."

He raised his eyebrows. "Did Lady Kinloch find out?"

"Thankfully, no. But she has quite the nose for sniffing out my misadventures. I feel faint with horror at the very idea that she might squeeze it out of someone."

"My lips are firmly sealed. And, again, there's no need to feel awkward about that encounter, or to avoid me."

She hesitated and then flashed him a rueful smile. "Is that what I've been doing?"

"I think so."

"Then I should stop behaving like such a chicken heart. But be warned, sir, that means I might start pestering you so much that you'll wish I would indeed avoid you. I did that when we were children, after all. You were so kind to put up with me then, when you must have been wishing me to perdition."

He smiled. "As I recall, you were a very sweet and interesting child. I enjoyed your company."

She looked dubious. "Really?"

"I particularly liked it when you bashed Andrew in the nose. How I could ever have forgotten that glorious moment is beyond me."

Charlie laughed, and the warm, lovely sound was as endearing as she was.

"I'll never forget it," she wryly replied. "Papa gave me a

right royal scold—and he never scolded me. In fact, I was sent to my room without supper."

"That hardly seems fair, since you were defending a friend from a bully."

"He was a rat, too. Ran right off to tattle to his father." She shook her head. "Andrew's lucky I didn't hit him again."

"It would seem the Campbells have much to answer for, in addition to Glencoe."

"Indeed." Then she gracefully dodged past him to a side table stacked with books. "I'll be out of your hair in a moment."

She still seemed a little too eager to escape his company. Why that should bother him so much was a mystery, but bother him it did.

"For a family that is apparently not musical," he said, trying another topic of conversation, "this room is very well kitted out."

Even in some of the bigger houses, it was rare to find a separate music room. This one was very handsome, with a great deal of natural light and elegantly decorated with gold wallpaper and matching drapes. A blue and gold Aubusson carpet covered most of the floor, and a stylish settee and matching armchairs composed an intimate seating arrangement before the large marble fireplace.

"And the piano is excellent," he added. "I couldn't ask for better."

He'd been expecting the usual mediocre instrument, played only when young ladies were encouraged to display their skills to prospective suitors or entertain at parties. The piano, in fact, was a superb and well-tuned Broadwood grand.

She glanced up from her books. "Well, I may have exaggerated a bit for effect. Melissa is certainly competent on the piano. She used to play the harp, too, although she gave that up a few years ago. And I'm also very fond of music."

Kade gave her an encouraging smile. "I'm not seeing the harp as your instrument, so I assume you play piano."

Charlie shook her head. "Nothing so grand. I play fiddle."

Now, *that* was interesting. Young ladies were generally discouraged from the string instruments, but for the harp.

"So you play the violin. Good for you."

She gave him a sheepish grin. "In my hands, it's definitely a fiddle. I learned my scales and some of the simpler classics from my teacher, of course. Mostly, though, I play Highland ballads and reels. It's the music that Papa enjoys, and he asks me to play it all the time."

"I've been playing jigs and reels since I was a child. My family also enjoys them."

"Hardly your usual concert repertoire, I suspect."

Kade waggled a hand. "Paying patrons generally expect something more highbrow, even if they would actually prefer country ballads or dances. I've spotted more than a few people dozing off in the audience when I play longer or more complicated works."

"Oh, dear. That must be rather . . ."

"Annoying?"

"I was going to say disconcerting."

"I do my best to ignore them, although sometimes the sound of snoring coming from the audience can be a trifle distracting."

She scoffed. "I refuse to believe that anyone would dare fall asleep during one of your concerts. You're an absolute master."

Then she blushed as if she'd said something salacious. Kade rather liked it when she blushed.

"May I ask who was your teacher, Miss Stewart?"

Charlie made a visible effort to collect herself. "I learned the basics on the piano from our governess, although I was truly dreadful. Our local vicar taught me the fiddle. He's quite an expert in Highland music, and was kind enough to say that I possessed natural aptitude. Papa supported me over Mamma's objections."

"Good for your father. Girls should be encouraged to play the violin. It's a splendid instrument."

Charlie studied him for several moments, as if trying to read him—or make a decision.

"It's because of you that I wanted to play it," she said in something of a rush. "I heard you practicing during that visit to Inveraray. I thought you sounded beautiful." She fluttered a hand. "Your violin playing, I mean. It sounded beautiful. I decided right then that I would learn to play it, too."

It took him a moment to recover from his surprise. "I am flattered to hear that, Miss Stewart. And honored."

"You might rethink that if you ever hear me play," she said with a shy smile. "I'm very much an amateur."

"Still, I would enjoy hearing you play."

She regarded him with a degree of skepticism before glancing at the piano. Kade had the distinct impression that she wanted to ask him a question.

"Yes?" he gently prompted.

Charlie crinkled her nose. "I apologize for being so nosy, but you're working on a new piece of music, aren't you? Not for the wedding, but for something else."

"Yes, I'm writing a concerto. Would you like to take a look at it?"

Her eyes went wide. "May I?"

"Of course."

Charlie gingerly took a seat next to him on the piano bench. She now reminded him of a nervous filly, and he found that odd, given her generally confident manner. She'd have to be confident to buck society's trends as she did and stand up to her strong-willed mother. Even though Glencoe was fairly remote, aristocratic young women were still expected to act like ladies.

She studied the musical notations for a few moments before glancing at him. Kade couldn't help noticing that her velvet-brown gaze contained flecks of gold. It made her eyes all the more striking, as if light were sparking from deep within their depths.

"Is something wrong?" she asked.

Dolt, staring at her like a witless boob.

"Not at all," he said.

She frowned, but then returned her gaze to his scribbled notations. "Is it written mainly for the piano?"

"Violin, as well as oboe. I'm trying to approximate the sound of bagpipes."

"That's rather unusual for a concerto, isn't it?"

He nodded. "This piece was especially commissioned by King George. He's mad for anything Scottish, as you know, so he asked me to write something that would extol the majesty and history of the Highlands."

"Including the part when the *Sassenach*s conquered us?" she dryly asked.

Kade laughed. "I thought I'd leave that part out. The old fellow has a rather rosy-eyed view of our history, thanks to Sir Walter Scott."

"I remember reading about the king's visit to Edinburgh," she said a little wistfully. "It sounded like fun."

"Several members of my family participated in the affair, and I think they have yet to recover from the ridiculousness of the experience."

"I wanted to go, but my parents aren't fond of travel, and Papa particularly dislikes the city."

"That's a bit of a shame."

"I suppose, but I expect I wouldn't much take to the city, either." She returned her attention to his music. "If you're trying to re-create the sound of a bagpipe, why not just use a bagpipe instead of an oboe?"

"Because my grandfather would insist on performing with me, which would result in the king charging me with treason—or at the very least the murder of anything resembling music."

"You must be joking."

"I am not. Angus is devoted to his bagpipes, and has spent the last several years trying to convince me that we should tour together."

Her eyes danced with amusement. "And he's really that bad?"

"Worse."

"We certainly can't have the king charging you with treason, so the oboe it is." She pointed to a particular section on the sheet. "You seem to be having a spot of trouble here."

"Noticed that, did you?"

Her smile was apologetic. "Sorry. Rather hard to miss, given all the cross outs."

"I thought it made sense to go with the B flat down to the A, then come down to the G. It seems to be the natural progression."

But no matter how much he'd tinkered, he couldn't seem to coax out the sound he wanted.

"You're trying for something that evokes melancholy?" she asked.

He blinked in surprise at her ability to read the sense of the passage. "Yes, exactly."

Charlie intently studied the notes. He held his peace, interested to see what she would come up with.

"Perhaps you could carry the F over for effect," she finally said. "And here." She pointed to the next bar. "I'd add a C."

Kade practically had to push his thumb up against his jaw to keep it from sagging open. Now that she'd pointed it out, the solution seemed obvious.

"I'm missing a bloody C, aren't I?" he said.

"I think so." Then she held up her hands. "But it's just a thought, and only because this passage somewhat reminds me of one of the old ballads the vicar taught me."

Kade couldn't help grinning at her. "Miss Stewart, you are a genius. That is exactly what the passage needs."

He put his hands on the keyboard and played the notes, incorporating her suggestions. The passage now captured what he'd struggled all morning to achieve.

"It's perfect," he said.

Her smile was both shy and pleased. "Just a lucky guess."

"Then I'm exceedingly grateful for your lucky guess, and I'm going to insist that you play some of those ballads for me. That might give me some genuine inspiration, which I am sorely lacking at the moment."

"I couldn't," she said, now looking slightly alarmed. She slid off the bench. "My playing is nothing out of the ordinary. Nor would my mother approve."

"But—"

Shouts coming from the garden interrupted him. Kade had left the French doors to the terrace slightly ajar to let in the soft summer air, but now a noisy commotion carried into the room. Boys were shouting at something, from the sound of it.

He twisted around to face the garden. "What is that about?"

"I think it's the stable boys," Charlie replied.

She strode to the doors and disappeared onto the terrace.

Kade followed at a more leisurely pace, stepping out onto the wide stone terrace to see Charlie down on the neatly mown lawn. It ran from the back of the house to a small stream that meandered through the grounds of the estate. Although flower beds ringed the manor, including bordering the terrace in a summer riot of color, most of the grounds were lawn interspersed with clusters of holly and juniper. Directly behind the terrace was a magnificent oak, its expansive branches casting shade onto the house.

The oak was the scene of the ruckus. Three young lads were pointing up at the tree while attempting to explain something to Charlie, loudly and all at once.

When Kade joined them, Charlie tapped the shoulder of one of the boys, who appeared to be about twelve and older than the others. She told them to hush, and they subsided with a mutter, obviously still fashed.

"Problem?" Kade asked.

Charlie rolled her eyes. "Maisy is stuck in the tree again."

The oldest boy, dressed to work in the stables, grimaced. "Sorry, Miss Charlotte, but it ain't her fault. She's just a wee one."

"Yes, Peter, I know. But after last week's episode, one would think she'd have learnt her lesson."

Kade could now hear the sound of Maisy's distressed mews. Peering up through the dense greenery, he could just spot the small gray cat about a quarter of the way up, clinging to a branch.

"Poor Maisy ain't very smart," piped up one of the little ones.

"Indeed," Charlie replied. "But you boys are supposed to keep the kittens in the stables and barns, remember? Your father was quite clear about that."

The two little ones, who appeared to be around six and eight, exchanged guilty glances.

Peter blew out an exasperated breath. "I know, Miss Charlotte. But Tommy and Billy keep forgettin' and takin' them out to play."

"They get bored in the stables, miss," piped up the middle one. "'Specially Maisy."

"Told you that, did she?" Charlie asked.

When the lad vigorously nodded, his big brother cuffed him on the shoulder. "Now don't ye be tellin' fibs to Miss Charlotte. She won't believe ye anyway."

The littlest one tugged on the hem of Kade's coat, his blue eyes in his snub-nosed face pleading with him. "Mister, can ye get Maisy down? She's scared."

Before Kade could reply, Charlie quickly marshaled the boys into a straight line.

"First, you will make a proper greeting to our guest," she said. "Mr. Kendrick, this is Peter, the oldest son of our stable-master, and his brothers Tommy and Billy."

"Guid day to ye, sir," Peter said, respectfully tipping his cap. "I'm right sorry that we made a fuss and interrupted ye at yer work."

Kade smiled at them. "No worries, lads. It's a pleasure to meet you."

Billy, the middle one, stared up at him with wide eyes. "Yer music, sir. We heard it earlier. It sounded right fancy. Almost as good as the curate playin' the big organ at church."

Charlie choked out a laugh, which she quickly covered with a cough.

"That's very kind of you, Billy," Kade said in a grave tone.

Another tug on his coat.

"Mister," said Tommy with single-minded determination, "can ye get puir Maisy down? She's right fashed."

From the increasingly frantic meows coming from above, it would seem Tommy was correct.

Kade gazed up at the tree. The branches were sturdy, and there were plenty of good footholds, so he should have no trouble.

"I think so, as long as Maisy cooperates," he said as he started to doff his coat.

"No, I'll do it," said Charlie. "You shouldn't be straining your shoulder."

Kade frowned. "How do you know about my shoulder?"

Instead of answering him, she leaned against the tree. "If you give me a leg up, I can catch that first branch. It's an easy scramble from that point."

"You cannot be serious," Kade said. "You're not properly dressed for it."

She glanced over her shoulder. "I've climbed this tree any number of times, including while wearing a dress."

"Aye," Billy said. "Maisy got up there last week, and Miss Charlotte got her down."

"And I do hope this will be the last time, Billy. I put a thundering rip in my dress the last time, and my maid was not best pleased."

Billy grimaced. "Sorry, miss. Did ye tell her ye got it climbin' the tree? My dad will give us a right paddlin' if he finds out about gettin' ye in trouble and all."

She winked at him. "Since I wish to avoid a paddling from my mother, it will forever remain our secret, as will today's adventure, all right?"

The boys vigorously nodded their heads.

"I'll do it," Kade said. "There's no need for you to rip any more dresses, or scrape your hands, for that matter. The bark is quite rough."

Charlie shook her head. "You're the one who shouldn't be scraping his hands. Besides, Maisy knows me, so she's more likely to let me grab her. The last thing we need is her climbing higher to get away from you."

"Miss Charlotte's a champion climber, sir," Billy said.

Kade glanced at the expectant faces of the lads, and then back at Charlie. She lifted her chin, her gaze determined and just a wee bit stubborn. In that moment, she looked much like the slip of a girl he used to know—feisty and fearless. And he had the feeling that if he insisted on climbing the tree, he would somehow let her down.

"Are your shoes up to the task?" he asked her.

She lifted up her skirts, displaying sturdy half boots and a nicely shaped calf.

Kade bent and cupped his hands.

Charlie flashed him a quick smile, and then she braced her hands on his shoulders and placed a foot in his hands. Since that brought her chest directly to eye level, he couldn't help noticing that her breasts were even more nicely curved than her calves.

"Are you ready, Mr. Kendrick?" she asked.

He snapped his attention back to the matter at hand. "All right, lass, up you go."

When Kade gave her a good boost, she launched herself and caught the lowest branch and pulled herself up. Deftly, and in a quick flurry of skirts, she swung a leg over the bough and settled into a sitting position. He stared up at her, somewhat dumbfounded at her ease in accomplishing the task.

"You see?" she said. "Easy-peasy."

"Apparently," he wryly replied.

"Miss Charlotte's just the best," Tommy said in an admiring voice.

"And now to get Maisy down before she attracts any more attention," Charlie said.

Although the kitten was now mewing even more frantically, perhaps sensing rescue close at hand, Kade suspected it was the oldest daughter of Lord Kinloch, up a tree in full view of the house, who was more likely to attract attention.

Charlie shimmied over to the trunk, bracing against it as she scrambled to her feet. The lass obviously knew what she was doing, but just in case, Kade stood directly beneath, ready to catch her if she fell.

That naturally afforded him a view up her skirts, with an even more fulsome glimpse of her shapely legs, all the way up to the tops of her stockings.

Don't look, you idiot.

Charlie glanced down. "Not to worry, Mr. Kendrick. I won't fall."

"I have complete trust in you, Miss Stewart."

Reaching for the next branch, she started to climb the tree. The kitten had a death grip on a branch several feet over Charlie's head, but she quickly reached it. Kade held his breath as she crouched down on the bough—fortunately a thick and sturdy one—and reached for Maisy.

"Come along, you silly thing," she crooned in a singsong voice.

When the kitten lifted a paw as if to reach for her, Charlie snatched her up. She wobbled a bit but managed to flatten herself against the trunk and keep her grip on the kitten.

"Careful, Charlie," Kade said in a sharp voice.

"I'm all right," she replied a moment later, a bit breathlessly.

When she plopped Maisy onto her shoulder, Kade could see the wee mite digging for purchase on Charlie's gown.

"Ouch, Maisy!"

"All right up there?" Kade asked.

"Yes. Poor thing is just scared, so she's got a good grip on me."

She made her way down to the lowest branch and carefully sat down on it.

"If I lean over and drop Maisy, will you catch her?" she asked Kade. "She could probably climb down from here herself, but if I put her onto the branch I'm afraid she'll go up again."

"No worries," Kade replied. "I'll catch her."

She wrinkled her nose. "She might scratch."

"I've survived worse."

"So I've heard."

And that cryptic remark demanded an explanation, as soon as her feet were on solid ground again.

Charlie pried the cat from her shoulder and gently clasped her by the scruff of the neck. "Now, be a good girl, Maisy, and don't claw Mr. Kendrick."

Then she braced one hand against the trunk and leaned down as far as she could as she prepared to drop the little bugger into Kade's outstretched hands. Thanks to that maneuver, he got an unexpected eyeful down the front of her bodice. Smooth, white breasts plumped out over the tops of her stays, and he fancied he could even see the rosy edges of her—

"Are you ready, Mr. Kendrick?"

He snapped his gaze up to meet hers, which, above her flushed cheeks, looked rather annoyed.

"Er, yes," he replied, mentally wincing. "Perfectly ready. Fire away, Miss Stewart."

She let go her mewling charge. Luckily, Maisy dropped straight into Kade's loose grip, and he managed to catch her around her ribs. But she immediately wriggled away and fell to the ground, taking off like a shot in the direction of the stables.

Tommy and Billy exploded in hot pursuit.

"Thanks, Miss Charlotte," they hollered over their shoulders as they pelted after the kitten. Peter doffed his cap and headed after his brothers.

Charlie shook her head. "Rascals. I have a sneaking suspicion I'll be doing this on a fairly regular basis until Maisy is big enough to get down on her own."

"Perhaps one of the grooms can go up next time. You keep tempting fate like that, and you might take a nasty tumble one day."

She looked down on him, gently swinging her feet and clearly at ease on her perch. "I've been climbing these trees since I was a little girl, and I've yet to take a tumble. Didn't you ever climb trees when you were a boy, Mr. Kendrick?"

"As a matter of fact, I did not."

"Of course not. Because you were sick." She grimaced. "Sorry. I can be such a ninny sometimes."

"There's no need to apologize. I suppose I could have climbed a tree if I'd had a burning desire to do so, though it surely would have sent my entire family into a lather."

"It must have been difficult not to be able to run about and raise Cain like the rest of your brothers."

He smiled up at her. "Or like you?"

She smiled back. "Or like me. I'm sure I could have given your siblings a run for their money."

"In all fairness, unlike the rest, my brother Braden was very well-behaved and serious. And I did have my music and studies, which kept me very happily occupied."

"Still, it must not have been easy."

To be so sickly—and so sick of being sickly—that sometimes he'd wanted to rampage from one end of Castle Kinglas to the other? No, it had been the opposite of easy.

He shrugged. "I was fortunate to have a family that loved me and did everything they could to make life easier for me."

"That part must have been nice," she said, again sounding wistful.

"Now, are you going to spend the rest of the day up there? Because I'm getting a crick in my neck, and you know how delicate my health is. I might have to retire to my bed with a hot compress and headache powders."

She huffed out a laugh. "For someone who used to be so sickly, you're *very* tall and quite as brawny as your brothers."

"I am, which means I am well able to catch you. Having practiced on Maisy, I feel sure I'm up to the task."

And having caught a glimpse of her various feminine attributes, Kade rather thought he'd very much enjoy catching her in his arms.

"That's not necessary, sir, but you should step back now."

He did so, and she pushed off from the branch, landing in front of him in a neat crouch.

Good God. The woman was a veritable Amazon.

Kade reached down to help her stand upright. "Impressive landing, Miss Stewart. That branch is a good nine feet off the ground."

"Oh, that was nothing." She brushed off her hands and then batted a few pieces of bark from her gown. "It's not as tricky in a kilt. Much less fabric to manage."

Kade suddenly decided that he would like to see her climb a tree in a kilt.

Get a hold of yerself, man.

"I can imagine," he said. "And congratulations on a successful rescue mission. I must say, however, that I am put to shame, forced to stand by while you did all the work."

"I'm sorry, but I couldn't let you hurt your shoulder. I know it's still healing, and your grandfather would never forgive me if you reinjured it."

Kade mentally sighed. Of course it had been Angus who'd told her. "What else did my grandfather tell you?"

"That you were injured in a knife fight in Paris." She frowned. "Mr. MacDonald grew quite mysterious when I asked him how you ended up in a knife fight. He claimed he was under a compulsion not to answer, which seemed an odd thing to say."

Despite his irritation, Kade almost laughed at his grandfather's phraseology.

"It was just an unfortunate incident with a thief," he said. "And my injury is well healed, I assure you."

"Not according to your grandfather," she said, turning serious. "He said you were almost killed. I was . . . was quite upset to hear that."

She grimaced and looked down at her feet, as if embarrassed by her show of emotion.

"My grandfather has a marked tendency to exaggerate," he gently replied. "I was never in any real danger."

She drew in a large breath before looking up. "I'm glad to hear that."

He found himself caught in her gaze, which shimmered like rich Baltic amber.

"I'm right as rain, lass," he rather gruffly replied. "In fact—"

"Charlotte Elizabeth Stewart, what in heaven's name are you doing?"

Kade turned to see Lady Kinloch marching down from

the terrace, her normally serene features hardened in lines of well-bred outrage.

"Blast," muttered Charlie. "Get ready for hell to rain down, Mr. Kendrick."

He choked back a laugh and turned to greet his irate hostess. "Lady Kinloch, Miss Stewart and I were just having a stroll about the garden. Would you care to join us?"

Lady Kinloch, for once, ignored him. "Charlotte, I have told you *repeatedly* not to climb trees. Now you do it in front of our guest, no less. Whatever were you thinking?"

"I was thinking I had to get Maisy out of the tree," her unrepentant daughter calmly replied. "Mr. Kendrick offered to do it, but of course I couldn't let him take such a risk."

That threw Lady Kinloch off a bit. She cast Kade an uncertain glance before recovering her parental stride.

"Then you should have sent for one of the grooms, or just left that ridiculous creature up there. Really, Charlotte, climbing trees at your age. Your sister almost had a fit when she saw you."

Charlie rolled her eyes. "So it was Melissa who grassed on me, was it?"

Her mother drew herself up, the very picture of offended dignity. "Please refrain from using horrid cant, especially in front of our distinguished guest."

"I'm really not that distinguished," Kade put in. "Just a regular fellow who also likes to climb trees."

Both ladies looked at him as if he'd just sprouted a pair of ram's horns.

"Of course you are distinguished, Mr. Kendrick," Lady Kinloch insisted. "That is why it is all the more embarrassing that I did not get down here in a timely manner. I do apologize, but Melissa was exceedingly shocked, so I was forced to spend a few minutes with her."

"In other words, Melissa had another bout of the vapors."

Charlie shook her head. "I do hope Colin knows what he's getting himself into by taking the poor girl on."

For a moment, Lady Kinloch was too horrified to respond. Kade, though, was finding it a challenge not to burst into laughter. It was usually his family causing scenes, so being a bystander instead of a participant was a refreshing change.

Lady Kinloch recovered herself. "That, miss, is *quite* enough out of you. Mr. Kendrick, again please accept my apologies for this unfortunate scene. I do hope you will forgive my daughter's *most* unfortunate behavior."

"My lady, I am not in the least bit offended," he said.

"And to be fair, Mamma," Charlie said, "I'm not actually the one causing a scene, at the moment."

Now looking like doom itself, Lady Kinloch took her daughter by the elbow and began marching her toward the house.

As Charlie was hustled onto the terrace, she glanced over her shoulder at Kade.

Sorry, she mouthed.

Then her mother rushed her through the French doors and out of sight.

Staring after them, Kade realized, much to his surprise, that Charlotte Stewart was the most interesting girl he'd met in a very, very long time.

CHAPTER 6

Royal's head appeared around Kade's bedroom door. "Ready to go, old man?"

Kade glanced up from his work. "Already?"

"It's going on seven. Didn't you notice?"

"I did not." Thankfully, at least he was dressed for dinner.

His brother strolled over to join him at the writing desk in the window alcove. "Lad, you've been at it all day."

Kade stretched his arms over his head, trying to work out the kink in his shoulder. "When the muse strikes, I must obey."

Charlie's perceptive comments about his troublesome variation had opened up his creative floodgates, causing Kade to accomplish more work this afternoon than he had in days. After the ridiculous cat rescue, he'd spent the rest of the afternoon working. If Ainsley hadn't popped in to remind him to get dressed for dinner, he'd still be down in the music room.

"Splendid, but you're done for the night," Royal said. "We're assembling in the drawing room to give a grand welcome to Richard Campbell, Miss Charlotte's ostensible fiancé."

"I've already met Richard Campbell." Kade had forgotten that the blighter was here to court Charlie, which annoyed him far more than it should.

"My encounters with Richard and his brother are engraved in my memory," he added. "I see no need to further the acquaintance any more than necessary."

Royal poked him in the arm. "Up, laddie boy. You're not leaving me alone with Grandda. You know he'll shoot death glares at the man for the simple act of being a Campbell—or he'll pick a fight with Lord Kinloch. While you've holed yourself up with your work, I've had to practically sit on Grandda to keep him from instigating a full-blown clan feud."

Kade got up and followed his brother from the room. "I will do my best to assist you in preventing an Angus eruption, or a lamentable sequel to Glencoe."

"An all too plausible outcome, given our grandfather."

They headed down the wide, carpeted staircase to the front hall, where Simmons, the family butler, awaited them. He led them at a stately pace down a long corridor. When they reached one of the drawing rooms, the butler ushered them in.

"Mr. Royal Kendrick and Mr. Kade Kendrick," Simmons announced in a solemn tone.

"How very proper we are tonight," Kade murmured to his brother.

"Trying to impress the prospective in-law, I imagine."

Lord Kinloch bustled over to greet them. "Good evening, gentlemen. We've been waiting for you."

"Please excuse us, my lord," Kade said. "My fault entirely."

Their host gave him a broad wink. "Working on that new music for Melissa's wedding, eh? We're all agog with anticipation for it. But you must also enjoy yourself, young man. All work and no play, and all that rot. Now, come along and say hallo to Richard. He tells me that you were great friends all those years ago."

That was certainly news to Kade.

"My dear, why are you keeping our poor guests standing by that drafty door?" called Lady Kinloch from across the room. "You'll give young Mr. Kendrick a chill. We cannot have him falling sick before the festivities."

Kade mentally sighed. God only knew what Angus had told Lady Kinloch about the state of his health.

"Come along, lads," Kinloch said.

"Not to worry," Royal murmured as they followed their host. "I've got smelling salts if you're feeling faint."

"Yes, and you know where you can put them," Kade murmured back.

Royal simply chuckled.

"Here we are, everyone," Lord Kinloch said as they joined the others at a grouping of sofas and armchairs at the far end of the cavernous space.

The formal drawing room was massive, with high stucco ceilings, gilded trim, two fireplaces, and several elegant seating arrangements that together could comfortably hold at least fifty people. Bay windows overlooked the back garden, affording a spectacular view of the mountains of Glencoe in the distance.

Lord and Lady Kinloch were clearly pulling out the stops to impress Richard Campbell.

The prospective fiancé rose to his feet and offered a smile that resembled nothing so much as a supercilious sneer. While Kade hadn't been friendly with Richard on that childhood visit, he'd found him more innocuous than not. So why the sneer now?

"Kade Kendrick," Richard said. "A pleasure to make your acquaintance again. I was just regaling the ladies with some amusing stories of our youthful hijinks. All quite in good fun, you know."

Angus, seated next to Ainsley on a sofa, glared at Richard. Grandda was obviously in a stew, provoked either by those stories or by the mere presence of a Campbell in their midst.

"About time ye lads showed up," he barked. "I was beginnin' to think ye'd given us the slip and headed out to the local pub.

Not that I could blame ye, except for not takin' yer old grandda with ye."

Ainsley patted his hand. "You know the lads would never go to the pub without you. What would be the fun in that?"

"Ye got that right, *Sassenach*. And an evenin' in the pub sounds just the ticket at the moment, ye ken."

Richard gave an indulgent chuckle. "Why, Mr. MacDonald, I would think you'd enjoy hearing stories from the old days. You have quite the talent for telling tales yourself." He winked at Kade. "At great length, I recall."

Angus narrowed his gaze on Richard, no doubt lamenting the fact that he'd failed to tuck a knife into the pocket of his coat. "And I recall that yer a pom—"

"And I recall that I don't have a drink," Royal cheerfully interrupted. He turned to Kade. "Can I get you something, old son?"

"Allow me," Richard said. "Something mild for Kade, I would imagine. We don't want to upset his delicate constitution. A sherry, perhaps?"

While Richard was some three inches shorter than Kade, the man seemed to be trim and fit, although it was a bit hard to be sure, given his fashionable outfit. The shoulders of his coat were well padded, and his trousers flared out from an oddly narrow waist. He was probably wearing stays, a recent and unfortunate development among the stylish set. Richard's thick red hair, which had been straight as a stick when he was a boy, was fashionably curled, and he sported thick sideburns that curved down almost to his chin.

Coxcomb.

Lord Kinloch waved Richard back down to his seat next to Charlie on a cozy divan. Although, to be fair, the lass had edged as far away from him as she could get without actually tumbling over the edge.

Charlie was looking very pretty in a yellow silk dress that did an excellent job of showcasing her lithe figure and gentle curves. Her usual gold braid highlighted her elfin features and enchanting, tip-tilted nose. Tonight, though, she'd threaded a Kinloch plaid ribbon through the braid. Her simple yet elegant styling stood in marked contrast to the elaborate and mostly ridiculous coiffures that adorned the heads of the other women.

She glanced up at Kade and smiled, and then rolled her eyes in Richard's direction. Kade had to swallow a laugh. Clearly, she was unimpressed with her new suitor.

"No, I'll fetch the drinks, Richard," said Lord Kinloch. "Can't have our guest of honor toadying for the rest of us."

Johnny, who'd been standing politely by, suddenly frowned. "I thought Kade was the guest of honor. After all, he's the big draw for Melissa's wedding. No offense to Richard, of course," he added with a placating smile.

"One never takes offense at these things, you know," Richard said, sounding quite offended. Then he turned to Charlie. "And I've claimed the greatest honor of the evening, which is the privilege of sitting with Miss Charlotte. Anything else pales in comparison to that, including one's tinklings on the piano."

Angus bristled like a jumped-up rooster. "Tinkling? Why, ye—"

When he suddenly clamped his mouth shut and scowled at Ainsley, Kade was quite sure she'd just elbowed him in the ribs.

Seated between her fiancé and Lady Kinloch on one of the other sofas, Melissa stared earnestly at Richard. "Of *course* Mr. Kade Kendrick is our guest of honor. He's very famous, you know, and quite the toast of the Continent. We are so, so lucky that he graciously agreed to gift us with his presence."

Royal started to laugh before covering it up with a cough.

"Something stuck in your throat, old boy?" Kade politely asked.

"Something," his brother managed.

"Naturally, you are all our honored guests," Lady Kinloch said, obviously keen to bring the absurd discussion to a conclusion. "Henry, why are you standing about like that? By all means, do please fetch the drinks. The dinner gong will be going off shortly."

Kinloch snapped his fingers. "Perfectly right, my dear. Mr. Royal, a whisky. And Mr. Kade, you'll be having a . . ."

"A whisky," Charlie firmly interjected. "Both Mr. Kendricks drink whisky, Papa. I, however, will have another sherry, if you don't mind."

Her father frowned at the glass in her hand. "But you haven't finished your first one."

Charlie brought the delicate glass to her lips and quickly drained the contents. Then she handed the glass to her father.

Richard looked shocked, while Melissa let out a horrified squeak.

"A lassie after my own heart," Angus said, winking at her.

Lady Kinloch, after casting Charlie an irritated glance, rose. She dredged up a smile for Kade. "Mr. Kendrick, do sit by Melissa. She would love to hear about your musical plans for the wedding."

Having quickly recovered from her shock at her sister's behavior, Melissa fluttered her eyelashes at Kade. "Yes, please. I am simply *agog* with excitement. I cannot *believe* you're going to play at my wedding. Dear sir, I grow positively light-headed just thinking about it."

Colin, Melissa's fiancé, leveled a glare at Kade. The evening was rapidly descending into a farce, and Kade had barely opened his mouth.

He took a seat next to Melissa. "It would be my pleasure, Miss Melissa."

Royal took pity on Colin and got him up for a discussion about hunting. Charlie soon joined in, as did Richard. Kade listened with half an ear, discerning with amusement that Charlie was a more accomplished hunter than either Richard or Colin. From the sour expression on Richard's face, it was obvious he didn't approve of her sporting prowess.

"Mr. Kendrick," Melissa said, "please do let me tell you about the decorations Mamma and I have planned for the reception room. I hope they'll meet with your approval."

"I'm sure they will," he said with a smile.

He listened politely as Melissa described the decorations and other wedding details. Everyone else in the room was now also engaged in conversation but for Johnny. He'd wandered off to the window and was absently staring out at the descending dusk. Kade sensed that something was bothering the lad. Of course, it seemed clear that his father didn't approve of him, so perhaps that was it. Still—

The gong sounded, interrupting his ruminations. A moment later, the door opened and Simmons paced back into the room.

"Dinner is served, my lady," he announced in a stentorian tone.

Kade stood and gave Melissa a hand up from the sofa. She fluttered off to Colin while Kade joined Ainsley and Angus.

"Finally," Angus grumbled. "If I had to listen to that jingle-brains of a Campbell one moment longer, I'd have gutted him like a maggot-ridden hog."

Ainsley sighed. "Grandda, you must stop threatening the guests, even if that guest is a Campbell."

Angus jerked his head toward Richard. "Just look at him, botherin' that bonny lass. She wants naught to do with him, and yet the idiot willna leave her alone."

Richard was now gallantly offering his arm to Charlie, insisting that he escort her into dinner. When she politely tried to put him off, Lady Kinloch intervened, directing her daughter to accept his offer.

Her ladyship then addressed Kade. "If you would be so kind as to escort your grandfather in to dinner."

"Elspeth, I've been gettin' myself in to dinner for yon

eighty years," Angus replied with asperity. "I dinna need to totter along on Kade's arm, ye ken."

"Do stop making such a fuss, Angus," Lady Kinloch replied. "You're holding up dinner."

She then turned and swept across the room, following the others already making their way to the dining room.

"Shall we, Grandda?" Kade asked.

His grandfather's gaze narrowed to fiery slits. "Offer me yer arm and I'll knock yer block off."

"I wouldn't dare."

"We should skip the whole bloody thing, if ye ask me," Angus grumbled as they started toward the dining room. "Best we nip down to the pub after all."

"No one is nipping down to the pub, and you *will* behave yourself at dinner," Kade firmly said. "For God's sake, we've socialized with Campbells any number of times over the years. This is no different."

"And if ye'd been quicker off the mark, ye could have taken Miss Charlie into dinner, instead of that niffy-naffy jinglebrains."

"I'm certain Charlotte would have preferred to go in with you, Kade," Ainsley said.

"I think she would have preferred to go in with just about anybody else," Kade replied.

"Och, ye dinna have the brains to see what's afoot, do ye?" Angus said with a derisive snort. "She's sweet on ye, lad, and that's a fact."

Fortunately, since they'd finally reached the dining room, Kade was able to ignore his grandfather's embarrassing—if flattering—assessment.

The formal dining room was just as impressive as the drawing room, although not as cavernous. The highly polished rosewood table all but groaned under elaborate place settings of her ladyship's best crystal and plate, obviously hauled out for the occasion. Silver trays contained carefully arranged displays of pineapples and oranges, and a large and quite ugly epergne held pride of place at the halfway point of the table.

It was quite the display for a small dinner party, all in the service of impressing the junior scion of a junior branch of the Campbell family. Kade could only assume that Lady Kinloch was trying to compensate for the fact that the intended object of the wooing was obviously less than enthusiastic about the wooer.

Kade took his seat directly across from Richard, who was on Charlie's right. The lass didn't seem best pleased by the arrangement; she glanced over and gave Kade a little grimace.

Angus, on Kade's left, elbowed him.

"Told ye the lassie would rather be with ye than that chuckleheaded twit," he said in a loud stage whisper.

Lady Kinloch hastily stepped into the breach.

"Mr. Kendrick," she said to Kade, "you must excuse the numbers at table tonight. We find ourselves uneven, I'm afraid. I'm sure it's nothing like what you've come to expect on your travels to the Continent."

"Not at all, my lady," he replied. "I have never seen a more beautiful table, even in Paris."

Lady Kinloch rewarded him with a pleased smile. "Surely you exaggerate, but I'm happy you find everything to your satisfaction."

"I do, and without a doubt, ma'am."

"I doubt any French hostess could match Lady Kinloch in terms of style or elegance," Richard said. "As for Parisians . . . well, Kade might find them to his taste, but I certainly do not."

"You've been to Paris?" Kade asked in a bland tone.

"I have, and once was more than enough. Dirtiest place I've ever seen. As for the morals of the French, especially the women, we all know about that, eh, old fellow?"

The man was an even worse prat than he remembered.

"I cannot say that I've noticed any difference in the morals of the French as opposed to anyone else," Kade politely replied.

"You seem to know quite a bit about the morals of French women," Charlie said to Richard as two footmen served out the soup course. "Why is that?"

He shot her a startled glance. "Er, I'm not really sure what you're asking, Miss Charlotte."

Angus chuckled. "I think the lassie is askin' if ye—"

"Cousin, please eat your soup before it gets cold," Lady Kinloch firmly interrupted. "I had the seafood bisque made especially for you, since I know how much you like it."

Angus frowned at her. "Elspeth, ye know I hate shellfish. There's nothing worse than slurpin' down a grisly old mussel or a manky oyster."

Richard chuckled. "I see the old fellow is just as outrageous as ever. I'd quite forgotten what an original you are, Mr. MacDonald."

"Ha," barked Lord Kinloch from the other end of the table. "'Original.' That's one way to describe it."

Lady Kinloch looked pained at the intrusion. "Charlotte, would you please ask Johnny to convey to your father that he should not shout down the table at us?"

Johnny, who'd been solely focused on his food, glanced up at his mother. "I can hear you, Mamma. I'm sure father can, too."

"Sorry, my dear," Kinloch said in a hearty voice. "I'm forgetting my manners, but we're just family and friends now, aren't we?"

Lady Kinloch turned her attention to Kade, trying to regroup. "Mr. Kendrick, while I hate to presume, might I be so bold as to ask you to play for us later?"

"Yes, please," exclaimed Melissa, clapping her hands. "That would be simply splendid."

"I should be happy to oblige," Kade said.

"Huzzah," enthused Kinloch, forgetting his wife's admonition. "You could play a little duet with Charlie, eh? I'm sure she wouldn't mind, would you, my dear?"

Charlie dropped her spoon and stared at her father with abject dismay. "Papa, I couldn't possibly do that. I'm simply an amateur."

Kinloch beamed at her. "Nonsense, pet. You play the prettiest ballads on that fiddle of yours. No one better in the county, save the vicar."

When Charlie's shoulders climbed up around her ears, Kade cudgeled his brain to find a polite way to get the lass off the hook.

"I didn't know you played the violin, Charlotte," Ainsley said. "That's an unusual choice for a lady, although I'm not sure why. It's such a lovely instrument, you'd think many a girl would wish to learn it. When Kade plays for us, it's such a treat."

Angus nodded. "Our lad is a wonder. He gets his talent from me."

Charlie, gamely recovering, smiled at Angus. "Mr. Kendrick told me that you play the bagpipes. I adore the bagpipes and wish I'd learned to play them."

Richard frowned at her. "Why would you want to play those infernal things? If you ask me, they always sound like a goat getting throttled."

"And have you actually heard a goat getting throttled?" Kade couldn't help asking.

"You know what I mean," Richard said, annoyed.

Angus exhaled a dramatic sigh. "Aye, that's a Campbell for ye. Doesna appreciate his own heritage. I'll be happy to give ye a few lessons on the pipes, Miss Charlotte, if we can rustle up a pair."

"Grandda, I'm sure Miss Charlotte will be too busy with wedding preparations," Royal tactfully put in.

"And thank God for that," Richard said with a smirk. "I quite recall Mr. MacDonald's efforts on the bagpipes. Words fail me, I'm afraid. Oh, wait . . . strangled goat, anyone?"

"Oh, Lord," Royal muttered.

While Kade prepared to grab onto his grandfather to forestall impending mayhem, Charlie glared at Richard.

"What an utterly mean-spirited remark," she said. "I'm shocked that you would say such a thing about my mother's cousin—or about anyone, for that matter."

A short, fraught silence took hold of the room. Even Lady Kinloch seemed at a loss.

Richard starched up. "It's just a little jest, Charlotte. I don't mean to be rude."

"Apparently you do," she replied.

"Charlotte, please remember yourself," Lady Kinloch exclaimed. "Richard is our guest."

Richard mustered up a smile. "It's quite all right, my lady. Miss Charlotte is just having a little sport with me. The ladies must have their fun, eh?"

Kade stared at him in disbelief. The man truly was an idiot.

Fortunately, the butler and several footmen trooped in and began serving the next course, providing a welcome distraction.

Angus, who'd been suspiciously calm despite Richard's digs, leaned forward and addressed him across the table. "Ho, Campbell. My memory is not as good as it was, ye ken. Remind me which branch of the clan yer from."

Richard had just been about to cut into a large slice of beef, but paused. "Er, the Loudoun branch, I think." He chuckled. "I've never paid much attention to that sort of thing. There are so many Campbells running about the country that it's hard to keep us all straight."

Even the amiable Lord Kinloch looked slightly shocked.

For a Scot not to know the details of his own clan lineage was tantamount to heresy.

Angus shook his head. "Ye have the wrong end of the stick on that one. Your ma's a Campbell of Craignish and yer da's from a cadet branch of Breadalbane. Campbells of Glenorchy, to be exact."

Richard bristled, as if he'd just been accused of something unsightly. "I'm not sure how you can be so certain about that. It's not like you're a Campbell."

"Thank the Lord for that," Angus said as he forked up a piece of potato.

Lady Kinloch hastily intervened. "I believe you're correct, Angus. Your knowledge of clan history is quite astonishing."

Richard looked even more annoyed now. "All I know is that I'm a Campbell, and I'm related to the Duke of Argyll, which should certainly be good enough for anyone."

"Yer a second cousin once removed, which is hardly worth mentioning," Angus replied. "Hard to believe ye think yer good enough for the likes of a fine Stewart lass like Miss Charlotte."

That observation naturally took the conversation off the proverbial cliff.

Lord Kinloch recovered first. "What in God's name are you talking about, man?"

Torn between irritation and amusement, Kade turned to his grandfather. "Angus, this is hardly the time or place to discuss family matters, especially ones that don't concern us."

"Of course they concern us, lad." He pointedly looked at Charlie before waggling his eyebrows at Kade. "We discussed this, remember?"

"No," he replied in a blighting tone.

His grandfather wasn't just twitting Richard. He was clearly trying to play matchmaker at the dinner table. And from the look on Charlie's face—her mouth slightly ajar—she was as stunned as everyone else.

When Richard swelled up with anger, he rather resembled a toad with sideburns. "Now see here, you old—"

Angus jabbed his fork at him. "Yer kin murdered my ancestors at Glencoe, which makes ye descended from traitors. To think ye have the nerve to court Miss Charlotte, when ye have such a stain on yer name. It's a crime, is what it is."

"Grandda, that's a bit much, even for you," Royal said.

"There's some things that canna be forgiven," Angus retorted. "Murder and treason are two of them."

Richard threw down his napkin. "Glencoe happened ages ago. And it wasn't like I was there, or had anything to do with the whole bloody mess."

"Emphasis on 'bloody,'" Ainsley quipped from the other side of the table.

Despite his better judgment, Kade had to work hard not to laugh. It was like watching the Highland version of a terrible French farce.

"Really, Ainsley?" Royal said to his wife.

She simply winked at him, and went back to eating her creamed peas.

"I say, MacDonald," Kinloch blustered. "Why you persist in hanging onto these dreary old feuds is beyond me. As Richard said, it happened ages ago. It's now the eighteen twenties, for God's sake."

Angus pressed a hand to his chest, looking tragic. "For a Stewart to forget our noble history is a sad sign of the times. Not to mention lettin' this ninny court yer daughter. It's that ashamed of ye, I am."

"It's none of your business who I court or don't court, you silly old fool," Richard hotly retorted. "And you would be wise—"

Kade leaned forward. "And *you* would be wise to choose your next words carefully, my friend."

When their gazes locked, Richard's flushed cheeks lost some of their color. Kade wasn't surprised. He'd spent years perfecting the icy Kendrick glare. His older brothers had always employed it to great effect, sending more than one hardheaded idiot into a scrambling retreat.

Richard struggled to regroup.

"I had no wish to offend," he said, mustering a smile for Lady Kinloch. "Please forgive me if I have."

"This conversation has been most irregular," Lady Kinloch replied. "I barely know where to look."

Melissa fluttered her napkin. "Indeed, Mamma. I feel quite, *quite* faint."

"Forgive me, Miss Melissa," Richard said. "I certainly had no intention of upsetting the ladies. I was simply trying to explain that my intentions to woo Miss Charlotte are not—"

Charlie suddenly stood, all but knocking over her chair. "Mamma, don't you think it's time we left the gentlemen to their port and whisky while we repair to the drawing room?"

Lady Kinloch peered at her daughter, obviously mystified by her behavior. Charlie simply shrugged, and then turned and strode from the room.

Ainsley rose to follow her.

"Enjoy your whiskies, gentlemen," she said in a voice suffused with laughter. "But don't keep us waiting too long."

CHAPTER 7

Charlie longingly eyed the whisky decanter on the sideboard. But she'd already downed two glasses of sherry before dinner and a glass of wine with dinner. If she added a shot of whisky on top of it, she'd likely pull an old claymore off the wall of the gallery and cleave Richard in half for being such an idiot.

Her mother, ensconced on a velvet divan, leveled another disapproving look her way. For the last ten minutes, Mamma had been fussing with her needlework in fraught silence, conveying her well-bred sense of disappointment without uttering a word. Charlie suspected she was debating the possibility of exiling her eldest daughter to the Outer Hebrides. Mamma hated scenes, and Charlie had just created one of fairly epic proportions.

Part of her wished her mother would indeed send her into exile, if it meant she'd never have to face Kade again. What he must think of her after that hideous scene—compounded by his grandfather's embarrassingly pointed comments—she couldn't begin to imagine.

"Really, Charlotte," Mamma said, finally breaking her tight-lipped silence. "I cannot imagine what you were thinking to behave in so outlandish a manner. To storm out like that . . . I was never more embarrassed in my life."

Charlie wrinkled her nose. "Sorry, Mamma, but it seemed a reasonable response at the time."

"Why you would think that is beyond me," her mother tartly replied. "But then again, I gave up trying to understand you some time ago."

Melissa, who was nervously twisting her tatting into a mess, cast Charlie a reproachful glance. "It was such a dreadful scene that Colin wanted to ask one of the footmen to fetch my smelling salts. I became quite light-headed, you know."

Charlie had to repress the urge to roll her eyes, since her sister was quite adept at throwing scenes of a different sort. Melissa could barely get through the day without recourse to her smelling salts, although her scenes garnered sympathy more often than not.

Mamma peered anxiously at Melissa. "You are looking quite pale, my love. Perhaps it might be best if you retired for the evening. You must keep up your strength for the wedding festivities. Colin will expect you to look your best."

Melissa adopted a heroic expression, as if she were Joan of Arc heading off to the stake. "Thank you, Mamma. But I will persevere this evening, for Colin's sake. He would be *quite* upset if I were to take to my bed from the shock of this evening's events."

This time, Charlie did roll her eyes. "For heaven's sake, Mel, it wasn't that bad. But if you want me to apologize to Colin, I shall be happy to do so. I would like to point out, however, that you have the good fortune to marry a man you actually love, and who loves you in return. In contrast, Richard is a boring old poop who doesn't love me one little bit, and yet everyone wants me to marry him."

Richard probably had a mild affection for her based on their tepid childhood friendship. What he had a great affection for was her dowry. Of that Charlie was dead certain. He had political ambitions, and her marriage settlements would come in handy in furthering those ambitions, as would a solid alliance with Lord Kinloch of Clan Stewart.

Mamma plunked her needlework back into her work-basket with an exasperated huff. "Richard is not a boring old poop, and no one is forcing you to do anything, Charlotte. We are simply asking you to give him a chance. Your father has allowed you to rattle around the estate for too long. It's past time for you to settle down, and Richard will make for an extremely eligible match."

"Mamma's right," Melissa earnestly said. "People are beginning to gossip about you, dearest, and that's quite uncomfortable for the rest of us."

Ainsley, who'd gone upstairs to check on her daughter, entered the room.

"Sorry to be late," she said as she took the seat next to Charlie on the sofa. "What have I missed?"

"Not much," Charlie wryly replied, "but for the fact that I've become an object of gossip amongst the locals. You're just in time to hear the gruesome details."

Mamma prepared a cup of tea for Ainsley. "As tonight's display illustrated, it's no wonder that people are gossiping."

Ainsley accepted her cup with a smile. "Kendricks are champion generators of gossip. We've simply learned to live with it."

For a moment, Mamma looked a bit daunted. "There is a great deal of difference between a man kicking up larks and a young woman in Charlotte's position. Surely you must agree."

"I've always thought it massively unfair, actually," Ainsley replied. "Why should the men have all the fun?"

Melissa let out a squeak of dismay.

"But you must see how dismaying it is that people are gossiping about Charlotte," Mamma protested.

Ainsley took a sip of tea before replying. "I find it's usually best to ignore gossip. People rarely mean well, and they would do better to keep their opinions to themselves."

"Yes, but it's *what* people are saying about Charlotte that's so distressing," Melissa said, sounding genuinely upset.

Charlie mentally sighed. As much as she loathed being pestered by her mother and sister, she did love them and knew they loved her. If Melissa was that disturbed, the gossip must be truly unpleasant.

"It's quite all right, Mel," she said. "You can tell me. I promise I won't get upset."

Her sister grimaced. "Well, people are saying that you're becoming . . . odd."

Of course she was odd, at least compared to the other young women in the district. "What, exactly, do they mean by odd?"

Melissa hesitated, and then tapped her head with one finger.

Charlie practically fell off the sofa. "Are you saying the locals think I'm dicked in the nob?"

"That's utterly ridiculous," Ainsley said, clearly annoyed. "Whoever is making such claims should be hauled out to the nearest field and shot."

Mamma eyed Ainsley with a degree of consternation that might signal she was beginning to wonder if she was the right woman to educate her daughter in the feminine social graces.

"As distressing as the situation is," Mamma finally said, "there is no need to exaggerate. Besides, no child of mine could possibly be dicked, er, weak in the head. That is not what Melissa meant."

"Sorry, Mamma, but it is," Melissa replied. "At least that's what Sarah and Rebecca Fielding told me. There was no mistaking their intent, I'm afraid."

Mamma scoffed. "The Fielding girls are dreadful gossips, as well as being excessively silly."

"But people are also saying that you're dwindling into an old maid, Charlotte," Melissa said. "And that no one wants to marry you because you're . . ."

"Dicked in the nob," Charlie dryly finished for her. "Yet Richard's presence would seem to suggest otherwise. Besides, I'm the one who doesn't want to get married, not the other way around."

Melissa's bluebell eyes went wide with shock. "But dwindling into an old maid would be awful, dearest. How could you bear it?"

"I will not allow you to dwindle into anything, Charlotte," their mother rapped out. "Much less an old maid."

Charlie couldn't hold back a sigh. "All right, but *not* Richard Campbell."

"Richard is a very nice man," said Mamma, "and he seems more than willing to disregard your eccentric behavior."

Ainsley let out a delicate snort. "That's generous of him. Personally, I think she'd be throwing herself away on Campbell. Charlotte deserves better."

Charlie smiled at her. "That's very kind of you."

"I tell only the truth, dear girl. You deserve someone who truly loves you."

Unfortunately, however much Charlie might wish for a certain man to be that someone, the chances of that occurring were stupidly remote.

The door opened and the men came into the room, interrupting their conversation. Richard joined them and perched on one of the wingback chairs, giving Charlie a hopeful look. She knew she should try to muster up an off-putting remark, but her heart just wasn't in it.

Ainsley glanced at her and then rose from her seat. "Kade, why don't you sit next to Charlotte? I need to speak to Royal for a minute."

"It would be my pleasure," Kade replied, sounding as if he meant it.

Charlie mustered up a smile as Kade sat beside her. For a moment, she stared at him, taking in the amusement in his wonderful cobalt gaze. She could get lost in that gaze, and that would be entirely too risky for her heart.

His mouth tilted up, matching the smile in his eyes. "Still bent on making mischief?"

The man was certainly blunt.

"Why, sir, whatever can you mean?" she replied, widening her eyes in mock innocence.

He inclined his head toward Richard. "Your hopeful suitor. You're trying to put him off—or make him jealous. I'm having trouble deciding. But he's staring daggers at me, so I'm leaning toward the second interpretation."

Startled, she glanced at Richard. Sure enough, he was directing a tremendously dirty look at Kade, as if he saw him as a rival for her attentions.

"That's ridiculous," she said. "Even Richard's not stupid enough to believe you would wish to court me."

Then she mentally kicked herself. When would she learn to control her blasted tongue?

Kade glanced at Richard before returning his attention to her. "Are you sure? If I even dared to flirt with you, I suspect he'd challenge me to a duel."

"Now you're just being silly."

"I am frequently silly," he admitted. "As any one of my brothers will tell you."

"I rather doubt that. Most of the time, you seem very serious to me."

He inclined his head. "My family does often scold me for being too serious and working too hard. The fault of my chosen profession, I'm afraid."

"One must be serious to attain the level of excellence you have achieved. But then why did you say you were frequently silly, when you're the exact opposite?"

"Because I would hate for you to think of me as a dull fellow like poor Richard over there. You've rather boxed him into a corner, haven't you?" He ducked his head a bit, to stare right into her eyes. "I don't want you to box me in, Charlotte."

For a panicky moment, she felt like she'd just been thrown into a deep pond. Men never panicked her, and yet right now her brain was scrambling to come up with a coherent reply.

"I . . . I would never compare you to Richard," she stammered.

"So, I'm not boring?"

She eyed him. "My dear sir, I believe you have now boxed *me* into a corner. At least conversationally."

Kade gave her a lazy smile that made her heart flutter madly. For a moment, she felt as light-headed as Melissa always claimed to be.

Fortunately, Angus appeared in front of them with a glass for Kade. "Here's yer whisky, lad."

"Thanks, Grandda. Perhaps you can also fetch a drink for Miss Charlotte."

"Please, call me Charlie," she automatically said. "Oh, but not in front of my mother."

"Yes, you mentioned that before," Kade replied, sounding amused. "Duly noted, though."

Perhaps she really was becoming dicked in the nob. At the moment, she was certainly coming off as weak in the head, as Mamma so daintily put it.

"So, lassie, ye'll be wantin' a drink?" Angus said.

"No, thank you, Mr. MacDonald. I'm fine."

"Then shove over," the old fellow said. "I've a mind to talk with ye."

He plunked down beside her. Kade shifted as best he could, but he was so big that Charlie found herself squeezed between the two men, and thigh to thigh with Kade. Suddenly, her dress and underskirts didn't feel nearly as sturdy as they normally did.

And, appallingly, she was absolutely riveted by the outline of Kade's muscled thighs through his trousers.

"Grandda, if you wish to speak to Miss Charlotte, I can move away," Kade said. "You practically sat on the poor girl."

"Nay, it's both of ye that I aim to be talkin' to."

While Angus's wrinkled features looked benign, the expression in his eyes could only be described as cagey.

"About what?" she cautiously asked.

"That booby Campbell. Surely yer not thinkin' of leg-shacklin' yerself to the fellow. Now, I think the world of yer mother, but she's far off the mark with this one, lassie."

"Grandda, this is not an appropriate topic for conversation," Kade said with a frown. "And you'll embarrass Miss Charlotte."

"I think I'm beyond embarrassment," she admitted. "Nor was I a paragon of good behavior at dinner myself, as my mother has made clear."

"Elspeth was always a bit of a stickler," Angus said. "I can have a wee chat with her if ye like."

Charlie knew that would be a very bad idea.

"Thank you, but I think she's best left alone, for now." She sighed. "I'm sorry I put you all in such an awkward position. My family and I are quite ridiculous."

Kade's answering smile was so full of warmth that Charlie's brain seemed to go fuzzy around the edges. She imagined legions of women all over the Continent being slain by that smile.

"Kendricks have been known to kick up a scene now and again," Kade said. "It's rather bred in the bone, much to my oldest brother's dismay."

"Nick caused a few scenes of his own, especially when he was courtin' Victoria." Angus gave Charlie a canny look. "I ken what yer doing with booby Campbell. Yer kickin' over the traces, hopin' to put him off."

"I suppose it's rather obvious," she admitted.

He tapped the side of his nose. "I can sniff out a scheme a mile away, lassie. It's a requirement when dealing with Kendricks."

Charlie suddenly discovered an avid curiosity about the Kendrick family, and of course one member in particular.

"Why is that?"

"Because some of my older brothers were regularly involved in harebrained schemes," Kade dryly offered. "Some of which sadly involved a degree of criminal behavior."

Angus shook his head. "I had my hands full with the lot of ye, back in the day."

"Grandda, half the time you were the mastermind behind the schemes."

"Yer dreamin'," Angus retorted. "Besides, my schemes always worked."

Kade leaned toward Charlie, covering one side of his mouth as if to share a secret. "They never worked."

Charlie couldn't hold back a laugh any more than the giddy feeling that his nearness produced in her.

"And I'll have no sass from ye, laddie boy," the old fellow said. "Dinna be forgettin' that yer nae too big for me to paddle yer bum."

Charlie clapped a hand over her mouth, practically choking on laughter. Kade was as big and brawny a man as she'd ever met, while Angus looked like an ancient Highland sprite who'd just popped out from the woodland realm.

Kade smiled. "Grandda, you've been threatening that for as long as I can remember, and yet you've never laid a hand on any of us."

"Aye, but there's a first time for everything. And dinna ye be tryin' to distract me. This is serious business, saving Miss Charlie from booby Campbell."

Charlie held up her hand, as if making a vow. "I solemnly

promise to do everything in my power to avoid marriage to Richard Campbell."

Angus patted her knee. "Good lass. Ye dinna want to be pollutin' yer foine bloodlines with that lot."

She could only blink at that comment.

"Grandda, that is *completely* inappropriate," Kade said.

"Clan bloodlines are that important, as ye well know. Miss Charlie is a Stewart, descended from kings and queens. Ye'll nae be wantin' any of those treacherous Campbells in the mix."

Charlie recovered her voice. "In all fairness, Richard is a pale imitation of a Campbell. He says he doesn't even know which branch of the family he comes from."

"Another reason why yer dear ma should nae be tryin' to make ye marry him," Angus replied, somewhat illogically. "And why ye need our help."

"Miss Charlotte is doing just fine without us," Kade sternly said. "Best to leave it alone."

His grandfather ignored him. "The best thing would be for our Kade here to pretend that he's courtin' ye."

Charlie's brain all but froze, whether from shock or embarrassment or both.

Kade breathed out a long-suffering sigh.

Embarrassment.

"Really not necessary, sir," she hastily said. "I'm sure I'll be able to—"

Angus interrupted her. "Nae, it's perfect. If booby Campbell thinks Kade is a-courtin', he'll back off and be on his way."

"I'm fairly sure it would produce the opposite effect," Kade said in a voice as dry as chalk.

He made a point of looking across the room at Richard. Charlie followed his gaze and winced. Her suitor had gone back to glaring daggers at Kade so obviously that her mother finally took notice.

Mamma frowned. "Charlotte, you're getting quite wrinkled, squashed between the gentlemen. Do get up."

"Yes, Mamma."

Kade rose first and gave her a hand.

"Thank you," she said, avoiding his eye.

"Pet," her father called from across the room, "why don't you give us a little tune on your fiddle? I'm sure Richard would love to hear you play."

Richard flashed her a broad smile. "Indeed. I know that Miss Charlotte is quite accomplished on the violin. I'm not used to ladies playing that particular instrument, mind you, but I'm sure it will be a treat."

Blood seemed to drain from Charlie's head as panic set in. "I'd really rather not. Melissa, why don't you play the pianoforte? Colin does love to hear you play, and you're so good."

"Richard has expressed an interest in hearing you play, my dear," Mamma said in a firm tone. "I would hate for you to disappoint him."

Richard gave an indulgent chuckle. "I would indeed be most disappointed, Miss Charlotte. You must know how much I love music."

She knew for a fact that he cared not a fig for music but was just trying to toady up to her parents.

"That's a good girl," said her father. "Play a few of the old Highland ballads."

"Ho, Kade," Angus said. "Ye can play along with Miss Charlotte. There's a dandy little pianoforte over there by the window."

"Even better," enthused Papa.

For a hideous moment, Charlie thought she would faint. Bad enough to have to play her fiddle in front of possibly the best violinist in the entire kingdom, but to actually play *with* him? She couldn't imagine a more appalling scenario.

She tried to muster a coherent response. "Uh, I don't think—"

Melissa clapped her hands. "Yes, please. I would *love* to hear Mr. Kendrick play again, even if it's only with Charlotte."

Charlie closed her eyes and contemplated the most effective way to murder both her family *and* Richard.

"I would be honored to play with Miss Charlotte," Kade said.

Her eyes flew open, and she met his gaze. He flashed her a brief, wry smile.

"Capital," said Papa. "I'll have one of the footmen dash to the music room to fetch Charlie's fiddle."

While her father made those arrangements, Kade escorted her to the pianoforte.

"I'm sorry about this," she quietly said.

"Don't be. I'm looking forward to hearing you play."

"I have a feeling you'll regret it."

He arranged the bench in front of the instrument. "There's nothing to worry about, Charlie. Just play something you're comfortable with, and I'll follow along."

She sighed. "I'm sorry to be such a die-away miss, and I'm also sorry this isn't a better instrument."

He sat down at the keyboard, deftly flipping his coat behind him. "We have a similar one at Kinglas, so I'm sure it will be fine. It's tuned, no doubt."

"Yes."

When he glanced at her hands, she realized she'd actually been wringing them.

Idiot.

"Charlotte, please don't fret about this." His deep, quiet voice seemed to resonate in her bones. "I promise everything will be fine. Just be yourself."

She let out a slow breath and felt some of the tension drain from her shoulders. "You're right, of course. I'm being silly."

He smiled. "Never."

As Papa bustled up with her case, the others rearranged their chairs to listen. Angus dragged a padded bench over and placed it directly in front of Richard before plunking down on the seat.

"Sir, must you sit right there?" Richard huffed.

"When yer as old as I am, ye can sit wherever ye want."

When Angus winked at Charlie, she was forced to stifle a laugh.

Papa opened her case and handed her the fiddle. Kade leaned over to look at the instrument.

"Ah, that looks like a Betts," he said. "I commend you on your excellent taste, Miss Charlotte."

Her father got a bit starchy. "I am well able to afford my daughter a good instrument, Kendrick. While we may be simple Highlanders, we are not lacking in taste."

Charlie widened her eyes at her father, but he refused to look at her.

"That is readily apparent, my lord," Kade replied with a friendly nod. "This pianoforte is also an excellent instrument. It's a privilege to be able to play it."

"Hrumph," said Papa, slightly mollified. He patted Charlie's shoulder and returned to his seat.

She tested the fiddle's strings, trying to think of a piece that might suit them both. But she was simply a girl from the Highlands, while he was . . . Kade Kendrick.

"Ready?" he asked.

"Do you know 'The Elfin Knight'?"

"I do, and it's an excellent choice."

Tucking the fiddle under her chin, Charlie sent a quick prayer up to the heavens. Then she lifted her bow and began to play. Thankfully, she knew the ballad so well she barely had to think, and it took several bars before she realized Kade had yet to join in.

Charlie faltered and stopped. "Is something wrong?"

Kade was staring at her with his eyebrows arched high.

He looked, well, astonished. Not really in a bad way. Just very, very surprised.

"Do you want me to choose another ballad?" she asked.

"Huh," he muttered.

She frowned. "Are you all right?"

His smile flashed, so quick and bright that it sparked an answering glow in her chest.

"Yes. Please continue, Miss Charlotte. I am happy to follow your lead."

CHAPTER 8

Leaving the piano, Kade wandered over to the French windows of the music room and absently gazed out over the garden. His work for the last two hours had met with very little success, largely thanks to an eccentric sprite of a woman who was taking up acres of space in his thoughts. Ever since their impromptu concert last night, he'd been sore put to think of anything but Charlie.

Truthfully, he hadn't known what to expect. But when she had started to play, she'd all but knocked him off the piano bench.

Her bowing technique was excellent and she played with deft assurance, bringing forth dynamic tones from her violin. Of course, there was room for improvement, as there was with any good musician. Kade had itched to make a small adjustment to the position of her wrist that would give her even more flexibility and mastery over her bow.

Her wrist wasn't the only thing you were itching to touch.

Kade sighed and rubbed his hands over his head, as if doing so might scrub away his muddled thinking. It wasn't really her technique or her mastery of the material that had captivated him. It was the woman herself, and the way she threw herself into the music, body and spirit. Charlie practically vibrated with life even when just sitting and reading a book. But when she took up her fiddle? Then the energy practically crackled in the air as her lithe form moved in time with the music.

As he'd watched her play, Kade had recalled their arrival at Laroch Manor, when he'd caught that glimpse of her riding in the glen. She'd been like quicksilver then. Or perhaps like a new piece of music, full of surprises, beauties, and promises.

He'd never been the sort of man to tumble over a woman—or stumble over his feelings for her. Had he enjoyed a few minor dalliances with willing ladies? Yes, and so had they. Each time, he and the lady had parted without regret.

Ever since he was a child at the mercy of illness, Kade had relentlessly worked to gain control over his life. Charlie's very presence threatened to upend that control, and he couldn't decide if that was good or bad.

"Stop overthinking it," he muttered as he stalked back to the piano.

He sat down, determined to polish off the second movement before dinner.

When the door opened a few seconds later and Ainsley marched in, he sighed. Clearly, the fates were conspiring against him.

"Goodness, Kade, what have you done with your hair? You look like somebody pulled you backwards through a thornbush."

"And good morning to you, too, Ainsley."

He stood and glanced in the mirror that hung over the fireplace. He had to admit his hair *was* looking rather ridiculous.

"It's noon already," his sister-in-law said. "I would have wished you good morning if I'd actually seen you this morning. But you skipped breakfast and dodged us all."

He smoothed down his hair. "I wanted to get an early start on my work."

He'd also wanted to avoid Charlie, so he'd made do with

the coffee and toast a footman had delivered as he was getting dressed.

Ainsley regarded him with disapproval. "You're still recovering, which means you need proper food and rest. You should not be slaving away for hours on your stupid concerto."

"May I remind you that the king himself has commissioned this concerto?" he countered. "By the way, your glares and scolds may terrify the other Kendrick men, but they've never worked on me. You may leave off at any time."

"Ah, yes, you've always been impervious to my scolds, even when the twins were climbing out windows to escape them."

"That's because I liked you from the beginning, remember? And you said that I was the best of the Kendricks—which I am."

"Sorry, no. You've been bumped down to second place behind Royal. After all, he is my husband."

"I'm sure he finds ways to keep himself in your good graces."

She waggled her eyebrows. "And does, on a regular basis, if you deduce my meaning."

"I do, and to quote your daughter, *ugh*."

She laughed. "For a man who generally drags a trail of eager women in his wake, you are decidedly unromantic."

"I don't have time to be romantic."

Ainsley crossed her arms and leaned on the piano, obviously settling in for a discussion.

"Yet you seemed quite taken with Charlie last night," she mused. "One might even say that the two of you seemed lost in each other."

"Lost in the music, you mean. Now, did you come in here simply to pester me, or is there a reason for this visit?"

"Kade Kendrick, I never pester anyone. I am the soul of courtesy."

"Yes, I've noticed that," he sarcastically replied.

"Actually, there is one thing. I'm to teach Charlie how to waltz. She'll be arriving shortly with Angus for her first lesson."

"At her age, she doesn't know how to waltz?"

"Apparently not."

"Then what's the rush now?"

"The wedding, dear boy. Her mamma is insistent that she be able to waltz properly. She cannot be allowed to embarrass the family, you know."

"That's ridiculous. Who cares if she can waltz or not?"

"Melissa, for one. And what Melissa wants, Melissa tends to get."

"Poor Charlie." He stood. "I'll get out of your way so the lesson can commence."

She waved him back down. "No, stay where you are. You're going to help."

"Are you sure?"

"Do not move."

Charlie might not be thrilled at the prospect of his presence during her dancing lessons, but he'd do his best to make her feel comfortable. He felt protective of the sweet lass, despite the uncertainty of his own emotions.

"Fine. If you need me to play, I'm happy to do so."

"Speaking of playing," Ainsley said, "I was rather stunned by Charlie's performance. She's very accomplished, isn't she?"

"Yes, she has clearly had an excellent instructor. But she also possesses a great deal of natural talent."

"Melissa, of course, was over the moon about you. She made sheep's eyes all evening, much to poor Colin's dismay."

Kade lifted his hands. "What can I say? The ladies do love me."

"Perhaps it's your swelled head they find so attractive. Richard Campbell certainly doesn't love you, though. Best watch him or you'll find another knife in your back."

Kade snorted. "Campbell's a complete thickhead. I was surprised Charlie didn't whack him with her bow after that stupid comment he made to her."

After he and Charlie had finished their performance to a hearty round of applause, Richard had come forward to escort Charlie back to her seat. He'd then made a jesting remark that she wouldn't have to bother with music and *such fripperies* once she became a wife and mother.

"What disturbs me is his attitude," Ainsley said. "He's already making the assumption that he has the right to make such judgments. As if everything is settled between them."

"No man has the right to make such a judgment about a woman, even if he is married to her."

Ainsley leaned over and patted him on the cheek. "You really are the nice Kendrick, aren't you?"

"I am, but all my brothers would agree with what I said. Fortunately, Charlie seems well able to defend herself from the likes of that booby."

''Thank goodness. Still, it's clear her parents are putting a great deal of pressure on her to marry—if not Richard, then someone else."

Kade disliked the sound of that more than he should. "I can't see her caving to those demands, no matter how much pressure they subject her to."

"I hope you're right. But I still worry about her future in that regard."

He thought for a moment, trying to get a handle on his muddled emotions. "On top of that, she's languishing away in this backwater. With a talent like hers, Charlie needs access to better teachers and opportunities than she'll find here."

Ainsley opened her eyes wide. "And do you have a specific teacher in mind?"

Kade refused to be baited. "There are some excellent violin masters in Edinburgh who could take her on."

"I think you're forgetting something, my boy."

"What?"

"How to be a Highlander," she replied. "That's what Charlie is, down to the bone. Be honest, Kade. Does she seem like she's languishing, or are you letting your own view of the matter obscure your vision?"

Again, that image of the first time he saw Charlie, when she was riding in glorious freedom, came charging into his head. "I see your point. She might not be happy anywhere else but here."

Ainsley waggled a hand. "Maybe. But I think that with the right man by her side, Charlie could take on the world. She simply needs someone who understands her, and accepts her for who she is."

"A tall order, it would appear."

"Is it?" she responded in a challenging tone.

The sound of footsteps approaching allowed him to dodge her too-perceptive question. The door opened and Angus stumped into the room, followed by Charlie.

"Had to rustle the lassie up," his grandfather said. "She was out in the stables with yon booby Campbell."

Charlie gave Kade a shy smile and a wave of the hand by way of greeting.

He eyed her kilted attire. "With the intention of annoying him, I assume."

"Only an idiot like Campbell would be annoyed by the sight of a proper kilt," Angus scornfully said. "And if I can wear one, why canna Miss Charlie?"

"She certainly looks much better in a kilt than you do," Kade replied.

"And hers is clean," Ainsley added.

Angus was wearing his oldest kilt and the shabby Highland bonnet he insisted was a relic handed down from Bonny Prince Charlie. Charlie, however, was neatly garbed in a beautiful kilt in Stewart plaid. Over it she wore a white linen blouse and a form-fitting leather vest suitable for riding. She completed the outfit with riding boots that reached to the hem of her kilt.

When home at Kinglas or attending formal occasions in Scotland, Kade often wore a kilt. He knew exactly what went under it and what didn't. And for a delirious moment, he was seized with an almost unconquerable desire to know what Charlie wore—or didn't wear—under *her* kilt.

Moron.

"How did Richard take your appearance?" he asked, trying to banish the image of a naked Charlie from his head.

She grinned. "I think he was quite shocked, although he did his best to pretend he wasn't."

"It's that fat dowry of yers," Angus said in his usual blunt manner. "You'll have to do more than lark about in a kilt to get yon twiddlepoop to shove off."

Charlie crinkled her adorable nose. Even dressed like a man—and a raffish one at that—she was an utter darling, from her gleaming gold hair to her polished boots.

"Drat," she said. "He's really becoming a nuisance, hasn't he?"

Angus patted her shoulder. "Never fear. We'll come up with something to scare booby Campbell off."

"I hope so," she said with a sigh.

"We will," Ainsley said in reassuring tones. "Meanwhile, we had best get on with your dancing lesson."

Charlie glanced at Kade. "My apologies, sir. We're disturbing your work."

"That's all our lad does is work," Angus said with a dismissive wave. "It's good for him to have a break. Get up and move his pins, ye ken."

Kade frowned at Ainsley. "I thought you needed me to play while you showed Charlie the steps?"

"I am entirely capable of playing a waltz on the piano,"

Ainsley said as she came round to join him. "Besides, who did you think was going to dance with Charlie? Grandda?"

Doing his best to look feeble, Angus tottered over to a nearby armchair. "My caperin' days are over. It's ready to be put out to pasture, I am."

Since his grandfather would be the first to rip up at any family member who would dare to suggest such a thing, Kade had to roll his eyes.

Charlie was now looking completely startled. "Oh, it's all right, Mr. Kendrick. You needn't put yourself out on my behalf."

"Nonsense, Kade will be delighted to help us," Ainsley replied.

"No, truly," she protested, her cheeks pink with embarrassment. "I can't possibly do this without stepping all over Mr. Kendrick's toes. There are my boots, for one thing, but I'm also hopeless when it comes to dancing and such. It's really quite sad."

Kade relinquished his seat at the piano. He was unable to bear the idea that she would think less of herself or feel the slightest bit uncomfortable on his account.

"Since I'm wearing boots as well, that should not be a problem. Besides, my feet are the size of clodhoppers, so I'm the one who'd best take care not to trample on you."

Charlie looked at Kade's feet and then up at him, her expression clearly dubious. "Are you sure? It's quite a lot to ask of you."

"I could use the practice, quite frankly," he replied. "It's been ages since I waltzed, and I expect I'll be required to do so at your sister's wedding."

"Well, as long as you don't mind."

He winked at her. "Absolutely. We can polish our capering skills together."

She blushed even more deeply, but this time a shy smile accompanied the roses in her cheeks. God, she was enchanting.

"Thank you," she said. "And I will do my best not to step on your toes."

"You'll be fine, dear," Ainsley said. "Now, shall we begin with a proper bow and curtsy?"

When Kade bowed and held out his hand, Charlie gave him a lopsided grin. She placed her hand in his and then dropped into a respectable curtsy, kilt and all.

"Charlie, do you remember any of the steps?" Ainsley asked.

"I think I recall the basics."

"Then let's try them without music first."

Kade smiled down on Charlie, as she barely came up to his chin. "Ready?"

She squared her shoulders, as if preparing for battle. "Ready."

He took her into his arms and immediately realized it *would* be something of a battle, at least for him. She was lovely and lithe, and the temptation to pull her close was almost overwhelming. Thank God she was wearing a kilt and a vest. If she were dressed in a typical evening gown, there would be naked shoulders and curves barely concealed by the silky flow of skirts.

He began to steer her through the movements as Ainsley counted off steps. Once, Charlie tripped and stumbled, but he was able to smoothly set her back on her feet.

"Thank you," she said with a little grimace. "I'm sorry I'm so clumsy."

"You're not. It's because we're wearing boots instead of dancing shoes. More foot to trip over."

When she glanced up and gave him a little smile, Kade felt a tug on his heart, like a memory. Then he realized it *was* a memory, from their first meeting at Inveraray. She'd followed him about whenever she could, happy to be in his presence and flashing that shy smile whenever he paid attention to her.

"Kade, I think we're ready for some music," Ainsley said.

Angus nodded. "Aye, yer both doin' grand. Ye fit together right nicely."

"Er, thank you," Charlie said.

Kade ignored his grandfather's blatant attempts at matchmaking. "Ready for some music, lass?"

Charlie's smile was wry. "It's now or never."

He glanced at Ainsley. "How about 'The Sussex Waltz'? It's got an easy tempo."

"Excellent choice."

Ainsley began to play, and Kade once more took Charlie in his arms, guiding her through the first turn. She followed his lead with an almost grim determination, her brow knit as she concentrated on her steps.

"You're doing very well," he assured her.

She muttered something under her breath.

"What's that?"

"Nothing. I'm sorry to put you all out like this. It's such a—"

She stumbled again. Kade held her steady, though, bringing her through the next turn.

"Drat," she muttered.

While Charlie was naturally graceful and athletic, right now she was as stiff as a hitching post. Was she still shy about him, or was it the pressure of living up to what her mother expected of her?

She needed a distraction.

"We didn't really have the chance to talk last night after we played together," he said. "You're a very talented violinist, Charlie. It was an honor to perform with you."

"Really?" she asked, her gaze firmly fixed on his shoulder.

"I would never lie about something as important as music. Especially not to another musician."

She finally glanced up to look at him. Her gaze was soft and lovely but also direct and honest. There was no artifice to Charlotte Stewart, and he found that enormously appealing.

She was exactly who she appeared to be, even when it ran her straight into a wall of disapproval.

"I've never really thought of myself as a musician," she said. "Just a fiddler."

"I know more than one violinist who would kill to be as good a fiddler as you are."

She responded with a smile so dazzling that *he* almost tripped over his own feet.

"Watch your steps, Kade," Ainsley called over the music.

"Yes, Mother."

When Charlie huffed out a chuckle, the enchanting little sound made him want to pull her even closer. Thank God his grandfather and sister-in-law were in the room, or he'd be inclined to do something stupid.

Like kiss the girl.

"Lady Ainsley is rather bossy, isn't she?" Charlie said, her eyes gleaming with amusement.

"I heard that," Ainsley said.

"Ears like a bat, too," Kade replied.

"Angus, your grandson just said I look like a bat," Ainsley said, not missing a beat.

Kade twirled Charlie through a turn. "Yes, Ainsley, but a very stylish bat."

Charlie's kilt briefly wrapped around his legs as her body brushed against his. And what a delightful sensation that provoked, although the location of that provocation could prove to be massively inconvenient. Thank God he wasn't the one wearing a kilt.

Angus, who'd been filling his pipe, snorted. "She's a *Sassenach* saucebox, is what she is, and she does have ears like a bat."

When Charlie laughed again, Kade felt the warmth curl through him. She was now pliant in his arms, her awkwardness seemingly forgotten. They moved as one, as if they'd been dancing partners for years.

"*Sassenach* saucebox," she said. "That's quite a nickname."

"Angus only dares to call me that because he knows he's too old for me to box his ears," Ainsley replied.

"Ye'd never be able to catch me, lassie."

"No, but Royal would. I'd send him after you."

"Och, he kens I'd give him a right paddle on the bum if he tried."

"You two are going to give Charlie all the wrong ideas about our family," Kade said.

Charlie smiled up at him. "No, I like your family. They're fun."

"They're certainly different," he wryly replied.

"It must be lovely to have a family that doesn't make you try to be something you're not," she said in a wistful tone.

And wasn't that a kick to the gut? Charlie had a rare and beautiful spirit, but both her family and society would see that as hindrance rather than help, especially as she grew older. The world would send storms her way and she would face them with courage, but he hated to think she might have to face them alone.

"Mr. Kendrick, is something wrong?" she asked.

That brought him back to the lithe, lovely girl in his arms. "Not at all. Why do you ask?"

"Because you're frowning, and I haven't even stepped on your toes."

"Oh, ah, something just occurred to me about my concerto. I was trying to figure it out in my head."

Then he mentally winced, knowing he'd sounded like a dunce.

Fortunately, the waltz was coming to an end. As Ainsley finished with a flourish, Kade twirled Charlie through the final turn and brought her to a halt by the piano.

"Very well done," Ainsley said. "Wasn't that lovely, Grandda?"

"Aye, by the perfect pair. Like they're made for each other, I ken."

Charlie made a funny little grimace. "Thank you, but I think that should be enough of dancing for the day. I'm keeping Mr. Kendrick from his work."

"Nonsense," Ainsley said. "Kade is happy to help."

He nodded. "Of course I am, and I'd be pleased to give it another go."

Charlie started to back away. "You're too kind, but I think I have the hang of it now. I know Mamma will be very pleased."

"We really should try a few variations, dear," Ainsley put in. "Just to be sure."

"Absolutely," Kade said, giving Charlie an encouraging smile.

Charlie's eyes grew wider as she continued to back toward the door. "Perhaps later. I've just thought of something I have to tell my father. Thank you all for your help."

She turned and bolted from the room, her kilt swirling around her legs.

Angus took his pipe out of his mouth. "Ye buggered that one up, son. So much for all yer fancy manners."

"I didn't do anything but dance with the girl," Kade protested. "Which is exactly what you both wanted me to do."

"Grandda's right," said Ainsley. "You buggered it up."

Kade studied their disapproving faces. He had indeed buggered it up, it seemed. Too bad he hadn't a clue how to set things right.

Or if he should even try.

CHAPTER 9

His shoulder propped against a stone column, Kade watched Charlie take to the ballroom floor for the first waltz of the evening. Her partner was a dandified fellow dressed in wide, pleated pants and sporting pomaded hair. He gave her a flourishing bow, and Charlie eyed him with a startled expression before dipping a shallow curtsy.

Kade had debated asking her for the first waltz. He was more attracted to Charlie than he cared to admit, and spending time with her would only strengthen that attraction. Since the Kendricks would be leaving Laroch Manor in a few days, it was wise to limit their time together as best he could without giving offense.

Of course, Charlie was doing her best to avoid *him*. Yes, there had been the last-minute flurry of wedding preparations, along with the arrival of numerous guests, to distract her. Still, it was clear she was dodging his company and not making the least effort to hide it.

That was beginning to annoy him more than it should.

When someone bumped into him, Kade straightened up. A petite young lady with an elaborately coiled and feathered coiffure that added almost a foot to her height gave him a blushing smile.

"I beg your pardon, miss," he said. "It's rather a crush, isn't it?"

"It's my fault entirely, Mr. Kendrick," she replied, madly fluttering her fan. "I didn't see you there, although I *have* been wanting to speak with you this last half hour. Your performance tonight was simply *wonderful*. I've never heard anything like it. Mamma—Lady Torbay, you know—said it was *utterly* transporting."

Ah, now he remembered her.

Kade had been introduced to Lady Torbay and her two daughters, as well as several dozen other guests whose names were now but a dim memory.

"You're very kind, Lady Constance. I'm glad you enjoyed it."

She gazed soulfully up at him. "I don't think I've heard anything more elevating in my life. Your playing seemed to take me right out of myself, as if I were . . ."

"Transported?" Kade said after a few moments of rather fraught silence.

She pressed a hand to his arm. "Exactly! My dear sir, Mamma was wondering if you would be so kind as to join us for tea." She shot him a coy look from under her eyelashes. "We've already secured a table in the supper room. It's quite cozy and away from all this dreadful noise and heat. I'm sure you must be *dreadfully* parched after your performance. After all, you play with such drama and *passion*."

She took a step closer, virtually backing him up against the column. From the blush in her cheeks and the determined glint in her gaze, Kade feared that Lady Constance might be overcome with passion right in the middle of the ballroom.

Angus suddenly appeared, having slipped deftly between two portly gentlemen. "Och, laddie, there ye are. I've been lookin' all over for ye."

"Grandda, do you remember Lady Constance? I believe you met her last night."

His grandfather eyed the young woman. "Aye, Torbay's daughter. Just saw yer da up in the cardroom, lass." He tapped the side of his nose. "Lookin' a wee bit worse for wear, I'm sorry to say. Probably best if he sits the next hand out, if ye catch my drift."

Lady Constance jerked her hand from Kade's arm as if stung by a wasp.

"I have no idea what you mean, Mr. MacDonald. If you'll forgive me, sir," she said to Kade, "I must return to my mother."

"Please give her my regards, and thank you for—"

Lady Constance turned on her heel and shoved her way between the portly—and now protesting—gentlemen.

Kade shook his head. "Grandda, you are utterly ruthless."

"Saved ye, didn't I? Torbay's a gambler, pockets to let all the time. And his lady will scold yer ears off. Best steer clear of that lot."

"Perhaps Lady Torbay is a scold because her husband keeps losing their money? Nor is that his daughter's fault."

Angus waved a hand. "I hate to break it to ye, but that lassie wasn't making sheep's eyes at ye because of yer good looks or yer piano noodlin'. It's Kendrick money she's after."

Kade laughed. "Now, there's a blow to my ego, but I thank you for the rescue all the same. She was trying to drag me off to tea with her mother."

"Never fear, lad. I willna let the dragons get their claws in ye." Angus glanced over at the dance floor. "There's another lassie ye should be dancin' with, though."

"And who is that, Grandda?"

"Jinglebrains. Ye ken exactly who it is. And why yer lettin' some idiot in balloon pants take yer place is beyond me. Ye should be protectin' Charlie now, not flirtin' with ninnies like that Torbay girl."

"I wasn't flirting with her or anyone," Kade protested.

"And that's yer problem."

Thankfully, before the conversation could become more ridiculous, Royal joined them.

"I see Angus has rescued you from another ardent fan," his brother said. "I hope you're properly grateful."

"I am in awe of his ruthless methods."

"Fah," Angus said. "Maybe if ye'd been more ruthless, ye wouldna have gotten yerself stabbed by that dancer."

"She was an opera singer, Grandda, not a dancer. And perhaps this is not the best place to be discussing such matters."

"That bloody orchestra is making so much noise that we could discuss the king's entire spy network and no one would hear a thing." Angus scowled in the direction of the elegant twelve-piece orchestra at the end of the ballroom. "Sounds like a barnyard full of brayin' donkeys in here. Nothin' like yer fine playin', although I did think ye could stand a bit more practice on that Holyrood strathspey. I fancy ye missed a few notes."

"At least I didn't sound like a donkey," Kade dryly replied.

Royal laughed. "Your performance was excellent. I'm sure Melissa and Lady Kinloch were over the moon."

"And thank the guid Lord this blasted waltz is comin' to an end," Angus said.

Kade glanced at the dance floor. Charlie had moved off to the opposite side of the room and was now chatting with her dance partner. Or, rather, he was chatting with her. She simply stood with her arms crossed over her chest, occasionally nodding. She seemed distracted and certainly not her usual bright self.

"I hope Melissa was pleased," he said. "Yet Lady Kinloch barely said a word to me afterwards. Something seems off with the entire family, especially Miss Charlotte."

Royal gave a slow nod. "I agree. Lord Kinloch has been looking positively grim all night. It makes no sense, since the festivities seem to be going well."

"Aye, somethin's amiss," Angus said. "They're all lookin' as queer as Dick's hatband."

"I thought Melissa was going to burst into tears at the altar," Kade replied. "And not from joy."

Angus nodded. "I felt fair sorry for young Colin, even if he is a bit of a dunce."

"Perhaps Ainsley will be able to get the truth out of Lady Kinloch," said Royal.

Kade transferred his attention to Charlie, who had left her dance partner and was making her way toward the hall. Despite the crowd, it was easy to track her, since she shone like a moonbeam in her silver-spangled gown with its snug bodice and wide skirts. A tartan sash in the colors of Clan Stewart fell from one shoulder to the opposite hip, nicely emphasizing her lovely shape. For such a slender lass, she had more than her share of delightful curves.

"Or I could just ask Charlie," he mused, half to himself.

Royal's eyebrows went up. "'Charlie,' is it? On quite good terms with her, are you?"

Kade looked at his brother and grandfather, who both regarded him with the same knowing expression. "There's nothing between us but a mild friendship, I assure you."

"There could be more if ye paid the lass a little attention," Angus retorted. "Ye spend all day locked up in that stupid music room when the fairest maid in the Highlands is ready to tumble into yer arms."

"Unbelievable," Kade said. "Aren't you the one who just told me that I needed more practice?"

His grandfather poked him in the chest. Yer nae gettin' any younger, laddie boy. It's time ye found a wife and settled down."

"I have no intention of settling down, nor does my career lend itself to that sort of life."

Angus suddenly switched tactics by lifting a trembling hand to his brow. "Och, I'm not long for this world, Kade.

Can ye blame me for wantin' to see my favorite grandson married before I shuffle off this immortal coil?"

"It's *mortal* coil, Grandda," Royal said. "And I thought I was your favorite grandson."

Kade snorted. "Each of us is his favorite grandson when he's trying to wheedle us around to something."

His grandfather scowled. "Ye can both quit yer sassin'. Ye ken exactly what I'm sayin', Kade. Yer lettin' someone like booby Campbell or an idiot in balloon pants steal a march on ye with Miss Charlie."

"I see no evidence that Miss Charlie has taken an interest in Mr. Balloon Pants or anyone else, including Richard."

Royal waggled a hand. "She has gotten quite a bit of attention from other gentlemen guests these last two days, though."

"Really? I hadn't noticed."

Except he had, and he was more than a wee bit irritated by the fact.

Angus eyed him. "It's a good thing ye gave up the spy work, because yer a terrible liar."

"Look, here's Ainsley," Kade said. "Perhaps she can bring an end to this ridiculous conversation."

Royal pulled his wife in for a hug. "Hullo, sweetheart. I'd love to give you a kiss, but I'm afraid one of those things sprouting out of your head will poke me in the eye."

She gave him a little swat on the chest. "Philistine. I'll have you know that it took my maid almost an hour to construct this masterpiece."

Kade eyed his sister-in-law's mad coiffure, a gravity-defying affair that featured a number of large combs that could easily double as weapons.

"Your head does look rather lethal," he said.

"In this family, no one can predict when the next varlet will be lurking about, ready to do something nefarious—like that nonsensical man dancing with Charlotte, for instance. Really, Kade, someone will cut you out if you're not careful."

Kade sighed. "Not you, too."

"I only speak the truth, dear boy. Now, what are you three whispering about? You look very suspicious."

"We're trying to figure out what's wrong with the Kinlochs," Royal said. "Especially Miss Charlotte."

Ainsley immediately turned serious. "Don't think I haven't tried to find out. According to my maid, Melissa had a bout of hysterics shortly before the ceremony. There was some concern as to whether she would even calm down enough to get married."

Royal elbowed Kade. "She's already regretting it, probably because she fancies our lad."

Ainsley rolled her eyes. "It's nothing like that. I asked Lady Kinloch, who was very tight-lipped about the whole thing. However, I got the distinct impression it had something to do with Charlotte."

Kade frowned. "Is she all right?"

Ainsley batted her eyelashes at him. "I don't know. Perhaps you should ask her."

"I have no intention of interrogating the poor girl in the middle of her sister's wedding," he replied. "Besides, it's none of our business. If Lady Kinloch had wished to tell you, she would have."

"Aye, but there's mystery afoot." Angus rubbed his hands. "And it's up to us to solve it."

"We're not solving anything," Kade replied in a firm voice. "As I said, it's none of our business."

Angus curled his lip. "Fah."

"Then, since you apparently have no interest in Charlotte," Ainsley said, "you should do your duty and dance with some of the other ladies. You're not holding up the Kendrick side, Kade. It is frankly quite embarrassing."

"I'm not about to prance about a ballroom in full dress kilt, Ainsley. Besides, I just played a bloody recital. Let Royal hold up the family side."

"Sorry, old son," his brother said, adopting an insincere expression of regret. "My bad leg is rather giving me fits tonight. Really, I shouldn't even be standing on it."

"Your leg is perfectly fine and you know it," Kade replied.

Ainsley ignored that interjection. "Grandda, please take Royal down to the supper room for a little rest, all right?"

"Why don't we all go down to the supper room for a little rest," Kade suggested.

She took a firm grip on his elbow. "You're coming with me. There are two very nice young ladies who want to meet you and would love to dance with you."

"Ainsley, I have no desire to meet young ladies or to dance," he replied, getting annoyed.

"Of course you do. What man doesn't like to dance with pretty ladies?"

"Our Kade, apparently," Royal said in a droll tone.

Angus shook his head. "Sad, that."

"Come along now, dear," Ainsley said. "It's time you had a little fun."

As she towed him off, Kade threw a dirty look over his shoulder at his brother and grandfather. Of course they were having a good chuckle at his expense.

"Good God," he muttered.

"You work too hard, Kade. If you won't dance with Charlotte—although for the life of me I cannot deduce why not—then there are other pretty girls who will fit the bill. I'm going to make sure you relax and enjoy yourself, even if it kills you."

"Then just shoot me now and get it over with."

Ignoring his absurd comment, Ainsley hauled him off to his fate.

* * *

Kade danced two sets of country dances, made polite conversation with three sweet but excitable girls and their even more excitable mothers, and dodged Lady Constance when she tried to lure him into a curtained alcove. After that last episode, he informed Ainsley that he was retiring to the music room and insisted that, under pain of death, she was to keep his whereabouts a secret. His sister-in-law merely rolled her eyes before sauntering off to find Royal.

As he turned into the wing leading to the music room, he exhaled a sigh of relief. This part of the manor was blessedly quiet, with only a few lamps to light his way toward the back of the house. He would have the room to himself and the peace he needed to work.

But when he strode through the door, he saw someone who'd also taken flight from the ballroom—in this case, a Highland Cinderella.

Charlie was curled up on the velvet sofa next to the open French doors, which let in the garden-scented night air. Her shoes had been discarded in the middle of the floor, and she was reading by the light of one lamp. Its soft glow made her hair gleam like gold and her silk gown shimmer like moonlight. Away from the lamp and a branch of candles on top of the piano, the rest of the room melted into shadow.

Not wishing to startle her, Kade cleared his throat.

Charlie glanced over, then dropped her book on the cushions and started to scramble up. Then she froze, obviously remembering she wasn't wearing shoes.

"Don't get up," he said. "It's only me."

He scooped up her shoes and brought them to her.

"Thank you," she said, looking rather embarrassed. "How shocking to leave my shoes lying about. I just wasn't expecting anyone."

"Don't feel you need to wear them on my account. I'm not the least bit shocked by you going about in your stocking feet."

She gave him a crooked smile. "Mamma would certainly scold me for acting in so vulgar a fashion."

"Charlotte, do you wish to put your shoes back on?"

"No. My feet are killing me," she ruefully admitted. "I'm not used to so much dancing, as you know."

"Well, you did splendidly."

"I noticed you watching when I was dancing that last waltz." Then she blushed, as if she'd said something salacious.

A tick of irritation flared in him. He hoped her blushes were not on account of Mr. Balloon Pants.

"Your partner was fortunate in his choice," he carefully replied. "Did you enjoy dancing with him?"

She rolled her eyes. "He stepped on *my* feet and didn't even notice, he was so busy talking about himself."

Kade laughed. "Och, lass. So you're hiding out to give your wee toes a rest?"

"It's dreadful of me, I know, but Mamma insisted that I stand up for every set *and* dance the next waltz with Richard. I simply couldn't force myself to do it." She patted her cheeks. "My face feels frozen from all the smiling, pretending to be enjoying myself."

"Not a fan of weddings, I take it."

"No, and I suppose that makes me quite hopeless. According to Melissa, females are meant to enjoy these sorts of things. Not that she's doing such a good job of it tonight," she added, more to herself than to him.

He couldn't resist the temptation to probe. "I noticed that. In fact, your entire family seemed a bit . . . flustered by events."

She gave him a sideways glance, as if weighing how to respond.

"Mr. Kendrick, would you like to join me in a brandy?"

she finally said. "Or a whisky." Then she blinked. "No, you must be here to work. So I'd best be on my way."

When she started to reach for her shoes, he took her hand and gently placed it back in her lap.

"My work is done for the evening," he said, jettisoning his plans without a second thought. "And in fact I'd love a whisky. Can I fetch you one?"

She glanced at the small tumbler on the table beside her, which he'd failed to notice until now. "Thank you, but I already have mine."

Kade smiled. "Settled in for the evening, are you?"

"If I'm lucky enough. I'm hoping no one will think to look for me here. Present company excepted, of course."

He gave her a flourishing bow, which made her laugh. "I'm honored. Allow me to fetch my drink and I will join you."

When he returned, she'd scooted over to make room for him on the sofa. He sat, making sure not to crumple her wide silk skirts. It occurred to him that their situation could be considered scandalous if they were discovered. Then again, they were more or less like family, were they not? They were simply having a friendly little chat. It wasn't as if he were going to kiss the girl.

Sure about that?

"So, Mr. Kendrick, who are you hiding from?" Charlie asked.

"Am I that obvious?"

"I recognize a fellow combatant when I see one."

He grinned. "If you must know, I'm avoiding some very enthusiastic young ladies, which makes me sound like a complete coxcomb."

"It's no wonder they're pestering you, given your splendid recital tonight. Lady Constance Torbay especially seemed quite taken with your, er, performance."

Obviously, Charlie had been watching him as much as he'd been watching her.

"Please, don't remind me," he replied. "When Lady Constance tried to corner me in a window alcove, I thought I might have to leap out the window to escape."

Her eyes danced with laughter. "How dreadful to be the object of adoration from so many ladies."

"I'm inclined to be more cynical, I'm afraid. I'm sure it's the lure of fame that's so attractive, not me. They probably envision a glamorous life—hobnobbing with royalty, dashing about the Continent. But much of that is nonsense, and not who I truly am."

Charlie rested her chin in her hands. "Then who are you, Kade Kendrick?"

It was a simple question but somehow seemed more like a challenge. The hell of it was he was no longer sure who he was.

"I suppose I'm still trying to figure that out for myself," he confessed.

She nodded, as if she knew. "It's hard, isn't it? Pretending to be something you're not, or trying to be what other people want you to be."

"Yes, but I cannot complain. I've been blessed to be able to do what I love. The rest of it . . ." He shrugged. "I don't really give a hang for that kind of life. It's the music I care about. That's what makes me who I am."

But he was beginning to wonder if the music was enough. If it was, why had he thrown himself so eagerly into those intelligence missions, almost at the cost of his life?

She let out a sad little sigh that rather broke his heart. "It must be wonderful to be able to do what you truly want."

Kade studied her for a moment. "Charlotte, you're not just hiding out from Richard or your mother. There's something else going on, isn't there?"

"Now I'm the one who's being rather obvious, I suppose," she admitted.

"Kendricks are busybodies, so we tend to notice things.

It's not just you, though. Your entire family is fashed about something."

Charlie rolled her lips into a tight line, as if holding in words that were struggling to escape.

When he took one of her hands, her gaze, wide and startled, met his. She didn't pull away, but nor did she return his clasp. She simply allowed her hand to rest in his palm, as if trusting him just enough for that but no more.

And Kade wanted more.

"I won't press you," he quietly said. "I just want to help if I can. That's what friends do, is it not?"

A genuine smile crept forth from Charlie. "Yes. However, it's a convoluted tale, so I think I need fortification. Do you mind handing over my drink?"

"Not at all."

He relinquished her hand, wondering if her request had been a way of getting him to do so. When he handed over the glass, she took a sip and then settled back against the sofa cushions, re-tucking her legs beneath her skirts. Charlie was the most unaffected girl he'd ever met. And yet there was a natural elegance to her that was more alluring than the languid graces and charms of the most sophisticated ladies.

"It's about the Clan Iain brooch," she said. "I don't think there's any harm in telling you, because the whole blasted mess is going to come out sooner or later. My parents and sister are simply waiting until the festivities are over before pitching a fit of absolutely monumental proportions."

Kade blinked. "That's quite the opening for your explanation."

"It's quite the pickle I'm in. My family is furious with me. For a moment this morning, I thought Papa was going to lock me in my room and tell everyone I'd been stricken by the grippe and couldn't attend the wedding."

He frowned. "That doesn't sound like Lord Kinloch. He obviously adores you."

"Not at the moment," she ruefully replied.

"How can I help?"

She waggled a hand. "While I'm tempted by the notion of securing the assistance of one of His Majesty's spies, I cannot possibly put you to the trouble. I'm sure I can sort it out if given a bit of time."

Kade rubbed his forehead. Clearly, the person who needed to be locked up wasn't Charlie but his loose-lipped grandfather. "You've been talking to Angus."

"He's been telling me about your adventures on the Continent. I was quite envious, since I never get to have that sort of dashing-around fun."

Thankfully, it didn't sound like Angus had revealed too much to her, and especially not about Paris.

"Remember, my grandfather tends to exaggerate matters. At the request of the Crown, I simply made a few discreet inquiries on some government matters whilst on my travels. Nothing very dramatic, I assure you."

She looked dubious. "According to your grandfather, you're something of a master spy."

Kade sighed. "Only in Grandda's head. But I do stand ready to help you, Charlie. That's a promise."

She gave him an uncertain smile, as if unsure how to take his offer.

"Perhaps you could tell me the problem?" he prompted.

"Right. Well, the Clan Iain thistle brooch is a family heirloom, always passed down from mother to eldest daughter when she comes of age. Legend has it that it was a present from Queen Margaret to one of our ancestors. It's to be worn at clan gatherings and formal occasions." She tapped her shoulder, where her tartan sash was fastened with a gold pin in the shape of a stag's head. "As you can see, no thistle brooch."

"Gone missing, has it?"

She grimaced. "When I went to fetch it this morning from my jewelry box, it was gone."

"When was the last time you wore it?"

"Last January, for our Hogmanay celebrations. I keep it in a leather pouch in the back of the box, so I always know where it is."

"No chance of misplacing it, then."

She shrugged. "I don't think so, although I don't precisely remember putting it back. Nor does my maid. Naturally, we tore my room apart looking for it, but came up empty."

Kade briefly squeezed her hand. "I'm sorry. That must have been very distressing."

"And exceedingly inconvenient, given the circumstances," she said with a sigh.

"Scots do tend to take their family heirlooms rather seriously. Is the brooch very valuable, aside from its historical significance?"

She nodded. "It's made of a very fine silver, and set with amethysts and diamonds. It's quite lovely and in very good shape, so one would never guess its age by looking at it."

"It sounds like just the sort of thing an enterprising thief would love to get his hands on."

"True, but my jewelry box is always locked and only Mamma and I know where the key is kept. I also have a valuable set of pearls with matching earrings, along with a few other good pieces, and they were untouched."

"That is rather odd."

"A disaster is what it is," she replied. "If I don't find the blasted thing, my family will never forgive me."

"Certainly I understand that your family would be distressed to lose such a valuable heirloom, but I fail to see why they would be so upset with you. Or why its disappearance would have the power to apparently ruin your sister's wedding."

Charlie looked embarrassed. "It's mostly because of the legend attached to the brooch."

Kade had to shake his head. "Of course there's a legend. It's the Highlands, after all."

"As I mentioned, the brooch is to be worn on all special occasions, and it signals that the oldest daughter is eligible for marriage."

Kade reached for his whisky. "Isn't it usually obvious by the fact that the young woman is unmarried?"

"Well . . . there's a bit more to it than that."

"No doubt something arcane and mysterious," he dryly replied.

She crinkled her nose. "Unfortunately, yes. The legend says that if the oldest daughter marries or even enters into a courtship without the brooch, she will never find true love, and misfortune will follow her all the days of her life."

Kade had just taken a mouthful of whisky, and his impulse to laugh caused a catch in his throat. He managed to force the brew down.

"You're joking," he rasped, his eyes watering.

Charlie eyed him with concern. "Do you need me to thump on your back? You look like that went down the wrong way."

He cleared his throat. "No, I'm fine. And I must say that's a hell of a nasty legend even for the Highlands. You don't really believe that, do you?"

She waved a hand. "Of course it's all stuff and nonsense, but Melissa has gotten it into her silly head that *her* marriage is now cursed, as is the rest of the family. She's convinced that the Four Horsemen of the Apocalypse will shortly be descending on Laroch Manor."

Kade tried to smother a laugh. "How unfortunate."

"If you'd been in my sister's bedroom this morning,

you'd be employing considerably stronger language than *unfortunate*."

"I completely understand. Angus has a revolting Highland bonnet he pulls out on special occasions. He claims one of our ancestors wore it at the Battle of Culloden, and any attempt to correct the historical record is inevitably met with dramatic eruptions. But do your parents also believe this nonsense?"

"Mamma isn't generally superstitious, but she and Melissa are very close and this has unnerved both of them. As for my father, he's exceedingly annoyed at the loss of a family heirloom and the fact that he has to listen to my mother and Melissa harp on about it." She shrugged. "I can't really blame any of them, since the brooch is my responsibility."

"So, it's up to you to find it."

"Yes." She held up a finger. "Although I intend to hold off until Richard leaves. If I don't have the brooch, he can't court me."

Kade laughed. "That's certainly convenient."

"Mamma has already accused me of losing the brooch for just that purpose. That was also a delightful discussion, as you can imagine. Believe me, losing it wouldn't be worth the trouble. At some point I'll simply tell poor Richard to bugger off and be done with it."

"Miss Charlotte Stewart, you are the most extraordinary girl."

Charlie gave him a cheeky smile. "Aren't I just? Still, I'd best get to it and find the blasted thing before my family throws me out on my ear."

Although Kade would only be here for a few days more, he resolved to help her as best he could. The likeliest explanation was that someone had stolen it, but it made sense to undertake a full search of the house and look for other explanations.

"I'll help you look for it, then."

"But you're leaving in a few days," she replied, sounding rather wistful. "And, truly, it's not necessary. I've imposed on you enough with my tale of woe."

"And, truly, it's no imposition."

He *did* want to help her, and for more than a few days. The prospect of saying farewell to Charlie, likely forever, was a starling and unwelcome realization.

She hesitated. "Really?"

"Really."

He was also realizing that he wanted to kiss her now, and keep on kissing her. Charlie had the most delightful mouth, pink and luscious and with a lovely shape that was perfect for smiling. All he had to do was lean a bit closer. Rather astonishingly, she seemed to be leaning in toward him, too, and it would only take a few more inches—

She jerked upright and threw a panicked glance at the door. "Oh, thunderbolts. Someone's coming."

It took a moment for Kade to pull his wits out of his Charlie-induced haze. But, yes, footsteps were coming their way down the hall.

She scrambled for her shoes. "Hell and damnation."

Kade did a bit of scrambling, too, straight to the piano. "I'll tell whoever it is that I'm in here working."

She barely had time to acknowledge his remark before the door opened and Sir Leslie Morgan, one of the wedding guests, sauntered into the room.

"Ah, there you are, my dear. I have come to—" Morgan came up short when he spotted Kade at the piano. "Kendrick, what the devil are you doing in here?"

Kade put down the pencil he'd just picked up and subjected Morgan to a calm perusal. *Dandy prat* was how Angus had described the man after meeting him yesterday. Kade wagered that Morgan spent more time and money on his wardrobe than did most fashionable ladies. But underneath his stylish if slightly absurd appearance Kade suspected lurked a hardened roué. He also cultivated an air of cynical amusement, which was both hackneyed and tiresome.

"I'm obviously working," Kade replied. "What's your excuse for wandering about the house looking for young ladies?"

"I'm looking for only one lady," Morgan answered in a supercilious tone. "And at Lady Kinloch's request. She tasked me with finding Miss Charlotte."

Charlie, who was now sitting demurely on the sofa, her properly shod feet firmly on the floor, tilted her head. "How odd of her. Why didn't she just send a footman to fetch me? She obviously guessed I'd be in the music room."

"I received the impression that your dear mamma was a trifle worried about gossip." He cast a pointed look at Kade. "Not without reason, it would appear."

Charlie scoffed. "If you're suggesting that Mr. Kendrick and I are engaged in any sort of improper behavior, you are very wide of the mark, Sir Leslie. Mr. Kendrick is working on his concerto, while I simply came in for a moment of rest and quiet."

Morgan spread his hands wide. "Of course, my dear. But appearances, you know, they can be tricky. To be seen closeted alone with another man is not quite—"

Charlie jumped to her feet. "Sir Leslie, I am neither a girl just released from the schoolroom nor a ninny. Mr. Kendrick is an old friend and a guest in our house. As such, I have encountered him more than once without any danger posed to my virtue." She shot a narrow-eyed look at Kade. "Did you say something, sir?"

Kade had managed to choke back his laugh. "No. Just something caught in my throat."

Morgan glared at him before trying to regain control of the

conversation. "Miss Stewart, your mother is clearly worried about you. Again, not without cause."

"If she was so worried about me, please explain why she sent only a gentleman I hardly know to look for me?"

That was a very good question.

Morgan looked momentarily flummoxed. "I . . . I suppose because I'm a friend of the family." Then he mustered a smile. "And of course because you're my supper partner, as you will recall. When we danced earlier, you graciously agreed to let me escort you down to the supper room."

Charlie frowned. "No, I didn't."

Now the man began to look cross. "I would never wish to contradict a lady—"

"Then don't," she replied.

Kade rose to his feet. "Miss Stewart, I would be happy to escort you to the supper room—or back to the ballroom, if you would prefer."

She waved him back to his seat. "Thank you, Mr. Kendrick, but I've disrupted your work for quite long enough."

"Excellent," Morgan said, throwing Kade a smug glance. "Then, Miss Stewart, I will be happy to escort you—"

"Also not necessary," she replied, cutting him off. "I'm perfectly capable of escorting myself down to the blasted supper room."

Then she strode out, leaving Morgan to stare after her, his sideburns all but bristling with ire.

"I don't suppose you'd like to hear what I've been working on, do you?" Kade asked in an innocent tone.

Morgan threw him an ugly glance and then turned on his heel and stomped out of the room.

For a few moments, Kade listened to footsteps retreating down the hall. Then the peace of the night, broken only by the sound of crickets in the garden, settled over him.

He pulled his music closer. Returning to the party held little appeal, so work it would be. It wasn't nearly as enticing as the idea of kissing Charlie, but nor would it lead to trouble. If he had a brain in his head, he'd realize he'd had a lucky escape tonight.

It was unfortunate, then, that he didn't seem to have a brain in his head, because with Charlie's lips only a few inches from his, escape had never even crossed his mind.

CHAPTER 10

Charlie was avoiding him—again.

This evening she was sitting on the other side of the private family drawing room, hiding behind Ainsley and refusing to meet Kade's eye. She was undoubtedly fashed about the missing brooch. And the fact that she also had Richard Campbell hard on her heels was another complication in a thicket of awkward situations.

Still, after their intimate conversation in the music room the other night, Kade hadn't expected her to be awkward with *him*. True, he'd been about to kiss her when Sir Leslie interrupted them, so it was possible that she now saw their little interlude as a mistake. But her efforts to evade him now had piqued his curiosity.

Angus joined him, handing him a whisky. "Ye look like ye could use this, what with yer scowlin' and black moods. What's amiss?"

Kade raised the glass in thanks. "Not scowling, Grandda. Just thinking."

His grandfather plopped down in the club chair next to him. "Och, I can always tell when yer frettin', Kade. Ye canna deny it."

He couldn't, unfortunately. Angus had an unfailing knack for reading his grandsons.

"I'm a bit concerned about Charlie," he quietly responded. "She's under a fair bit of pressure, and I wish I could help her."

"Did ye actually offer to help her?"

When Kade shot him a disbelieving look, Angus smiled.

"Of course ye did. It's a kind heart ye have, and I'm sure the lassie was grateful."

"I thought so, but now she's dodging me."

Angus glanced over at the small group on the divans by the fireplace. Ainsley was talking to Melissa—or, rather, Melissa was talking *at* Ainsley. Charlie sat quietly, doing her best to ignore Richard, who was hovering close by, much like an annoying gnat.

"Mayhap her ma is puttin' pressure on the lass to avoid ye," Angus said.

Kade shot him a startled glance. "Why would she do that?"

"Because yer competition for yon booby Campbell, who looks like a complete ninny next to ye. Why my cousin is trying to match poor Charlie up with that jackanapes instead of ye is a mystery."

"Possibly because I'm not actually courting her daughter?" Kade sarcastically replied.

Angus ignored that comment. "And there's that bloody brooch. Kinloch's cross as crabs, and he's pesterin' the poor lassie, too. What with all her problems, I reckon our Charlie's not in the mood to talk to anyone. Not even ye."

"She has no trouble talking to Ainsley."

In fact, Ainsley seemed to be the only Kendrick Charlie spent any time with.

"She's not talkin' so much as hidin' behind her, from her parents as well as ye." Angus shook his head. "And that sister. She's a piece of work."

"Yes, Melissa has been something of a trial."

The bride had spent the last two days crying one minute and then dramatically swearing the next that her family had been cursed forever. Her poor husband seemed entirely flummoxed.

"How is Colin holding up?" Kade asked. "You and Royal were chatting with him. Giving comfort and advice, I presume?"

"He's a bit of a dull fellow, but a good lad. I feel right sorry for him. I'm told Melissa was so upset on their wedding night that Colin had to fetch Elspeth to give her sleeping powders." He snorted. "Just the person ye wish to see in the bridal bower—yer mother-in-law."

Kade was forced to smother a laugh. "Did he actually tell you that?"

"Nay, Elspeth did. I told her that Melissa was actin' like a ninny and that next time she should toss a glass of water in her face. That's what I do when the terriers fall to scrapin'. Dump a pot of cold water on them. Works every time."

"I'm sure Lady Kinloch was thrilled to hear you compare her daughter to one of your terriers."

"Laddie, I only speak the truth."

"In this case, I would agree with you. Speaking of foolishness, what do you think about this legend of the brooch? I cannot believe anyone in the family would take it seriously."

Angus tapped his nose, looking wise. "As Robert the Bruce once said, 'There are more things in heaven and earth, ye ken, than can be dreamt of in all yer philosophical thinkin'.'"

"That is not how the saying goes, Grandda. And it's a quotation from *Hamlet*, not the Bruce."

"Who do ye think that *Sassenach* nincompoop stole it from?"

"Not a term one generally applies to the Bard," Kade dryly replied.

"Lad, have ye actually read *Macbeth*? Those bloody witches capering about like half-wits, spouting their hubble-bubble bad poetry. It's nae Robbie Burns, I tell ye."

Kade tried to pull the conversation back on course. "While your literary analysis is fascinating, I'm more interested in the brooch. You don't believe that curse nonsense, do you?"

Angus rolled his eyes. "Of course it's nae cursed, but ye canna blame Kinloch and Elspeth for being fashed. The thistle brooch is verra valuable. It's nae good to be losing family heirlooms."

"It might have been stolen. I don't understand why Charlie's family is so hell-bent on blaming her."

"Aye, it's nae fair, so ye'd best put on yer spy cap and figure it out."

"I can't do a bloody thing if Charlie won't talk to me."

"Well, yer so bloody cautious, she likely hasn't a clue yer sweet on her."

Kade throttled back his irritation. "Grandda, I am not sweet on her."

Angus shook his head. "Ye always were a bad liar, son. No wonder ye couldna fool the other spies with yer sad stories."

Lord and Lady Kinloch entered the drawing room, sparing Kade no doubt even more unflattering commentary on his career of espionage.

Ainsley smiled at their hostess. "Are your cousins now safely away?"

With a weary sigh, Lady Kinloch sank into an elegant French-style chair opposite Ainsley. "Yes, that's the last of my family. I'm pleased the wedding festivities went off so well . . ." She paused to narrow her eyes at Charlie. "But it's a relief to have the house back to ourselves."

"Weddings are dreadfully exhausting, but you pulled it off in great style," Ainsley replied. "Everyone agreed that Melissa was the most beautiful bride in all the Highlands, and that Colin is a very lucky man."

"I reckon there's nae much luck between the sheets, though," Angus whispered to Kade.

Since Grandda's whispers were usually loud enough to be heard halfway across the room, Kade winced. Thankfully, only Charlie seemed to have caught the comment. She shot them a startled glance and then bit her lower lip, obviously trying not to laugh.

Kade experienced a sudden and inconvenient surge of lust—and the conviction that he'd like nothing better than to give that sweet lip a gentle bite, too.

"Thank you, Lady Ainsley," Melissa said with a wan smile. "Only my determination not to dishonor Colin and my family kept me from completely collapsing. Charlotte's news has been a terrible shock."

"It's my brooch, so I think I'm the one who suffered the most shock," Charlie replied in a wry tone. "But as Lady Ainsley said, your wedding was bang up to the mark, old girl."

Lady Kinloch looked pained. "Charlotte, please refrain from using cant. Nor should you make light of the disaster that has befallen this family, thanks to your carelessness."

"But I didn't do anything," Charlie protested.

Lord Kinloch, who'd been brooding over a whisky, scowled at his daughter. "Of course you did. You misplaced the Clan Iain brooch. Such a thing has never happened before, not once."

Charlie grimaced. "I'm truly sorry, but I didn't do it on purpose."

"Of course not," Richard said, coming to her defense. "It could have happened to anyone."

"Unfortunately, it happened to Charlotte," Lady Kinloch replied in a withering tone.

Richard wilted under her stare and slunk off to join Royal and Colin.

Johnny, who'd been lounging in one of the window seats chatting with Sir Leslie Morgan, finally entered the conversation. "Mamma, I'm sure poor Charlie feels blue-deviled about it. It'll turn up sooner or later. Bound to, you know."

"Unless someone stole it," Morgan said with a certain degree of relish.

Melissa let out a small shriek and fell back against the cushions. "Heaven forfend! Then we are surely doomed."

Colin hurried over, pulling a small bottle of smelling salts out of his coat pocket. "Here, my darling. Use this."

"She's got him trained already," Angus muttered. "That lad's better than a retriever."

Charlie rose from the divan. "Here, Colin, take my seat."

When Richard hurried up and tried to take her arm, she evaded him by stalking over to join Angus and Kade.

"Miss Stewart, please take my seat," Kade said, coming to his feet.

Angus sprang up with remarkable alacrity. "Nay, take mine. I'll just be toppin' off my drink."

Charlie looked hesitant but then shrugged and sat in Angus's spot.

"How are you?" Kade quietly asked as he resumed his seat. "Really?"

"Running out of patience. I'm afraid I might be forced to murder my sister before the week is out."

"My offer still stands, Charlotte. I'm happy to help you search for the brooch."

She ducked her head, avoiding his gaze. "Thank you."
More evasion.

Morgan strolled over to the drinks trolley to refresh his glass. "Now that the festivities are over, perhaps we could all help Miss Charlotte search for the brooch. You know, like a treasure hunt. I'm sure we'd find it in a trice."

Lord Kinloch shot him a startled glance. "Treasure hunt? This is no joking matter, sir."

"Of course not, my dear sir," Morgan replied. "And not a treasure hunt, precisely. But at least the men could mount a search. We could even place wagers as to who would find it first. Nothing extravagant, of course, just a trifling thing to make it more interesting."

Johnny perked up. "That's a splendid idea, old fellow. Lighten the mood, eh?"

Kade felt Charlie go rigid beside him. "No, it's a terrible idea," she said.

"I quite agree," Lady Kinloch sternly intoned. "There will be no wagering in my household, especially over such a serious matter."

Morgan bowed in her direction. "My apologies, dear ma'am. I certainly do not wish to cause offense."

Lady Kinloch gathered herself and returned a polite smile. "We really shouldn't bore our guests with a little family problem. Do forgive us."

The baronet pressed a hand to his chest. "I consider myself quite one of the family, my lady. It was so kind of you to ask me to stay and join this cozy little group."

"That was me," Johnny said. "It never even occurred to Mamma until I asked her."

Lady Kinloch looked discreetly appalled by her son's admission. Even Morgan seemed taken aback.

Charlie sighed. "Really, could my family be any more ridiculous?"

Kade smiled at her. "Just another day in the Highlands, if you ask me." He leaned in a bit. "By the way, I'm happy for the opportunity to spend more time with you, although I get the distinct impression you're trying to avoid me."

Her eyes went wide and she stared at him. She truly had lovely eyes, like the softest of velvet.

"A-*hem*."

Kade glanced up to find Richard hovering a few feet away, glaring daggers of death at him. "Ah, Campbell. Did you wish to say something?"

The man squared his shoulders. "As a matter of fact—"

Charlie jumped up, forcing Richard to step back. "Oh, Mamma, look at the time. Surely dinner is ready by now."

Lady Kinloch looked momentarily confused. "Oh, yes. I quite forgot that we're eating a cold buffet tonight."

"Splendid," Colin said from across the room. "I'm positively famished."

Melissa looked reproachfully at her husband. "Dearest, how can you even *think* of eating with all this uproar?"

"Well, because it's dinnertime, I suppose," Colin replied.

"Quite right," Lord Kinloch put in. "And enough of your die-away airs, Melissa. Poor Colin will begin to wonder why he ever married you."

That unfortunate comment unsurprisingly caused a bit of a kerfuffle. Ainsley and Lady Kinloch soothed Melissa's ruffled nerves, and Lord Kinloch herded the rest of them toward the dining room.

"Rather like a flock of poorly behaved sheep," Royal said to Kade as they followed the others. "I believe the Stewart family is almost as bad as our family."

"That is beyond the limits of natural law," Kade replied. "Since they have neither Angus nor the twins."

"Ho," Angus retorted. "No sass from ye. Now, make sure ye sit next to Miss Charlie. Ye'll nae be wantin' to let booby Campbell get a march on you."

Royal shot Kade a startled glance. "Oh, is that the way the wind blows?"

"Only in our grandfather's fevered brain," he replied.

Angus snorted. "I ken what I ken, and so does Ainsley."

"Ainsley hasn't said a word to me," Royal said. "Of course, we've been rather busy with other matters. It's not often we get a chance to spend time away from the little ones, if you catch my meaning."

"If I didn't, your smirk would have tipped me off," Kade replied.

"Papa, you shouldn't talk about such things in company," said Tira, from behind them.

Royal winced, then turned to smile at his daughter, who'd seemingly appeared out of nowhere. Tira obviously shared the Kendrick trait for sneaking up on others with nary a sound.

"There you are, sweetheart," he said. "I didn't know you were joining us for dinner."

"Mamma said I could, because it's just family now. And don't worry, Papa. I won't tell her that you were making in . . . innuendos."

"Good for you, lassie," Angus said with approval. "Yer never too young to be practicin' the family code."

Royal sighed. "Angus, there *is* no family code."

"Yes there is, Papa," Tira earnestly replied. "Grandda's been teaching me all about it."

"Well, that's alarming," said Kade.

Royal narrowed his gaze on Angus. "What, exactly, have you been teaching my daughter?"

"If ye dinna ken, then yer a sad excuse for a Kendrick," Angus replied in a lofty tone.

Kade held out his hand to Tira. "Come sit with me, sweet lass. I want to hear all about your day."

Angus scowled at him. "Yer supposed to be sittin' next to Miss Charlie."

"Too late," Kade replied as they walked into the dining room.

Booby Campbell had already taken his place.

Charlie sat halfway down the long, polished table, with Richard on one side and smarmy Sir Leslie Morgan on the other. She didn't look happy about it, but her mother had clearly engineered the seating arrangements.

Ainsley waved them over and did a bit of engineering herself. Kade found himself seated directly across from Charlie and flanked by his sister-in-law and Tira. Charlie glanced left and right at her dinner partners before fixing her gaze on Kade and wrinkling her nose.

He covered up his laugh with a cough as he reached for his napkin.

Tira yanked on his sleeve, pulling him down so she could whisper in his ear. "I think Miss Charlie likes you, Uncle Kade."

"I hope so. After all, I'm a very likable fellow. Everyone says so."

"Not Mr. Campbell. He thinks you're a pompous ass."

Startled, he couldn't help a frown. "Did he say that to you, Tira?"

"No, I overheard him say it to someone when you were playing after the wedding. I thought about kicking him in the shins but decided Mamma probably wouldn't like it. I did tell Grandda, though."

"And what did Grandda do?"

"He accidentally spilled a glass of red wine down the front of Mr. Campbell's shirt."

Kade had to smile. "Good for Grandda, although I suppose I shouldn't encourage you—or him—in such behavior. Your mamma wouldn't approve."

"What wouldn't I approve?" Ainsley asked, leaning around Kade to speak to her daughter.

"Nothing," Tira and Kade replied in unison.

Ainsley scoffed. "And you're supposed to be the good one in the family, Kade Kendrick."

"Don't blame me," he protested. "Blame Angus."

"I'm beginning to think you're as bad as he is."

"That is literally impossible."

Ainsley snapped open her napkin. "Recent events in Paris would suggest otherwise."

Ouch.

Kade glanced across the table to again meet Charlie's gaze. It seemed she'd been listening, though now she quickly focused her attention on the footman serving the first course.

Conversation around the table was subdued. Lord Kinloch was clearly distracted, and Melissa dolefully picked at her food while her husband fussed over her. Morgan and Richard competed for Charlie's attention, but she barely uttered a word in response. Young Johnny also seemed out of sorts. While Lady Kinloch, Royal, and Ainsley did their best to keep the conversation going, it was an uphill climb.

Tira bumped her shoulder into Kade. "This isn't a very fun party, is it?"

"Sorry, lass. Maybe after the dessert course you and I can make our escape."

She giggled. "I'd like that."

"I have something to say," Lord Kinloch suddenly announced in a loud voice.

Lady Kinloch put down her wineglass. "Goodness, sir, must you shout down the table at us?"

Kinloch shoved back his chair and stood. "I've come to a decision, and you all need to hear it."

"But we're in the middle of dinner," his wife protested. "Can't it wait until we have tea in the drawing room?"

"No," Kinloch rapped out. "It's about the Clan Iain brooch and what we're going to do about it."

Charlie frowned. "Papa, I don't think there's anything to be done about it. I've looked everywhere, and it's just gone."

"I refuse to accept that. And although I don't hold to any nonsense about curses and such, like your silly sister—"

"Papa!" Melissa plaintively exclaimed.

"The loss is still a stain on our family honor," Kinloch firmly said. "Your mamma is *very* disappointed in you, Charlotte, as am I."

"I say, Papa," Johnny nervously interjected. "Might it not be best if we discussed this with just family? Don't want to embarrass the guests, airing our dirty linen."

"Not to mention the servants," Ainsley dryly put in.

Morgan smirked. "Air away, my lord. We're almost like family, don't you know? Anyway, who cares about the servants? Pay them no never mind."

Charlie cut him an evil glance before looking back to her father. "It's not like I lost the brooch on purpose. In fact, I don't even know if I *did* lose it."

"What the devil does that mean?" Kinloch demanded.

"It might have been stolen."

"From your locked jewel box? When nothing else is missing?"

Charlie seemed to miss a beat. "I'm sorry, Papa, but I can't explain it. You can bluster at me all you like, but it won't do any good."

Kinloch slammed his fist down on the table, rattling the cutlery. "I won't stand for it, I tell you."

Angus threw down his napkin. "Yer actin' like a jingle-brains, Kinloch. It's nae yer daughter's fault the bloody thing disappeared. Yellin' at her like a fishwife willna make it come back."

Kinloch glared down the table at him. "Now, see here, you old—"

Lady Kinloch hastily intervened. "My dear sir, of course I share your dismay. But what is to be done? Bring in the local authorities to investigate a possible theft?"

Her husband waved an irritated hand. "I won't have some fool constable running about the place. No, I have a better idea."

"What idea is that, Papa?" Charlie asked.

"I'm going to offer a reward for its safe return."

"But the brooch is invaluable," Lady Kinloch patiently said. "How could we even put a price on such a thing?"

Kinloch waved an impatient hand. "Not that kind of reward."

Charlie warily eyed her father. "Then what?"

Her father pinned her with a steely gaze. "I do not believe the brooch has been stolen. I'm certain you have misplaced it through some careless act, one that has caused our family a great deal of distress and embarrassment. You know I love you, Charlotte, but I have had enough of your reckless, indeed outrageous, behavior. You are becoming too old for this sort of nonsense. Therefore, the first eligible gentleman to find the brooch will receive your hand in marriage, along with a sizable addition to your dowry. That, I trust, will be incentive enough to find the blasted thing *and* get you safely wed."

Charlie sprang to her feet. "What?"

Tira clapped her hands over her ears, and Kade didn't blame her, because Charlie's shriek was epic. Everyone else froze in shock, including the now-gaping footman serving dinner, who stood with a spoonful of buttered potatoes, one of which dropped off and missed Johnny's plate.

Morgan broke the silence with an uproarious laugh. "I say," he gasped. "It's to be a treasure hunt, after all."

Charlie took a hasty step toward her father. "You cannot be serious, Papa. That is the most ridiculous thing I've ever heard."

Lady Kinloch also came to her feet, alarmed. "Indeed, my dear. It does seem like a rather rash proposal."

"It's bloody deranged, even for Kinloch," Angus said. "Yer husband's a ninny, Elspeth. I told ye that before ye married him."

Kinloch started to round on Angus, but Ainsley cut him off. "Really, my lord, full marks for creativity. But it's an unenforceable proposition, unless you're going to march the poor girl to the altar at gunpoint."

"I'm not marrying anyone," Charlie tersely said.

"I say," protested Richard, finally entering the fray. "That's not fair. After all, I'm supposed to be courting you, Charlotte. Your father and mother said so."

Charlie spun around, jabbing her oyster fork at him. "If you say another word, I swear I will stab you."

And with that, Melissa descended into full-on hysterics. Colin waved his napkin at her, Morgan continued to laugh, and most of the others erupted into loud disputes. Charlie remained silent as she studied her father with a narrow, assessing gaze.

"It's not boring anymore, is it?" Tira whispered to Kade.

"I've never seen anything like it," he answered.

"Poor Miss Charlotte. I think her father's being very mean to her."

"So do I, pet."

Charlie suddenly glanced at Kade. Her lips were compressed into an irritated line, but she now seemed to have full control over her temper. She was, in fact, the calm eye of the storm.

"This is such utter nonsense," she said.

Then she stalked from the room, and because of the general uproar, no one seemed to notice but Kade and Tira.

"I think you should go after her, Uncle Kade," Tira said.

"Right as always, lassie. You stay here and report back to me later."

She gave him a salute. "Aye, aye, sir."

Kade pushed back his chair and strode after Charlie. Exiting the dining room, he saw her whisk around the corner of the hall. He caught up with her just as she was about to fling open one of the doors that led out to the gardens.

"Mind if I join you?" he asked. "It was getting rather fraught in there. Not good for my nerves."

"*Your* nerves? You're not the one whose father is trying to auction you off to the highest bidder."

"Sorry to contradict a lady, but it seems rather the opposite," Kade said as he followed her out onto the terrace.

She huffed. "Sadly true. He's trying to bribe someone—anyone—to take me off his hands."

"He did stipulate eligible gentlemen only."

Charlie stopped short at the path that wound through the flower beds. "Are you intentionally trying to annoy me, Mr. Kendrick? If so, I will regret having left my oyster fork in the dining room."

Kade held up his hands. "Sorry, lass, but I couldn't help teasing. The whole thing is farcical."

Her lips twitched into a reluctant smile. "You're right. It is a farce. The only question is why my normally level-headed father came up with the deranged notion. I'll admit that I am rather outrageous on occasion, but this does seem an over-reaction to events."

"It is odd, indeed."

"Mamma and Melissa have been endlessly pestering him to do something, so that's part of it. Then I suppose he got the idea from Sir Leslie's stupid suggestion." She gazed out into the garden, now softly shrouded in evening shadows. "I'm so sorry that you and your family were subjected to such a foolish scene."

"Don't be. Scenes are a Kendrick specialty."

She started down the path. "I suspect that Kendricks do not descend into hysterics."

"Only because Angus would run us through with a dirk."

"His intervention just now was very colorful."

"Aye, he's a wonder. But truly, Charlie, I hope you're not too upset. Your father surely does not intend to go through with that mad scheme."

"I'm afraid he does," she ruefully replied. "Once he makes up his mind, he tends to bull ahead."

"But he *cannot* force you to marry."

She waved a hand. "Of course not. But what this hare-brained idea will do is bring more suitors to our doorstep, and *that* my mother will approve of. She'll natter at me endlessly, driving me quite mad."

"And let's not forget Melissa and her poor nerves."

"Oh, Lord. Poor Colin."

"He married her, so he can't give her back. That must be a great comfort to your parents."

She laughed. "You are a very bad man, Mr. Kendrick."

I'd like to show you just how bad I can be.

"No, I'm the nice Kendrick. Ask anyone."

He caught her glimmer of a smile. "I have not forgotten how truly nice you are, sir."

That sounded . . . tepid.

They walked in silence but for their footsteps crunching on the gravel. A soft breeze wafted about them as flower beds gave way to shrubbery and a stand of oaks lining the path. After a few minutes, they reached a small gazebo overlooking a pond. It was a charming scene and decidedly intimate.

You're in trouble now, mate.

Kade ignored the warning voice in his head.

"So what are you going to do?" he asked as she led him up the steps.

Charlie flopped down onto a cushioned bench that ringed the inside of the gazebo. "Hold my ground, I suppose. Papa has the bit between his teeth, and I'm not sure if even my mother can pry it loose this time. Not that she'll want to, once she's thought about it. She can't wait to marry me off."

He propped a shoulder against the wrought iron column at the entrance, refusing to give in to the temptation to sit next to her. "That's rather dreadful."

Charlie curled her legs up under her skirts and leaned an

arm along the railing as she gazed out over the water. In the deepening dusk, somehow she seemed very alone at the moment.

"I can't really blame them, since *I'm* rather dreadful. They've been very patient with me, especially my father."

The touch of sadness in her voice twisted his heart. Tossing his caution into the pond, Kade went over and sat next to her.

Charlie twisted a bit to glance up at him, her eyes shadowed and full of hidden depths. She was *impossibly* beautiful.

Kade took her hand. "You are the opposite of dreadful. You are smart, funny, and very talented. Your parents are beyond fortunate to have such a splendid daughter."

She blinked a few times, as if startled by his praise. Then she flashed a quicksilver smile. "Perhaps you could give them a recommendation? They might actually listen to it, coming from you."

"It would be my pleasure."

She squeezed his fingers before pulling her hand free.

And thank God.

He was—they were—courting enough trouble as it was.

"And what about you, Mr. Kendrick?" she asked in a lighter tone. "Are you going to join in the infamous treasure hunt, or do you intend to flee our fair shores? I recommend the latter. Life is only bound to get more ridiculous in the days ahead."

While she undoubtedly appreciated the absurdity of the situation, Kade also heard something else—embarrassment. Underneath her rather brash exterior lurked a sensitive soul, one that took refuge in music and nature. No one in her family understood her. That such knowledge pained her was evident, at least to him.

Kade knew what it was like to feel alone, even when surrounded by people who loved you. Sometimes, even with the best of intentions, love didn't always know or understand.

He gently turned her to face him. "I told you that I would help you, and I meant it."

"Thank you," she whispered. Then she crinkled her nose. "You do realize that Papa will think you're in the hunt for my hand. Or, properly speaking, my dowry."

"Charlie, I don't need your dowry," he gruffly replied.

And what the hell did he mean by that?

Kade found that he didn't give a damn. Charlie looked so beguiling in the soft light of a just-rising moon that all he could think about was kissing her.

He started to dip his head. She breathed out a fluttery sigh and tilted her chin up, as if to meet him. Her lips parted, and—

"Och, finally. I've been lookin' all over for ye," intruded a most unwelcome voice.

Charlie jerked back, almost falling off the bench. Kade grabbed for her, but she quickly recovered.

Sighing, he turned to face his grandfather. Angus waited on the gazebo steps, practically vibrating with impatience.

"Mr. MacDonald, I didn't see you there," Charlie brightly said.

"Aye, ye were both *occupied*," Angus meaningfully replied.

Kade stood. "Grandda, next time you might trying making a little noise before startling people out of their wits."

"I wasn't exactly sneaking up on ye, laddie. No wonder ye got stabbed in Paris by that Russian spy."

Charlie gaped at Kade. "Is that what happened?"

"It was nothing," he replied, trying not to grind his molars into dust. "Grandda, could you please not bandy about that subject so carelessly? It's supposed to be a secret, remember?"

Angus batted his objection away like a fly. "I only told Miss Charlie a wee bit, and I'll wager she can keep a secret."

"You have no idea," she muttered.

Kade shot her a sideways glance before answering Angus. "All right, you found us. What's amiss?"

"Everything! Kinloch refuses to give up that barmy idea about offering Miss Charlie up as a prize, even though I did my best to make him see he was bein' a jinglebrains. And that scabby Sir Leslie is winding everyone up, too."

"If that's how you expressed it to Lord Kinloch, no wonder you failed. I presume Ainsley and Royal did their best to inject some sense into the discussion?"

"Both Royal and young Johnny did, but Ainsley had to help cart Melissa up to her room." He shook his head. "I hate to criticize yer family, Miss Charlie, but that girl's a piece of work."

"At least you don't have to live with her," she drolly replied.

"As fascinating as all this is, Grandda," Kade said, "you have yet to explain why you sought us out."

"Because ye need to start lookin' for that blasted brooch right away, ye noddy. Scabby Sir Leslie is now swearin' to find it, which made ninny Campbell pitch a fit. That's what set Melissa off again, just after her puir ma finally got her calmed down."

Charlie stood up. "I'd best go back in and see if I can help my mother with Melissa."

"Ainsley will get her sorted, never fear," Angus said. "But ye and Kade need to start searchin' for the brooch. Work together, as it were."

Kade could practically hear the cogs and wheels churning away in his grandfather's head.

"And it looks like ye already were doin' that," the old fellow added.

"We were simply discussing the situation," Kade replied. "Nothing more."

"Ye need to do more than jaw about it, so get off yer arse and get to work. If someone else finds the brooch, then Miss Charlie will be in a right pickle." Angus waved a finger at him. "And ye dinna want to let the fair lassie slip through yer fingers. That's a prize ye should be happy to claim, lad."

Bloody hell.

Charlie started flapping her arms like a gull about to take flight. "No one needs to do anything. I'm sure the brooch will turn up on its own. Or not. Likely not because it was probably stolen. Or something. Besides, I have no intention of getting married, regardless of my father's ridiculous ideas."

Charlotte Stewart was not the sort of woman to incoherently babble, but now she definitely was. And she was more agitated than Kade had ever seen her.

"I'm happy to help, Charlie," he said. "With no strings attached, I promise."

"That's very kind but entirely unnecessary. Now, if you'll excuse me, I must see to my sister."

Then she was off like a shot, heading up the path without a backward glance.

His grandfather flopped down on the bench. "Ye buggered that one up, lad. Ye'd best be careful or someone will steal a march on ye."

"We were doing perfectly fine until you showed up."

"About to kiss her, were ye? She seems a mite skittish now. Ye'll have to work on that."

"I'm not working on anything."

He tried to tell himself that his grandfather's intervention had been a blessing in disguise. If Kade had kissed Charlie, who knows what it would have led to.

You know what.

Which was precisely why moonlight kisses in romantic gazebos were so dangerous.

"Are ye tellin' me yer not helpin' that puir girl?" Angus exclaimed, outraged.

"Of course I'm going to help her, but as a friend. She's under enough pressure from her family as it is. Besides, the entire thing is ridiculous. Charlie has no marital intentions, something she has made abundantly clear."

"Och, she'll nae be able to withstand yer charm once ye

actually start usin' it instead of prancing about like a die-away *Sassenach*."

"What the hell is that supposed to mean?"

"Yer a Highlander, so start actin' like one. That's what the lassie needs."

Kade hoisted his grandfather up from the bench. "As is too often the case, I have no idea what you're talking about. Which suggests that you've had too much whisky."

"I have not," Angus indignantly replied. "In fact, I could do with one right now."

"Splendid. Let's get one. And while we're having that drink, I'll explain exactly why we need to approach this situation with caution. If we're not careful, we'll end up in a right mess."

And he might very well end up in love.

CHAPTER 11

The length of the corridor was shrouded in darkness but for the small circle of light cast by Charlie's candle. Since there were no family rooms in this wing, lamps were never left burning, and the junior footman who kept the night watch spent most of his time in the kitchen, making his rounds once on the hour.

Everyone was now in bed, including Johnny, who'd developed the unfortunate habit of playing cards with Sir Leslie late into the night. Her brother seemed more changeable lately, no longer the sunny, even-tempered lad of his youth. Charlie was convinced Sir Leslie was a bad influence. Unfortunately, no one agreed with her, because Sir Leslie came from an old Scottish family that was above reproach.

Charlie would have to sort out her brother herself—once she got her own life in order.

She slipped into the music room, her bare feet silent on the polished floorboards, and crossed to the mahogany, glass-fronted cabinet. Papa had once been an avid collector of Chinese lacquered boxes and had amassed several dozen specimens of very good quality. Eventually, though, he'd lost interest and had moved the collection case to a corner of the music room, where it now collected nothing but dust.

Setting her candle down, she pulled the cabinet key from

her wrapper. As she bent over to insert the small key into the lock, she heard a quick scratching sound. When light flared behind her, she whipped around and tripped over the edge of the area rug. Biting back a yelp, she waved her arms for balance but went arse over teakettle, landing with a thump on the floor.

"Bloody hell," she muttered.

A moment later, Kade crouched in front of her and studied her with concern. "Are you all right, lass?"

She glanced across the room to the reading nook. A candle now softly shed its light on the armchair where he'd obviously been seated.

Or lurking.

Charlie narrowed her gaze as she stared up at him. Normally, she'd be entranced to be only inches away from his too-handsome face. Right now, though, she was tempted to give him a good shove and put *him* on his arse.

"You're spying on me," she accused.

"No, I was simply waiting to talk to you."

"And you didn't feel the need to talk to me when I came into the blasted room?"

"I didn't want to startle you while you were still holding the candle."

"You made a poor job of not startling me."

He grimaced. "You can give me a proper scold once we get you up off the floor. I also want to make sure you didn't injure yourself."

"I'm not a porcelain figurine, sir," she tartly replied. "I'm perfectly fine."

Her backside had taken a painful thump, though. If she'd been alone, she would have given it a bit of a rub.

You could always ask Kade to do it for you.

Ignoring that idiotic thought, Charlie planted her hands flat on the floor, preparing to push herself up. "If you'll get out of my way—"

She bit back another yelp when Kade slipped his hands under her arms and stood in one fluid movement, bringing her straight up with him. He did it effortlessly, as if she'd been nothing more than a child's rag doll.

"Thank you," she said, rather breathless, "though I was perfectly capable of getting myself up."

His smile was charmingly rueful. "Since I'm the one who put you there, I thought I could at least be a gentleman and help you up."

And now her brain tossed up the most alarming image of both of them on the blasted floor, in each other's arms and with very little clothing on. Her deranged mind seemed to think that would be a good thing.

You're a ninny.

She straightened her wrapper. "Gentlemen don't generally lie in wait for people like a common footpad."

"I'm truly sorry for startling you," he said, looking contrite. "But if you knew I was in here, you would not have come in."

"Well, I am in my nightclothes, in case you failed to notice."

His smile flashed again. "I noticed, but that's not the real reason you would have retreated, is it? Charlie, I know what you're up to, and it's fine. I promise I won't betray you."

She silently fumed at him for a few moments and then decided there was no point. He obviously did know, which was both annoying and impressive.

"How did you catch me out?"

He steered her to the chaise. "Sit first and catch your breath. Are you sure you didn't hurt yourself? That was quite a tumble."

She sank down onto the soft cushions. "I've taken more than my share of tumbles off the back of a horse. A few inches to the floor can't compare."

He crossed his arms, still concerned. "But it was bound

to be a shock. Would you like something to drink, perhaps a sherry?"

She pointed to the decanter on the sideboard. "We've only got whisky in here, but that should dull the pain."

"Charlotte, I am truly sorry—"

"Goodness, I'm not that fragile. If I'm being honest, I need a drink to bolster my courage for the conversation we're about to have, not for imaginary injuries."

"I promise to be gentle," he wryly said.

"I'll hold you to that promise, Mr. Kendrick."

He fetched the candle from the reading nook and lit a branch of them on the piano. A soft glow pushed back the shadows, and Charlie self-consciously tucked her bare feet under her wrapper. God only knew what Kade thought of her, creeping about the house like a deranged ghost.

Kade poured out two glasses of whisky and handed her one. "This will warm you up, especially your wee toes."

She mentally sighed, wishing the blasted man wasn't so observant.

The welcome heat of the whisky slid down her throat to warm her stomach and steady her nerves. It wasn't just the impending conversation that made her jumpy, or the fact that he'd discovered her secret. Kade had discarded his coat and rolled up his sleeves, which showcased his muscular arms as well as his broad shoulders and chest. For someone who'd been such a sickly boy, he was now so brawny that she truly felt, possibly for the first time, both dainty and rather petite.

As he stood there, his tall, masculine form outlined by the soft glow of candlelight, she became intensely aware of her scandalously flimsy attire—although her robe *was* flannel, so hardly the stuff of seduction. She'd never actually thought about seducing a man, much less pondered the appropriate garb for undertaking such a venture. But Kade had a knack for putting all sorts of ideas into her head, and they were ones best ignored.

"How did you catch me out?" she asked with feigned nonchalance. "Here I thought I was making such a good job of it."

"You did make a good job of it. But before we get to that, I need to say something to you."

He sat next to her and stretched out his long legs, propping one foot on top of the other.

"Settling in for a nice chat, are we?" she asked, trying to ignore the way his very presence seemed to bring the blood rushing to her head.

"An apology first," he replied. "On my grandfather's behalf. I'm afraid he embarrassed you in the gazebo."

Charlie had been embarrassed, but probably not in the way he assumed. She'd taken his grandfather's measure some days ago and found his behavior amusing rather than embarrassing.

"Are you referring to his assumption that you are participating in my father's scheme to catch me a husband?" she asked.

Kade snorted. "An assumption delivered with all the subtlety of a sledgehammer, I'm afraid."

Charlie smiled. "I like your grandfather, Kade. He's fun, although I do wish he wouldn't twit my father so much. He's driving Papa rather mad."

"Royal has tried to lay down the law in that regard but, alas, to no avail."

"My mother is more than capable of managing the both of them. Or, rather, she is as long as Melissa isn't having an episode."

He canted sideways to face her. "But you were embarrassed earlier, Charlie, and I am truly sorry for that."

She waved a hand. "He's no worse than my parents. Our relatives seem quite determined to embarrass us with their matchmaking."

"It's practically an avocation among Highlanders. They're

obsessed with strengthening and preserving the family and the clans."

"I suppose you can't blame them," she replied. "The Highland clans did not have an easy time of it for a very long spell. But nobody's trying to kill us anymore, and we get along perfectly well with the *Sassenachs*. Look at your family. Royal and Ainsley seem like the perfect example of peaceful coexistence."

"The Kendricks have been thoroughly conquered by Englishwomen, with an Irish lass thrown in for good measure. But as for peaceful coexistence . . ." He waggled a hand. "Let's just say, most of the time."

"Well, we *are* Highlanders. Fighting is in our blood, is it not?"

"You certainly have more than your fair share of the Highland warrior flowing through your veins."

She eyed him, feeling dubious. Was he teasing her?

"I hope that's a good thing," she said.

"Absolutely it is. My brother Braden's wife, Samantha, is a true Highland warrior. She even brought down a criminal gang, with a wee spot of Kendrick help."

Charlie perked up. "How exciting. Were you there when it happened? I'd love to hear all about it."

"And I'll be happy to tell you some other time." Kade hesitated, and then tapped a finger on the cushion between them. "I'm glad you weren't embarrassed tonight, because I would truly hate for you to feel uncomfortable around me."

She'd only been embarrassed because they'd been interrupted in the middle of an almost kiss. At least she thought Kade had been about to kiss her. It would be doubly mortifying if he hadn't been and she'd misread him so badly.

"Thank you," she said. "And you don't make me uncomfortable at all."

At least not the way he meant.

"So," she added, "how did you figure me out? Here I thought I was being so clever."

"You were, actually. No sane person would ever believe you would willingly subject yourself to your family's disapproval, much less to Melissa's hysterics."

"Since poor Melissa has the vapors on a regular basis, it was only a matter of degree. But what led you to believe that I had stolen the brooch?"

He shrugged. "It was partly a reasoned deduction and partly a guess. It was one way to spike Richard's guns, so that was my first thought."

"I was more interested in spiking my mother's guns. But how did you know where I hid it and when I would retrieve it?" She shook her head. "I'm really quite annoyed with you, Mr. Kendrick. I was very careful."

He grinned. "Sorry, lass. My suspicions were ratcheted up this morning at breakfast. You were startled when Lady Kinloch mentioned to me that the maids would be thoroughly cleaning the music room in the next day or so."

Charlie grimaced. "Yes, that did startle me. I knew the girls would wish to dust the inside of the cabinet and my father's boxes. I hid the brooch in a box on the bottom shelf. But was that all it took to crack the riddle?"

"What really tipped me off was how you reacted to your father's harebrained announcement at dinner tonight. After you recovered from your initial shock, you were calmer than the rest of your family, and most of the other guests."

He was a clever one, and fatally observant.

"Because I knew the brooch would be found only if I allowed it to be found." She shook her head. "Who knew that *not* flying off the handle would prove to be my undoing?"

When Kade smiled at her, she felt almost lit within from its warmth, as if he'd set off a spark in the middle of her chest.

"If it's any comfort, I only noticed because I was watching

you," he said. "And since I was also not flying off the handle, I was capable of rational thought."

Charlie adopted a stern expression. "Well, you have thrown quite a spoke into my plans, sir, and I do not approve."

He held up a hand, as if taking an oath. "Never fear, my lady. I would not betray your secret, even under the most hideous of tortures."

"You'd best steer clear of Melissa, then. If I don't think of some way out of this mess, the poor dear will descend into a permanent state of nervous excitement, and that will be torture for all of us."

He laughed. Charlie could learn to be quite addicted to that laugh, given half a chance.

"What else led you to believe that the music room was my hiding place?" she asked. "Surely not just my reaction at breakfast this morning."

"Well, you spend much of your time here, after all. Your bedroom would be the first place your mother and the servants would search, but you would still want to keep the brooch close by. Therefore, all that was left was to sit here and wait, and let you do the rest."

Charlie shook her head. "That's both impressive and annoying. Although I suppose I shouldn't be annoyed, since you are an intelligence agent."

"Is that what Angus told you?" He blew out an exasperated sigh. "No doubt highly exaggerated tales of my prowess."

"He was rather mysterious, although he did say you were one of the king's best spies."

"No, that would be my brother Graeme."

She blinked. "You're joking."

"No, and he used to be a spy," he amended. "I'm obviously as bad as my grandfather for telling you that. But since the cat is now clearly out of the bag, I will admit to doing a spot of intelligence work for the Crown now and again. My work and my travels abroad allow me access to, shall we say, certain people."

"Important people."

He hesitated for a moment. "Yes, and others, too."

Like the person who'd stabbed him. When Angus had first told her of Kade's adventures, it had all seemed terribly exciting. But now the reality of it struck home. Someone had tried to hurt him, perhaps even kill him. And the idea of that, of a world without Kade, suddenly became too devastating to contemplate.

She grabbed his arm. "You mustn't put yourself in danger, do you hear me? You're not to do that again."

He blinked, as if startled by her reaction.

"Sorry," she muttered, feeling like an idiot.

Before she could unclench her fingers, his hand covered hers. "I promise I will be fine, Charlie. There's no need to worry."

His tone was so kind and tender that she found herself having to fight against the impulse to cry.

"It's just that I don't want you to get hurt," she gruffly said, trying to compensate. "If you were injured, you might not be able to play anymore."

There, that sounded like a reasonable explanation for her emotional outburst.

His eyebrows lifted in a comical tilt. "Believe me, I was very aware of that in Paris. Thankfully, no permanent damage was done."

"You're certain?"

"Absolutely. It was just a silly misunderstanding, mostly on my part."

She scoffed. "Silly misunderstandings don't usually end up with a knife to the back, do they?"

He responded with a sly grin. "Sorry, but didn't you say you were from the Highlands?"

"I see, and I must surrender the point, sir," she wryly replied.

"I should hope so."

For several long seconds, they simply stared at each other. Something changed in his amazing cobalt gaze, something that flashed heat through her veins. Her mind seemed to go fuzzy around the edges.

"But why did you do it?" she asked, blurting out the first thing that came to mind. "The intelligence work, I mean."

Kade didn't seem at all discomposed by her abrupt change in behavior. "I was doing it for my country, of course. But if I'm honest, it was also for the thrill of it. And that makes me sound like a bit of a prat, doesn't it?"

"No, but it seems to me that your life was already quite thrilling to begin with. Traveling everywhere, meeting interesting people. It all sounds very glamorous to me."

"So I am an ungrateful prat," he wryly said. "I thought so."

Appalled, Charlie started to stutter. "Oh . . . oh, Mr. Kendrick, please don't think I would ever say such a thing."

He gently tapped her cheek. "Charlie, I'm just teasing. And please stop calling me Mr. Kendrick. We've been friends for a very long time, have we not?"

"I . . . I suppose," she replied, feeling rather foolish.

"And you don't object to me calling you Charlie, do you?"

"No, I like it," she confessed. "And just to be completely clear, I don't think you're a prat or ungrateful. Not at all. It's just that your life is so different from mine that I have trouble imagining what it's like."

"My life is everything I wished it to be, and I'm enormously grateful for that," he said, turning serious. "But it's been hard work and I've been doing it for a long time to the exclusion of almost everything else. I suppose I got a bit bored for a spell."

"Do you regret any of it?" she softly asked.

"Not one bit. But it does come with a price—loss of privacy, and not seeing my family as much as I'd like."

"Still, all that travel must be wonderful," she said, feeling rather wistful. "Paris, Vienna, Madrid . . . it sounds quite amazing to me."

He cocked his head. "Charlie, are you bored with your life?"

That took her aback. Was she? She'd never really thought in those terms.

"Maybe sometimes, I suppose. But of course that's silly, because I have a perfectly good life and I love my family." She rolled her eyes. "Most of the time."

Kade smiled. "I know the feeling."

"And I do love the freedom that comes with living in the Highlands. It's so beautiful, too. Still, I've only been to Edinburgh twice in my life, and I've never been south of the borderlands." She shrugged. "So Paris and Madrid will simply have to live in my imagination."

Kade's mouth curled up in a smile that seemed to hold so many secrets. She had to resist the impulse to lean over and press her lips against his, as if in doing so she would some- how gain access to all those secrets.

When his smile turned quizzical, Charlie mentally shook herself. Kade and his life would never be hers, and he would soon be leaving, anyway. That was just as it should be. She no more belonged in his world than she would in a traveling circus.

She patted his hand and stood. "It's late. I'd best retrieve my silly brooch and be off to bed. Heaven knows I've caused you enough trouble for one night."

He also rose. "No trouble, lass. I've enjoyed our talk very much."

"Thank you," she said with a smile. "I enjoyed it, too. I'm

just sorry that you had to sit through that dreadful spectacle at dinner."

"My dear girl, that was the most entertaining part of the evening. I wouldn't have missed it for anything."

Charlie doffed an imaginary cap. "We aim to please, sir. Now, if you'll just give me a moment to retrieve my brooch, we can sneak back upstairs undetected. As a spy, I'm sure you're very good at that."

She opened the cabinet and reached for the small lacquered box on the bottom shelf. When it felt too light, her brain tripped and stumbled to a halt. With trembling hands, she flipped up the lid.

Kade was at her side in an instant. "What's wrong?"

Unable to speak past the constriction in her throat, she simply showed him the empty box.

He frowned. "Charlie, are you sure this is the right one? The blasted things all look the same to me."

She *had* been rushing that day, so perhaps . . .

Hastily, she checked the boxes on the two bottom shelves, then the others. All were empty.

"It's gone," she said, as panic punched through her shock. "It's really, really gone."

"Well, that's no good," he replied.

"And that is a ridiculous understatement," she snapped, unable to stop herself.

He ran a hand down her arm. "Charlie, it'll be all right, I promise. We'll figure it out."

Full-blown panic was now surging through her body like a roiling thunderstorm, along with the hideous conviction that she'd brought this dreadful state of affairs upon herself.

Stupid, stupid, stupid.

"The bloody thing is gone and somebody obviously took it," she exclaimed, waving her arms.

She spun on her heel and paced the room, too agitated to

remain still. Her thoughts whirled about inside her skull, making it hard to think rationally.

"Perhaps one of the maids found it," he suggested. "Might they have come in early to dust?"

"No, because they would have returned it to Papa immediately."

Then she stopped pacing, struck by a hideous thought.

"What if Richard already found it, or Sir Leslie? Papa will be an absolute terror. He'll *insist* that I marry them. Him. Whomever." She covered her face, feeling ill. "This is a disaster."

A moment later, Kade gently pulled her hands away and gathered them to his chest. His gaze was tender and more than slightly amused.

"If you dare to laugh, Kade Kendrick, I swear I will throw you out the window."

"I wouldn't dream of it, sweetheart. But you know as well as I do that your father cannot make you marry anyone."

"No, but he and Mamma would pester me endlessly. And *everyone* will be talking about it, and *everyone* will be pressuring me to uphold the family honor. Either way, my life will be ruined."

She knew she sounded dramatic, but she couldn't help it. She'd tumbled into more than a few scrapes in her life, but nothing compared to this. This one was a monumental disaster.

He shook his head. "I won't allow that to happen."

"Kade, you don't understand. This is going to be—"

He let go of her hands and tipped up her chin. Then he lowered his head and . . .

Kissed her.

Every thought scattered to the four winds, and she felt like she was falling—falling *up* and into him.

She dug her fingers into his waistcoat, trying to find her bearings as his firm, warm lips brushed over hers. Then she stopped trying because, well, Kade was *kissing* her. And it was the most *wonderful* kiss, so tender and alluring that her anxieties and frustrations faded away. His caress was everything she'd imagined it would be in the foolish dreams of a schoolgirl, and in the quiet longings of a woman grown. His mouth seduced her with softness and heat, and a gentle passion that stole into the depths of her soul.

When Charlie sighed her pleasure against his lips, he slid a big hand to the nape of her neck, gently cradling her. At the touch of his fingertips, she shivered. Kade murmured deep in his throat and moved his other hand down to her waist, pulling her closer. And thank God for that, because every one of her muscles had gone weak with a yearning so intense it made her dizzy. For a silly, delirious moment, she imagined she might faint from the sheer wonder of it all.

Kade's tongue slid along the seam of her lips, silently asking permission to enter. Then Charlie forgot all about fainting and focused on feeling instead. When she opened to him, he swept in with a bold, possessive kiss. She melted against him, desperately eager to take as much as he wanted to give.

But when she stretched up on her toes, reaching for more, Kade began a slow retreat. His lips wandered over to press a kiss to her cheek, before returning to briefly nuzzle her mouth one last time. Then he straightened up, although his hand still rested gently against her neck.

Charlie sucked in a deep breath and gazed up into his eyes. They glittered like blue flame. How could something so hot make one shiver? Then she realized that she was gaping at him like a booby, her eyes no doubt as round as saucers. She clamped her mouth shut, and she and Kade stared at each other for several long seconds before he ticked up an eyebrow.

"All right, lass?" he asked, his voice holding a hint of a Highland growl.

She frowned, slightly perplexed by the question. "Why wouldn't I be?"

His other brow went up.

God, she was acting like a complete nincompoop. "Yes, I'm perfectly well, thank you. Splendid, in fact."

His mouth—his truly wonderful mouth—suddenly split into a grin. "Excellent. Now, Charlie, as you pointed out some minutes ago, it's very late, so it's off to bed with you. I'll snuff out the candles and follow in a few minutes. That way, we should escape detection."

She tried to gather her wits. "Yes, that makes perfect sense."

He tapped the side of his head. "Master spy. We think about these things."

His joke brought her problems roaring back. That kiss had knocked them right out of her head, but now they loomed as hideous as before.

"But what about my brooch? And what about—"

He swooped down and pressed a brief, firm kiss to her lips. The man was ridiculously good at deflecting her questions.

"You're not to worry about that tonight," he said. "We'll regroup in the morning and come up with a plan."

Then he took her by the shoulders and walked her to the door. He cracked it a few inches, listened, and then nodded his head.

"Can you see without a candle?" he murmured as he opened the door wider.

She peeked down the hall. Moonlight filtered through the windows that lined the corridor, providing a soft illumination.

"Yes," she whispered.

"Off with you, then."

He gave her a gentle push to get her started, but his voice stopped her a few moments later.

"And, Charlie?"

She turned and took in his mysterious, tender smile. She stood fast, resisting the urge to throw herself into his arms.

"Yes?" she managed.

"Sweet dreams." Then he quietly closed the door.

Charlie forced her feet to move. If she did dream tonight, her dreams would be only of him.

CHAPTER 12

"Ye'll find breakfast in the small dining room today, Mr. Kendrick," said the footman waiting for Kade at the foot of the central staircase. "I just brought a fresh pot of coffee."

Kade smiled. "Thank you. Coffee sounds just the thing."

He'd tossed and turned for hours. Thoughts about Charlie had bedeviled him all night, including what to do about the missing brooch. More importantly, though, what to do about his feelings for Charlie? Kade told himself that he'd only kissed her on impulse, just to arrest her growing sense of panic.

That was a lie, of course. He'd kissed her because he'd wanted to. He'd wanted it more than anything he'd ever wanted in his life.

As for calming her down, it had done the opposite for him. Only a mighty act of willpower had stopped him from sweeping her off to the sofa for more kisses and many other delightful activities his brain had readily conjured up. He'd never thought of himself as the flannel wrapper, bare feet, and messy braid sort of fellow, but last night Charlie had proven him wrong.

He'd crossed a line in that music room, one from which there was no return. So now he needed at least three cups of coffee before he could get his brain functioning clearly enough to figure out the problem—or problems—posed by Charlotte Stewart.

"Is anyone else in the dining room?" he asked the footman.

"Mr. Royal Kendrick, as well as yer grandfather and Miss Tira, sir. Lord Kinloch and the other gentlemen are out riding, Miss Charlotte ate earlier, and Lady Kinloch and Miss Melissa—I mean, Mrs. MacMillan—have yet to come down."

"For the best. It's always a happy thing when one can avoid hysterics at the breakfast table."

The footman made a slight, choking sound. "Indeed, sir. Now, if ye'll excuse me."

He hurried off in the direction of the kitchen.

"Really, Kade, you shouldn't tease the staff," Ainsley said as she descended the stairs to join him.

"I know, but you must admit that this visit has turned into something of a farce."

She took his arm. "I feel like I've wandered into one of Molière's ridiculous comedies, and I'm beginning to think Charlie's the only sane one in the lot."

"I think Johnny's all right, if a bit rattled by the fireworks," he replied as he escorted her toward the dining room.

"Yes, he's a very nice boy, which makes me wonder why he is hanging about with Sir Leslie. That man is a bounder and a complication."

"He's definitely a bounder, but why a complication?"

"Because he's joined in the hunt for that ridiculous brooch, and if he finds it, Lord Kinloch will pressure poor Charlotte into marrying him."

"It wouldn't work. Charlie told me last night that she has no intention of getting married at all."

Except to me.

His brain stumbled over that thought.

Ainsley paused outside the door of the dining room. "And when did she tell you this?"

"I had a little chat with her last night," he replied.

"Do tell all, dear boy. I am now ravenous with curiosity."

"I will be happy to assuage that curiosity once I have assuaged my need for coffee."

He opened the door and ushered her into the elegantly appointed room with its wide sash windows that showcased the rugged peaks in the distance. No one with a drop of Highland blood could gaze upon the outstanding view and not feel the stir of something ancient. It was like the call of a hunting horn in a distant glen, or the faint skirl of bagpipes carried away on the breeze.

Angus looked up from his breakfast. "So yon lazybones has finally decided to join us, with the morning half gone and so much work to be done."

"I'm going to assume that remark was not directed at me," Ainsley said. "I've already discussed today's outings with Lady Kinloch and spoken to the cook on her behalf. Poor woman needed a bit of bucking up, I'm sorry to say."

Angus frowned. "Why would the bloody cook need buckin' up?"

Royal put down his coffee cup. "Language, Grandda. There's a child in the room."

"Och, the lassie's heard worse from me."

"That's true, Papa," Tira said as she slathered marmalade on a scone.

Royal sighed.

Ainsley took a seat next to her husband. "Darling, that ship sailed long ago. We just have to trust in Tira's good judgment, which we know is considerably better than her great-grandfather's."

"Ho, *Sassenach*," Angus said, "I'll nae have ye insultin' me at the breakfast table. And I'd still like to know why the bloody cook needs buckin' up."

"Not the cook," Ainsley replied. "Elspeth, your cousin. Remember her?"

"Of course I remember her. I already told Elspeth to tell

Kinloch to stop shootin' off his mouth like an arseling, and to give booby Campbell and Sir Leslie the boot. And," he added, pointing his spoon at Ainsley, "to ship Melissa off with Colin on their blasted wedding trip so the rest of us can have some peace."

Ainsley rolled her eyes. "Please do us a favor, Grandda, and cease giving advice—to anyone."

"Why? I give the best advice of anyone in this family. Not that ye seem to appreciate it."

Kade fetched a cup of coffee from the sideboard. "I wonder why that is?"

"No sass from ye, either, laddie boy. Dinna forget that yer nae too old for me to paddle yer bum."

Kade had been hearing that empty threat for so long that he barely registered it now.

"What events required you to consult with the cook?" he asked Ainsley as he took a seat.

"There's to be a special picnic on Eilean Munde Island this afternoon," Tira cut in. "We're taking a boat ride and everything."

Kade eyed Ainsley askance. "A picnic while the entire house is in an uproar? Seems rather dotty, doesn't it?"

"I agree, but it was planned some weeks ago as part of the wedding festivities, and will include a few local families as well. Elspeth told me that she refuses to let Charlie's poor behavior ruin the entire wedding."

"I'd say it's the rest of the family that's been behaving poorly, not Charlie."

"Too true," Ainsley said, selecting a ginger biscuit from the pastry tray. "It's all such a mess."

Angus finished sawing away at a piece of ham and pointed his knife at Kade. "It's up to the great spy to straighten it out, because yer the one best able to find the brooch. So what's the plan?"

Kade thought for a moment but then decided the truth

would serve best, since he would probably need his family's help. "I'm afraid we have a bit of a problem on that score."

"If there's a problem," Tira piped up, "I'd like to help. I think Miss Charlotte's a pip."

Kade smiled at his niece. "Aye, that she is."

"She'll make a fine wife for ye, lad, and that's a fact," Angus said.

"You're getting a bit ahead of yourself, Grandda."

Ainsley widened her eyes at Kade with faux innocence. "Is he?"

"Let's return to the discussion at hand," he firmly said. "Charlie's problem is more complicated than we thought, because the brooch wasn't misplaced. It was stolen by its owner."

"Ah," Ainsley replied. "I suspected as much."

Royal cast her a startled glance. "You did?"

"I knew how determined she was to put Richard off. In order to do so, she had to put her parents off, too. But I suspect she didn't think the uproar would be this bad."

Kade nodded. "I finally picked up the scent yesterday and confronted her about the matter last night."

Angus waggled his eyebrows. "Was that when ye were out in the gazebo together, bein' so kissy-face?"

When Royal choked on a sip of coffee, Ainsley thumped him on the back.

"Really, Grandda," she said. "That is quite childish of you."

"I ken what I ken."

Kade frowned at his grandfather. "I was not kissing Charlie in the gazebo. Nor did she reveal at that time that she'd stolen the brooch. I found out later, when she went to retrieve it from its hiding place in the music room."

"I'll wager she was not best pleased about that," Ainsley said with a wry smile.

"She was not."

Although she'd seemed quite pleased once he'd gotten around to kissing her.

"She'll get over it," Angus said. "So I reckon the plan is to keep hidin' the brooch until booby Richard and Sir Leslie hie themselves off, and then ye can be the hero and find the bloody thing." He beamed at Kade. "It's a fine plan, lad. Good on ye."

"I'm afraid I won't have the chance to play hero, because someone else has now stolen the blasted thing from under Charlie's nose."

Royal sighed. "And thus the real problem."

"Yes."

"Och, that's nae good," Angus said with disapproval. "And shame on ye for lettin' it slip away like that."

"Grandda, I was only guessing where it might be. I had to wait until Charlie actually told me, and by then it was gone."

"Is it possible that one of the servants could have found it?" Royal asked.

"Charlie feels that's highly unlikely."

"And if booby Campbell had it, he'd be crowing all over the place by now," Angus said.

"True," Kade said.

His grandfather pushed back his chair and stood. "Then it's a good thing ye have me to help. I'm a wonder at solvin' mysteries, as ye well ken."

"Grandda, what are you doing now?" Kade asked.

"Goin' to the music room, ye jinglebrains. That's the scene of the crime, so that's where we'll start our detectin'."

Kade couldn't hold back a deep sigh.

"Angus is right," Royal said, clearly trying not to laugh. "Best crack on."

"I searched the room last night," Kade said. He'd gone over every inch of the room after he'd sent Charlie to bed and had found nothing.

Angus waved a hand. "Ye might have missed somethin'. It being dark and all."

"I did not miss anything. And I'd like another cup of coffee first, if you don't mind."

"Fine, I'll start searchin' myself." Angus stomped out of the room.

"You'd best go after him, Kade," Ainsley said. "You know he'll just cause trouble on his own."

Tira put her napkin down and stood. "I can help, too, Uncle Kade. I'm very good at finding things."

"Tira, we're going to help Lady Kinloch get ready for the picnic, remember?" Ainsley said. "There's an awful lot to be done before we can leave."

When Tira rolled her eyes, Kade winked at her. "You can help me search later, pet. Maybe we'll do some snooping on the island while the others are having their picnic."

His niece grinned at him. "That would be so fun."

"Aye that, lassie."

He swiped a scone from the sideboard, gulping it down as he went after his grandfather.

When he caught up to Angus, he was surprised to see him standing quietly in the doorway to the music room, just listening . . . to the sound of Kade's violin, its tones unmistakable. For a moment, irritation flared. He *never* let anyone touch the rare and expensive instrument.

But irritation quickly gave way to an astonishment that nailed him to the floorboards. His Guarneri was pouring forth a haunting melody that seemed to echo his thoughts and emotions. It was Charlie, of course, playing from his unfinished concerto. Her deft touch was drawing forth the beauty and passion he'd struggled so mightily to convey. Kade could hardly believe they were the same notes he'd written and rewritten with so much frustration.

He quietly joined his grandfather in the doorway to watch. Sunlight streamed in from the terrace, bathing Charlie in golden rays. Although her gaze was fixed intently on the sheet music on top of the piano, she moved with unconscious grace, as if the music flowed naturally through her body and into the instrument. In her plain white gown, with hair pulled back in a simple braid, he supposed some men might find her merely pretty, or perhaps even somewhat dowdy. Certainly they would think her odd. But to Kade, Charlie seemed lit from within, radiant with life and music. She devastated him, and made his heart ache with a thousand untold dreams.

Angus glanced at him.

"Aye, yer fairly caught now, laddie," he murmured.

Kade was tempted to laugh. *Caught* couldn't even begin to describe it. "So it would seem."

"She's a bonny lass. Ye couldna do better."

The notes poured forth in golden tones as Charlie, swept up in the music, played on.

"It won't be easy," Kade quietly replied. "Our lives are so different."

"Anything worth havin' is nae easy. Just ask yer brothers."

"Aye, that."

To gaze at Charlie was to gaze at his future—at least he hoped so. But would the sweet lass be willing to leave the only home she'd ever known? She likely had little idea what she'd be in for with him and his life.

He kept watching her, reluctant to break the spell. Because once that happened, life would come rushing back at them. The problems would all become real.

The first of which was finding her ridiculous brooch.

Angus elbowed him. "Are ye goin' to stand there all day, just gawping at her?"

"I don't want to startle her."

"Good point. She might drop that fiddle of yers, and ye paid a small fortune for it."

At the moment, Kade would have gladly tossed his fiddle—

violin—out the window for Charlie. Still, it was a fair point. He waited till she reached the end of the movement and then cleared his throat.

Charlie froze with the bow suspended over the strings. Then she sighed and put the bow down on the piano before carefully placing the instrument back in its case.

"I'm sorry. You must be appalled," she said with a grimace. "I had no right to touch your violin. But I couldn't seem to help myself."

Kade joined her at the piano. "Not appalled but astonished, actually. That section sounds much better than I thought it would. All credit to you, of course. Your playing was exceptional."

She eyed him. "You're very kind, but it was still wrong of me. This is your work, and I had no right to snoop."

"Charlie, you can snoop whenever you want. I'm not being polite when I say you brought that particular passage to life. I was beginning to wonder if I was on the right course at all."

"You mustn't think that way," she earnestly replied. "It's spectacular, Kade. It truly is."

"Och, it was your playin', lassie," Angus said as he joined them. "I have nae doubt ye'll be givin' Kade more than a wee bit of necessary inspiration." He winked at her. "He needs it, because he's been complainin' about that stupid concerto for weeks."

"You're exaggerating, Grandda," Kade said.

He struck a dramatic pose. "Me, exaggerate? Ye must be thinkin' of someone else."

Charlie actually giggled, and it was . . . delightful. It took a tremendous amount of willpower for Kade not to sweep her up and kiss her until she melted into him. Even the presence of his annoying grandfather barely stopped him.

"I agree with you about her playing," Kade said. "It was grand."

She gave him a shy smile. "Thank you. It was your violin, really. Playing such a fine instrument was very inspiring."

"Perhaps I should leave ye two musicians alone," said Angus, suggestively waggling his eyebrows. "Ye could make beautiful music together, I have nae doubt."

Charlie immediately blushed, while Kade had to repress the impulse to scowl at his irritatingly obvious grandfather.

"I . . . I really should be going," she said. "I'm sure you need to work."

Kade held up a hand. "No, please stay. I thought to search the room again, in case we missed anything last night."

Angus nodded. "Right, lad, let's get on it. The sooner ye find that bloody brooch, the sooner ye and Miss Charlie can get back to makin' beautiful music."

"You told my grandfather about my brooch?" Charlie asked in a surprisingly squeaky voice.

Kade froze.

Dammit.

"Well, yes," he admitted. "Just now at breakfast. Ainsley and Royal were there, too. I'm sorry, Charlie. I should have asked your permission before I did so."

Clearly, he *was* an arrogant prat, too used to working alone.

She gazed at him, wide-eyed and flushed. "What, exactly, did you tell them?"

Kade frowned, slightly perplexed. "Simply that you'd hidden the brooch yourself—"

"Completely understandable," Angus broke in. "Especially with booby Campbell bein' such a pest. Well done for ye, lassie."

"But that someone had taken it from your hiding place," Kade finished.

She crossed her arms over her chest. "And that's all?"

Kade nodded.

When she breathed out a sigh of relief, he suddenly understood. It was their romantic interlude she was worried about, not that the others now knew she was the original thief. Kade didn't know whether to be amused or annoyed by that.

"Ye needn't worry that we'll grass on ye," Angus said, patting her shoulder. "We're loyal to the bone, and we'll do everything to help."

"No one will say a word, Charlie," said Kade. "But I do apologize for not consulting you first. It was your secret to tell, not mine."

She gave him a hesitant smile. "Thank you, but it's fine. And I'm certainly not one to be casting stones, since I stole the blasted thing in the first place."

"Kade will get it back," Angus assured her. "The rest of us will help as best we can."

"But you'll all be leaving in a few days, won't you?" she asked.

"I'll stay as long as you need me," Kade replied.

He hoped she would need him for a very long time.

"That's so kind of you," she said, sounding rather shy.

Angus rubbed his hands together. "Tell me where to start, lassie. We'll turn the room upside down if we have to."

"I already have," she ruefully said. "I was down here at dawn, and I've looked everywhere several times. It's just . . . gone."

She looked so woeful that Kade had to clench his hands to keep from pulling her in for a comforting hug.

"I even looked up the chimney, which perhaps was not very wise," she added with a comical grimace.

Kade bit back a smile. "Then we'll just expand our search. But we should come up with a plan first. That will partly depend on who you think might have removed the brooch from its hiding place, and why."

Angus slapped him on his good shoulder. "Good thinkin', lad. Why don't ye go for a wee stroll with Miss Charlie to the gazebo? It's nice and private there, and no one will bother ye. Ye can plan away to yer heart's content out there, if ye get my drift."

His grandfather followed up that appalling remark by giving Kade a broad wink.

Wide-eyed, Charlie started to back away towards the door. "Yes, um, I do think we need to come up with a plan. But I have to change for the picnic. And help my mother. I promised to help her, you know. I . . . I'll see you both later."

She turned and fled.

"Thank you for that mortifying scene," Kade said to his grandfather. "You've been such a help."

Angus pointed a finger at him. "It's time ye learned something, son."

"And what is that, Grandda?"

"Ye canna fight Cupid. Now, stir yer stumps. Ye have a lassie to rescue."

CHAPTER 13

Charlie studied her brother as their small sailing vessel approached Eilean Munde. He sat in the prow with Sir Leslie, chatting away. But she knew Johnny, and something was wrong. It showed in the jittery bounce of his leg and a restless gaze that darted about, refusing to settle.

Sir Leslie, however, seemed entirely at ease as he lounged on the boat cushions. His friendship with Johnny was a complete mystery to her. Not only was he at least five years older, but he was very much the jaded man about town. Johnny was anything but, only occasionally indulging in the harmless pranks typical of young men his age.

Something was very much amiss, and she was beginning to think that something involved her brooch.

Ainsley, seated next to her, tapped her arm. "Dear girl, where are you?"

Charlie forced a weak smile. "I'm sorry. I've been ignoring you, which is terribly rude."

"You do seem rather lost in thought." Her stylish friend glanced toward the front of the boat. "I take it you don't approve of Sir Leslie."

"I had no idea they were so close until Johnny insisted that he stay on with us. It's so odd, since they have nothing in common."

"Another mystery. They're rather thick on the ground, aren't they?"

Charlie crinkled her nose. "And you're supposed to be on holiday, but instead, you're all pulled into my stupid problems."

"It's hard to feel celebratory when one is anxious. But you needn't worry. Everything will sort itself out, I promise."

"But how? It seems a complete mess to me, and to be mostly my fault."

"It's a mess you can put aside for the afternoon. It's a beautiful day, and we're taking a charming boat ride to a picnic. What could be more enchanting?"

"Finding my brooch?" Charlie wryly replied.

"I have every confidence that you and Kade will find it. Dearest, you're looking a bit pulled around the edges, so a relaxing outing is just what you need."

If she indeed looked pulled around the edges, Charlie attributed it to the fact that she'd been awake most of the night, fretting about Kade.

"And it's such a perfect day," Ainsley added. "The fresh air is so lovely."

The weather was ideal for their trip to Eilean Munde, a small island off Ballachulish. Their party, which included two other families from the district, was divided between three tidy sailing vessels. The largest carried Ainsley and Charlie, plus the rest of her family and two sailors.

Kade, fortunately, was in a boat with Royal, Angus, and Tira. After that embarrassing scene in the music room this morning—hard on the heels of last night's kissing episode—Charlie wasn't ready to face him. Yet once they reached the island, she would need to ask for his help, and that would mean being alone with him. Although part of her longed for that, she had a sneaking suspicion that his wonderful kiss had been just an impulsive gesture, a way to calm her panic in the moment. The notion that Kade might pity her was too appalling to contemplate.

When she glanced over at his boat, her stomach swooped in a little dive, because he was staring straight at her. Even though his face was partly shadowed by his hat, she sensed the intensity of his gaze and his annoyance. At the dock, he'd tried to talk to her but she'd evaded him, all but dragging Ainsley into the boat and thus forcing Kade to get in another one.

"I'm sorry, what were you saying?" Charlie said after realizing that she hadn't been listening to Ainsley.

"I was just commenting on the day's excursion," Ainsley replied. "Picnics in an island graveyard don't seem to be your mother's style. Surely there are plenty of scenic spots where an outing like this would make more sense."

"She thought Angus would enjoy a visit to the MacDonald graveyard. It's very historic. Mamma is actually quite interested in our family's history, much more so than Papa."

Her father had decided to sit this excursion out, although Charlie suspected that had more to do with avoiding Angus than from lack of interest in history. In another stroke of good luck, Papa had invited Richard to go riding with him. Her erstwhile suitor had seemed torn, but an invitation to spend the day with his prospective father-in-law had obviously been too flattering to decline. Given Charlie's steadfast attempts to keep Richard at arm's length, he probably felt he'd make better progress toadying up to her father.

Ainsley smiled. "Yes, Angus will enjoy that. And Tira is quite excited at the prospect of poking around in an old graveyard. She's determined to turn up a ghost."

"On Eilean Munde, she just might."

The small, picturesque island, which held about three hundred graves, was the burial place of three clans, including the Stewarts and the MacDonalds of Glencoe. Among the number of warriors and clan chiefs who were buried on the island, some were killed in the Glencoe massacre.

"It's a bit of a challenge to see Melissa enjoying this sort of outing, though," Ainsley said.

"Perhaps, but it's really not ghoulish. Many of the graves are quite picturesque. It's even rather cozy, for lack of a better word. I expect it would be different at night, but during the day, with these views?"

She opened a hand to the rugged mountains on the north side of the loch, their granite-gray tops giving way to a tumble of fir trees and heather on the lower slopes. Sea, sky, and mountain met in a dramatic sweep of beauty both ancient and steadfast and yet ever changing with the seasons and vagaries of weather. Charlie had spent her entire life tucked away in this corner of the Highlands, and yet she never grew bored with it. The place was too grand and elemental for her to ever feel mundane.

Ainsley looked thoughtful. "You love it here."

"It was a wonderful place to grow up. I can't imagine anything in a city topping this."

"You also had more freedom here than a girl—much less a young woman—would have in the city, or even a less remote locale."

Charlie couldn't help but smile. "I'm sure the freedom is one of the reasons I love it."

"Would you ever consider living anywhere else?"

She hesitated, sensing more behind the question than mere curiosity. "I'm not really sure why I would."

Ainsley arched a sardonic brow. "I can think of one reason."

And his name is Kade Kendrick.

Fortunately, circumstances came to her rescue.

"Look—we're just about to beach," she said. "You'd best hang on."

Her friend looked vaguely alarmed. "You mean we're going to sail right up onto the island?"

"How else did you think we'd get to shore?"

"I assumed there was a dock on which we could disembark, like civilized people."

Charlie lifted the hem of her skirts to show off her riding boots. "Why do you think I wore these?"

"Oh, Lord," Ainsley said with a sigh. "I'm going to get soaked, aren't I? How utterly dreadful the Highlands can be."

Charlie laughed. "Not to worry, lassie. Ye'll nae get a drop on those pretty feet of yers."

A few moments later, the sailors ran the boat through the shallows and up onto the beach. They came to rest with a bit of a jerk on the pebbled shoreline.

"See?" Charlie said. "Easy as pie."

After they made their way to the front of the boat, Johnny helped Ainsley onto the beach, while Sir Leslie bowed and extended a hand to Charlie.

"Miss Charlotte, may I be of assistance?" he said with a smile that held a bit of a leer.

"No need to fuss," Johnny said over his shoulder. "Charlie can manage."

Sir Leslie darted him an irritated look. "A gentleman always offers to help whenever he can." Then he reached for Charlie again. "My dear?"

Charlie saw Kade stalking over from the other boat, which had landed right next to theirs. He brushed past Sir Leslie and extended his hand to her.

"Allow me, Miss Charlotte," he said in a voice that brooked no opposition.

When Sir Leslie glared at him, Kade narrowed his gaze into a lethal stare, as if daring the other man to challenge him. Charlie mentally rolled her eyes but took Kade's hand nonetheless.

"Thank you, sir. God knows I would hate to get even a drop of water on my boots."

Kade took in her sturdy riding boots and then winked at her.

Charlie bit back a smile. He knew perfectly well she didn't need help, but it was also clear he was determined to cut Sir Leslie out. That was both amusing . . . and flattering.

It was also effective, since the baronet promptly stalked off to join Ainsley and Johnny.

"I don't know what I would have done without you to rescue me," Charlie wryly said.

"I imagine you would have continued in your efforts to avoid me," Kade replied.

She widened her eyes. "Goodness, is that what I've been doing?"

He snorted. "Vixen."

No one had ever called her a vixen before. She quite liked it.

But now she needed to screw her courage to the sticking point, because she needed his help. There was a mystery to be solved, and he was clearly the man for the job.

"Actually," she said, "I have been meaning to talk to you."

Kade raised a politely incredulous eyebrow.

Charlie flapped a hand. "Yes, yes, you've made your point. I'm sorry I've been such a ninny about . . . about everything."

A slow smile curled up his mouth. It made her brain go fuzzy around the edges, because that smile was positively *killing*. At least it certainly killed her ability to think clearly.

"Sweetheart, you could never be a ninny," he said. "Elusive, yes, and I admit to finding that a bit frustrating under the circumstances."

She crinkled her nose. "Sorry. It's just a lot to take in."

"I know," he gently replied. "And I will never push you."

Really, he was the *nicest* man in the world. He was also the most fascinating one she'd ever met, so it was no wonder she'd fallen in love with him.

For a moment, her mind went totally blank. Then it seemed to sputter back to life, bringing with it what felt like an entirely new way of looking at the world. Of course, she'd always had feelings for Kade, and had harbored dreams she had known would never come to fruition. But love him? That had always seemed nothing but a silly hope to cherish in her heart.

Kade's piercing blue gaze tracked over her. "Is something wrong?"

"Not at all," she managed.

"You'd tell me if there was, I hope."

"You mean something wrong besides my missing brooch?"

He smiled. "Yes."

"Ho, laddie," called Angus from farther up the beach. "Why are ye keepin' Miss Charlie standin' about in the muck? The others are waitin' on us."

"Coming, Grandda." Kade took her elbow and guided her along the narrow beach.

"I do need to talk to you soon," she said in a low voice. "I need your help today."

"I'm at your disposal. But what sort of help do you need on a picnic?"

"I'll explain later. After we eat."

"Another mystery?"

"No, it's still my blasted brooch. I just have a few ideas about where we might find it."

He shot her a surprised glance. "You mean on the island? Why the devil would it be over here?"

She shushed him, seeing her mother and Angus waiting just ahead on the path to the top of the embankment that overlooked the landing site.

"Charlotte, why are you dawdling with Mr. Kendrick?" Mamma asked, obviously suspicious. "Everyone is waiting."

Angus patted her arm. "Och, there's nae need to fret, Elspeth. They're just chattin', as young people are wont to do."

"They should not be wandering off alone, Angus. People will talk."

Charlie sighed. Clearly, her mother still had her sights set on Richard as her daughter's prospective husband, and no other candidate would do.

"Mamma, even if I wanted to be private with Mr. Kendrick—and I'm not saying I do," she hastily added when her mother looked offended, "you know it would be all but impossible on Eilean Munde, where you can walk from one end to the other in twenty minutes."

"I should certainly hope you do not wish to be private with Mr. Kendrick," her mother huffily replied.

"You're the one suggesting it, Mamma, not me."

"Liar," Kade murmured under his breath.

She resisted the impulse to elbow him. "Mr. Kendrick was simply helping me get out of the boat, not taking liberties."

"Yer daughter could sneak off with Kade as much as she liked, and he'd nae be takin' any liberties." Angus wagged a finger at Charlie's mother. "That booby Campbell's the one ye have to watch out for. Ye canna trust a Campbell as far as ye can throw him."

"This is a ridiculous conversation," Mamma declared. "Now, come along. The footmen went ahead and have already set up the picnic. So tell your brother and Sir Leslie to stop dawdling as well."

Charlie mentally rolled her eyes. "Yes, Mamma."

As her mother and Angus proceeded up the trail, Kade leaned down, close to her ear.

"I promise I won't take any liberties," he murmured. "Unless of course you want me to."

She ignored the little thrill that shivered up her spine and gave him a little shove. "Do stop being an idiot. You're as bad as booby Campbell."

"No one's as bad as booby Campbell." He offered his arm. "Shall we?"

She glanced over her shoulder. Johnny and Sir Leslie were still on the beach, although they'd moved away from the boats. They appeared deep in discussion, and not a happy one.

"Huh," she said.

"Problem?" Kade asked.

"I don't know."

He glanced down the beach. "Your brother and Sir Leslie appear to be having an argument."

"You go on ahead. I'll fetch Johnny."

"I can go," he offered. "I'm happy to play errand boy."

"No, it's fine." She flapped her hands, shooing him. "Now, please go. I'll take care of it."

Kade narrowed his gaze. "Charlie—"

"Go—I'll be right there."

Ignoring his irritated expression, she turned and hurried down the beach. It was something of a revelation that Kade Kendrick could be the bossy, overprotective sort.

She nodded to the boatmen as she passed. They politely tipped their caps, although their attention was on the little scene between Johnny and Sir Leslie. Her brother and Sir Leslie were clearly engaged in some sort of dispute, and Johnny was doing most of the talking, in an agitated manner.

"Ho, Johnny," she called while still several yards away. "You mustn't linger. Everyone's waiting for us."

When Sir Leslie glanced over, she got a bit of a shock. The man had always struck her as a cad, but a rather genial one for all that. Right now, he seemed anything but genial. His mouth was flat and unforgiving, and anger crackled in his hard gaze.

Then he blinked and his nasty expression vanished, replaced with a smile. Charlie could almost doubt what she'd seen. And perhaps she would have, if not for the look on her brother's face. Johnny was pale and clearly rattled. When their gazes met, he turned away from her.

"What's going on here?" she asked.

"Why, nothing, Miss Charlotte," Sir Leslie replied in a friendly tone. "How kind of you to come fetch us."

She propped her hands on her hips. "Really? Because it didn't seem like nothing."

"It was nothing, Charlie," Johnny said. "We were just talking."

She knew her brother's every intonation, his every expression. Right now, she'd bet ten bob that he was anxious, even scared.

Sir Leslie wagged a finger at her. "You're too perceptive by half, my dear. Johnny and I *were* having a little dispute, but I promise it was not serious. The dear fellow wishes to depart for Edinburgh tomorrow, but I was explaining to him that your father asked us to stay for several more days, and I feel it would be rude to ignore Lord Kinloch's kind invitation."

"Is that true?" Charlie asked her brother. "You wish to leave tomorrow?"

"The blasted wedding is over," he replied in a surly tone. "No point in hanging about, which I was trying to explain to Sir Leslie. Unfortunately, he seems to think several more days in Ballachulish would be just the thing, instead of the complete bore that it actually is."

"Come now," responded Sir Leslie in an indulgent tone. "It's the perfect retreat from the heat and the dust of the city, especially at this time of year."

Johnny scoffed. "If you say so."

Charlie gave him an encouraging smile. "You've hardly been home these last several months. Don't you want to spend more time with us?"

He shrugged a shoulder. "I suppose."

"And you must admit it's the perfect place to rusticate." Sir Leslie winked at Charlie. "Sometimes us fellows need a bit of rustication, you know."

Rustication often meant a forced retreat from society.

Charlie tilted her head. "And why would you need to rusticate, Sir Leslie? Or why would Johnny, for that matter?"

He put up his hands. "Just a figure of speech, dear lady. And you're perfectly right. We mustn't keep the others waiting. Come along, Johnny."

When he turned and headed along the beach and Johnny started to trudge after him, Charlie caught her brother's arm.

"You go ahead, Sir Leslie," she said. "I'll walk back with Johnny."

"As you wish, my dears." He waved a cheery hand.

They followed in Sir Leslie's wake, but at a much slower pace. Johnny all but vibrated with impatience, but he matched his steps to hers.

"You don't have to worry," he said. "Leslie has convinced me to stay."

She pressed his arm. "I'm glad, but I'm not sure why you wanted to run away. I've missed you, Johnny. I feel like we hardly talk anymore."

"Ha. You're the one whose always busy, what with one fellow or another. If it's not that idiot Richard Campbell, it's Kade Kendrick you're mooning after."

She repressed a flare of irritation. Johnny was upset, or else he wouldn't be so snappish with her.

"I'm not mooning after Mr. Kendrick, but he is a friend. It's not so unusual that I would spend time with him, is it?"

"I suppose not. But please tell me that you won't accept Campbell's offer. He's only after your money and the influence it could buy him for his stupid political ambitions."

"Thank you for that flattering assessment," she wryly said as they started up the path to the graveyard.

He grimaced. "I didn't mean it like that, Charlie."

"I know, and you are quite right. Fortunately, I have no intention of marrying the blighter."

"Thank God." He cast her a sideways glance. "But what about Kendrick? You do like him, don't you? Quite a lot, I'll wager."

Charlie ignored the little flutter of her heart. "I do, but it doesn't mean anything, dear. He's just a friend."

And she needed to keep telling herself that, no matter how bossy and overprotective Kade might be.

"I'm sorry, Sis. You deserve someone as grand as you are. I hope you find him someday."

"I'll bump along just fine. But I'm worried about you, Johnny. Something's wrong, and I wish you'd tell me what it is."

She felt him jerk under her hand.

"Why do you keep saying that?"

"Because I know you," she quietly replied. "I can always tell when something is wrong. It's why you want to leave, isn't it?"

"I want to leave because Father is being his usual awful self to me," he said, going back to surly. "I can't say two words without him biting my head off."

"I know, dearest, and I'm sorry about that. Papa is worried about you, as am I. That's why he's short with you sometimes."

"Well, I'm fine, I assure you."

They'd climbed up the path and could now hear the voices of the others up ahead. Charlie held her brother back.

"What now?" he said with an aggrieved sigh.

She searched his face. "Cut line, Johnny. I know it's something bad. Is it money?"

He pressed his lips tight and looked past her for several painfully long seconds. She forced herself to wait it out.

"It's nothing I can't handle," he finally said.

"Johnny—"

"No." He chopped down a hand. "I'm telling you, Charlie, leave it alone."

As he started to turn away, she grabbed his arm and pulled him back. For a moment, he refused to meet her gaze. When he finally looked at her, defiance shimmered in the brown eyes so like her own.

"Johnny, did you steal my brooch?"

His eyes went wide with shock. Unfortunately, she couldn't

tell if it was because she'd guessed the truth or because he was simply startled by the question.

"Of course I didn't," he blustered. "Why would you even ask me that?"

"I'm asking because I need the truth."

He angrily jerked his arm from her grasp. "You're daft, Charlie. Someone might have stolen your stupid brooch, but it wasn't me."

They were interrupted by footsteps, and in a moment Sir Leslie appeared at the head of the path.

"Lady Kinloch is asking after the both of you," he said. "Everyone's waiting."

"Coming," Johnny replied.

He quickly started back up the path. Charlie followed, her mind spinning with more questions than answers. The secrets were piling up. In Johnny's case, she feared they obscured something that put him at risk.

In the muddle of her brain, only one thing stood out in sharp relief. She needed help, and right now there was really only one person she fully trusted to hold all her secrets and to help her.

CHAPTER 14

Kade sat with his back against a nearby tree, finishing his ale as he watched Charlie, who, like the rest of the ladies, was seated on a tartan blanket. She was sipping sherry from one of the absurdly dainty crystal glasses that had been stowed in the wicker baskets the footmen had lugged onto the island. Luncheon was over, and most of the men now stood about the small clearing, smoking pipes or cigars.

The picnic so far had been a rousing success. The weather was sunny and the breeze gentle. Food was plentiful and so were sherry and lemonade for the ladies and port and ale for the men. The guests had engaged in easy chatter, and Morgan had told amusing stories about Edinburgh's social scene. Even Melissa seemed to be enjoying herself, talking vivaciously with Ainsley and bestowing sweet smiles on her clearly relieved husband.

Everyone was having a grand time except Charlie and Johnny. She'd barely uttered a word, her attention focused on her brother. Johnny, who'd retreated to the other side of the clearing, looked so morose that his mother had asked him if he was bilious. That had simply made him scowl more.

Secrets were rather thick on the ground at the moment, and so were the emotional crosscurrents that Kade was doing his best to parse. Morgan somehow played a part. His little scene on the beach with Johnny had made that obvious, as had Charlie's stone-faced responses to the bounder whenever he'd tried to engage her in conversation.

Whatever the problem was, Kade intended to get to the bottom of it as soon as he could get Charlie alone. That might prove a challenge, though, since Eilean Munde was a very small island. Still, there seemed to be enough secluded spots around the graveyard where they might be able to have a private conversation.

And perhaps steal a kiss or three?

Just then, Charlie looked up and gazed straight at him. Then she blinked, and a blush colored her cheeks. Apparently, she'd been able to read his mind with very little trouble.

"Charlotte, you're quite red in the face," Lady Kinloch said with a frown. "I do hope you're not getting overheated."

Charlie winced. "Of course not. You know the weather never bothers me."

"You should not have taken off your bonnet. You will quite ruin your complexion, if you haven't done so already."

"Nonsense, Lady Kinloch," Morgan chimed in. "Your daughter's complexion is ravishing, quite like a bowl of cherries and cream. With such beauty, one hardly cares about finding Miss Charlotte's brooch, because she is certainly prize enough."

"Very kind," her ladyship replied in blighting tones. "But Charlotte should still put on her bonnet."

With a sigh, Charlie retrieved her wide-brimmed hat and jammed it back on her head.

"After such a such a large repast, I'm in need of a stroll," Ainsley said cheerily. "Lady Kinloch, would you care to join me? I'm simply dying to see the rest of the island."

"No pun intended," Royal wryly commented.

"I want to see the gravestones," Tira said. "Grandda says Alastair MacIain is buried here. He was the twelfth chief of

Glencoe, but he got slaughtered by those nasty poltroons from Clan Campbell."

Angus, sitting next to Tira, heaved a sigh. "Aye, lassie. Slaughtered like a hog, he was. Practically cleaved in half with a dirk."

"Goodness," squeaked Melissa.

Lady Kinloch frowned. "Really, Angus, there's no need to be so graphic."

"We canna forget our sacred history, Elspeth."

"No chance of that with you around, old boy," Morgan said with a smirk.

Angus narrowed his gaze on him but declined to answer.

Kade pushed himself up and went to his grandfather. "Come on, Grandda, I'll help you up. Then you and Tira can go grave hunting."

"Thanks, lad."

"Would you also like me to push Morgan off a cliff?" Kade murmured as he helped his grandfather rise.

Angus snorted. "Dandy prat, that one."

"I don't like that man," Tira said in a whisper loud enough to be heard halfway across the clearing. "He's a twiddlepoop."

Since his niece was generally soft-spoken, Kade was fairly certain her comment was purposeful.

Morgan ignored the gibe and gave Charlie a flourishing bow. "Dear Miss Charlotte, allow me to help you."

Charlie all but hopped to her feet. "That's not necessary, but perhaps you could help my mother."

Morgan looked momentarily irritated but then turned to Lady Kinloch. "Allow me, dear ma'am."

"Thank you," she coolly replied.

Obviously, Lady Kinloch didn't think much of Morgan, either.

"If you follow me, everyone," she said to the group. "The MacDonald section of the graveyard is this way."

Most of the others trailed after her, although a few of the local guests went off toward the beach. Johnny started after his mother but stopped when Morgan took his arm. They held a low-voiced conversation before heading toward the opposite side of the clearing.

Charlie, who'd wandered over to Kade, muttered something under her breath.

"What's that?" Kade asked.

She ignored him. "Where are you off to, Johnny?"

"Can't a fellow go for a smoke with his friend?" her brother replied, clearly irritated.

"I promise to bring him back safe and sound, Miss Charlotte," Morgan said with a wink. "Not to worry."

"Do come along, Leslie," Johnny snapped.

He stalked out of the clearing, while Morgan strolled behind.

"That man is truly beginning to annoy me," Charlie said.

"He's a dandy prat, according to my grandfather."

"He's worse than that."

Kade raised an eyebrow. "Care to elucidate?"

"Perhaps later."

She took his arm and started to propel him toward another path that led from the clearing to the center of the island.

"I do love a masterful lass," Kade said, "but I'm quite willing to go anywhere with you, Charlie. No need to drag me."

She grimaced and let go of his arm. "Sorry. Sometimes I forget myself."

"You can forget yourself with me any time you like, sweetheart."

When she stopped dead in her tracks, he almost ran over her.

"Mr. Kendrick, I really wish you'd stop flirting with me. It's . . . it's frustrating."

"It's Kade, and I am not flirting with you."

She propped her hands on her hips. "Then what are you doing?"

He studied her, trying not to smile. "Telling you how I feel?"

Charlie looked blank for a second before her eyes popped wide. "Do you actually mean—"

She pointed to herself, and then to him.

"You and me?" Kade said. "Yes."

"Huh," she said, looking flummoxed.

"Is that so hard to believe?"

"Well . . . yes, actually."

Amusement gave way to a tenderness he'd never felt until he met this woman. "Then perhaps you'll let me show you."

For a moment, her chestnut brown eyes grew soft as velvet, and one hand fluttered up to rest on his shoulder. Kade was just dipping his head when she suddenly gave him a little shove.

"You *cannot* kiss me here," she hissed. "The servants are right behind us."

Kade glanced over his shoulder at the footmen, who were busy packing up the picnic baskets. "I'm sure they won't mind."

"I'll mind, and so will Mamma when she hears about it." She grabbed his arm again. "Stop acting like a jinglebrains and come along."

"Jinglebrains, eh? You've clearly been talking to my grandfather."

He let her tow him down the little path. She was right, of course. He shouldn't be kissing her in front of the servants, or anywhere else on this bloody island. The place was so small you could shout from one end to the other and be heard. Each of the clan graveyards had its own plot of land, but it wouldn't take much wandering about to bump into someone.

"Would it be impolite for me to ask why you're dragging me off?"

"Certainly not to have my way with you."

When Kade burst into laughter—because, really, he couldn't help it—she scowled at him.

"It's not that funny," she grumbled.

"No, of course not."

She stopped and sighed. "I'm sorry for acting like such a twit. It's just that you've thrown me off my game."

"Lass, you are the furthest thing from a twit I could ever imagine. And I'm sorry for throwing you off your game."

"No, you're not."

"Touché," he admitted. "But since I am also off my game, perhaps it's best to defer this discussion to a time when we're not at risk of one of our blasted relatives stumbling upon us."

"What a gruesome thought. My mother would likely toss me into the loch," she replied as she started them along the path again. "She has her heart set on Richard."

"Then she's going to be disappointed."

"Are you going to challenge Richard to a duel for my hand, mayhap?"

"No, I'll get Angus to do it."

That surprised a laugh out of her. "You're being ridiculous now."

"I'm trying," he said. "Now, perhaps you can enlighten me as to the nature of our expedition."

"I'm taking you to the chapel. It's just up ahead."

"There wouldn't happen to be a parson about, would there? That would be convenient."

Charlie rounded on him and pointed a finger at his nose. "Kade Kendrick, you will cease being nonsensical this instant. This is serious business, ye ken. *Very* serious."

He tried to look contrite. "Sorry, love. I promise to behave from now on."

She blushed at his endearment. "You will absolutely *not* behave, from what I can see. And to think everyone calls you the good Kendrick."

He waggled his eyebrows. "Give me a chance, and I'll show you just how good I can be."

"Lord, you're worse than your grandfather."

"But surely that would defy all the laws of nature."

She rolled her eyes. "Hopeless."

"Aye, that."

Kade couldn't remember the last time he'd had so much fun. In fact, he felt bloody euphoric. And it was all down to the adorable lass looking askance at him.

"You do realize," she said, "that if *we* don't find that blasted brooch before someone else does, I could end up riveted to the wrong man."

"Well, then, we'd best find it first."

She led the way past a small clearing overgrown with larkspur, heather, and wild grasses. A dozen old gravestones and a few Celtic crosses languished in the grass, some leaning sideways and covered with lichen. It was a picturesque, peaceful scene.

"This is one of the older sections," Charlie said. "Stewarts, for the most part. The MacDonalds are on the other side of the island."

"So, we're looking at your father's noble ancestors."

"He's not very sentimental about them, so he rarely visits. He told Mamma that if she buried him out on this dreary island, he'd come back and haunt her."

"I can't say as I would relish the thought of eternity spent out here, either."

"Goodness, your grandfather would be horrified by such an attitude."

"Too true. Angus believes I've forgotten how to be a Highlander. 'Citified' is the term he recently used to describe me."

She glanced up at him. "And have you forgotten?"

"No. I love the Highlands and I greatly respect family and clan traditions. But that doesn't mean I can't also appreciate other ways of life or seek to expand my horizons. I don't have to give up one to have the other."

"Don't you find it difficult, sometimes?"

"On occasion, yes. But with a little effort, it works, if one desires it hard enough."

"Huh," she said again, more to herself than to him.

Kade held his peace. He was certain now that she'd developed strong feelings for him. Yet did she love him enough to leave her beloved Highlands and her life here behind?

Charlie brushed away a tangle of ferns. "Here we are."

He eyed what initially appeared to be nothing more than a tangle of vines and creepers growing out of a tumbledown wall. Then, on closer inspection, he managed to make out the shape of a small building with a stone archway. Most of the chapel's roof had caved in, with vines and a large, flowering shrub overtopping it.

"How long has it been in disrepair?" he asked.

"Well over a hundred years. Johnny and I used to play here when we were children, when the family came to visit the graveyard or have a picnic. When we were older, we'd sail over because it was the perfect place to sneak away from our parents. Sometimes we would hide things out here, too. Notes to each other, special trinkets . . . that sort of thing."

"Ah, so you think someone might have stashed the brooch here. Your brother, I presume."

Charlie gave him a grimace by way of answer.

Kade frowned. "Why would your brother steal the brooch when he knows how upsetting it would be for you and your family?"

She opened her hands in a helpless gesture. "To pawn it, perhaps? He's fallen in with a fast crowd—people like Sir Leslie. Johnny obviously owes him or someone else money, although he wouldn't tell me how much."

"Do you really think he would steal a priceless family

heirloom to pay off his debts?" Kade shook his head. "I imagine it wouldn't be easy to pawn, either."

"He doesn't always exercise the best judgment, I'm afraid."

"I take it you asked him about the brooch when you were on the beach."

She wrinkled her nose. "He got quite angry with me for even suggesting he took it."

"Do you believe him?"

"I don't know, which is rather awful of me."

Kade gently cupped her cheek. "There's nothing awful about you, Charlotte Stewart. In fact, you are exactly the opposite of that."

Her gaze filled with something akin to wonder at his mild compliment. Did no one in her family or amongst her friends really appreciate this wonderful girl? Her display of emotion made him long to pull her into his arms and shelter her for the rest of their days.

"Thank you," she whispered.

"You're welcome," he whispered back.

A few moments later, she gave him a rueful smile. "Well, we can't stand about mooning at each other like a pair of ninnies. We have to conduct a search before the others start wondering where we are."

"Good point. Why don't you let me go first and try to clear a path? It's quite a tangle."

He pushed his way through the heavy undergrowth and finally broke through to a small patch of dirt in front of the chapel door.

Charlie followed him through and crouched down to peer inside the chapel. "Doesn't look like anyone's been here recently. Not that you can really tell."

When she straightened up, she caught the brim of her hat on an overhanging vine, knocking it half off.

"Allow me," Kade said, reaching to straighten it.

She shook her head, then took off the hat and carefully placed it on a pile of broken slate. "It will only get covered with cobwebs and dead leaves once we're inside."

"Better than your hair getting dirty."

"Actually, no. If my hat gets dirty, Mamma will become suspicious. If my hair gets dirty, I can simply put my hat back on and no one's the wiser."

"Very logical of you."

"You have to work to keep ahead of my mother." She waved him in. "After you, sir."

Kade ducked under the low arch, Charlie following closely behind.

They found themselves standing in a patch of dappled sunlight. The chapel had obviously lost its roof long ago, but it was shaded by an enormous bush covered in white blooms. The stone floor was strewn with dry leaves and dirt, and vines draped down the walls like rustic curtains. There were a few slate gravestones embedded in the stones, and the remains of a Celtic cross stood in one corner, half-covered by a patch of ferns.

"It's a shame it's fallen into such disrepair," Kade said. "Some of the engravings seem quite good."

Charlie pointed to the wall on his right. "Take a look at that one."

He crouched down to get a better view. "Good God. He's putting an ax through that poor fellow's head."

She bent down and traced a fingertip along the outline of a figure wielding a massive sword. "That's the gravestone for Big Duncan MacKenzie, a famous Jacobite warrior. He's slicing open the head of a British dragoon."

"Angus would love this. Depictions of bloodthirsty battles on one's gravestone—what could be better?"

"It's one way to be remembered."

She ran her fingers around the edges of the thick slate. "We used to hide trinkets behind Duncan's gravestone." She glanced at him. "Why don't you start on the other side of the chapel, and we can meet in the middle. Be sure to move the pieces of broken slate and look behind the cross. We used to hide things there, too."

"Aye, that."

He began to search, moving up and down the walls and examining any suitable hiding place. Once, he had to jerk back a hand when he dislodged a nest of spiders.

"Sorry," Charlie said with a grimace. "I forgot about the cellar spiders. They don't usually bite, but they are rather gruesome looking."

"No worse than a nest of spies, I suppose."

She straightened up, looking interested. "Did you ever discover a nest of spies?"

"Legions of them, actually."

She rolled her eyes and went back to the search.

A few minutes later, they were done.

"Drat," Charlie said as she slapped her hands together to dust off her gloves. "I was so hoping we'd find it here."

"Is there anywhere else on the island that Johnny might have hidden it?"

"Possibly at the base of one of the gravestones."

"Charlie, there seem to be quite a few gravestones on this island," Kade said.

"Over three hundred."

"Well, that's a pity."

"I'm afraid it's a goose chase," she said, sounding morose. "And it's not very likely, in all honesty. But I had to be certain."

He smiled at her. "No worries, lass. At least we've eliminated one hiding place."

"Yes, but I'm not really sure what to do next."

"I'd say keep searching Laroch Manor, as well as keep an eye on Johnny. If he did take it, he'll probably check on it at some point."

"All right. Though I'm not sure how we can keep a constant

eye on him without rousing his suspicion—especially since I already barged right up and asked him."

"Royal and Angus will help. Johnny won't suspect them— or me, for that matter."

She reached up to rub her nose and then thought better of it, since her gloves were still rather dirty. Instead, she gave an endearing little sniff. "You're all so kind. I truly don't know how to thank you."

"I can think of one way."

He carefully tipped up her chin with a knuckle that wasn't dirty and lowered his mouth to hers. Charlie's hands stole around his waist as she let out a happy sigh, sinking into his embrace. Kade held her lightly, relishing the softness of her luscious mouth.

The first time he'd kissed her, he'd been all too aware of how vulnerable she was and of the risks they were taking. So he'd forced himself to hold back. Now, though, all doubts were resolved and he knew what he wanted.

He wanted Charlie, for the rest of their lives.

For long, delicious moments, their mouths played with each other. Kade had never felt so much for a woman. It was a passion that set his heart throbbing with longing and his body vibrating with need. In this tumbledown old chapel, dappled with sunlight and shadow, he felt something shift, something deep and elemental. He'd finally found his forever lass, the one he would never let go.

When he teased along the seam of her lips, she responded with an eagerness that almost took him out at the knees. He slipped inside, savoring a hint of sherry, along with a warmth and sweetness that was all Charlie.

She hummed deep in her throat and gripped the fabric of his coat. When she drew back a few seconds later, Kade almost groaned. But then she traced the shape of his mouth with the delicate tip of her tongue, sending fire through his veins. Instinctively, he responded by capturing her lips, pouring all his need into the kiss. Charlie wriggled closer, her slim body pressing against him, driving every rational thought from his brain. There was only his beautiful lass— and a desire that would take a lifetime of passion to satisfy.

For a lunatic moment, Kade thought about pulling her down onto the soft, moss-covered ground and having his way with her.

Idiot.

He clamped down on his rampant desire, easing back to nuzzle her lips with a gentle caress. This was neither the time nor the place for lovemaking. And he'd be damned if he rushed things, both for her sake and for his. But, oh, she tempted him, and—

When a faint sound penetrated his consciousness, Kade forced himself to retreat. Charlie's eyes fluttered open, and she smiled dreamily up at him, her lips plump and rosy from his kiss.

"Why did you stop?" she murmured.

"I didn't want to, but I think I heard voices."

Charlie's eyes snapped wide open. "Mamma! We've got to hurry."

She brushed passed him and ducked under the archway. Kade followed.

"Oh, Lord," she said, glancing down at herself. "We both look a mess."

He studied her. "Mostly just the hem of your skirt, but your hair is looking a bit dusty. Best you get your hat on."

She'd bent over to retrieve her hat from the stack of slate when Kade noticed a massive, disgusting spider crawling up the back of her skirt, heading for her waist.

"Hold still," he said firmly.

She craned around to look at him. "Why?"

"Spider on your back."

Carefully, he started to brush it off, scooping it off the swell of her backside and then whacking it into the dirt.

"Mr. Kendrick!" yelped an all-too-familiar voice. "What are you doing?"

Kade spun on his heel. Glaring at him from the other side of the clearing were Lady Kinloch and Angus.

"My lady," he said. "I didn't see you there."

"Obviously," she replied in a horrified voice. "Mr. Kendrick, why was your hand on my daughter's . . . er, form?"

Charlie rammed her hat sideways onto her head and took a hasty step forward. "It's fine, Mamma. He was only—"

"Why are you so disheveled, Charlotte?" her mother interrupted. "And *why* were you bent over in so . . . so unseemly a fashion?"

"Aye, that's what I'd like to ken, too," Angus barked. "Yer lookin' mighty guilty there, laddie boy. With ye and Miss Charlie sneakin' off, I hope there's nae been any canoodlin' amongst the gravestones."

"What?" Lady Kinloch all but shrieked.

"Not now, Angus," Kade warned, glaring at his grandfather.

"Oh, God," Charlie muttered.

"Charlotte Stewart, you will come over here right now and explain yourself," her mother ordered. "I am *utterly* mortified by your behavior."

"Mamma, it's not what—"

"And I'll be havin' a word with ye, Kade," Angus said with heavy disapproval. "This is not the proper way to be wooin' the lassie."

Lady Kinloch rounded on Angus. "No one will be wooing anyone without my permission. Besides, Charlotte is all but promised to Richard."

Now, *that* was irritating.

"I would like to point out—" Kade started.

Charlotte elbowed him, hard.

"Ouch," he muttered.

"Don't argue with her," she hissed.

"I'm simply trying to explain to your mother—"

A terrified scream from beyond the trees cut him off. They all froze, staring at each other.

Charlie recovered first. "That sounded like Johnny."

"Came from the south side of the island," Kade said.

Lady Kinloch gasped. "That's where the high banks are. They're very unstable."

She spun, picked up her skirts, and rushed back up the path.

"Wait, Mamma," Charlie called.

She ran after her mother, scrambling through the undergrowth. Kade followed, pausing only for a moment beside Angus.

"Don't run, Grandda," he said. "We don't need you falling, too."

Angus waved at him. "I'm fine. Get ye goin' and help them."

Kade took off, jogging after Charlie. He broke through the trees and saw the embankment up ahead, topped with a few scrubby pines. Ainsley and a few of the other guests were standing on it, peering over the edge.

He strode over to his sister-in-law. "Was that Johnny screaming?"

Ainsley pointed straight down. "Yes, he apparently took a tumble and hurt himself."

Kade looked over the edge of the embankment. It was a straight drop down of at least twenty feet, onto a rocky beach. Johnny, supported by Royal and a footman, was struggling to sit up just as Charlie and Lady Kinloch scrambled down a steep path to the beach. Tira was there, along with Morgan, Colin, and a very upset Melissa.

From the grimace on Johnny's face and the way he was cradling his right arm, it was clear he was injured.

"How the devil did he manage to fall?" Kade asked his sister-in-law.

"It looks like the edge of the embankment might have

given away. Don't get too close, Kade," Ainsley warned. "It might crumble right out from beneath you."

One of Kinloch's neighbors joined them. "It's been known to happen, especially after a good rainstorm."

"Yet there has been little rain for the past few weeks," Kade replied.

The young man shrugged.

Crouching down, Kade ran his hand along the edge of the small cliff. It seemed fine to him, dry and quite firm. He stood and paced several feet in both directions, looking for the likely spot of Johnny's fall. But the embankment appeared undisturbed, with a solid cover of grass and heather right up to the edge.

Angus came puffing up beside him and glanced down. "Och, the poor laddie took a tumble."

"Kade," Royal called from down below. "Can you come down and lend a hand?"

"On it." Kade glanced at Ainsley. "Where's the path to the beach?"

She pointed to the left. "It's behind those bushes. Be careful, though. We don't need you tumbling down."

"Not to worry. I have no intention of taking a tumble," he said as he headed for the path.

"Neither did Johnny," she called after him.

Kade suspected that Ainsley was more right than she knew.

It had taken a bit of maneuvering, but they finally got Johnny safely loaded into the biggest of the boats. Although it looked like the poor lad had broken his collarbone, matters could have been much worse. Kade thought it something of a miracle that Johnny hadn't cracked his skull on the rocky beach.

After helping one of the sailors shove the boat into the

water, Kade hopped in and then clambered to the front to check on Johnny, who was lying on a stack of boat cushions that Charlie had gathered into a pile. Lady Kinloch sat beside her son, dabbing his brow with a cloth while speaking to him in a soothing tone. The lad would be fine with rest and a bit of time. Still, Kade knew that sort of injury hurt like the devil.

Lady Kinloch glanced up at him, looking harried. "Oh, Mr. Kendrick, I'm so sorry you had to splash about in the water with the sailors. What a dreadful way to treat our guests."

Apparently, his little contretemps with Charlie back at the chapel had been forgotten, at least for the moment. Between Johnny's fall and Melissa's descent into a fit of the vapors, the poor woman's hands had been full.

"I was happy to help, my lady." Kade smiled down at Johnny. "How are you feeling, old son?"

Johnny, although pale and sweating, managed a smile. "I'll be fine. Thanks for your help, by the way. Sorry to be such an awful pain."

Kade braced himself against the side of the boat as it heeled around and headed toward Ballachulish. "No worries, lad. We'll get you back home in no time. There's a good, stiff breeze behind us now."

Charlie smoothed a lock of damp hair off her brother's forehead. "Johnny, how did you fall? The embankments are quite firm and dry at this time of year."

He started to shrug but then grimaced. "I . . . I don't know. It all happened so fast. I suppose I just slipped."

Charlie frowned. "You were walking along and then just slipped?"

"What difference does it make?" he snapped. "I slipped and fell like a damn fool. There's nothing more to it."

"Charlotte, there's no need to pester your poor brother," Lady Kinloch said. "I do believe there's a bottle of port in one of the picnic baskets. Please fetch Johnny a glass. It will help with the pain."

Charlie blew out a sigh. "All right."

Kade helped her up and moved with her toward the back of the boat.

"It makes no sense," she said in a low voice. "Johnny and I know where all the dodgy bits are on that island. It's hard to believe he'd fall like that, especially in such dry weather."

"Yes, I checked the edge of the cliff myself and there was no evidence of the edge crumbling. The grass was trampled down a bit, but that's all."

"You're sure?"

He nodded.

"Charlotte," her mother called. "Stop dawdling with Mr. Kendrick. You've caused quite enough trouble on that score for one day."

Ouch.

Apparently, her ladyship had not forgotten after all.

Charlie grimaced. "Sorry," she said to Kade.

"Don't be. We'll talk later."

She nodded and made her way forward with a glass and the port.

Kade joined his niece on one of the benches in the center of the boat. Tira had come aboard with Angus and was keeping quietly out of the way but observing everything with a sharp eye. Angus, meanwhile, had plopped down in the stern and was indulging in a fortifying glass of ale while chatting with the boatmen.

"How did you manage to escape your parents?" Kade asked Tira.

"Papa was organizing things for one of the other boats, and Mamma was helping Mr. MacMillan take care of Melissa. So I thought it made sense to get in with you and Grandda."

He glanced at the boat on their port side, several dozen yards away. Melissa was leaning against her husband's shoulder, while Ainsley waved what Kade assumed were smelling salts under her nose.

"You dodged a bullet there, lass," he said.

"Melissa thinks that Johnny fell because of the curse. That's why she's so fashed."

"Because of the lost brooch?"

The girl nodded. "Losing the brooch means the whole family will suffer bad luck."

"You do realize there's no curse, sweetheart. It was just a bit of bad luck that Johnny fell."

Tira scrunched up her face. "I'm not so sure, Uncle Kade."

He studied her for a few moments. "I'm beginning to think you got into this boat for a reason, and not just to avoid Melissa's hysterics."

"You're awfully smart, Uncle Kade. How did you know?"

"I used to be a spy, remember? Now, out with it, lass. What's bothering you?"

She glanced around before leaning in close. "I think Sir Leslie pushed Johnny off that cliff."

"Tira, why don't you start from the beginning and tell me everything," he replied, keeping his voice low and level.

"I was on the beach looking for shells. Papa and Mamma were farther down, *pretending* to look for shells." She rolled her eyes. "They were kissing."

"Good Lord, how revolting of them."

"They're always doing that. Anyway, when I heard people arguing, I went up the beach and saw Johnny and Sir Leslie standing on top of the cliff. Sir Leslie was doing most of the talking, though. He seemed very mad, and he kept jabbing Johnny in the chest." She scowled. "I don't think Sir Leslie a good person at all."

"I agree with you, pet. Then what happened?"

"Johnny yelled at him to bugger off, and then he turned around and left. Sir Leslie followed him, but I lost sight of them because of the trees. So I went back to looking for shells. It was almost right after that when I heard Johnny scream. Then he fell and landed on the beach up ahead of me."

Kade gave her a little hug. "I'm so sorry you had to see that, sweet girl."

"It was scary for a minute, but when I ran up to Johnny he was cursing a lot, so that was good. When he saw me he stopped cursing, though, and started to look upset."

"Where was Sir Leslie?"

"He came running down the path to the beach a couple of minutes later."

"Think hard, pet. Was it really a couple of minutes, or less than that?"

She shook her head. "No, it was a couple of minutes, because Papa was already running up by then, too."

"And what did Sir Leslie do?"

"He tried to help Johnny up, but Johnny yelled at him. Then the footmen ran up, and so did Lady Kinloch and Charlie. Mamma went to look for you and Grandda."

Kade gave her a little squeeze before letting go. "That is an excellent report, Tira. Thank you."

She grinned at him. "I think I would make a good spy someday, don't you?"

"An excellent spy, but don't tell your mother I said that. And speaking of which, did you tell either of your parents about this?"

"I didn't get a chance."

"We'll tell them together later. But I don't want you talking to anyone else about this, all right? Not even Grandda, for now."

"I thought you'd say that, so I didn't."

"That's my grand lassie."

"There's something else, Uncle Kade." Tira hesitated.

"While we were waiting to get into the boats, Sir Leslie talked to me."

Kade went hard and still inside.

"What did he say?" he asked, keeping his voice calm.

"He asked if I saw or heard anything when Johnny fell. He tried to be nice about it, but I could tell he was . . ." She scrunched up her nose. "Mad, I guess, although he pretended he wasn't. I didn't like it."

I'll throttle the bastard.

Kade forced himself to remain calm in front of his niece. "What did you tell him?"

"I just said I heard Johnny yell, and then saw him tumble down to the beach."

"Do you think he believed you?"

"Yes. I don't think he's very smart, Uncle Kade."

He blew out a relieved breath. "You, however, are incredibly smart. You kept your wits about you. Well done, lassie."

She beamed at him. "I'm much smarter than my brothers, aren't I? They probably would have blabbed their mouths off."

"You're the smartest Kendrick of them all, but I'll take this matter up from here, all right?"

Tira nodded.

"Good girl," Kade said, smiling at her. "Now, did you have the chance to find any good shells before all this unpleasantness occurred? What else did you do on your adventures?"

"Grandda and I found the gravestone of the chief of Glencoe. It was quite dirty, so Grandda got fashed. Mamma had to calm him down."

"That sounds like Grandda."

While Tira chattered on about her explorations, Kade studied the other boat. Morgan was seated with the remaining guests, holding forth with what looked like great bonhomie. He seemed entirely at his ease, not like a man who'd pushed another man off a cliff, or one who'd tried to intimidate a little girl.

Not that Kade had any proof of Morgan's guilt at this point. He'd find it, though. The search for the brooch was no longer a foolish lark or even an unfortunate inconvenience. Matters had suddenly become very serious, and that meant it was time for him to get serious, too.

CHAPTER 15

Charlie opened the door to Johnny's bedroom and stuck her head in. "Knock, knock. Mind a visit?"

She slipped in before he could answer. Given Kade's brief, whispered warning as they were leaving the drawing room for dinner, she wasn't about to give her brother a chance to refuse. Clearly, matters between Sir Leslie and Johnny were worse than she'd thought, and even dangerous.

Johnny warily eyed her from his canopy bed. "I suppose not. As long as you don't pester me."

Charlie wandered over and braced a hand against a scrolled bedpost as she studied her brother. Johnny was dressed in a nightshirt, his arm immobilized by a sturdy sling, his strain evident as he rested against the mountain of pillows that all but swallowed up his reedy form. He looked more like the little boy she'd watched over throughout their childhood than the grown man he was becoming.

She silently castigated herself for not doing a better job of protecting him—not just today, but over these last few years. Ever since he'd left for university, life had been difficult for the poor fellow. Between an overcritical father and an overprotective mother, he struggled to find his place. Now he was really in trouble, and it was up to her to pull him out of it.

"How are you feeling, Johnny?"

"Pretty banged up," he said with a sigh. "Getting home wasn't much fun."

"Yes, it was dreadful."

Thankfully, the Kendricks had stepped into the chaos, helping to get her brother transferred from the island to Ballachulish. Johnny had been tight-lipped and stoic throughout the entire ordeal, only losing his temper when Sir Leslie made a show of trying to help him from the boat to the carriage. Johnny had snapped, telling him to sod off and leave him alone. Fortunately, Kade had intervened, hoisting Johnny out of the boat with an impressive display of strength and more or less carrying him to the carriage. Best of all, he'd done it with a minimum of fuss, while treating Johnny with a kind manner that had defused the situation.

Sir Leslie had been displeased at that but had made an effort to hide it. He'd then loudly blamed himself for Johnny's injury, since he hadn't been close enough to prevent the *dear boy* from falling down the embankment in the first place.

Now, of course, Charlie knew that he'd probably pushed Johnny off that embankment, and it had taken all her willpower during dinner not to smash the soup tureen over the blighter's head.

"Did the doctor give you something for the pain?" she asked.

"Mamma wanted him to give me laudanum drops, but I said no. I feel woolly-headed enough without that nonsense. He did leave me some headache powders."

Alarmed, she straightened up. "You didn't hit your head, did you?"

"No, which was a lucky thing. If you can call falling down a stupid cliff lucky," he bitterly added. "And of course it would be my right collarbone. So now the doctor said I'm to wear this stupid sling for at least a month and not use my right arm at all. How the devil am I supposed to do that, Charlie? And God knows when Mamma will even let me get out of bed."

Charlie patted her brother's foot through the bed coverings. "I know, dearest, but look on the bright side. At least you no longer have to pretend to be social, or listen to Melissa crying."

Johnny let out a spurt of laughter but then winced. "Melissa did make rather a fuss, didn't she? You'd think she was the one who fell down a cliff."

"Poor Colin must be wondering what he's gotten himself into. It's all this nonsense about the brooch, though. Melissa is convinced that your injury is the result of the curse."

"I can't believe Mamma puts up with her nonsense. It was just a careless fall. My own fault."

She looked her brother straight in the eye. "Are you sure it was your fault?"

He seemed to flinch but quickly recovered. "Of course it was. I swear everyone in this family has lost their minds, even Mamma. You'd think I was maimed for life."

Charlie tried a different tack. "Speaking of Mamma, I really should be thanking you, Johnny. Your timing was excellent."

Her brother relaxed a bit. "What do you mean?"

She perched on the bed next to him. "Mamma and Mr. MacDonald came upon Kade and me in a rather awkward situation. Our dear mother, of course, immediately jumped to the wrong conclusion and was getting ready to pitch an absolute fit when you let out that bloodcurdling shriek. Fortuitously, your tumble served as an excellent distraction."

Of course, Mamma's instincts were actually bang-on, even though Kade's hand on her backside had been perfectly innocent. Their kiss in the chapel, though? There'd been nothing innocent about that.

"I'm glad it was good for something," he replied. "But what were you and Kendrick doing that would make Mamma pitch a fit?"

"It was all rather silly, really. We were looking about the old chapel when a spider crawled up the back of my skirt. Kade was knocking it off me when Mamma and Mr. MacDonald appeared out of nowhere."

"Are you telling me that Kendrick's hand was on your arse when Mamma waltzed up? Good God, I'm surprised she didn't shoot the poor fellow on the spot—or force you to marry him."

"She'd definitely prefer to shoot him," Charlie dryly replied.

Though Johnny's fall had served to distract their mother in the moment, she'd later made it clear that she was immensely displeased with Charlie's behavior.

"I suppose it's because she's so set on you marrying Richard." Johnny snorted. "As if you'd ever marry that dead bore."

"In all fairness, I don't think Richard can help being a bore—which is precisely why Mamma likes him so much. But you're right on both counts. Both Mamma and Richard's parents are determined that we marry, and I am equally determined to say no."

"That's good, because you should marry Kendrick. He's not at all swellheaded, even though he's so famous. Top of the trees, if you ask me."

Charlie had been doing her best *not* to think about the future, with or without Kade. On top of all the other problems in her life at the moment, it was simply too big to contemplate and too hard to imagine what a life with Kade might look like. But Johnny's casual comment brought it all home with a force that stole her breath.

"I . . . I . . . well, we're just friends, Johnny. Nothing more."

Liar.

She was madly in love with Kade Kendrick and hadn't a clue what to do about it—or if she even should do anything about it. Part of her couldn't help thinking that being with her was nothing more than a pleasant interlude for him, a way to pass the time at an otherwise boring social occasion. Except that didn't feel right or true. Kade would never carelessly dally with a woman, of that she felt absolutely certain.

So what, exactly, did he want from her? It was a mystery, because they were *hopelessly* mismatched.

Johnny shook his head. "I think he likes you, Charlie. Quite a lot, from what I can tell."

She mustered a smile. "That's very flattering, dear. But it's silly to think a man like Kade would wish to marry a Highland bumpkin like me."

"Of course he would. You're the best of us, Charlie. God knows you're the only person in this family who's ever cared about what I think or didn't bang on about what a failure I was."

Then he stared down at his lap, as if embarrassed that he'd said too much.

Charlie rested a hand on his knee. "Johnny, you're not a failure, and everyone in this family loves you very much."

"Our father sure as hell doesn't," he bitterly replied.

"Papa is just worried about you. As am I."

He just pressed his lips into a flat line.

Charlie gently jiggled his knee. "Johnny, I know something's wrong. I've always been able to tell, ever since you were a little boy."

He glanced up, looking both defensive and anxious. "I'm not a little boy anymore, Sis. You needn't treat me like one."

"I know, but it's not just children who get into trouble."

She comically crossed her eyes. "Just look at me. I'm up to my elbows in the muck."

His face crumpled a bit and Charlie's heart ached for him. He looked so lost.

"Dearest, please tell me what's wrong," she quietly said. "I want to help you."

He hesitated. "And you won't tell our parents?"

"Do you really need to ask?"

He smoothed a hand over the coverlet, refusing to meet her gaze. "All right, but it's nothing, really. Nothing that other fellows don't do all the time. It's . . . it's just more than it usually is, that's all."

It was easy to guess what he was talking about. "Are your pockets to let, Johnny?"

He gave a morose little nod.

"How much do you owe?"

"Three hundred quid, thereabouts."

Charlie sucked in a startled breath, stunned by the amount. "Good God."

He scowled. "You needn't be so missish. I've seen fellows drop even bigger sums in one game without even blinking an eye. Everyone does, you know."

She forced down her dismayed reaction. "I have no doubt. It's just that I'm not used to town ways. I'm a bumpkin, remember?"

He gave her a tentative smile. "I think you're the sharpest one of us all."

She doffed an imaginary cap. "Very kind, sir. Now, I'm assuming this awkward situation was caused by spending a wee bit too much time at the card tables?"

He grimaced. "Actually, it was mostly from one game. I knew the stakes were too high, but I . . . I didn't want . . ."

"To seem like a greenhead?" she gently finished.

He nodded, his expression miserable.

"Whom do you owe it to?"

"Sir Leslie. He was holding the bank."

It all made perfect sense. "Of course he was. And I'm assuming he's now demanding you pay it back."

Another grim nod. "The full sum, or he'll go to Papa."

She shook her head in disgust. "What a disgusting pig. I've a mind to take him out behind the stables and horsewhip him."

"I wouldn't stop you," he said with a heavy sigh.

She gently took his left hand. "Now, I have to ask this, Johnny. Did you steal my brooch?"

He jerked his hand away. "What? Why would you say that?"

"Because you know all my hiding places, like the boxes in the music room."

His tone turned defensive. "If anyone took that stupid brooch, it was you. To put Richard off the scent."

"Maybe," she acknowledged. "But it's really missing now, and I didn't take it. Quite frankly, I don't give a hang about the stupid thing, but I care about you. You're in trouble, and I want to help you."

"Well, it's not helpful to accuse me of theft." He snorted. "Good Lord."

Despite his apparent bravado, she knew he was scared and desperate.

"Is Sir Leslie threatening you? And I don't mean just ratting on you to Papa. Is he trying to intimidate you in any way?"

For a moment, panic leapt into his gaze. Then he lifted a defiant chin. "Don't be silly."

She leaned forward. "Kade told me before dinner that you and Sir Leslie had a bad argument a minute or two before you fell. Did he get so angry that he pushed you off the embankment?"

Her brother went as pale as a slipper moon. "I . . . I . . . that's ridiculous. Of course he didn't. I just slipped off. That was all."

"Now, *that* is ridiculous, because you know the island as well as I do. You would never have been so careless."

He mustered a glare, although he remained deathly pale. "If you're going to throw around wild accusations, you should just leave. Besides, it's none of your business, and you wouldn't understand, anyway. It's a matter of honor, between *men*."

Charlie repressed the impulse to give him a good shake. She couldn't do it anyway, because of his blasted shoulder.

"I don't think it's a wild accusation, though, is it?" she calmly asked.

"Just shut it, Charlie, would you? Let it—"

A knock sounded on the door, cutting him off.

She stifled a curse and stalked over to the door, yanking it open. Their housekeeper stood in the hall, tray in hand, looking apologetic.

"Beggin' yer pardon, Miss Charlotte. I've got Mr. Johnny's tea, as well as his headache powders."

Charlie stepped aside. "Of course. Please come in, Mrs. Martin."

The housekeeper bustled over to the bedside table. As she began to mix the powders into a glass of water, Johnny threw Charlie a veiled look.

"You needn't stay," he said. "I've got a thundering headache, and I'd like to rest."

Mrs. Martin glanced over her shoulder. "Her ladyship asked ye to come down to the drawin' room, miss. The men have come in, and they're waitin' on ye for tea."

"Please go, Charlie," her brother said, his voice now holding a pleading note. "I don't need Mamma coming up here and ringing a peal over the both of us."

Clearly, she wasn't going to get anything more from him tonight. "All right. I'll see you tomorrow, then."

When he didn't reply, she left and closed the door, frustration nipping at her heels. Another evening of tea and fraught conversation lay ahead, when all she wanted to do was mull things over. Should she confront Sir Leslie directly? Doing so could make things worse for Johnny.

If her brother continued to insist that he'd simply taken a tumble, she couldn't go around accusing Sir Leslie of assaulting him. And had it been intended to be a violent attack, or had the bastard simply lost his temper and given her poor brother a shove? Although injury was all too likely, the embankment wasn't steep enough to kill someone, unless one was very lucky—or unlucky, if on the receiving end of things.

Charlie took the staircase down to the first floor and stopped at the bottom, resting a hand on the polished banister. Everything was such a muddle, and she hadn't a clue what to do next. The problems were piling up, with no ready solution in sight.

Talk to Kade.

She closed her eyes, fighting desperately against the desire to seek him out. What right did she have to pull him further into this mess? Yes, he'd offered to help her search for the brooch, but this situation? Johnny would be furious if she breathed a word to anyone.

"Ahem," said a sweet little voice.

Charlie opened her eyes to see Tira standing a few feet away.

"How are you, Tira?" she replied, dredging up a smile.

"I'm fine. I was just in the drawing room, saying good night." She shook her head. "Everyone was arguing, so I think most of them didn't even notice I was there."

"That was rude of them. What were they arguing about?"

"You, mostly," the girl candidly replied. "And your brooch. And Johnny's accident. And the curse on your family."

Charlie couldn't help smiling. "There really isn't a curse."

"I know. That was mostly your sister who said that. Then Grandda called her a jinglebrains . . ." She twirled a hand. "Not to her face, but everyone heard it. So Melissa started crying, and then Lord Kinloch and Grandda started yelling at each other. And then Mr. Campbell started yelling, too. He said that he should be able to court you anyway, even without the blasted brooch."

"Oh, dear."

Tira gave her a sympathetic grimace. "That's when Grandda told him that he was a booby and a descendent of traitors, and that he should be thrown into Loch Leven as his just deserts. Everybody started yelling then, except my mother. She never yells. But people were starting to use bad language, so Mamma thought it best that I leave."

Charlie rubbed her forehead, unsure whether she should burst into laughter or make her escape. "Very wise of your mother."

"Mamma is very smart. She was trying hard to get everyone to calm down." The little girl glanced down the hall, in the direction of the drawing room. "They're still arguing, though."

Sure enough, Charlie could hear muffled but decidedly agitated voices filtering their way toward them.

"I wouldn't go in there, if I were you," Tira added.

Charlie laughed. "I agree with you. In fact, I think a little stroll in the garden might be just the thing. Would you care to join me?"

"Thank you, but I'm on my way to the library. I found a very good book yesterday, and Mamma said I could read for a half hour before I go to bed."

"Then I'll wish you a good night." She bent down and gave the little girl a hug. "Thank you for the warning."

Tira flashed an enchanting little grin. "You're welcome. Good night, Miss Charlie."

She skipped off in the direction of the library, while Charlie made her way down the central staircase to the ground floor.

A footman stationed by the front door bobbed his head. "Good evenin', Miss Charlotte. Can I get ye anythin'?"

"Good evening, Hamish. I don't suppose you have a spare family hanging about, do you? I'm thinking of replacing mine."

The young man rubbed a hand over his mouth. "I'm afraid not, miss."

"How disappointing. Well, I'm going for a stroll about the gardens before I brave the lion's den. Good night, Hamish."

"Good night, Miss Charlotte."

She slipped out to the terrace, bathed in a glow of lights from the drawing room one floor above. Through the open window, she could hear her father and Angus shouting at each other, and her mother vainly attempting to calm them down.

Really, it might be best to avoid the whole thing altogether.

Since it was a mild night, with a half-moon softly illuminating the path, she decided to walk to the gazebo. She'd always loved the gardens at night. As a child, she'd chased phantom hobgoblins and searched for fairies amongst the rosebushes and lavender. As she grew up, she imagined meeting a handsome man in the gazebo or down by the stream, a dashing beau who would carry her away into the wide, wide world.

Not that she'd ever had a beau, not really. But she occasionally still dreamed of one who would sweep her off her feet. Not surprisingly, that imaginary beau always possessed the most amazing cobalt blue eyes and a smile that made her heart ache with longing.

It was Kade, always Kade. And now he was here, and he more than lived up to her youthful dreams. He'd also made it clear that he was interested in *her*. She found that astonishing, because she'd never been the sort of girl a man like him would sweep away to the wide, wide world—especially not *his* world.

She stepped into the gazebo and plopped down onto the cushioned bench. It was time to stop mooning over Kade and deal with her problems, which now included Johnny's problems. Her little brother was in trouble up to his neck, and she could only hope he still had the brooch. The notion of slimy Sir Leslie getting his hands on it was simply unacceptable.

When she heard footsteps crunching on the gravel, she craned her neck out to see who it was.

Hell and damnation.

It was Richard, heading right for her.

"There you are, you sneaky thing," he exclaimed. "I've been stumbling about like a blasted fool, trying to find the right path to this gazebo. Although it's a mighty romantic setting, Charlotte, I'll give you that."

He flashed what he probably thought was a charming smile. Sadly, it more resembled a leer.

Mentally sighing, Charlie rose. "What the devil are you doing out here, Richard?"

That gave him pause. "What?"

"How did you find me?"

"Things were getting rather hideous in the drawing room, so I decided to nip out and get away from all the brangling. I just happened to hear you telling the footman that you were going out to the garden, so I decided to find you." Again, his unctuous smile. "Carpe diem and all that, eh?"

"Oh, God," she muttered.

"What's that?"

"Nothing. Actually, I was just about to join the others in the drawing room."

Richard shook his head. "Don't want to do that. Trust me."

"Then I suppose I'll just excuse myself and go to bed. Good night, Ri—"

He suddenly seized her hand and clasped it to his chest.

"Please do not flee me again," he announced dramatically.

"Allow me to make my case, once and for all. Surely you know how I feel about you, and yet you push me away at every turn. You are too cruel, my beautiful Charlotte. But please take pity on your helpless swain and make me the happiest of men."

When he tried to kiss her, Charlotte dodged and yanked her hand from his grasp. "Really, Richard, you forget yourself."

He tried to back her up against the cushioned bench. "If I do, it's because you're so lovely in the moonlight. A veritable Diana, a goddess of the hunt."

She dodged him again. "I don't mean to be rude, but would you please stop blithering such twaddle?"

"It's not twaddle," he replied, offended. "It's how a fellow is supposed to talk to a lady he's courting."

"What a gruesome notion. But in any event, I've made it quite clear that I don't want you to court me. You know we would not suit."

"Of course we would. Your parents are keen on it, and so are mine."

"I'm not going to marry you—or anyone—just because my parents are keen on it."

Now he was scowling at her. "But I'm keen on it, too. Or I would be, if you gave me half the chance."

Charlie checked her rising temper. "Richard, your father is pushing you onto me because of my dowry. We both know that it's the main attraction. So, I repeat, we will not suit."

"You'd be perfectly happy to let me court you if it wasn't for Kendrick sniffing about your skirts like a hound," he said in a surly tone. "He's ruining *everything*."

Charlie's anger flared, and she had to repress the urge to pop his cork. "What an incredibly rude thing to say. Now, if you'll excuse me, I'm going back to the house."

When she started to march past him, Richard grabbed her arm and tried to pull her against him.

"Let me go, Richard," she said through clenched teeth. "Or you'll regret it."

"I bet you let *him* kiss you," he retorted. "So maybe you should let me kiss you and see if you like it better."

He bobbed his head, trying to kiss her. Charlie was about to knee him in the privates when a large hand landed on Richard's shoulder and jerked him back.

"Keep yer dirty hands off her, ye bastard," Kade growled, his voice a guttural snarl. "Or I'll rip yer bleedin' head off yer shoulders."

CHAPTER 16

Robert let out a strangled yelp as he released his grip on her. Kade then tossed him to the side, where he landed on the bench in a hard sprawl.

Charlie sighed. "Kade, please don't hurt your shoulder."

Seething at Richard, he snapped his attention back to her, and her heart skipped a beat. Kade looked positively murderous, his gaze glittering with cold fury, his features sharp as shards of ice.

He ignored her comment. "Are ye all right, lass? Did he hurt ye?"

"I'm the one who's hurt," Richard blustered as he struggled to right himself. "Bloody hell, man! It's a wonder you didn't break my arm."

Charlie rounded on him. "You should be grateful for Mr. Kendrick's intervention, Richard. I was just about to knee you directly in the privates. And I *never* miss."

That precipitated another round of protests from Richard, which she ignored.

"Are you sure you're all right?" she asked Kade.

He was staring at her, looking a trifle bemused. "Were you really about to knee him there?"

"Yes, and I believe the colloquial term is *nutmegs*."

He choked out a laugh.

Richard had awkwardly clambered to his feet. "Really, Charlotte, what would your mother say at such language and behavior?"

"What would my mother say if I told her that you accosted me in the gazebo?" she replied.

Richard drew himself up. "Both your parents approve of me. I'm supposed to be courting you, and that's what I was doing."

"You don't have my blessing, and if that's your idea of courtship, it's appalling," she sternly replied. "When a girl doesn't wish to be kissed, you must respect her wishes."

"I thought you were just being coy," he protested.

When Kade took a menacing step forward, Richard retreated back to the bench.

"Let me tell you something, Campbell," Kade said in a lethal voice. "When a woman tells you no, that is *exactly* what she means."

"Richard," Charlie said, exasperated, "in all the years that you've known me, when have I ever been coy?"

"Well, never, I suppose. But your mother said I was being too cautious, and that I should make a go of it." He twirled a hand. "You know."

"Did my mother actually send you looking for me?"

He bristled. "I didn't need her to tell me. You're not the first girl I've wooed."

Kade snorted. "Obviously with a complete lack of success."

"I'll take no insults from you, Kendrick," Richard huffed. "If it wasn't for you, Charlotte and I would be doing just fine."

"No, we would not," she said.

"But if I find the brooch, you have to marry me," he replied. "It's a matter of family honor. Besides, your mother said—"

Charlie jabbed a finger at him, having had quite enough.

"If you bring my mother up one more time, I will toss you into the pond."

"And if she doesn't, I will," Kade added.

"This is ridiculous," Richard snapped. "I'm going back to the house."

He stomped past them, then turned to glare at Charlie. "Are you coming, Charlotte?"

She frowned. "Why would I?"

"Because if it's not proper for you to be alone with me, then you certainly shouldn't be alone with Kendrick."

She gave him a smile that was mostly teeth. "Why not? We're just old friends, you know."

Richard flapped an agitated arm. "He's not. He's . . . he's . . ."

"Yes?"

"A rogue."

She felt her mouth sag open. The man was truly an idiot.

"A rogue?" Kade said with disbelief. "I thought you said I was a pompous ass?"

"That too," Richard retorted. "In any event, you're not to be trusted with an innocent girl."

"It's a little late to be worrying about my virtue," Charlie said. "But if it's any consolation, I promise I will knee Mr. Kendrick in the nutmegs if he starts behaving like a rogue."

While Kade started to laugh, Richard swelled with outrage—rather like a frog in high dudgeon—and then turned on his heel and stormed out to the path.

"This isn't the end, Charlotte," he yelled over his shoulder. "Your mother is going to be *most* displeased."

"You don't have to tell her," she called back as he disappeared into the night.

Kade was doubled over with laughter.

Charlie poked his arm. "You're only laughing because you won't have to face an epic scold. No doubt Richard will tell Mamma every gory detail of this hideous encounter."

He straightened, trying to catch his breath.

"Not every detail, I suspect," he managed to gasp.

Charlie eyed him with concern. "Are you all right? Do you want me to thump you on the back?"

He wiped his eyes. "I'm fine. I'm astonished, however, that I could go so quickly from almost throttling Richard to thinking he's an utter boob."

"Yes, but he's mostly harmless."

"What he was doing didn't look harmless when I first came upon you."

"But twenty seconds later you would have come upon a much different scene. I really *was* going to knee him in the privates."

Kade shook his head. "It's still risky, though. You shouldn't have been outside here by yourself, not with everything that's going on."

"How did I know my ridiculous mother was going to send Richard out looking for me?"

"What if she'd sent Sir Leslie?"

"He's not interested in me."

"He is now, apparently."

She winced at that unappealing notion. "Really? That's annoying."

"Charlotte—"

"It's fine." She took his arm and steered him to the bench. "It's you I worry about. I'm afraid you hurt your shoulder when you threw Richard off me."

"My shoulder is fine."

She gently pushed him down and then sat beside him. "Stab wounds are nothing to be sneezed at."

"I'm well aware. Fortunately, we have a doctor in the family, and he took excellent care of me."

She hesitated for a moment before letting curiosity overcome caution. "You still haven't told me how you got stabbed by a Russian spy. It sounds . . ."

"Idiotic?" he dryly replied.

"I was going to say dangerous. Are you ever going to tell me what happened in Paris?"

He affected astonishment. "Do you mean my grandfather has yet to disclose the details?"

"Yes. He's been annoyingly closemouthed since you scolded him."

"Will wonders never cease?"

"Kade," she said in a warning tone.

His smile briefly flashed in the moonlight. "Someday I'll tell you. But for now, we have other matters to discuss."

"I'm aware, but can you at least tell me what transpired in the drawing room? The arguments, and such."

He cocked his head. "How do you know about that?"

"Your niece very kindly warned me off." She frowned. "How did you know where to find me?"

"I happened to glance out the drawing room window when you were crossing the terrace. Unfortunately, I couldn't make my escape immediately, but I came down as soon as I realized Richard had slipped out."

"Lucky for him," she wryly said. "Tira did say that Richard thinks he should be able to marry me, even without the brooch. And Sir Leslie has decided to enter the fray. Do I have that right?"

"Mostly. Your father also wants to put out a discreet word to local swains who might be interested in pursuing both you and the brooch."

"There is nothing discreet about my father, I'm afraid."

"Yes, my grandfather told him just that, in slightly more colorful terms."

She smiled. "I would have liked to have heard that."

"Especially when your mother began yelling at them," he wryly replied.

She winced. "If Mamma's yelling, matters are getting out of hand."

"So we need to find that damned brooch before your entire family comes apart at the seams or someone really gets hurt. Which brings us to Johnny. How did you get on with him?"

She waggled a hand. "As I suspected, he's lost a considerable sum playing cards."

"Most of which he owes to Morgan, I assume."

"Yes, although I'm to mind my own business, Johnny insists. It's a matter of honor, you see."

Kade's mouth turned down with disgust. "There's nothing honorable in a genuine rogue taking advantage of a boy like Johnny."

"Johnny thinks he's man enough to handle the situation on his own, unfortunately. He also rejected the suggestion that his fall was anything but an accident."

"Hmm."

Kade stretched an arm along the top of the bench, brushing her shoulders. He was probably just settling in for a chat, but Charlie had to resist the overwhelming temptation to snuggle against him. This was a serious discussion and not the time for mooning over the man of her dreams—or climbing into his lap and making mad, passionate love to him.

"Did you ask him about the brooch?" he asked.

"Yes. Point-blank. And he denied it, which I expected. Johnny is frightened."

"Of Morgan."

"Yes, but of my father finding out, too."

"Your father won't shove him off an embankment," Kade dryly commented.

She grimaced. "I know, but no one will believe that Sir Leslie would hurt Johnny. And I'm not sure it was even done deliberately. Perhaps it was a shove done in the heat of the moment, and Sir Leslie didn't intend for him to take such a tumble."

Kade shook his head. "I'm fairly certain it was deliberate."

Charlie frowned. "Why?"

"I know the type. He's a bad actor, and he's obviously desperate for the money. That's why he's thrown his hat in the ring to find the brooch."

"How flattering," she wryly said.

Kade looked sideways at her. "Och, lass. You know what I mean."

"Yes. I know I'm not the main attraction in this absurd mess."

He turned toward her, and a hand drifted down to settle on her shoulder. She was now all but cradled against his chest, without having had to do a thing.

"I beg to differ, Miss Charlotte," he murmured.

Though they were in deep shadow, she could see the glimmer of heat in his gaze and his seductive smile.

She had to swallow twice before she could answer. "In what way?"

"To me, you are the only attraction. Not your dowry, and certainly not your bloody brooch."

She rested a gentle hand on his cheek. "That's nice of you to say. So, what are you going to do about it?"

Kade brought his hand up to capture hers, then turned it over and pressed a kiss against her palm that made her shiver. His mouth was warm and enticing, and she longed to feel it against her lips.

But when she startled to snuggle closer, he put her hand back in her lap—reluctantly, it seemed—and drew away.

"What we're going to do next is keep watch," he said, his voice slightly husky. "Especially on Johnny. And we're going to wait. Something will break sooner or later."

She tapped his chest. "That's not what I'm talking about. Aren't you going to kiss me?"

He stood, pulling her up with him. "I would very much like to kiss you, but at the moment that's a bad idea."

"I think it depends on your definition of *bad*."

He chuckled. "Sweetheart, your mother could come barreling down that path any minute, along with half the household. That would be massively inconvenient, you have to admit."

She sighed. "You're no fun."

"As I am well aware. For now, though, it's best not to get distracted. We need to solve our problems first."

When he took her hand and began to lead her out of the gazebo, she resisted.

"Not even one kiss?" she asked.

"You are a menace, Charlotte Stewart," he said with a wry smile. "Come along before we both get in trouble."

He towed her along the path, ignoring her grumpy protests all the way back to the house.

Kade opened his eyes. It was pitch-dark and the house was dead silent, so what—

The sound of a violin filtered in through the open window of his bedroom, a haunting lament that likely commemorated a lost battle of days gone by.

With an exasperated sigh, he threw back the coverlet and stalked over to the window. The music was coming from above, not below. He leaned out, trying to pinpoint the exact location. As far as he could tell, it was coming from the roof.

What the devil was she up to now?

He retreated back inside and threw on some clothes. When he went out to the hall, flickering candlelight wavered into view. Angus appeared, garbed in kilt and nightshirt and, bizarrely, with his old Highland bonnet crammed down on his puffy white head.

"That's a charming outfit, Grandda."

"Just what came to hand. What's our lassie up to now?"

"Haven't a clue, but I'm going to find out. You've been up to the nursery floor. Any idea how to get to the roof?"

Another door opened, and Royal stuck his head out. "Where's that music coming from? Not from you, obviously."

"I generally don't practice in the middle of the night," Kade replied. "Are you coming out?"

"Sorry, old fellow, but I'm in the altogether."

"Royal, why aren't you in bed?" called a sleepy voice from inside the room.

The plaintive notes of the violin were getting louder and more dramatic.

"How the hell did Ainsley sleep through that?" Kade asked.

"She's a very heavy sleeper. Unless I decide to wake her up," Royal added with a wink.

Kade rolled his eyes. "Go back to bed, you idiot. Grandda and I will find out what's going on."

"Happy hunting," his brother replied.

By now, they could hear voices coming from the next corridor, which housed more bedrooms and the family apartments. Kade strode toward the central staircase, Angus scurrying along in his wake.

"Hold up, lad," his grandfather said. "I'm not as young as I used to be."

Kade slowed his pace. "Why don't you go back to bed, Grandda? I'll let you know what I find out."

"Och, I might as well see what all the fuss is about. Besides, ye'll probably need my help when Elspeth and Kinloch start kickin' up a fuss."

"I suspect that kicking up a fuss is precisely the point of this musical escapade."

Angus chuckled. "Aye. That lassie will keep ye on yer toes, I reckon."

"No doubt."

Kade took the stairs two at a time to the nursery floor, then waited for his grandfather.

"That way, I think," Angus said, pointing off to the left.

A door opened and Tira appeared, neatly garbed in her nightgown and robe. "Are you trying to get to the roof, Uncle Kade? It's this way, at the end of the hall."

He and Angus reversed course.

"Thanks, lass," Kade said. "Now, back to bed with you."

"Miss Charlie is up to something, isn't she?" Tira asked.

"Apparently."

His niece gave a nod. "I think she's pretending to be a ghost."

"That's seems a rather odd way to pass the time."

"It's kind of like that time Grandda played his bagpipes to try to scare Aunt Vicky away. Before she and Uncle Nick got married."

"It almost worked, too," Angus said with a grin.

Now servants were beginning to appear, their clothes obviously hastily thrown on.

"What's going on, sir?" one of the maids asked in a nervous voice. "What's that strange music?"

"I'm just on my way to find out," Kade replied.

He found the narrow, winding staircase to the roof and started up. He'd almost reached the top landing when the music ceased, as if someone had dropped a curtain on the performance.

"Dammit," he muttered.

He opened the door and strode onto the roof, wincing when a toe caught the edge of a rough piece of slate.

Laroch Manor was a sprawling edifice with some flat roofs but also several gables and a central tower. Right now, he and Angus stood over the north wing, which was separated from the rest of the house by the tower and a steep gable. He didn't fancy breaking his neck trying to scale the blasted gable in the dark. Nor did it matter—his fiddle-playing nightingale had fled the scene, no doubt anticipating that he'd come looking for her.

Angus, who'd wandered over to the left, returned. "Must be another way off this bloody roof."

"Several, I would think. But I expect she wasn't on this part of the roof to begin with."

"Closer to the family rooms, I reckon."

Kade headed back to the door. "Might as well go down and see the resulting uproar."

They returned to the nursery floor. Several maids now huddled there, with their nightcaps practically quivering with excitement.

"Did ye see anythin', sir?" one of them asked.

"Not a thing," he said with a smile. "It's probably best if you all returned to bed. The excitement is over for the night."

"I couldn't sleep a wink now," exclaimed one of the younger girls. "Not with the Kinloch Fiddler makin' an appearance."

"It's been years since anyone heard him," one of the other maids piped up. "And it nae bodes any good."

Kade sighed and headed down the hall, Angus following.

"Told you," Tira said, joining them. "It's supposed to be a ghost."

"Shouldn't you be in bed?" he asked her.

"I want to see all the fun."

Angus held out his hand. "Stick with me, lassie. We'll get to the bottom of this."

"I think we already know who *this* is," Kade tartly replied. "The only question is why?"

As they descended the central staircase to the lower floor, they heard voices, some quite loud. Kade wasn't surprised to see a small crowd now milling about the hall, guests and family alike—including Charlie. She was standing next to Ainsley at the back of the group, holding a candle and looking demure in her flannel wrapper, her hair properly tucked under her plain white nightcap.

Kade had to give her full marks for getting there so quickly, thus giving herself an alibi.

Lord Kinloch, who'd been arguing with his wife, spun around, flipping the tassel of his nightcap out of his face.

"Well, Kendrick," he demanded. "What did you find?"

"Not a thing. By the time I got up there, the music had stopped."

Lady Kinloch, resplendent in a lavishly trimmed pink wrapper with matching nightcap, skewered him with a disapproving look. "You saw no one?"

"I'm sorry, my lady," he replied. "Unfortunately, the configuration of the roof prevented me from conducting a full search."

"That's convenient," Richard sarcastically piped up.

Kade didn't respond, partly because he was awestruck by Richard's attire. The fellow was garbed in a floor-length green paisley robe that sported enormous velvet lapels, padded shoulders, and a family crest. His feet were shod in velvet slippers also bearing the crest.

"Ho, Campbell," Angus said. "Keep yer snotty opinions to yerself."

Richard sneered at him. "It was obviously your grandson up on the roof, waking us with his stupid prank."

"And why would I do that?" Kade asked.

"To cause trouble. That's all you Kendricks do."

Angus bristled like a hedgehog. "Why, ye scabby—"

Kade put a restraining hand on his grandfather's shoulder.

"To be clear, I was certainly not engaging in an impromptu performance on the roof. And my grandfather was with me when we searched."

"As if he would tell the truth," Richard contemptuously replied.

"Richard," Lady Kinloch sternly intoned. "If Mr. Kendrick states he wasn't playing his violin, then I'm sure he wasn't."

Tira piped up. "I saw Uncle Kade and Grandda go up to the roof while the music was still playing."

Richard snorted. "And we're supposed to believe Kendrick's niece? I think not."

Royal, who'd been looking mostly amused by the ridiculous scene, leveled a narrow-eyed gaze on Richard.

"Campbell, are you calling my daughter a liar?" he said, his voice so cold one could almost feel the north wind.

Ainsley joined her husband. "It certainly seemed like it to me. How distressing."

Tira, who had inherited her mother's dramatic skills, rubbed the corner of one eye. "Mamma, you know I would never do such a thing. You and Papa taught me that lying was wrong."

Ainsley opened her arms. "I know, darling. Come here."

Tira ran into her mother's arms. "I don't like that man," she said in a muffled voice. "He's mean."

"If it wasn't the middle of the night, I would ask your father to challenge Mr. Campbell to a duel." Ainsley smiled at Lady Kinloch. "Royal was the most accomplished swordsman in his regiment. His nickname was the Terror of the Black Watch."

"Heavens!" cried Melissa.

Kade glanced at Charlie. The imp had a hand clamped over her mouth, clearly stifling laughter at the Kendricks' stellar performance.

"You exaggerate my prowess, my love," Royal said to Ainsley in a powder-dry voice.

"Och," said Angus. "Ye'd run booby Campbell through in a trice."

"I say," exclaimed Richard, obviously a little alarmed.

Kade decided it was time to intervene. "Lady Kinloch, you need only inquire of the maids. They also saw Angus and I go up to the roof while the music was still playing."

She gave him a gracious smile. "I trust you and my cousin completely, of course."

"Of course it wasn't Kendrick," Lord Kinloch said, looking mightily aggrieved. "It was obviously Charlotte, although why the devil she'd do such a thing is beyond me."

"But, Papa," Charlie protested, "I too came out into the hall when I heard the music, just like the rest of you. How could I possibly do that and be up on the roof?"

"Well, I didn't see you come out," he said, "and neither did your mother. You just popped up in the back a few minutes ago."

"I saw her," Ainsley said. "She came out of her room at the same time as Royal and me."

Kinloch whipped around and scowled at Royal. "Is that true, Kendrick?"

"Of course. Absolutely," said Royal, with a commendably straight face.

"Then if it wasn't Kendrick and it wasn't Charlie, who the devil was it?" Kinloch demanded.

"It must be the Kinloch Fiddler," Melissa said, her voice quavering. "It's the only explanation."

Then she promptly burst into tears, throwing herself into her husband's arms. Colin clumsily patted his wife's back while casting a pleading gaze at Lady Kinloch.

Her ladyship sighed. "Everyone, please go back to bed. There has been quite enough nonsense for one night."

She took Melissa by the arm and hustled her off, Colin trailing gloomily in their wake.

Morgan had been sitting in a window alcove looking bored

by the proceedings and now finally spoke up. "I'm almost afraid to ask, but who is this Kinloch Fiddler and why is our dear little Melissa so upset about him?"

"He's some blasted, stupid ghost," Kinloch snapped. "Stuff and nonsense."

"They say he shows up and plays his fiddle when something bad is about to happen," Charlie helpfully supplied. "It's been a legend in the family for centuries. Something to do with an ancient battle between the clans."

Morgan roared with laughter, slapping his knee. "How splendid. Just what this party needed—a bloody musical ghost foretelling doom."

Kinloch glared at him. "I'll thank you not to spread stories about inane ghosts, sir. You'll frighten half the servants out of their wits."

"Wouldn't dream of it, my dear sir."

"Still, it's nae good to disrespect the old ways," Angus said, thoughtfully stroking his chin. "It's verra bad luck."

"There is no stupid ghost hanging about my bloody house," Kinloch retorted. "It was obviously Charlotte playing tricks on us."

She held up her hands. "You just heard that it couldn't have been me, Papa."

"Ye must admit that trouble has dogged the family since the Clan Iain brooch was lost," Angus said. "Just look at puir Johnny, laid up in his bed."

"This has all been very amusing," Morgan drawled, coming to his feet. "But now that the show is over, I'm for bed."

"Everyone should go to bed," Kinloch snapped.

He started to stalk off, but then turned and glared at Charlie. "Don't dawdle, Charlotte. Come along."

"Yes, Papa," she said in a meek voice.

She crinkled her nose at Kade and then hurried after her father. Morgan gave the rest of them a little salute before sauntering down the hall, a morose Richard following in his footsteps.

Once they were alone, Kade slowly clapped his hands. "Splendid performance, everyone. Well done."

Ainsley gave him a flourishing bow. "Thank you, dear boy. I thought it was one of our best. Don't you agree, Royal?"

"Certainly one of our more ridiculous ones," he responded. "And so much for teaching our daughter not to lie."

"Och, the bairn knows it was all for a good cause." Angus ruffled Tira's hair. "Well done, lassie."

The girl beamed at him. "Thank you, Grandda. It was just to help Miss Charlie. I know I'm not supposed to lie about serious things, or ever to Papa and Mamma."

Ainsley hugged her. "That's my girl. Seriously, though, I cannot imagine what Charlotte hoped to accomplish with this little adventure."

"Scared the servants good and proper, she did," Angus said.

"Surely that was not her intention." Royal cocked an eyebrow at Kade. "Any ideas?"

He shook his head. "No, and believe me—I intend to find out."

CHAPTER 17

Breakfast was a rather subdued affair. Lord Kinloch chewed his way through his beefsteak as if chewing nails, while Colin looked quietly morose. Johnny was lost in a brown study as he toyed with a cup of tea and a slice of toast.

As for Richard, he'd spent the last fifteen minutes glaring at Kade over his eggs and kippers, as he obviously still believed him to be the midnight fiddler. Only Angus ate with unimpaired gusto, ignoring the dark looks cast his way by Kinloch. Tira, seated next to Kade, also seemed undisturbed by a roomful of gloomy adults.

"Uncle Kade," she asked, "do you think the Kinloch Fiddler is real? One of the maids told me he was. She said the last time the fiddler appeared was before the Battle of Culloden, and we all know what happened there."

Kinloch sighed and put down his knife. "My dear child, we lost at Culloden because we were outnumbered and outgunned. There was nothing magical or mysterious about it."

"If some of the clans had fought the good fight instead of actin' like traitors," Angus said, pointedly eyeing Richard, "we might have won that battle."

Richard switched his ire to Angus. "Is that comment directed at me? Because I'll have you know that I don't give a damn about either the bloody Battle of Culloden or your bloody Kinloch Fiddler."

Angus pointed his fork at him. "Ho, none of yer foul language around the bairn, ye ken."

Richard snorted. "I'm sure the girl has heard far worse from you."

"The girl's name is Tira," Kade said in a warning tone. "And since she is a child, I would expect you to moderate your language in her presence."

Kinloch nodded. "Quite right. As ridiculous as this conversation is, there's no excuse to use off-color language around children."

Tira graced him a sweet smile. "Thank you, Lord Kinloch. Mamma would be quite upset to hear that I was exposed to rough language."

Kade had to bite the inside of his cheek to hold back a laugh.

"But I hardly said anything," Richard protested.

Kinloch glared at him. "Oh, do be quiet, man. I can't stand brangling at the breakfast table."

Richard subsided, no doubt not wishing to further alienate his prospective father-in-law.

The door opened and Lady Kinloch and Ainsley came into the room, followed by Royal. When the gentlemen started to stand, Lady Kinloch waved them back down.

"Good morning, my dear," Kinloch said, trying for an assumption of cheer. "I didn't expect to see you at breakfast this morning."

Lady Kinloch took her seat at the opposite end of the table. "Yes, it was a late night, but the Kendricks are departing, as you recall."

Royal and Ainsley had always intended to leave this morning. Although they'd offered to stay to assist in the search for the brooch, Kade had advised them to leave as scheduled. There was suspicious business afoot, and things might get a bit dicey, possibly even dangerous. He wanted his sister-in-law and niece well out of harm's way.

"Besides," Lady Kinloch added, "I could scarcely sleep a wink thinking about that dreadful Fiddler."

"Elspeth, there is no damned Kinloch Fiddler," her husband replied, forgetting his admonition about cursing around little girls.

"Of course there is," Charlie said as she sailed into the room. "The legend of the Kinloch Fiddler has been in the family for generations. And whenever he plays—"

"You mean whenever *she* plays," her father sarcastically interrupted.

"—disaster or even death is sure to occur," Charlie continued, undeterred. "And it certainly wasn't me up on the roof, Papa."

"It was Kendrick," Richard muttered.

Charlie poured herself a cup of tea. "It wasn't Mr. Kendrick, either. I checked with the maids, and they confirmed his report."

"There's only one explanation," Lady Kinloch said.

Her husband held up a hand. "Do *not* say it, Elspeth."

"The Kinloch Fiddler is real," she stated firmly. "And he's giving us a warning that something dreadful is about to occur."

Charlie glanced at her brother. "Some dreadful things have already occurred. My brooch disappeared and poor Johnny fell off a cliff."

"Who knows what will happen next?" Angus said, wiggling his fingers.

"Nothing is going to happen next," Kinloch thundered. "I won't allow it."

Lady Kinloch winced. "My dear, please don't yell whilst at table."

"I certainly will yell if you all don't cease this nonsense."

"Papa's right," Johnny said. "It was my own fault that I fell off that stupid embankment. Just a silly accident."

Charlie tilted her head to study him. "Are you sure that's all it was?"

"Of course it was an accident," he angrily replied. "What else would it be?"

Morgan strolled into the room. "Dear boy, I could hear you spouting off from out in the hall. Such a fuss."

Johnny flushed. "I'm not fussing. I'm just saying that it's nonsense to make out that my fall was anything but an accident."

"Of course it was an accident," Morgan said as he took the chair next to the young man. "What else could it be?"

"Nothing," the lad muttered, turning his shoulder on the blighter.

Lady Kinloch frowned with concern. "You are looking rather peaked, my son. Perhaps it wasn't wise for you to come downstairs just yet."

"I can't stand sitting in bed like a lump, Mamma. It's bad enough I have to wear this stupid sling for the next month."

"Not to worry, old boy," said Morgan with jovial cheer. "I'm happy to stay and lend a helping hand at keeping you occupied. A friend in need, and all that."

Lady Kinloch bristled, clearly offended. "Really, Sir Leslie, we're quite capable of looking after Johnny."

"No doubt, my lady, but I can do all sorts of little things to assist. Why, I can help him butter his toast, for one."

Johnny sat silently while Morgan made a show of buttering the toast. Kade glanced at Charlie, who returned his questioning look with a slight grimace. Clearly, her suspicions regarding Morgan had not abated, and Kade had to agree with her.

"No need to stay on Johnny's account, or ours," Kinloch said, glowering at Morgan. "All the Kendricks are leaving today, so you might as well be off, too. Shame, that, but all good things must come to an end, as they say."

"My dear, have you forgotten that Kade and Angus are staying on with us?" Lady Kinloch asked.

Her husband stared at her, thunderstruck. "What?"

"Yes, they've decided to stay a bit longer. I felt sure that I told you."

"You . . . you did not," Kinloch blustered. "And why the devil are they staying?"

"To help search for the Clan Iain brooch," Angus said. "Yer puir daughter needs all the help she can get." He leaned over to Ainsley and put a hand to the side of his mouth, whispering loudly. "Especially with a da like Kinloch."

Naturally, everyone in the room heard his comment.

"Goodness, look at the time," Ainsley said brightly. "We really must be getting along."

Ignoring her intervention, Kinloch fixed a disapproving gaze on Kade. "And I suppose you're also going to be dashing about after Charlie? Just like the rest of these fellows?"

Charlie stared at her father in disbelief. "Papa, you do remember that this was your idea in the first place, do you not? Angus and Mr. Kendrick are simply being kind. There's no need to read anything else into their actions."

Kade raised his eyebrows at her, but she refused to return his gaze.

"Just think, Grandda," Tira exclaimed, beaming at Angus. "You might find the brooch and end up saving everyone from the Kinloch Fiddler. That's so exciting!"

Angus winked at her. "Aye that, lassie."

Kinloch swelled up like a rooster about to crow and threw his napkin down. Without another word, he rose and stalked from the room.

"Oh, dear," Lady Kinloch said with a sigh. "I'd best go after him."

"Well, this has been quite the entertaining morning, eh?" Morgan said as their hostess hurried out. "What say you, Johnny? Up for another round of the treasure hunt?"

"Do shut up, Leslie," Johnny groused.

Richard pushed back his chair, almost knocking it over. "You all belong in a madhouse."

"Goodness, that's not very polite," said Ainsley.

Angus shrugged. "What else can ye expect of a Campbell?"

"Insane," Richard snapped before stomping out of the room.

"More coffee, anyone?" Charlie asked in a cheerful voice. "I can ring for a footman."

Kade rose. "Angus, I'd like a word."

"Now? I haven't finished my breakfast."

Kade held his gaze. "Yes, now."

His grandfather rolled his eyes. "I have a feelin' I'm goin' to need that coffee."

Kade glanced at his pocket watch as he left Royal's room and headed down the hall. His family was almost ready to depart and so would soon be out of harm's way. Now he needed to find Charlie and convince her to cease stirring the pot, at least for the moment. He had a plan and didn't want unexpected bombshells disrupting it—no matter how entertaining those bombshells might be.

The entrance hall was a hive of activity, as two footmen were carrying luggage out the front door to be loaded onto the Kendrick carriage. A third footman was about to haul out two overstuffed bags under the anxious eye of a supercilious fellow who, if Kade wasn't mistaken, was Richard Campbell's valet.

The man himself emerged from the back hallway, garbed

for travel in a voluminous greatcoat that featured enormous lapels.

As Kade reached the bottom of the staircase, Richard glanced over and scowled. "Kendrick. Of course I would have to run into you."

"Going somewhere, Richard?"

"I'm leaving and returning to Edinburgh immediately."

Kade leaned against the banister. "Then am I to believe that you're giving up your courtship of Miss Charlotte?"

"Why I ever agreed to try to court the blasted woman is beyond me. The entire family's deranged, and no amount of money could make it worth putting up with their mad antics." He let out a derisive snort. "The Kinloch Fiddler. It's pure insanity."

"A very wise decision," Kade said. "Who knows what kind of trouble you would attract by marrying Charlotte without the brooch. Doom would surely come upon you. You might even fall out a window or get flattened by a runaway carriage."

"Being leg-shackled to Charlotte would be misfortune enough," Richard tartly replied. "Her mother's right. She's a Highland hooligan."

Kade affected a heavy brogue. "Aye, she's a high-spirited lassie. She needs a true Highlander to keep up with her, ye ken."

Richard sneered at him. "I suppose you're just the man to do that, are you?"

"Ye canna blame her for having good taste, can ye?"

Richard's furious gaze threatened death—or, at the very least, a proper scold.

"You're an arrogant prat, Kendrick—intolerable, really. What Charlotte sees in you is a complete mystery."

"It must be my sunny temperament and impeccable manners."

"Bugger you," Richard snapped. "You're welcome to Charlotte and her crazy family. I've had more than enough."

Then he turned and stormed out the door, almost tripping over his greatcoat as his valet scurried after him.

Kade couldn't hold back a smile. Lord and Lady Kinloch might be dismayed by Richard's precipitous retreat, but he hoped to soon convince them of the merits of his replacement as their daughter's primary suitor. Of course, he would have to persuade the daughter of those merits, too.

He found Charlie in the music room, standing at the open terrace doors as she stared absently out over the gardens.

"Ho, lassie. What's amiss?"

She glanced back at him, her expression slightly incredulous. "Do you truly need to ask?"

"No, but for once I bring good news."

"I could use some," she ruefully replied.

"Booby Campbell has just taken his departure in high dudgeon. I very much doubt he will return."

Her eyes popped wide. "Truly?"

"Apparently, the Kinloch Fiddler was a bridge too far for him. Well done, you."

She grabbed his arms and planted a brief but enthusiastic kiss on his mouth. Kade reached for her but she'd already pulled back, her eyes sparkling with laughter.

"To tell you the truth," she said, "I questioned my sanity. It seemed like such a ridiculous scheme, even for me. Did Richard really believe there was a Kinloch Fiddler?"

"No, he knew it was you. But he says it convinced him that your entire family was deranged, and that you were little better than a hooligan."

She held up a finger. "A Highland hooligan, if you please."

Kade smiled. "Frankly, I didn't expect Richard to give up so easily."

"Nor I, because I do have a rather splendid dowry, as you know. Plus, my parents were very encouraging."

Kade took her hand and led her to the sofa. "Sweetheart,

it wasn't just your money. Last night's unfortunate scene in the gazebo with Richard made that very clear."

She wrinkled her nose. "That's when I decided I really needed to be rid of him."

"And so the Kinloch Fiddler made her appearance. A bit of a risk, though, since there are currently two accomplished fiddlers in residence."

"I am sorry that Richard tried to pin my ridiculous stunt on you," she replied, looking guilty.

"No worries, lass. But how did you know it would even work?"

"I wasn't entirely sure it would," she confessed. "But I knew Melissa would believe it, and I suspected Mamma would, too. She's a bit more superstitious than she likes to admit. I was simply hoping to create enough of an uproar to put Richard off. He's very staid, and his father is also a stickler for propriety. Even my dowry wouldn't compensate for having a hellion as a daughter-in-law."

"I applaud both your creative thinking and your success."

She smiled. "I owe you and your family a real debt of gratitude for supporting my absurd scheme. You were all quite splendid."

"Kendricks excel at absurd scenes." He gently tapped the end of her nose. "Which is why you should have told me about it. You must know by now that you have my support."

She blushed the enchanting shade of pink he'd come to love. "Yes, I know, but I didn't want to put you in an awkward position in case you didn't approve of what I was doing."

"You certainly won the approval of my family. They wholeheartedly enjoyed playing their parts, even on a moment's notice."

"And what about you? Were you shocked by my less-than-ladylike behavior?"

"Lass, you were so prim and proper that I could hardly

keep a straight face. But from now on, please give me fair warning so I can be better prepared. And on that note, do you have any plans to surprise Johnny into admitting the truth?"

She sighed. "No. I did try to buttonhole him before breakfast, but he's avoiding me. I really don't know why he insisted on getting out of bed today. He's so clearly in pain."

"That's a bit of a mystery, isn't it?"

"One I'm not sure how to solve, if he won't talk to me."

"I've put Angus on him. As you can imagine, Grandda has had a great deal of experience in dealing with young men over the years. I can't tell you how many secrets my brothers and I inadvertently divulged to him."

"I'm not sure your grandfather will be able to separate Johnny from Sir Leslie. That dreadful man is sticking to him like fish slime."

"An apt if disgusting analogy."

"Perhaps I should try to draw Sir Leslie off. Since he's entered the hunt for the brooch, he must also be interested in courting me." Charlie snapped her fingers. "I'll ask him to go riding with me. That would get him well away from Johnny."

Kade wasn't having it. "Absolutely not. You're not to go anywhere near that bastard, much less be alone with him."

She blinked in surprise before her lovely features rearranged themselves into a scowl. "Are you truly telling me what I can and cannot do, sir?"

"In this case, yes. Leslie Morgan is untrustworthy and potentially dangerous, and I don't want him within ten feet of you."

She scoffed. "If you think I can't manage that coxcomb, you are much mistaken."

"Have you forgotten this is the man who pushed your brother off a cliff?"

"No, but rest assured that if necessary I would be the one doing the pushing, not Morgan."

Kade pinched the bridge of his nose, trying to throttle back his temper and his worry. But every instinct he possessed cried out that Morgan could be dangerous.

"Look, Charlie," he said, trying for a more reasonable tone. "You are strong and incredibly capable. But Morgan will not be as easily handled as Richard. So if we need to get him away from Johnny, I will do it."

When she crossed her arms under her breasts, plumping them up over the top of her bodice, it was a distraction he didn't need at the moment.

"Kade, I realize that you are trying to protect me, and I'm grateful. But I do not need protection. If Sir Leslie tried anything, he would be *quite* sorry. I'm faster, smarter, and I suspect my left hook is better, too."

That failed to reassure him. "Charlotte, while I am well aware of your abilities, bad people, male or female, are adept at getting the jump on others. The woman who stabbed me in Paris barely came up to my chin and only weighed eight stone soaking wet."

That gave her pause. "But you weren't anticipating an attack, were you?"

"That is exactly my point," he replied, exasperated.

Charlie tapped her chest. "I, however, would be expecting one and would be on my guard, because we already know Sir Leslie could be dangerous."

Again, he tried to throttle back his temper and failed. When he pointed a finger at the tip of her nose, her eyes momentarily crossed.

"Charlotte Stewart, I forbid you to go anywhere near Morgan," he growled. "Is that clear?"

Charlie jumped up from the sofa and strode to the piano. She stood there for a few moments before turning around and jabbing a finger at him. "You're not to tell me what I can and cannot do, Kade Kendrick. And stop acting like a Highland oaf."

Little red sparks seemed to dart around in his brain. Kade couldn't believe they were even having this conversation.

He got up and stalked over to join her at the piano, looming over her. She had to crane her head back to meet his gaze.

"Charlie, if you will just—"

"Stop trying to intimidate me," she interrupted. "It won't work."

"I'm not trying to intimidate you. I'm trying to keep you safe."

She poked him in the chest. "No, you're trying to control me. There's a difference."

Kade wrapped his hands around her shoulders, bringing her up on her toes. "You are the most exasperating woman I've ever met, do you know that?"

"And you are the most annoying man I've ever met."

"I highly doubt that."

For several long seconds, they glared at each other. Charlie's color was high, and her velvet gaze crackled with anger. And she was so bloody enticing that he was tempted to drag her over to the sofa and have his way with her.

Moron.

He started to lower her back down when Charlie blew out an angry little huff.

"Hell and damnation," she muttered.

She reached up and clamped her hands around his head, pulled him down, and planted a kiss on his mouth that almost knocked him out of his boots. Nearly staggering, he braced his hands on the piano behind her. With Charlie all but wrapping herself around him, pressing her body to his, Kade quickly found himself at the very limits of his self-control.

When she slipped her tongue between his lips, all hell broke loose inside him.

He gripped the piano, fighting the urge to sweep her up into his arms—to lay her flat out on the sofa and make love to her. It was utter madness, but the temptation to claim her swept through him like a summer storm on a Highland peak.

Charlie wound her arms around his neck, kissing him with an urgency that was both sweetly innocent and sensually devastating. Naturally, he kissed her back, because she had the most delicious pair of lips he'd ever tasted. He nudged them wider, slipping inside to plunder her mouth. And his lass gave as good as she got, wriggling closer as she eagerly explored him back.

And weren't her curves just a delight, too? Her breasts were soft as pillows, and he could already imagine her nipples growing stiff and flushed as he played with her. And her arse . . . he'd definitely noticed those curves. Kade let a hand drift down, gently squeezing one cheek. When she sighed her approval into his mouth, he cupped her with both hands, kneading her pretty bottom and nudging her tight against him.

But then Charlie suddenly stilled, going stiff as a poker in his arms.

Kade mentally cursed himself. For all her boldness, she was an innocent and he was all but ravishing her against the piano.

He forced himself to ease back, clamping down hard on a desire that throbbed in every muscle of his body.

That's not the only part that's throbbing, ye randy bastard.

Charlie stared up at him, wide-eyed and flushed, her lips pink and swollen from his kisses. She was temptation incarnate.

"Sorry," he gruffly managed. "I shouldn't be manhandling you like this."

But as he started to step away, she whipped down her hands and clamped them on *his* arse, holding him tightly against her. That was a colossal mistake, because his cock was now perfectly wedged against the notch of her thighs.

Not that his cock—or the rest of his body—minded one bit.

"Lass, what are you doing?" he gritted out.

"I should think it obvious, by now," she pertly replied.

He frowned. "So . . . you want me to manhandle you?"

"I believe I'm doing the manhandling, at the moment."

He snorted. "Och, lass."

She narrowed her gaze. "Why did you stop, Kade?"

"Because *you* stopped."

"I was simply a bit startled. By the size of . . ." She released him, twirling a hand. "You know."

"Trust me, I do know," he dryly replied.

"Well, I'm no longer startled, so you can go back to doing what you were doing."

He shook his head. "Charlie, that is a very bad idea. For one thing, anyone could—"

She interrupted him. "Kade, *do* be quiet, would you?"

Once again, she clamped her hands around his head and pulled him down for a kiss. And what a kiss it was—full of softness and heat, and deliciously demanding. It shredded the last bit of sense in his brain.

Kade wrapped his hands around her waist and picked her straight up. Charlie wrapped herself around him, never breaking the kiss as he walked backwards. When his legs hit the edge of the sofa, he sat, bringing her down with him. They landed in a bit of a sprawl, Kade half reclining against the cushions.

Charlie broke free with a gasp. "Kade, don't hurt your shoulder!"

"My blasted shoulder is fine."

He wrapped his hands around her hips and lifted, plopping her fully onto his lap. She squeaked a bit, wriggling against his now-massive erection. Kade hissed out a breath. It took a stupendous exertion of will to keep from spreading her wide and exploring her most intimate parts.

Instead, he carefully positioned her to straddle his thighs. That hiked up her gown and brought her breasts to his eye level. Her bodice had pulled down a bit, revealing the top of her stays—and the tops of her breasts. Unable to resist, he ran his tongue along the plump swell, briefly dipping down to taste the edge of one nipple.

Charlie let out a moan, one that shot fire through his veins. He shifted her slightly so that her round backside was now snug against his erection, with nothing between them but the fall of his breeches and her thin gown. The thought of her tight little channel clenched around him was so enticing that he flexed his hips, nudging against her. He couldn't hold back a groan as her bottom pressed onto his cock.

"Oh . . . oh, my goodness," Charlie said with a gasp.

Kade trailed a hand down to her thigh, finding the top of her garter. "Too much?"

She hesitated, and then gave him a dreamy little smile. "No, it's perfect."

Placing a hand on her back, Kade brought her down for a kiss. With a happy sigh, she nestled close. She nuzzled his lips, sweetly playing. Her mouth was silky and warm and he knew he could spend hours kissing her—not just her mouth but also every delicious part of her. When the time was right he would do just that, lingering between her thighs and tasting the deepest, most intimate parts of her.

Soon.

When he gently bit her lower lip, she responded by wriggling her bottom. His erection thoroughly approved. Leaving her mouth, he kissed his way along her dainty jawline, nudging up her chin as he moved down her slender throat.

He paused to lick the tender hollow where her pulse fluttered. When she quivered, he held her steady. With his other hand, he gently tugged on her bodice. The tops of her breasts plumped up over her stays, partly exposing her nipples. He could see they were already flushed and plump, and oh-so-ready for his tongue.

"Now, there's a sight to behold," he murmured.

When he swiped a thumb across one nipple, Charlie let out a whimper. Kade leaned closer and—

"A*hem*," came a female voice from close by.

Charlie froze. A moment later, she pushed up and scrambled out of his arms, almost landing on the floor before she recovered.

Kade swallowed a curse and carefully sat up, trying not to wince. In her mad scramble, Charlie's hip bone had dealt a glancing blow to his privates. Thankfully, she'd not fully connected, or he'd be writhing in considerable agony.

He glared at his sister-in-law. She was garbed for travel and regarding them with open amusement. "Ainsley, have you ever heard of knocking?"

"Dear boy, it's the music room, which I believe is in a public part of the house. How was I to know you would be, er, indisposed?"

Charlie, cheeks now red as autumn apples, continued to yank her clothing back into some semblance of order.

"I'm so sorry, Ainsley," she blurted out as she smoothed her wrinkled skirts. "I . . . we didn't hear you. How embarrassing for you."

Ainsley gave an insouciant wave. "Please, I am rarely embarrassed. But perhaps you and Kade might think about a more private setting in which to engage in such . . . intimate conversations."

"Is that what we're calling it?" he said as he tugged his own clothing back into place.

When Charlie shot him a dirty look, he held up his hands. "Sorry. Just trying to lighten the mood."

She switched her attention back to Ainsley. "Were you looking for us?"

"Yes, to let you know that we're leaving." Ainsley eyed her. "I would, however, advise that you not come to the entrance hall to make your farewells. Both your parents will be there."

Charlie's shoulders went up around her ears. "Oh, dear, that's unfortunate. I mean, well, do you think . . ."

"Never fear," Ainsley replied. "I will simply tell your parents that we already said our farewells. Royal and Tira will perfectly understand the situation."

Charlie blushed an even deeper shade of red, which Kade would not have thought possible.

"Um, thank you," she said.

Ainsley opened her arms. "Give me a hug, my dear, and then be off with you. Via the back staircase, obviously."

Charlie enveloped her in a fierce hug. "Thank you for everything. You've been so wonderful."

Ainsley patted her back. "You're very easy to love, Charlotte. Never forget that, nor that you deserve all the happiness in the world."

"Thank you," she replied in a muffled tone. Then she released Ainsley and fled the room without even a backwards glance for Kade.

He rubbed his forehead. "Well, that was fun."

Ainsley crossed her arms. "Aren't you going to get up and give me a hug?"

"Normally I would, but circumstances dictate otherwise."

"Got you in the bollocks, did she? I thought so."

He couldn't hold back a laugh. "You are absolutely incorrigible."

She flopped gracefully down next to him. "Believe me, I understand. I did the same thing to Royal when we were first married. When Angus walked in on us, I reacted as Charlie did."

"Thank God for small favors. I'd much rather have you walk in on us than Grandda."

"But we *were* married, I might add," she said. "What if Lord or Lady Kinloch had walked in on you?"

He shrugged. "I'm assuming we would have been marched

off to the nearest parson, which would certainly have made life simpler."

Ainsley frowned. "Are you actually having trouble persuading Charlie to marry you?"

He scratched his chin. "Well . . . I haven't gotten around to asking her yet."

Her frown turned into a fiery glare. "Kade Kendrick, if you are toying with that girl, I will beat you to a bloody pulp. Her clothes were halfway off, for heaven's sake!"

"Of course I'm going to marry Charlie. But we never seem to get that far in the discussion. She's as slippery as an eel, that lassie."

"She didn't seem to be putting up much resistance when I walked in on you," she dryly replied.

"If you'd arrived a bit earlier, you would have heard her refer to me as a Highland oaf. I think that what followed was as much of a surprise to her as it was to me."

"Arguing, were you?" She waggled her eyebrows. "Sometimes a good argument can be quite stimulating."

"Apparently."

"What were you arguing about?"

"Sir Leslie Morgan. I want her to steer clear of the bounder. Charlie seemed to think I was questioning her ability to take care of herself."

"It rather sounds like you were, dear."

Kade rolled his eyes. "I know she can take care of herself. I know it better than anyone. But Morgan is a dangerous man, and I don't want her anywhere near him."

"Then you'd best marry the girl, or at least announce your betrothal. That might be enough to send Sir Leslie on his way."

"I'd like nothing better. But I'm not sure I understand why she's so elusive. At times, I can almost imagine she's toying with *me*."

Ainsley pressed a dramatic hand to her forehead. "What a blow to the great Kade Kendrick."

"Go ahead and have your laugh. Then please give me the benefit of your feminine wisdom so I can get the girl I've been waiting for all my life to say yes."

"Really, it's a wonder any of the Kendrick men ever found a wife. You're all so thickheaded. Except for Royal, of course. He fell in love with me instantly."

"He did, which is an enduring mystery to the rest of us."

She laughed. "Wretch. All right, here are my words of wisdom: Charlotte is madly in love with you and probably has been since she was a girl. But part of her is convinced that she's not good enough for you. I also believe she's having trouble imagining what your future together might look like."

Kade shook his head in disbelief. "Not good enough? She's the most amazing woman I've ever met. There's no one like her."

"She is amazing, and she would make you the perfect wife. For one thing, she would take care of you." She poked him in the arm. "And you do need taking care of, now and again. You're not a sickly little boy anymore, Kade, but we all need help sometimes. That would also equalize the situation between you and Charlotte, at least from her point of view."

He thought about Ainsley's words for a few moments. "All right, I see your point. But I still don't understand how Charlie could possibly think she's not good enough for me. It's ridiculous."

"Her entire life, Charlotte has been told that she's eccentric or even downright odd. Given that, it's quite astounding that she's grown up with the degree of self-confidence that she possesses. But somewhere deep down, she's still not sure about herself. That's the part you need to reach to assuage her fears."

Ainsley's assessment, while it made perfect sense, twisted

his heart. To him, Charlie was like music, the most beautiful he'd ever heard.

"You know, you're more than just a pretty face," he said. "You're actually quite perceptive for a *Sassenach*."

She snorted. "You are a dreadful boy. But now, I must be off. If we leave too late, we'll no doubt get stuck on some dreadful moor full of annoying Highland ghosts."

"Tira would like that."

"And I would not."

They stood, and Ainsley reached up and brushed a kiss across his cheek. "I'll make your goodbyes to Royal and Tira, since you're looking worse for wear."

He smiled. "Thank you. And thank you for your advice."

"See that you apply it. And keep out of trouble, Kade, you and Charlie both."

"Aye, that."

"Do not leave here until she promises to marry you."

"Yes, Mother."

Ainsley rolled her eyes and swept from the room.

CHAPTER 18

Charlie snuck past her mother's bedchamber and made her way along the pitch-dark hall. All was now quiet. The family was abed after repeated assurances by her father that the Kinloch Fiddler was gone for good.

Papa had buttonholed her earlier in the evening, extracting a promise to ensure just that.

"You've already managed to send Richard scampering off," he'd said, "so there's no need for your continued antics. I love you, Charlotte, but I will throw you off the tower if I hear one squeak from your blasted fiddle tonight."

Since her deranged scheme had yielded the proper result, Charlie had meekly promised that the Fiddler was forever consigned to the grave.

But while the Kinloch Fiddler's days were over, the family's troubles were not. She hadn't a clue how to get through to Johnny, and scabby Sir Leslie hung over their heads like the Sword of Damocles. Plus there was the still-missing brooch. She needed help, and from the only person capable of providing what she required.

Kade.

After their torrid and ultimately embarrassing encounter in the music room this morning, Charlie had made a point of avoiding him. He'd not been pleased about that. Whenever she'd glanced his way this evening, his narrow-eyed gaze had promised a reckoning would soon be at hand. But if there was to be a reckoning, she preferred it to be on her terms.

And perhaps that might include a few more kisses?

Charlie mentally winced at her own foolish thoughts. At her age, one would think she'd have better self-control.

She turned into the guest wing, which was dark save for one ray of light filtering out from beneath Kade's door. He was probably working.

Thank God.

The thought of sneaking into his bedroom and waking him up had given her distinct pause—especially after her brain had been seized by the image that he might be sleeping in the altogether. That was almost too stimulating to contemplate.

She inhaled a deep, calming breath and then tapped on the heavy oak door. Several agonizing seconds crept by until finally she heard a footstep. The door quietly swung open—thank God for well-oiled hinges—and Kade loomed over her. He'd discarded his frock coat and vest but was still dressed in trousers and shirt.

His eyebrows rose in a sardonic tilt as he took in her kilted attire. "The Kinloch Fiddler, I presume?"

"Shh," she hissed, pushing him back inside and stepping in. "Papa will have my head on a platter if he finds out I'm here. I promised to behave myself, at least for tonight."

"I'm not sure sneaking into my bedroom in the middle of the night falls under the heading of proper behavior, at least by your father's standards."

"Yes, it's quite shocking of me. But it couldn't be helped."

His smile broke free, shedding more warmth than the cozy fire burning in the grate. A corresponding glow lit up her heart.

"We can be shocking together." Kade led her to a pair of wing chairs in front of the fireplace. "I suspect, however, that you're here for another reason. Unfortunately for me."

She tried to ignore the heat rising in her cheeks. Charlie had never been the blushing type, but Kade had a knack for charging straight past her defenses.

Taking a seat, she averted her gaze from the large and inviting bed with its cozy wool coverlets and mound of pillows. Instead, she glanced at the writing desk tucked into a nook between the windows. Well lit by two lamps, it held music scores and writing implements.

"I'm sorry to interrupt your work," she said. "It's a miracle you've been able to get anything accomplished while visiting our Highland version of Bedlam."

Kade propped a shoulder against the mantel, his broad shoulders and tall form outlined by the gentle glow cast by the peat fire. She couldn't help thinking back to the first time she'd met him, when he'd been a slight, sickly boy. The passage of years had left a dramatic mark on him, and yet his eyes hadn't changed, nor had his smile. Both were as warm and as kind as they'd ever been, perfectly reflecting his generous heart.

"I was almost finished for the night," he replied. "And contrary to my expectations, I've been remarkably productive." He gently tapped the end of her nose. "That's down to you, Charlie. You've inspired me, and I will be forever grateful."

The breath seemed to seize in her lungs as she gazed up into his handsome features. The fact that this man now held her heart in his hands was both terrifying and wonderful.

"I don't think anyone's ever said that about the Kinloch Fiddler before," she managed to lightly reply.

Better to make a jest than let him see how nervous she was. She was so far out of her depth that she might as well be in the middle of the North Sea.

He grinned. "There's no accounting for the muse. Now, can I get you a drink, sweetheart? I've just got whisky up here, I'm afraid."

"No, thank you. I need a clear head for this conversation."

"Ah, we are to be serious, then."

He pulled the other chair around and sat down facing her. With his hands loosely clasped between his thighs, his gaze steady, Kade waited patiently for her to begin.

Doing her best to ignore her jangled nerves, Charlie smoothed down the soft wool of her kilt. "First, I need to apologize. I was dreadfully rude to you today."

An amused gleam crept back into his gaze. "When was that?"

"Well . . . I believe I called you a Highland oaf at one point."

"True."

"Then I ignored you at dinner and positively snubbed you later, in the drawing room."

"Also true. I admit I was cut to the quick. In fact, I almost borrowed Melissa's smelling salts to aid my recovery."

Clearly, he was not going to make it easy for her. "Kade Kendrick, you're acting like a jinglebrains."

He smiled. "Sorry, sweetheart. I will do my best to behave. Now, is there anything else you'd like to apologize for, while we're on the subject?"

"Yes. Earlier, in the music room . . . I threw myself at you in the most disgraceful fashion. And then Ainsley burst in, and it was utterly mortifying, and that's why I ran out of the room," she finished in a humiliated rush.

"Charlie, I didn't mind that part in the least." He held up a finger. "When you threw yourself at me, that is, not when Ainsley so annoyingly interrupted us."

"It was *so* embarrassing, though. What must Ainsley think of me?"

"She thinks you're a wonderful girl. However, it was probably a good thing that my sister-in-law walked in on us. I was not exercising the best judgment in the moment."

Charlie's stomach started to twist, but she forced herself

to calmly meet his gaze. "I'm so sorry, Kade. I put you in a terrible position, and I sincerely regret doing so."

He frowned. "Love, I think we're talking past each other. Our encounter was delightful. I'm simply noting that passionate interludes are best conducted in private. Anyone could have walked in on us. We were fortunate it was Ainsley."

Relief seeped through her. Still, she felt compelled to press the point. After all, proper young women didn't throw themselves at respectable men. Nor did they run about in kilts, for that matter. By any standard, her behavior was shocking.

"You truly didn't mind? Mamma says I'm a great deal too forward, and *that* was far beyond forward, even for me."

Kade reached over and wound their fingers together. His hands were strong and sure, as befitted a musician. Charlie longed for the wonderful feel of them roving over her body again, as they had this afternoon.

"Sweet lass," he murmured, his voice low and tinged with a brogue. "Ye can be forward with me anytime. In fact, I look forward to it."

Again, she felt a blush rise to her cheeks. For all that, she couldn't help smiling. "Thank you."

"Are we now finished with the apologies?"

She nodded, but forced herself to extract her hands from his gentle clasp. As much as she longed for his touch, there were things to discuss and questions that must be answered.

He sat back, probably sensing her need for some distance. While Charlie desperately wanted him, she needed to think— and she needed to face facts, whatever those facts might be. Whenever Kade touched her, her brain tended to go fuzzy around the edges.

"What else is bothering you?" he quietly asked. "You can tell me anything, Charlie. You must know you're safe with me."

She had to swallow past the sudden lump in her throat. "I do know. And at the risk of repeating myself, I can't help wondering about . . . us. What are we doing here, Kade?"

Whatever it was between them still felt so unreal, and too new and fragile to survive beyond the confines of her small world.

"You mean besides annoying your parents and looking for your brooch?" he wryly asked.

"Are you being deliberately obtuse, Kade Kendrick?"

"No, I'm just teasing you, love."

"Well, I wish you wouldn't."

And, yes, she sounded grumpy. It was because she was just about vibrating with suppressed anxiety.

"I'm courting you, sweetheart, or so I thought," he replied. "But I'm beginning to suspect that I've not made a very good job of it. Then again, it's hard to compete with so accomplished a swain as Richard Campbell."

His observation was so ridiculous that she had to first laugh and then give him a jab in the knee. "Oaf."

He waggled his eyebrows. "Aye, that."

"Really, sir, you are having too much fun when I'm trying to be serious."

"I can't seem to help it. It's because I'm happy. *You* make me happy, Charlie, and that's the most splendid thing that's ever happened to me."

She worked mightily to let those words—those impossible words—settle into her mind and heart. "Are . . . are you saying that you love me?"

His handsome features took on a serious, almost earnest, cast. It was an echo of the solemn, quiet boy who'd offered her friendship and so much more those many years ago.

"Yes," he replied.

It was such a simple word, but a fiat that would change her life forever.

"And you're sure?" she whispered.

He smiled. "I am."

Her entire world seemed to stop for a moment before slowly starting to rotate in the opposite direction, as if a child had slapped a hand down on a spinning globe and then sent it going the other way.

Kade leaned forward again. "Now let me ask you a question, Charlie. What do you want?"

She hardly knew how to answer, since she wanted so much. But was she actually up to the change and the challenge? "You mean from you."

"Yes, but also from your life. What do you want your life to be?"

Charlie took a deep breath, trying to slow the spinning enough to think. "You, obviously. Beyond that, though, it's hard for me to imagine. And that's *incredibly* annoying. For someone who claims to be neck-or-nothing, it's like I'm afraid to take the jump. I'm beginning to feel rather cowardly, to tell you the truth."

Kade took her hand again. "You're much too hard on yourself. Has this been a surprise to both of us? Yes, but that doesn't mean it's wrong, or somehow false."

The only true surprise was that he actually returned her feelings. Since that sounded rather mawkish, she would keep that to herself.

"It's this blasted brooch," she said instead. "And Johnny. I can't think clearly."

He studied her for a moment. "What you could do with is a bit of a drink. You're rather jittery around the edges."

Charlie sighed. "I think you're right."

He got up and went to fetch her a whisky.

"By the way," he said as he poured a glass for her, "why are you dressed in a kilt?"

"I went for a walk by the stream before coming here, to try to clear my head. I didn't want to get my evening gown dirty, so I changed." She pointed at her stocking feet. "Obviously, I took my boots off once I got back. Better for sneaking."

Kade muttered something as he handed her the whisky. Then he folded his arms, looking quite cross.

"What?" she asked.

"Charlotte, you should not be wandering about the grounds alone, especially at night. We talked about this."

She managed not to roll her eyes before taking a drink. As the whisky settled in her stomach, she could feel her shoulders start to relax. Kade, however, looked like he was fuming.

"I was perfectly fine," she said. "Everyone's in bed, including scabby Sir Leslie. Besides, I was armed."

He looked blank for a moment. "You were?"

"I took my new Deringer pistol with me. It's an excellent weapon. Now, please sit down, Kade. You're looming over me like . . . like . . ."

"A Highland oaf?" he dryly replied.

She gave him an apologetic smile. "Rather."

He rubbed a hand over his head as he sat. It made his thick black hair stand on end, which she found rather adorable.

"I'm sorry," he replied. "I just don't like you taking unnecessary risks right now. It unnerves me."

She scoffed. "Nothing unnerves you."

"Nothing used to, but that has officially changed since you entered my life. And if there's one thing Paris has taught me, it's that events can quickly go sideways."

She rounded her eyes at him. "Do tell. Then I'm assuming it was you who sent my brother-in-law as chaperone when I rode with Sir Leslie this afternoon?"

Kade waggled a hand. "I may have dropped a hint that such an escort would be appropriate."

"More than a hint, I suspect, since Colin took his duties very seriously. He rode between Sir Leslie and me whenever possible, and he changed the conversation whenever my would-be suitor tried to engage in even a mild flirtation. When Sir Leslie got a bit snappish, Colin refused to be moved."

He laughed. "Well done, Colin. He's a truly estimable fellow, in my opinion."

"Yes, he's a very good sort. I will also admit, although it

kills me to do so, that your plan was a good one. It saved me from Sir Leslie's slimy attentions while giving your grandfather a chance to spend time with Johnny. So thank you for that."

Kade leaned forward and tipped up her chin with one finger. Then he pressed a soft kiss to her lips. But when Charlie reached for him, wanting to deepen the caress, he pulled back.

She eyed him. "You shouldn't start things you have no intention of finishing. It's rude, ye ken."

His deep, blue gaze glittered with devilment. "Who said I'm not going to finish? But since we still have important matters to discuss, it's best not to get distracted."

Charlie sighed. "I suppose that means your grandfather had little success with Johnny. I was afraid that might be the case."

Instead of replying, Kade went to the bedside table and opened its single drawer. He took something out and then rejoined her.

"I believe this belongs to you," he said as he sat down.

She stared at the small leather pouch he'd placed in her palm and comprehension dawned. With trembling fingers, she loosened the pouch strings and tipped the contents into her hand.

The Clan Iain brooch, its silver, amethysts, and diamonds glittering like starlight in her palm, was none the worse for wear. Her heart thudded with a heady mix of relief and astonishment, making it hard to breathe.

Kade watched her, a slight smile tilting up the corners of his mouth.

"How did you find it?" she finally managed.

"Angus did. Your brother did his best to avoid him, but the old fellow is cannier than he looks. At one point, Johnny snuck down to the gazebo. He spent some minutes there and then retreated to the house in what my grandfather described as a furtive manner. So we searched the gazebo and found it."

"But I looked in the gazebo," Charlie protested. "It was one of the first places I searched."

"One of the wooden panels beneath the bench was loose, and that's where Johnny hid it. There was some scratching on the panel, so he probably pried it off—after you searched the gazebo, obviously. Otherwise, you would have noticed it, like Angus and I did."

She grimaced. "Johnny lied to me, when he had it all along. I told him that he could trust me, but he still lied to me."

Tears suddenly prickled as disappointment swept through her. Even though she'd had her suspicions about her brother—more than suspicions—she'd clung to a faint hope that Johnny was telling the truth. It was crushing to know he'd had the brooch all along.

She pinched the end of her nose, trying to stifle the urge to cry. "He's never lied to me before. Not like this."

Kade took the brooch and placed it on the small round table next to his chair before taking her hands.

"I know it's bitter," he gently said. "I think Johnny is very scared, and as young men often are, he's concerned with the appearance of honor. He got himself into trouble and is trying to find a way out of it by himself. You mentioned that your father can be quite hard on him, and I suspect that incurring Lord Kinloch's displeasure is almost as frightening to Johnny as Morgan's threats."

Charlie struggled for a few seconds, her anger warring with the instinct to protect her foolish little brother. "So the solution was to steal my brooch. That is hardly an act of honor."

"He wouldn't be the first person to steal it."

Kade's expression was so wry that she couldn't possibly take offense. Besides, he was right.

"Yes, I've set a terrible example for him, haven't I?" she

said with a sigh. "I still wish he'd come to me, though. I would have helped him."

"Running to his big sister for help? Perish the thought."

When she started to protest, he gently tugged on her hands. "I'm not trying to excuse him, love. Of course he should have told you. But the fact that he didn't, given how close you are, illustrates how fearful he is."

She mulled that over. "I wonder what he thought he was going to do with it. Give it to Sir Leslie? Pawn it? It would be quite difficult to pawn, since it's so distinctive."

"Who knows? But you can take comfort in the fact that he refused to give Morgan the brooch, even under duress. That refusal leads me to conclude that your brother didn't really know what to do. So he simply hid the brooch away until he could find a way out of his dilemma."

That was true. While Johnny had been terribly foolish, he hadn't betrayed her. "Thank you for that, and for finding the brooch."

He smiled. "Thank Angus, although I fear you'll give him a swelled head. He's quite chuffed at the success of his 'spy work,' as he calls it."

"He's earned my undying gratitude. But what happens now?"

"We should sit back and wait to see how matters develop."

Charlie couldn't help feeling skeptical. "Shouldn't we just say we found the brooch? Once we do that, Sir Leslie will have no choice but to leave Johnny alone."

"We could, and of course the decision is up to you. However, I very much doubt Morgan will leave Johnny alone—not with the money he owes him."

Charlie could feel the beginning of a headache coming on. The situation was *so* blasted complicated and *so* frustrating.

"He'll go to my father, and poor Johnny will really be in the soup."

God only knew how their father would react. If he became

angry enough, he might force Johnny to leave university. He might even disinherit him from those parts of the estate not entailed.

"Kade, this could be bad," she added with a grimace.

"I know. The problem isn't your brother. It's Morgan. The bastard has no business preying on someone who is hardly more than a boy. I have no intention of allowing that to stand. I will not watch him wreak havoc on you and your family."

Kade's cobalt gaze was now hard as flint. His entire attitude had transformed from one of quiet sympathy to a steely resolve. It was, she realized, a glimpse at the man who'd spent two years roaming the Continent as an agent of the Crown.

"I agree entirely," she said. "But how do we accomplish that?"

"It won't be in a court of law."

When he didn't elaborate, Charlie gave him a wry smile. "In other words, you intend to put the fear of God into him."

"Or at least the fear of Clan Kendrick. First, though, we need to catch him in the act of threatening Johnny. Then we've got him."

"That makes sense, I suppose," she said, a bit dubious. "But we cannot put Johnny in harm's way."

"Charlie, I give you my word that Johnny will come to no harm," he firmly replied. "His injury is fortuitous in that respect, since it will confine him to the house or the garden. Between you, me, and Angus, it should be easy enough to keep an eye on him."

"We might enlist Colin. We could tell him that Sir Leslie is a bad influence and he's trying to get Johnny to gamble at cards."

Kade gave her an encouraging smile. "That's an excellent idea, lass."

"Good. Since that's settled, what do we do with the brooch?"

He slipped it back into its pouch. "I'll keep it for now, if you don't mind. No one will think to look for it here."

"That makes sense, but I have to be the one who supposedly finds it. If *you* return it, my father will pressure you to marry me. He'll pester you endlessly, since he now sees it as a matter of honor. I won't put you in that position."

He frowned. "Of course I'm going to give you the brooch. I'm also going to marry you, so you needn't worry about your father's reaction."

His blunt pronouncement was . . . thrilling, she supposed. It was also exceedingly unloverlike.

"Kade, that's so nice of you, but—"

His eyebrows shot up. "'Nice'? Really?"

Her patience started to slip a wee bit. "We have yet to even discuss marriage, much less what our life together would be like. For instance, where would we live? And would you wish me to travel with you when you're touring? If not, where would I live? With your family? With my family? These are matters we must discuss before charging ahead."

She hated to admit it, but there were a few significant obstacles standing between them. For one thing, she truly was a country bumpkin who'd barely set foot out of the Highlands. What did she know about the kind of life he led?

"Of course we'll discuss all that, but I do know what I want, Charlie. I want you."

His confident reply eased her onset of nerves. He probably thought her a ninny for asking those questions, but she had to be certain that *he* was certain. Because if even a smidgen of doubt existed between them, Charlie knew the obstacles might be too large to overcome.

She twirled a hand. "So you've no doubts at all?"

His smile suddenly flashed. "Ah. Now I see the problem."

"You do?"

"Yes, and I know just how to solve it."

A moment later—so quickly that she gasped—Charlie found herself sprawled on his lap.

"What . . . what are you doing?" she yelped as she grabbed his shoulders.

"I'm fixing the problem."

A moment later his mouth came down on hers and knocked every doubt right out of her head.

CHAPTER 19

When Kade finally pulled back, Charlie struggled to catch her breath. Humor gleamed in his eyes, along with a fiery desire that made her knees go wobbly as custard.

Good thing you're sitting down.

Of course, where she was sitting was on his lap, and in a decidedly inelegant sprawl. When she wiggled a bit to regain her balance, Kade hissed out a sharp breath.

"Sorry," she gasped. "Did I hurt you?"

"Not really," he replied through gritted teeth.

When he shifted her into a more comfortable position, Charlie bit back a squeak. *Now* she knew what his problem was. And it was a large one, currently pressing against her backside.

"Oh," she weakly replied. "That's good now."

His smile was wry. "Yes, it's actually very good."

Charlie had to smile back as she tentatively rested a hand on his cheek. His night beard tickled her palm, making her shiver. When she stroked her fingertips along his jawline, Kade moved a hand to her thigh and gently gripped it through the fabric of her kilt.

For several moments, she let herself enjoy the feel of him and the desire that sparked in his gaze—desire for *her*. But then she realized he had yet to answer her question. She silently ordered herself to focus on that, not on his kisses.

"At the risk of repeating myself," she said. "I still wonder how this—"

Kade once more captured her mouth, and when his tongue flicked between her lips, slipping inside to taste her, Charlie couldn't hold back a moan. She clutched at his shoulders as he ravished her mouth until every nerve in her body vibrated like the strings of a violin.

After reducing her to a state of near idiocy, Kade again drew back.

"You were saying, Miss Stewart?" he murmured with a satisfied smile.

It took a moment for his question to register. "Er, was I?"

When he grinned, Charlie let out a sigh. Really, the man had an astounding ability to chase every sensible thought from her head.

"You're a brute, Kade Kendrick," she said. "I'm trying to ask you a question and you keep distracting me."

His hand moved farther down her thigh and came to rest on her bare skin.

Bare skin?

She glanced down to see that her kilt had ridden up to the point where a respectable woman would quickly move to restore order, or at least order the gentleman in question to behave himself.

Apparently, however, she was not a respectable woman.

"How dreadful of me," he replied. "Please accept my apology."

"I would if I thought you were actually sorry. I'm trying to be serious, Kade, at least for a moment."

He adopted a contrite expression that didn't fool her one bit. "Of course, my darling. Ask away."

She ignored the flutter in her chest his endearment had produced, and instead adopted what she hoped was an appropriately stern expression. But when Kade actually chuckled, she could only assume her attempt was a failure.

"As delightful as this is—" she started.

When his fingers crept up under the hem of her kilt, caressing her thigh, Charlie again lost her breath.

"You mean sitting on my lap?" he murmured.

"Yes, and stop interrupting me. Now, as delightful as this is, I'm wondering how it's going to solve our problem. Although," she added after a moment, "I seem to be having trouble actually articulating the problem. Which is your fault, because you're mucking up my brain."

Was he really the problem? Or was it her lack of confidence holding her back? But, really, how could Kade truly love her after such a short time? After all, he'd completely forgotten about her until she'd crashed into his life less than two weeks ago.

As Kade studied her, his hand continued to caress her thigh, but with a soothing touch as if to reassure her.

"You're wondering if my love is true, or if it's simply a passing fancy," he said. "One that won't survive this moment or place."

She grimaced, feeling rather exposed. "I know that sounds as if I don't think you're trustworthy. But I do trust you, Kade. More than I've trusted anyone in my entire life."

"It's fine, sweet lass," he gently replied. "As we noted the other day, this has caught us both by surprise. But please know that I think you're the most wonderful woman I've ever met. You're brave, beautiful, smart, and incredibly talented. I count myself extremely fortunate that the men of Glencoe are too moronic to have seen the jewel in their midst, since it meant I had a chance at winning your hand."

The sincerity of his words and the tenderness of his gaze sent warmth flowing over her skin.

"I'm afraid you didn't have to work very hard at that, Kade," she admitted. "I've loved you for the longest time, which is rather embarrassing, since I haven't seen you in years. Girls aren't supposed to moon about after youthful crushes or make their feelings so obvious."

"Charlie, you have every right to express your feelings—and your doubts, too."

She fiddled with a button on his shirt. "It makes me feel vulnerable, though."

Even as a child, she'd tried to remain in control of her life in whatever small way she could. As she grew older, that was the reason she never wished to marry or move away from Laroch Manor. Here, she'd been able to be who she was and who she wanted to be—until her parents had upended the apple cart.

Kade, in his own way, was doing the same now.

"It's never easy to be different," he replied. "But you're safe with me, Charlie. You can be as strong or as vulnerable as you wish. I will always be there to catch you, or to stand by your side."

He tipped up her chin. His gaze was steady, sure, and full of promise—a promise, she realized with a sense of wonder, he fully intended to keep.

"I love you, Charlotte Stewart," he quietly vowed. "I want to spend the rest of my life with you. I want to make you happy. Everything else is secondary, including the problems we might face now or in the future. So, I'm asking you to give us a chance."

Her throat went tight, and she had the most ridiculous impulse to burst into tears. But it was silly to cry when everything she'd ever longed for was right in front of her.

"Thank you," she whispered.

His slow smile held a hint of mischief. "You don't need to thank me, love. You just need to kiss me."

"All right, but—"

"Later."

Then he took her mouth, kissing her with relentless, beautiful passion until her mind and body were infused with heat. His kisses were wonderful, but suddenly she wanted more.

She wanted *everything*.

Breaking free, she tried to catch her breath. "Kade, you're driving me insane."

Unlike her, Kade seemed to be very much in control, although his gaze did glitter with blue fire.

"That's rather unfortunate," he replied. "Any suggestions?"

"You're the expert. You tell me."

He choked out a laugh. "I'm not sure whether to be flattered or offended. I'll have to think about that."

Deciding that he needed a bit of his own medicine, Charlie wriggled a bit as she slipped a hand to the back of his neck, gently caressing him. His body seemed to go hard as iron as his arm tightened around her waist. "Please don't think too long. I get bored rather easily, ye ken."

"We canna have ye gettin' bored," he growled in reply, his voice descending to a deep brogue.

He deftly unlaced her old-fashioned shirt and eased it open, exposing the tops of her stays. Gently, he ran a finger along her collarbone and then dipped it under her stays, just brushing the edge of one nipple. She clutched at his shoulders, shivering under his touch.

"Och, that's my sweet lass," he murmured.

He wriggled two fingers under her stays, rubbing over her nipple. His touch was magnetic, like nothing she'd ever experienced before.

"Goodness," she gasped.

He didn't reply, since he was apparently too busy unlacing her stays. When they gaped a bit, he swiped a thumb over the now-stiff peak. Charlie bit her lip, trying not to moan, but he did it again. Sensation shot from the tip of her breast to deep between her thighs, causing her to squirm in his arms.

Kade groaned. "Hell and damnation, sweetheart. You're going to drive *me* to the madhouse."

She reached up and pressed a kiss to the side of his mouth. "As long as they lock us up together, I don't mind."

He snorted and returned his attention to her body, cupping

her breast. "I don't mean to be rude, but your shirt is beginning to annoy me."

"I can fix that," she replied.

When she straightened up, her bottom—and other parts of her—pressed down on his rock-hard erection. She froze, fighting the urge to wriggle against him to assuage the growing ache between her thighs.

Kade studied her through eyes that had narrowed to glittering cobalt slits. "You were saying?"

"Right. My shirt."

Taking her courage—and her shirt—between her hands, she yanked it straight over her head and tossed it to the floor. She obviously surprised Kade even more than she did herself, because his eyes opened wide and a dark flush glazed his cheeks.

Her stays sagged down, partially exposing her breasts, and the cool night air nipped her skin. But the heat in his gaze meant that she barely felt it.

"God, lass," he said in a rough voice. "You are the most beautiful thing I've ever seen."

His look was so riveting, so voracious, that she had to swallow twice before she could answer. "I'm glad you approve."

"I more than approve."

He pressed a lingering kiss to her lips as one hand cupped her breast. Through the fabric of her stays, he thumbed her nipple, teasing and stroking until a sultry heat cascaded through her body. He stroked his fingers up over the swell of her breast, and then slipped them under her sagging stays. When he gently tugged on her nipple, she almost cried out. The sensation was electrifying.

"Kade," she gasped.

"More?"

"Yes."

"Good, because I want to see everything," he growled.

He nudged the straps of her stays down and then tugged on the front. Her breasts popped free. Her nipples, dark and stiff, seemed to grow even tighter under his avid gaze.

"You are so damn lovely," he murmured.

His voice alone seemed to melt every bone in her body

Kade lowered his head, and his tongue flicked out, wetting the stiff peak of her nipple. Charlie tried to squirm, silently urging him to increase the pressure, but he held her firmly as he tormented her. He went from one breast to the other, teasing and flicking his tongue over them until they were equally flushed and hard. Sensation rocked her body, and she couldn't hold back a moan.

"That's it, sweetheart," he rasped, glancing up.

She tightened her hand on the back of his skull and pulled him in for a frenzied kiss. Too soon, he broke free of her.

"Kade," she moaned. "Don't stop—"

She almost choked when he squeezed a flushed nipple between his fingertips. Then his mouth was on her. She jerked, but he held her tightly, lavishing attention on her breasts. For long, delicious moments he played with her, before sucking the stiff peak into his mouth.

Charlie felt herself go up in flames, as everything inside turned hot and wet. She arched her back, pressing against his lips, wanting to give him everything.

But a moment later, he pulled back. Again.

Frustrated, she tried to pull him back down, but he resisted, his mouth curled up in a wry smile.

She couldn't help scowling at him. "Why are you stopping now?"

"I'm not. I just want to see something else."

He grasped the hem of her kilt and flipped it up to her hips. Charlie blinked, a little shocked to be so suddenly exposed.

Well, mostly exposed.

Kade glanced up, his eyes glittering with laughter. "Well, that answers the question of what you wear under your kilt."

She wrinkled her nose. "I know it makes me something of a failure as a true Highlander, but it wouldn't be very comfortable riding a horse without some sort of undergarment. Besides, Mamma would have a fit if I didn't wear them."

He huffed out a chuckle. "Let's leave your mother out of the discussion, shall we? These are very pretty, Charlie, if unconventional. Almost like men's smalls."

"That's what they basically are. Our seamstress made them from a boy's pattern."

Kade's hand drifted over the delicate fabric of her undergarment, which tied at the waist and had legs extending halfway down her thighs. The modified garment protected her while riding and she didn't have to wear a shift. She'd have been happy with a plain garment, but Mamma's seamstress had insisted on trimming the legs with lace and using blue ribbon ties at the waist.

He smiled as he slipped his fingers under the silly lace trim. "I don't know too many Highland lads who would wear lace and ribbons on their smalls."

Charlie narrowed her gaze. "If you laugh, Kade Kendrick, I swear I will murder you."

His smile turned into a full-on grin. "Sweetheart, I love them. And I especially love what's *under* them."

She felt herself blushing. Even though she was covered, the material was thin enough that he could certainly see her intimate parts. She'd also grown damp, which she found both embarrassing and exciting.

When he cupped her sex a moment later, she went breathless.

Kade glanced up. "All right, love?"

"Y . . . yes," she managed.

"Excellent."

He began to gently stroke her through the thin fabric. Instinctively, her knees parted, giving him greater access. Her body grew hot and tight as he caressed her, and it took all her strength not to squirm like a mad thing in his arms.

But just as she began to arch against his hand, pushing into the delicious ache building between her thighs, Kade stilled, lightly cupping her.

Charlie blinked and then peered up at him. "What's wrong?"

After another gentle caress, Kade eased her kilt down over her thighs, smoothing it with a hand that wasn't quite steady.

"Nothing," he replied in a gravelly voice.

"Then why are you stopping?"

"Because if we go on like this, I will very quickly have you flat on your back on that big, comfortable bed over there. And then I'll bury myself deep inside you, love. Of that you can be certain."

Her stomach seemed to do a little flip at that unnerving and yet terribly exciting image. "Oh, and would that be such a bad thing?"

Then she winced. Somewhere along the way, she'd sent her modesty catapulting out the window. Not that she really cared about her modesty at this point. She wanted Kade—all of him—more than she'd ever wanted anything in her life.

He drew in a harsh breath before answering. "No, it would be an excellent thing, especially for me. But it's not how I want to do things with you, Charlie."

"Then how do you want to do things?" she asked, rather perplexed.

"In the appropriate order. That means I make a proper proposal of marriage, we have a proper wedding, and *then* we have a proper wedding night."

Now she began to feel rather grumpy—and frustrated. "But we can still have a proper wedding night, even if we . . ." She twirled a hand.

Kade bit back a smile. "True. And trust me, you tempt me more than I can put into words. But while we were lost in the throes of passion, some dim portion of my brain was not entirely addled with lust, nor was my hearing. And I heard—"

"Oh, Lord," she said with a sigh. "The night footman making his rounds."

"Exactly. It would not do to be discovered like this, Charlie. I will not have you embarrassed, for one thing. And if your parents found out, your father would likely murder me before I managed to explain that I'm going to marry you."

She patted him on the chest. "That's very noble of you, but the footman only patrols once every hour, so we should be fine."

"It's not noble at all. It's bloody inconvenient. But there's too much going on for us to do this properly. Scabby Sir Leslie could be wandering about the place, up to God knows what, or—"

She grimaced. "Or it could be my father. Even though I promised I wouldn't cause any more trouble, I don't think he's convinced."

"So he might check to see if you're in your room."

"He probably won't, though." She gave him an encouraging smile. "And if we're quick—"

Kade tipped her upright into a sitting position. "I have no intention of rushing this, Charlie. We'll have all the time we need soon enough."

When she crossed her arms under her naked breasts, plumping them up, she could practically hear him grinding his molars.

"Are you sure?" she asked in a coaxing voice.

His laugh sounded more like a groan. "No, I'm not. And you're a vixen to keep tempting me like this."

Charlie couldn't help smiling. "No one's ever called me a vixen before except you."

"Then they haven't been paying attention. Now, up with you, lass."

"Very well," she grumbled.

She climbed off his lap, doing her best to ignore the massive erection that was tenting the front of his trousers. Wincing a bit, Kade stood and then helped her restore her stays to order and put on her shirt.

Finally, he leaned down and kissed the tip of her nose. "There, all is well now. Even if you do run into someone, you look perfectly respectable."

"I don't feel very respectable," she replied. "I feel frustrated."

"I share your pain."

"It's a rather large pain, from what I can see."

He snorted. "Och, lass."

"It's just that I've been waiting forever," she said.

And, yes, she sounded cross, but that was his fault for so thoroughly working her up.

Kade took her hand and led her to the door. "I promise to make it worth your wait."

"You'd better, or I'll be *quite* annoyed with you."

When he laughed, she flapped a hand. "Sorry, it's just that I'm not quite sure how to behave under the circumstances—not that I've ever been very good at behaving, really. According to Mamma I'm much too forward, as my actions tonight would seem to bear out."

Kade leaned down and brushed a soft kiss across her lips. "As long as you're only forward with me."

"You have no competition, I assure you. Until you showed up, I was quite convinced that I would end my days as a spinster."

"I hope you're happy with your impending change in circumstances," he replied as he reached for the doorknob.

"Of course I am. But there are still more than a few things we need to discuss, and—"

He gently shushed her as he opened the door and sent a quick glance down the hall.

"All is quiet," he murmured and led her out.

"Kade, I'm perfectly capable of finding my way back to my room," she whispered as he accompanied her toward the family wing.

"I'm not letting you wander around alone," he whispered back. "It's not safe."

There was no point in arguing with the stubborn man, since he was clearly the overprotective sort. And even though she didn't really need protecting, Charlie had to admit that it made her feel cherished in a way she'd never felt before.

They soft-footed their way to the corridor that led to her bedroom, and a quick glance showed that it was empty.

Kade leaned down to murmur in her ear. "I'll wait till you're safely inside."

She nodded, and then stretched up on her tiptoes to kiss him. He lingered for a moment, his hand caressing her shoulder.

"Good night, love," he whispered. "Sweet dreams."

Charlie smiled at him and then quietly pattered down to her room. A glance over her shoulder showed he still waited, now merely a shadow in the darkness. She raised a hand in farewell and then slipped into her bedroom, carefully shutting the door without a sound.

She leaned against it as she eyed her big, empty bed. She suspected that sleep would elude her tonight. Her nerves still vibrated with lingering desire, and a dozen questions buzzed inside her skull. Once again, those questions had gone unanswered. Kade was the most wonderful man in the world, but also annoyingly adept at avoiding issues he wasn't ready to discuss. He'd obviously decided that solving their immediate problems came first. Only then could they truly talk about their future.

Or make mad, passionate love, finally.

Feeling almost as frustrated as when she'd first knocked on his door, Charlie trudged off to bed. Answers—and lovemaking—would have to wait.

CHAPTER 20

Charlie leaned against the terrace balustrade and peered out over the garden, looking for Kade.

After a restless night, she'd risen well past her normal time and had hurried down to breakfast, hoping to catch him. Unfortunately, Kade had already been and gone. She'd tried the music room next, but she'd had no better luck there.

"Where is the dratted man?" she muttered to herself.

Her reputed fiancé was, as usual, proving elusive. Had the clear light of day brought him second thoughts about his promises to her? As hard as she tried, she couldn't shake the unwelcome notion that Kade had put a stop to their love-making because he still harbored doubts about their future. If he did, of course she wouldn't press him or stop him from walking away. But it would break her heart into a thousand pieces, and how would she survive that?

She blew out an exasperated breath, disgusted with her inability to control her emotions. They continued to spin around in her head like a top.

You're as silly and as mawkish as Melissa.

That thought made her snort with laughter. Love and lack of sleep had clearly addled her brain. Still, Charlie knew she couldn't be easy again until she saw Kade.

She was about to go inside when she heard footsteps on

the path from the stables. Kade appeared, dressed in riding gear. He took the terrace steps two at a time and crossed to join her.

"Good morning," he said. "I'm sorry I didn't see you at breakfast. Did you sleep in a bit?"

Charlie took a moment to appreciate how splendid he looked in the well-cut breeches that outlined his long, muscular legs and the hacking jacket that showcased his broad shoulders.

Then she frowned. "You've been out riding."

When his eyebrows ticked up at her unfortunately chippy tone, she winced.

"Oh, dear," she added quickly. "I don't mean to sound rude. It's just that I've been looking for you."

"I thought to go for an early ride. I was up anyway, and I needed to clear my head."

That did *not* sound good.

Still, Charlie forced herself to respond calmly. "Kade, are you having second thoughts about us? It's quite all right if you are, you know. I understand. It's . . . it's a very big decision."

Now his eyebrows went up almost comically high, and his expression suggested he thought her dicked in the nob.

She flapped a hand. "Never mind. Forget I said anything. How was your ride?"

Kade cast a quick glance around and then clamped his hands on her shoulders and backed her up against the house. He kissed her with a passion as intense as a summer storm. Her knees buckled with relief, and she clutched at the lapels of his jacket to keep her balance.

And just like a summer storm, the kiss ended as quickly as it had swept in. When Kade released her and took a step back, Charlie flattened her hands against the warm brick wall at her back, barely able to catch her breath.

"Daft girl," he said, a hint of brogue roughening his deep voice. "Does that answer your question?"

Charlie somehow managed a coherent response. "Yes, thank you. That was quite satisfactory."

"Only 'quite'?" Devilment gleamed in his eyes. "I'm crushed."

She crossed her arms. "Kade Kendrick, you have legions of girls mooning after you all the time. You'll get a swelled head if you don't watch out."

His smile was slow, sensual, and stole the breath she'd only just recovered.

"You're the only girl I want mooning after me, Charlie. And I'll be happy to have another go at kissing, if you think I'm in need of improvement."

Laughter and relief combined to fizz through her veins like sweet autumn cider.

"Hmm," she said. "I'll have to think about that."

He scoffed. "Is that a challenge?"

"I rather think it is."

She was stretching out a hand, intending to pull him back in, when heavy footsteps crunched on the gravel path. Kade glanced over his shoulder and took a step back.

"Rats," she grumbled.

Her father rounded the corner of the house, dressed in riding togs; it was apparent he'd just come from the stables as well.

He joined them on the terrace, eyeing them with a frown. "Am I interrupting a private discussion?"

Charlie crossed her fingers behind her back. "Don't be silly, Papa. I just happened to be in the music room when Kade, I mean, Mr. Kendrick, came out from the stables."

Her father's gaze narrowed with suspicion. "Kade, is it? I hope you're not engaging in a silly flirtation with Mr.

Kendrick, Charlotte. Your mother does not approve of silly flirtations."

Heat crawled up her neck and onto her face, no doubt turning her cheeks apple red. Kade, however, merely adopted an expression of vague surprise, as if such a thought would never occur to him. He was really *very* good at hiding his emotions. It was a talent she'd love to acquire someday.

Charlie spread her hands wide. "Papa, when have you ever known me to flirt with anyone?"

"Humph." He still looked disgruntled.

As Kade studied her with a bland expression, his cobalt gaze gleamed with unholy amusement.

"Nor would I ever assume that so worldly a man as Mr. Kendrick would be interested in a country bumpkin like me," she tartly added. "How silly would that be?"

"I must object, Miss Stewart," Kade politely stated. "You greatly underestimate your charms."

She rounded her eyes at him. "And what charms would those be, sir? Perhaps you would care to list them for me?"

Kade's lips twitched.

Charlie's father leveled a scowl at her. "I certainly hope you're not twitting me, my girl. You've caused enough trouble these last few days, what with your blasted Kinloch Fiddler driving off poor Richard. Your mamma is very disappointed about that, you know. As am I."

"I'm sorry, Papa. But you could plainly see that Richard and I didn't suit. We probably would have killed each other within weeks of the wedding."

"You mean you would have killed him," Papa said with a snort.

Charlie flashed him a sheepish smile. "Probably."

"Well, I suppose you're right," he said. "Richard was a disappointment with those ridiculous outfits and that ghastly curled hair. No decent fellow ever thought to curl his hair

back in my day, or wear a corset, for God's sake." He looked
at Kade. "You don't wear a corset, do you?"

"Really, Papa," Charlie protested. "That's a bit much."

Kade, however, was unflappable. "I do not, sir. My brother,
Lord Arnprior, would throw me off the battlements of Castle
Kinglas if I resorted to such affectations."

"Quite right, too," Papa said. "Good head on his shoulders, that brother of yours. And I'll admit that you're a very
sensible fellow as well, even though the young ladies are
always flocking around you like magpies. Even Melissa,
which seems a bit odd since she just got riveted to poor
Colin."

That, rather comically, was true.

"Let's hope he doesn't challenge Mr. Kendrick to a duel,"
Charlie joked.

Her father looked rather aghast. "Good God, Charlotte.
Don't even jest about such a thing. You'll give Melissa the
vapors, and your poor mother already has enough to deal
with, what with Johnny being laid up."

She patted his arm. "Sorry, Papa."

He scoffed. "You're not the least bit sorry. Now, I'm going
to change and then see how Johnny is doing. Try to stay out
of trouble, all right? And stop pestering Mr. Kendrick. I'm
sure he has better things to do than lark about with your
nonsense."

"Yes, Papa."

After a nod to Kade, her father stomped into the house.

Charlie stared after him. "I wonder what's got him so lath-
ered up. Did you see him when you were out riding? Did he
say anything to you?"

"No, I just ran into him back at the stables," he replied.

She sensed that Kade was not being entirely forthcoming.
"And he didn't seemed fashed, or worried about anything in
particular? Besides booby Richard, I mean."

"Not at all, though now it seems he's worried that we

might be engaging in a mad flirtation," he replied with a wry smile.

She sighed. "Yes, that was a rather awkward discussion—imagine asking if you wore a corset! Even for Papa, that was too much."

Kade took her hand and twinned their fingers together. "Since, as I previously noted, my family excels at awkward discussions, I'd say we're perfectly well matched."

"I'm afraid my father might not agree."

"I'll bring him around, love. Try not to worry."

"I'll try," she said. "It's still so unreal to me, as if we couldn't possibly work out there in the wider world. And if Papa doesn't approve . . ."

It would be yet another obstacle in their path.

Kade brushed a soft kiss across her lips. "It is entirely real, and it will absolutely work. Although your parents might be a bit surprised, I'm sure they'll approve once they realize how much I love their daughter and wish to take care of her."

Charlie mustered a smile. "That's so lovely, Kade. Still, I don't want you thinking that you need to take care of me. I'm not to be a burden to you." She held up a hand, as if making a vow. "And I solemnly promise never to fall into hysterics, no matter what happens."

Her secret fear, she supposed, was that she wouldn't fit into his world and would therefore be a hindrance to him. The very idea that she might be a burden to him made her queasy.

"You could never be a burden, love, and everyone needs taking care of now and again," he gently replied. "I certainly do. Besides, I'm hoping we'll take care of each other."

She patted his chest. "That sounds nice."

Yet, there were many unanswered questions. Where would they live? Would he want her to go on tour with him? Charlie was quite certain that her happiness involved more than simply being married to Kade. Her happiness would be found in *being* with him, in every way. But would he feel the same?

"Speaking of taking care of each other," she said, "I'm hoping that we can finally have that discussion about—"

"Absolutely," he said. "Later, perhaps?"

Charlie exhaled a frustrated sigh. "That's what you said last night."

"I thought we worked through quite a few problems last night."

"Yes, but—"

A moment later, he had her once more backed up against the house. As he tilted up her chin, his gaze glittered with sensual intent. For a moment, Charlie was tempted to give him a scold, but then she realized she wanted to kiss him as much as he apparently wanted to kiss her.

She stretched up to meet—

Angus exploded out of the French doors beside them, and Charlie almost jumped out of her shoes.

"There's nae time for canoodling," Angus barked. "There's trouble afoot."

"Good God, Angus," Kade exclaimed. "You almost gave me a bloody heart attack. What the hell is going on?"

"Yer needed upstairs. The lassie, too."

Charlie's heart skipped a beat. Although Angus was highly prone to drama, his wrinkled features expressed genuine concern.

"What's wrong?" she asked.

"It's Johnny. He's nae good."

Kade frowned. "Explain, Grandda."

Angus flapped his hands to shoo them inside. "When he didna come down for breakfast, yer ma went up to check on him. Johnny didna want to wake up, and now he's verra lethargic."

Charlie's stomach took a sharp dip as anxiety gripped her.

"That makes no sense," she said as the three of them hurried to the front of the house. "Except for some pain in his shoulder last night, he seemed fine."

Kade rested a comforting hand on her back before they started up the central staircase.

"Does he have a fever?" he asked Angus. "Is his injury inflamed?"

"I only ken what Elspeth just told me, but it doesna seem likely to me. It was a clean break."

"Has a doctor been sent for?" Charlie asked.

"I dinna ken. I talked to Elspeth and then came straight for ye."

When they reached the top of the stairs, she picked up her skirts and ran to her brother's room.

Kade caught up just as she was about to yank open the door to Johnny's room.

"Wait, love, wait," he said, grabbing hold of her wrist.

By now, her heart was racing so fast she could barely catch her breath.

"Why? I need to get in there," she gasped.

His gaze was warm with sympathy. "Better to catch your breath for a moment first. It won't do to go bursting in like the room is on fire."

Charlie sucked in a deep breath, forcing her heart and mind to settle a bit. "You're right, of course. I just lost my head for a minute."

Along with fear had come the sudden realization that they'd—she'd—left Johnny exposed. Had Sir Leslie tried to hurt him again, or even made an attempt on his life?

Kade gently chafed her hands. "You're fine, sweetheart."

Angus came puffing up to join them. "Yer ma and Melissa are in there. Yer housekeeper, too. They'll be lookin' after wee Johnny."

Kade winced. "Melissa is in a sickroom?"

"I know it seems strange," Charlie said, "but Melissa has been a surprisingly good nurse when any of us has fallen ill."

"She was a right mess when Johnny fell, though," Angus commented in a skeptical tone.

"She was simply startled. Besides, we could all tell right away that Johnny wasn't really in danger. It's when Melissa isn't hysterical that one has to worry."

Like now.

Angus grimaced. "That's nae good."

Riven with guilt, Charlie squeezed her eyes shut. "This is all my fault."

Kade gently tugged on her hands. "Charlie, how could this be your fault?"

She opened her eyes, staring miserably up to meet his infinitely kind gaze. "Because I should have been keeping a better eye on him. What if Sir Leslie got in during the night and did something to him? Tried to . . ."

Poison him.

Her throat constricted around those words. If that brute had hurt Johnny in any way, she would never forgive herself.

"Lassie's got a point," Angus admitted. "The timin' is too suspicious for my likin'. I wouldna put anything past that scabby varlet."

"Nor would I," Kade replied. "But Sir Leslie didn't leave his room last night, so I'm not yet sure if we can blame this on him."

Charlie blinked. "How do you know that?"

"Because I locked him in after he retired. I unlocked his door shortly after dawn, once I knew the servants were stirring."

"How did you manage that?" she asked. "The keys are kept in the butler's quarters."

Kade shrugged. "I didn't need a key to lock him in."

Angus tapped the side of his nose. "Spycraft, I reckon."

For a moment, Charlie was diverted. "That sounds very interesting. Will you teach me how to do it?"

"Of course, love," he said with a fleeting smile. "I hope you won't use it on me, though."

Angus rolled his eyes. "We have nae time for yer flirtin',

laddie boy. We've got to find out what happened to Johnny. I still have my suspicions that Sir Leslie somehow got to the poor fellow. We need to be keepin' a close eye on the varlet, in case he gives anythin' away."

"He's a canny one," Kade replied, "so I doubt he'll express any emotion other than concern for Johnny. Still, we must certainly watch him."

Just then, Charlie's father hurried toward them from the other end of the hall. He was dressed in his riding gear but looked rather disheveled, as if he'd started to change but had then hastily thrown his clothes back on.

"What's this I hear about Johnny?" he asked, clearly agitated. "Is it the fever? What in God's name is going on?"

When Kade threw Charlie a warning glance, she gave him a slight nod in return. Obviously, he wasn't yet ready to raise suspicions against Sir Leslie.

She pressed a reassuring hand to her father's arm. "No, it's not a fever. But apparently he was quite lethargic this morning."

"Has anyone sent for a doctor?" Papa asked.

Charlie shook her head. "I don't think so."

"I can fetch him, sir," Kade said. "Anything I can do to help."

"No, I'll send one of the grooms," Papa brusquely replied. "But someone needs to tell me now what the hell is wrong with my son so the blasted doctor will know what he's going to be dealing with."

The bedroom door suddenly opened, and Charlie's mother stepped out. "Please stop shouting, Henry. It is not helpful to have such a commotion."

Papa immediately looked contrite. "Sorry, my dear. My valet just informed me that Johnny has taken a bad turn, so you can't blame a father for being upset."

"From what I saw earlier," Angus observed, "ye could shoot off a cannon in the lad's room without wakin' him."

"Good God," Papa exclaimed. "What's wrong with the lad?"

"I don't know," Mamma replied. "Melissa and I finally managed to rouse him, but the doctor should certainly be sent for. Johnny is clearly not himself."

"I'll send a groom to fetch . . . no, hang it, I'll go myself. I'm already dressed for it. What do I need to tell the doctor, so he brings the right gear to treat the boy?"

"I'll walk with you to the stables. We can talk on the way." Mamma glanced at Charlie. "Please go in and help your sister, my dear."

Once her parents hurried off, Charlie glanced at Kade. "You'll find Sir Leslie and keep an eye on him?"

He gave her a reassuring smile. "Yes, and don't worry. Just take care of your brother."

Then he strode off in the direction of the guest wing.

"I need to go in with ye, lass," Angus said. "I might be able to tell what's wrong with wee Johnny and get a jump on treatin' him."

"But shouldn't we wait for the physician?" she asked.

He regarded her with a kind but serious expression. "The lads like to twit me about my doctorin' skills, but I do ken a great deal about herbs and medicinals. My dear wife taught me. If someone's slipped Johnny somethin', I might be able to tell what it is."

Charlie nodded as she opened the door. "Of course. That makes perfect sense."

Only one lamp and the small peat fire in the grate lighted the room. Johnny, clad in a wool robe, was in a chair by the fire. Melissa knelt in front of him, helping him drink a glass of water while their housekeeper was putting fresh linens on the bed.

Thank God.

If her brother was out of bed, he must be feeling somewhat better.

"Och, it's as dark as a dungeon in here," Angus said,

crossing to the closed curtains. "Johnny could stand a wee bit of light and fresh air, I reckon."

"Don't open the curtains too much," Melissa warned. "The light hurts his eyes."

Angus cast her a sharp glance. "Does it, now? Well, that's somethin' to think about."

Charlie went to her brother and sister. Johnny, rumpled and bleary-eyed, seemed to be having trouble focusing on her.

When she took his hands, they felt clammy. "How are you, dearest?"

"I feel like the devil," he slowly replied, his words a bit slurred. "Don't know what's wrong with me."

When Angus drew aside one of the curtains, letting light into the room, Charlie had to bite back a gasp. Johnny looked ill as death. His features were wan and pasty and sweat had plastered the hair to his forehead.

"Ugh," he muttered, scrunching his eyes against the light.

Charlie cast a worried glance at her sister.

"He's better than he was," Melissa said. "At least he's now awake and talking."

Angus joined them and leaned in to peer at Johnny. "Can ye open yer eyes wider, lad? Just for a wee second or two."

Johnny opened his eyes, hissing with the effort.

Angus studied his face for a few seconds and then patted him on the shoulder. "Ye can close yer eyes and rest now, young fella. Ye've nothing to worry about."

With a grateful sigh, Johnny did just that.

Charlie rose, took the water glass from Melissa, and helped her to stand. They moved out of the way as Mrs. Martin brought over a light blanket and gently tucked it around Johnny.

"Is he really better?" Charlie whispered to Melissa.

"Yes. At first, Mamma and I couldn't even rouse him. We finally just hauled him up, and Mamma splashed cold water on his face. That did the trick, thank heavens."

Angus stroked his chin. "Do ye ken what time he went to bed last night?"

"The same time as the rest of us," Charlie said. "Mamma insisted on it."

Melissa nodded. "That's right. In fact, Colin helped him up to bed before coming to our room."

Angus flashed her a smile. "He's a good one, is your Colin."

"I think so, too," Melissa shyly replied.

The housekeeper joined them. "Mr. Johnny is dozin' right now. But his breathin' is better. Regular, as it should be."

"Havin' trouble breathin', was he?" Angus asked.

"Yes," replied Melissa. "That's what really worried us. He wasn't in a natural sleep."

"Hmm," Angus murmured. "I dinna remember him being in his cups last night."

"I've seen Johnny in his cups," Charlie said, "and it's nothing like this. He's actually got a very hard head."

"Mr. Johnny did ask for a glass of wine to bring up to bed, though," Mrs. Martin said. "To help him sleep."

Angus frowned. "Does he often do that?"

"Nae, sir."

"Is that the glass?" Angus asked, glancing at the bedside table.

"Yes." Mrs. Martin quickly fetched it.

"Thank ye," he said. "Now, will ye be so kind as to bring wee Johnny a pot of tea? Make it nice and strong."

The housekeeper bobbed a curtsy. "Aye, sir. I'll bring it right up."

Angus waited until she left the room and then held the wineglass up to the light. There were only dregs left in the bottom.

"It simply looks like red wine," Charlie said.

"Aye, but looks can be deceivin'." He sniffed the contents.

Frowning, he dipped a finger into the glass and took a cautious taste of the dregs.

Melissa gasped. "Was the wine bad? I do hope no one else drank it!"

"Easy, lass," Angus replied in a soothing tone. "It's nae the wine that's the problem."

Poison, then?

Charlie worked to keep her voice steady as that thought hammered her brain. "Do you think something has been added to the wine?"

Melissa cast her a startled glance. "Charlotte, what are you talking about?"

"Does anyone in the house use laudanum drops?" Angus asked.

Melissa hesitated for a few seconds. "I do, which I suppose is no surprise. But I don't use them very often. They make me feel too fuzzy and sometimes upset my stomach." Then her eyes popped wide. "But I never gave them to Johnny, I promise!"

"Of course ye didn't," Angus said, patting her shoulder. "Does yer local sawbones make the drops up for ye? Do ye ken what he adds to the bottle?"

Charlie frowned. "What sort of things might he add?"

"The drops themselves taste very bitter," Melissa explained. "You add sugar and other flavorings to make it more palatable." She looked at Angus. "When the chemist makes up my drops, he adds cloves and cinnamon."

When he held the glass out to Melissa, she took a sniff and nodded.

"Yes, that's what my drops smell like." She grimaced. "Johnny must have taken them from my room and added them to his wine. To help with the pain, I'm sure."

"Nae doubt that's what he did," Angus said in an easy tone. "The lad just overdid it a bit."

Given the way Johnny had twitted Melissa about her

drops in the past, Charlie knew very well that he'd not given himself a dose of laudanum. She could tell that Angus was also keeping any doubts to himself, thank God. If Melissa were to find out that Sir Leslie had possibly attempted to poison poor Johnny, all hell would break loose.

Her hand curled into an involuntary fist as she struggled to keep her anger from showing.

All hell *would* break loose soon enough, and it would come from her. Because if Sir Leslie had indeed dosed Johnny, and she had little doubt that he had, Charlie would haul the bastard to the top of the tower and toss him right off.

She took a deep breath, forcing calm. "Is Johnny going to be all right?"

"Nae worries, lass," Angus replied. "Yer sawbones will likely give him a purgative, which is nae fun, but it'll help. And we'll give him lots of strong tea and get him drinkin' water, too. He'll be right as rain in no time."

Melissa expelled a shaky breath. "Thank goodness. I'd never forgive myself if something happened to poor Johnny."

Angus winked at her. "It was just a foolish mistake, ye ken. My grandsons were always gettin' into trouble, back in the day. Johnny's nae different."

Yes, it was a foolish mistake, but it was on Sir Leslie's part, not Johnny's. Because Charlie was now coming for him, and the villain would live to regret it.

CHAPTER 21

"Taking the day off, are you, Kendrick?" Morgan commented as he strolled into the drawing room. "You've got a concerto or some such to finish, don't you? Odd, then, that I find you sitting at your leisure this morning, reading the papers."

Angus, trailing in behind Morgan, rolled his eyes before wandering over to have a chat with Colin on the other side of the room. Kade had tasked his grandfather with keeping an eye on their suspect at breakfast, because it would leave him free to search Morgan's room. While doing so, he'd had to dodge a chambermaid's sudden appearance by ducking out an open window and hanging about on the windowsill until she left, but that barely qualified as an inconvenience.

All in all, keeping an eye on Morgan hadn't exactly been a stretch, since the blighter had made it blindingly easy.

Kade gave him a polite smile. "Yes, I thought I'd take the day off."

"How delightfully madcap of you," Morgan drawled. "But how will you fill the hours, old boy? You're such a slave to your work."

Kade studied him for a moment, pondering how to answer. *Why not push it?*

"As a matter of fact," he replied, "I thought I'd go on a

treasure hunt. Now that Johnny's feeling better, I'll look for Miss Charlotte's brooch. It's not going to find itself, after all."

Morgan's left eye twitched, but he mustered a credibly amused smile. "Oh, ho, so that's the way the wind blows. Didn't know you intended to throw your hat in the ring for that one."

Kade folded his paper and set it on the gateleg table beside him. "I'm only trying to help recover a cherished family heirloom, although Miss Charlotte's gratitude will certainly be a bonus."

Morgan winked at him. "Ah, playing your cards close to the chest. You sly dog! Not that I'm in the running, you understand. The field is all yours."

"I understood from Johnny that you are indeed in the running."

"I was simply jesting. Not really looking to get leg-shackled at the moment." He waggled his eyebrows. "Although Miss Charlotte is certainly quite the filly, isn't she? She'd give a fellow a run for the money."

For a moment, Kade seriously contemplated drilling his fist into the smug bastard's face.

Later.

"Indeed," he blandly said.

"And what splendid news about Johnny, I must say." He gave an indulgent chuckle. "Although I need to give the dear boy a bit of a scold when he's up to receiving visitors. He should know by now how to properly dose himself with those bloody drops. Can't imagine how he made such a silly mistake."

Kade raised his eyebrows. "I hadn't realized Johnny used laudanum on a regular basis."

Morgan waved a dismissive hand. "Only occasionally, when he has the headache or suffers from a bout of nerves." He leaned close, as if confiding a secret. "Seems to run in the family, if you know what I mean."

Kade abruptly stood, forcing Morgan to step back. "Johnny never struck me as the nervous type. Of course, you would know better than me, since you're such good friends. But I wonder if perhaps you should inform Lady Kinloch that Johnny has been using drops."

Morgan shifted his feet. "I'd hate to grass on the poor boy. But I'll be sure to drop a hint in Johnny's ear when next I see him. I assume he'll be coming downstairs today?"

"I believe the doctor advised Lady Kinloch that it would be best for Johnny to remain in his room for the next few days. The effects of an overdose can take some time to wear off, I understand."

After the physician's call on Johnny yesterday—and the administration of unpleasant but apparently effective purgatives—the young man had slept for the rest of the day and much of the night. While the lad would likely be fine today, Kade had every intention of keeping him safely out of the way until his tormentor was locked up tight.

Morgan nodded. "Very sensible. I'll simply have to wait until tomorrow to visit with him. By the way, old man, are you finished with those papers?"

After Kade handed them over, Morgan sauntered over to one of the club chairs by the fireplace and made a show of settling in. Kade glanced at Angus, who returned a slight nod to indicate that he would keep a weather eye on their prey.

Kade left the room and headed upstairs. He needed to speak with Charlie, and then they both needed to speak with Johnny. Hopefully, yesterday's scare would convince the lad that it was time to open up.

Charlie had insisted on spending the night in Johnny's room, watching over her brother like a mother fox with one kit—armed with a pistol, no less. It had been an unnecessary precaution, because once Morgan had retired for the night, Kade had again locked him in.

He'd not tried to talk Charlie out of standing watch. She

felt a great deal of responsibility for her brother and more than a little guilt. Kade well understood the protective instincts of older siblings. When he was a boy and quite ill, Nick had often remained by his side into the deep watches of the night, as if doing so could hold back whatever dangers might threaten Kade. Charlie felt the same kind of loyalty toward her little brother, but he hoped his lass would soon realize that she wasn't alone anymore. Kade was more than willing to fight for her and with her, and for Johnny, too.

As he paused outside the lad's bedroom door, he heard the muffled murmur of voices and hoped Johnny was finally confiding in his sister. They needed the full truth if there was to be any chance of bringing Morgan to heel.

That the blighter was a canny one was beyond doubt. So far, he'd not give them much in the way of incriminating evidence, nor had he attempted to visit Johnny. Instead, he'd attended to the rest of the family with great solicitude. He'd been at pains to spend time with Lady Kinloch and Melissa and had played billiards with Lord Kinloch and Colin. At one point, Morgan had asked about Charlie's whereabouts. When informed that she was keeping a strict watch on her brother, he'd simply nodded and gone back to helping Melissa sort her embroidery threads, all while telling amusing stories about life in Edinburgh.

In other words, the suspect was doing his utmost to deflect any suspicion that he might have something to do with Johnny's troubles.

Kade knocked, and a few moments later Charlie opened the door.

"Good morning, Kade. I was wondering when you would show up."

He cast a quick glance down the hall before bending to give her a kiss. Charlie's hand came fleetingly to rest on his chest. Then she gave him a little push and stepped out into the hall, closing the door behind her.

"Sorry," he said. "I couldn't resist. Is Johnny all right?"

"Yes, thank goodness. He's tired and his shoulder is bothering him, which is to be expected. It's his state of mind that worries me. He's quite despondent and afraid, although he's doing his best to hide it from me."

"He'll feel better once he tells us the truth."

"I hope so. He slept quite late, and then Mamma spent time with him this morning, so we haven't had much chance to talk."

Kade took in her kilt and riding boots. "I take it you were able to go for a ride this morning while your mother was with him."

"Yes, I thought a bit of fresh air and a gallop would clear the cobwebs from my brain."

He studied her face, noting the shadows under her eyes. "Did you get any sleep?"

"A bit, and you're not to worry about me. I'm perfectly fine."

"I can't help but worry. You're looking a bit pulled around the edges, love."

"That, sir, is your fault," she wryly replied. "You're the one who kept me up so late the previous night."

"True, but let's not forget the Kinloch Fiddler's appearance," Kade said. "You've been burning the candle at both ends, my darling, and sadly not with me."

Charlie blushed a bit and gave him such a sweet smile that he was hard-pressed not to back her up against the door and start kissing her. Or pick her up and carry her off to his bed.

"Then the sooner we bring this to an end, the sooner I'll be able to get a good night's sleep," she replied. "Since you're up here, I take it that Angus is shadowing Sir Leslie."

"Yes, although I'm afraid the old boy is in for a boring time of it. Morgan is being very careful."

"Not for long, I suspect. He needs to get his hands on the

brooch, which means he needs to get to my brother. We can't keep Johnny locked up in his room indefinitely."

"No, so we need to have a frank conversation with him. Do you think he's ready to talk now?"

She waggled a hand. "I haven't wanted to push him. I'm hoping you'll have better luck."

"I'm sure the poor lad is mortified. Whenever one of my brothers did something particularly idiotic, they invariably clammed up."

"I suspect no one was trying to kill them, though."

"You'd be surprised. I will say, however, that I don't think Morgan is actually trying to kill Johnny."

Charlie frowned. "He seems to be making a fairly good go of it."

He reached around her and opened the door. "Patience, love. We'll get to that."

She blew out a frustrated breath but let him shepherd her into the room.

Johnny was ensconced in an armchair by the fire, covered in a blanket. He was awkwardly trying to manage a cup of tea with his injured arm.

"Charlie, could you help me with this blasted—" He broke off, his eyes going wide when he saw Kade.

"Of course, dearest." She relieved him of the cup. "You're not supposed to be using that hand, remember?"

He winced as he adjusted his arm in its sling. "I tried to use my left hand, but I ended up spilling a glass of water down the front of my nightshirt. Mamma had to help me change the stupid thing."

"I injured my shoulder some weeks back," Kade said, giving him a friendly smile. "It's a bloody nuisance, isn't it?"

Johnny grimaced. "Sorry, I don't mean to complain, but I'm getting rather tired of being an invalid. First my collarbone, and now this stupid . . . well, me being stupid, I suppose."

Kade studied him. "Except you weren't being stupid, were you, Johnny?"

The lad blinked a few times and then looked away. "I . . . I'm not sure what you're talking about."

Charlie crossed her arms and gave him a rather stern look. "Johnny, you didn't dose yourself with laudanum, accidental or otherwise. And it certainly wasn't Melissa. So that only leaves one other person."

"You don't know anything about it," he replied in a chippy tone. "You should just leave it alone."

Charlie shook her head. "Johnny—"

"You don't know what he's like!" her brother suddenly burst out as he struggled to his feet. "You need to stay out of it, Charlie. I can manage it."

"Present circumstances would suggest otherwise," she retorted.

For several seconds, sister and brother glared at each other, their jawlines set in identical, stubborn lines.

"Well, this is getting us nowhere," Kade finally said. "Perhaps we might all take a seat and have a sensible conversation like the adults that we are."

Charlie grimaced. "I suppose we do sound rather like squabbling children, don't we?"

Kade held his thumb and forefinger about an inch apart.

"Wretch," she said with a little snort.

She dragged over an armchair from the other side of the fireplace, while Kade fetched a padded bench from under the window.

"I know it's been a frightening time," Kade said to Johnny, once they were seated. "But let me just say that I don't think Morgan is trying to kill you. And he's certainly not going to harm anyone in your family, so I think matters aren't as dire as they seem."

Charlie frowned at him. "Not trying to kill him? In both

incidents, Johnny could have been seriously harmed, if not killed."

"*Could* being the operative word," Kade replied. "I'm guessing that Sir Leslie lost his temper and acted on impulse when he shoved your brother down that embankment. Isn't that right, Johnny?"

The young man simply stared miserably into the fire.

"It's all right, lad. You can tell us," Kade gently urged. "Morgan's not going to hurt you or anyone else, I promise you that."

Charlie rested a hand on her brother's knee. "We've always been honest with each other, haven't we? You can trust me, dearest. You know that."

The young man sighed. "I know, Charlie. But I've made such a cock-up of things. And I betrayed you, too."

"You did no such thing."

"I took your brooch and then lied about it," he whispered, finally meeting her gaze.

Charlie flashed him a rueful smile. "I took it first, remember? I'm the idiot who started this whole thing, so there's plenty of blame to go around."

"You were just protecting yourself, though," Johnny said. "I'm the one who made it so much worse. I've been trying to find a way out of it, but I just can't see it. And if Papa finds out, he'll probably disinherit me."

She patted his knee. "You leave Papa to me. Now, will you answer Kade's question? Do you think Sir Leslie acted on impulse when he shoved you off the embankment?"

"I suppose I might as well tell you everything," Johnny said after a long moment. "You seemed to have guessed it all anyway. And I'll tell you where I hid the brooch."

"I've already retrieved the brooch and am keeping it safe, so you needn't worry about that," Kade replied.

Johnny's eyes popped rather wide. "You found it on your own? Then I guess you are a master spy after all."

Kade found himself unable to stifle a weary sigh. "Angus strikes again, I assume."

"He did mention quite casually that you were a very important agent for the Crown. I wondered at the time why he would tell me something like that. It seemed rather fantastical," Johnny said with an apologetic smile.

"The fantasy is mostly in my grandfather's head," Kade dryly replied. "But I can help you. That's why Charlie and I need you to tell us everything you can."

The lad nodded. "All right. I do think Sir Leslie just lost his temper. We had a blazing row, and I told him that I had no intention of giving him the brooch. Then I told him to sod off. The next thing I knew, I was tumbling down the embankment."

"Did Morgan say anything to you afterwards?" Kade asked.

"He came to my room after the doctor and tried to apologize." Johnny huffed out a bitter laugh. "He tried to blame the whole thing on me because I'd gone back on my word. He said no one could blame him for losing his temper, since it was a matter of honor."

"What bollocks," Charlie muttered.

"Because you lost money to him at cards?" Kade asked.

"Yes."

Charlie shook her head in disgust. "Sir Leslie doesn't have a shred of honor in his entire body."

"I'm sorry, Sis," Johnny said, sounding miserable again.

"Apology accepted, dearest. But how did you know it was me who stole the brooch in the first place?"

When Johnny started to shrug his shoulders, he winced and shifted uncomfortably. "It made the most sense. I know how careful you are with the brooch, but I also knew how much you wanted to get rid of Richard."

"Well done, you," she wryly replied. "So you searched all our secret hiding places and found it."

"It was unbelievably selfish of me, I know. But Sir Leslie was due here in a few days, and he'd already told me that he would tell Papa everything if I didn't pay up. I thought that if I gave him the brooch, he would be satisfied. I . . . I suppose I just lost my head."

"Then why didn't you simply give it to him?" Kade asked.

The young man's gaze turned angry. "I couldn't betray Charlie, especially not after Sir Leslie started making noises about using the brooch to force her to marry him. Bad enough that he would get his grubby hands on the brooch, but the thought of him marrying Charlie to get her dowry? I'd rather die first."

"Did that idiot really think I would marry him?" Charlie asked.

"He thought Papa could pressure you, what with family honor and all. Plus, you may have noticed that Sir Leslie has a rather good opinion of himself. He believed he'd be able to charm you once he had his hands on the brooch."

Charlie shook her head, muttering under her breath.

"Morgan seemed to give that notion up in short order," Kade said.

Johnny cast him a meaningful glance. "I think he realized pretty quickly that Charlie would never marry him, under any circumstance."

"Still, how could he hope to recoup his money?" Charlie asked. "The brooch is so recognizable that it would be almost impossible to pawn. He could sell the gems separately, but that would greatly reduce their worth."

"Sir Leslie said he knew a collector who would pay handsomely for a piece with such historical value," her brother replied.

Disgusted, Kade shook his head. "Well, isn't he the clever fellow? Morgan clearly put some thought into this particular swindle."

Charlie's amber gaze sparked with anger. "'Clever'? I can

think of other things to call him, starting with *blackmailing bastard*."

"I am in complete agreement with you, my love."

Johnny blinked, then quickly flashed his sister a broad smile. "I knew I was right about the two of you. Are congratulations in order, old girl?"

"Yes, I think so," she said, returning her brother's smile with a shy one of her own.

Kade repressed a sigh. "You think so?"

She crinkled her nose at him. "Sorry. Yes, Johnny, Kade and I are getting married, but you're to keep that to yourself for now. We need to get this mess sorted first."

"Hmm," Johnny said. "Our parents had their hearts set on Richard. I hope they don't kick up a fuss."

Kade shared his hope. "We'll cross that bridge later. As Charlie noted, we need to get this sorted as quickly as possible."

"Before Morgan makes another attempt on poor Johnny," Charlie said, her expression once more turning fierce.

"If he killed me," Johnny asked, "how would he ever find the brooch?"

"Don't forget, he could easily make a mistake," Charlie argued. "The laudanum drops. If he'd miscalculated . . ."

She broke off and took a deep, shaky breath. Her hands curled into fists in her lap.

Kade reached over and took one of them, easing open her tightly clenched fingers. "I know, but he didn't. That suggests to me that he's used drops before, either for his own use or on someone else."

Johnny's mouth gaped open for a moment. "Do you think he's done this to someone else?"

"It's entirely possible. He's obviously comfortable in employing such a repulsive method of persuasion."

Charlie had gone back to looking utterly murderous. "That man needs to be put out of his misery before he harms anyone else."

A warning bell sounded in the back of Kade's mind. He studied his sweet lass for a few moments, taking in her ramrod-straight posture and fierce expression. In her dashing kilted attire, she seemed rather like a Highland princess—one ready to go to war.

"Never fear," he calmly replied. "We'll bring him to heel. Johnny, do you have any idea how he was able to dose your wine?"

"When I was leaving the drawing room to go to bed, I asked our butler to have a glass sent up to my room. I suppose he could have somehow done it then."

Kade flicked through his memories of the previous evening. "I recall him loitering about the drinks trolley at that point."

"I am such an idiot," Johnny said in a bitter tone. "I always knew Sir Leslie was too fast for me, but I let him suck me in anyway."

"People like Morgan excel at what they do. They're predators."

"He certainly preyed on me," Johnny glumly replied.

"What puzzles me, though, is why Morgan hasn't carried through on his threat to inform your father. Why all these deranged plots?"

Johnny grimaced. "I told him that my father would never repay my gambling debts. Papa would be far more likely to throw me out on my ear."

"Papa detests gambling," Charlie explained. "Our uncle—Mamma's younger brother—was fleeced several times in gaming hells. Mamma kept lending him money until our father put a stop to it. I still remember the huge row they had over it."

Kade thought for a few moments before replying. "Then in order to bring an end to this, we either need to get Morgan to admit what he's been doing to Johnny or catch him in the act of whatever he's planning next."

Charlie shot out of her chair. "We are *not* putting Johnny in any more danger. I won't have it."

Kade stood and took her hand. "Johnny will be well protected at all times."

"I'll be fine, Sis," Johnny earnestly said. "We need to do this."

"The man's a poltroon and a blackmailer. A dangerous one," she gritted out.

Kade smiled at her. "I think between the two of us, we're rather more dangerous than he is. Wouldn't you agree?"

She glowered for a few seconds longer before her mouth twitched, as if she was trying to hold back an answering smile. "Yes, I believe we are."

"Maybe we should tell Papa, even if he does blow his top," Johnny hesitantly suggested. "I'm sure he can do something. After all, he is a magistrate."

Kade shook his head. "Morgan comes from a respected and well-connected family. He'll simply deny everything, and it would come down to your word against his. Your sister and I would back you, of course, but that would mean little in a court of law. We need proof."

Charlie grimaced. "Unfortunately, I seem to be drawing a blank on ideas at the moment. Which is tremendously frustrating."

"I take it Morgan has your vowels?" Kade asked Johnny.

"Yes. He's been quite obnoxious about flaunting them in my face."

"Then let's start there. We need to retrieve them so that's one less point of pressure on you. Without the vowels, there's no proof that you actually owe him money."

"How is that going to extract a confession from him?" Johnny asked, sounding dubious.

"It won't, but I take it that he needs the money quite badly."

"He is in Dun territory, from what I've heard," Johnny admitted. "I think he's quite desperate, to tell you the truth."

Kade nodded. "Exactly, and if there's one thing desperate men tend to do, it's make mistakes. I also twisted the knife a bit by letting it slip that I was back in the hunt for the brooch. Morgan wasn't best pleased to hear that."

Charlie frowned, clearly thinking it through. "I suppose that might work. Of course, I could also try my hand at extracting a confession from him. Pointing my pistol at his head should do the job nicely."

Kade was fairly certain she was not making that threat in jest.

"One step at a time, love," he replied. "First we get the vowels, and then we start to apply more pressure, all right?"

She gave a reluctant nod. "Very well. But if Morgan tries to hurt Johnny, we do it my way, understood?"

"Absolutely."

While the plan forming in Kade's head did involve a certain degree of risk, it would not be to Johnny or Charlie. It would be to him. That wee detail, however, he intended to keep to himself.

CHAPTER 22

"You know what to do, Grandda?" Kade quietly asked as he joined his grandfather at the drinks trolley.

"Aye. We've gone over yer bloody plan three times, and I still think it's dodgy."

"All we need to do is keep everyone occupied so I can do a proper search of Morgan's bedroom for Johnny's vowels. I didn't have much time this morning, but now with all the servants belowstairs having dinner, I should be undisturbed."

His grandfather cast a dubious glance towards the card table at the other end of the drawing room, where Melissa and Lady Kinloch were pairing up against Colin and Morgan.

"How did ye get them all lined up like that, especially Morgan?"

"I suggested to Colin that given all the recent turmoil, cards might be a good distraction for the ladies. Since Lord Kinloch doesn't play, Colin was perfectly capable of arriving at the conclusion that Morgan would be needed as the fourth."

Angus snorted. "Nae doubt he's delirious with joy to be playin' for chicken stakes with the ladies. Yer pullin' quite a few strings here, laddie boy. Let's hope yer luck doesn't run out."

"It's not luck. It's thinking ahead and foreseeing possible sticking points."

"Is Charlie one of those stickin' points? That's why ye sent her up to sit with Johnny, I reckon. Gettin' her out of the way."

"Given that she spent most of dinner glaring death threats across the table at Morgan," Kade dryly replied, "it seemed the wisest course of action."

Angus nodded. "If that lass doesn't kill the blighter before we're done with this, it'll be a miracle. I thought she was going to leap across the table and stab his eyes out with the butter knife."

Dinner had proved an awkward affair, to put it mildly. Johnny had agreed to stay safely in his room, claiming that he was feeling poorly. That, naturally, had set both Lady Kinloch and Melissa to fretting. Lord Kinloch had gloomily chewed his way through the meal, barely saying a word and ignoring any attempts to engage him in conversation.

Thankfully, Charlie had kept the peace. Although she'd spent most of dinner glowering at Morgan, so had Angus. Because his grandfather had muttered a few choice insults about jaw-me-dead twiddlepoops that could be heard by everyone at the table, Kade doubted that Morgan had even noticed Charlie's murderous glances.

But even with the insults and glowers the blighter remained unperturbed as he bored them all with yet another round of stories about society life and quizzed Kade about his efforts to find the brooch.

Kade had responded politely, simply stating that he had a few ideas about where to look next and that he hoped to find it very soon. Morgan had reacted as hoped—with a flare of alarm. He'd quickly recovered, though. Winking at Kade, he'd wished him good hunting, and congratulated him on his impending success in claiming his prize. At that point,

Kinloch had roused from his gloom and snapped at the idiot, telling him to keep his chuckleheaded comments to himself.

Shortly after that trenchant remark, the ladies had risen from the table and thankfully brought dinner to a close.

"Charlie is best kept out of the way for now," Kade said to his grandfather. "But she also understands that Morgan won't be able to get to Johnny as long as she's with him."

Angus cocked a bushy white eyebrow. "But what if Morgan decides to try to get her out of the way?"

"The only thing that worries me in that regard is the very real possibility that Charlie would shoot the bastard," Kade replied. "Since I would prefer my betrothed to avoid possible murder charges, I intend to keep her as far away from Morgan as possible."

"Aye, yer lady's a prime one. Still, I'm nae happy aboot leavin' the scabby blighter without a minder. Are ye sure ye don't want me to stay down here to keep watch on him?"

Kade had no intention of letting either Charlie or his grandfather get mixed up in his actual plans for the evening— not that either of them needed to know that.

"Morgan will be safely ensconced at the card table until the tea tray comes in," he replied. "That should give me plenty of time to search."

Angus still looked dubious but finally shrugged. "I expect ye know what yer about."

"I am the master spy, after all."

"But dinna forget ye got stabbed in Paris, laddie boy."

Kade held up his hands. "*You're* the one who keeps telling everyone I'm a master spy."

"Only because I dinna want ye to feel bad."

"How very kind. Now, if you would also be so kind as to go up to Charlie. She'll be stewing and could use the distraction of your visit," Kade said as he steered Angus to the door.

"All right, I'm goin'. I'll be back down in an hour to see how ye got on."

"I'll see you then."

With any luck, by that time Morgan would be rolled up and the mystery of the Clan Iain brooch safely resolved.

Lady Kinloch glanced up from her cards as Angus left the room. "Is your grandfather going to bed already? Dear me, everyone is abandoning us this evening."

Kade smiled. "He's just going to sit with Miss Charlotte and Johnny for a spell."

"No doubt to entertain them with his amusing stories," Morgan said with a smirk. "Quite the colorful character, your dear grandfather."

Blackmailer, bully, and complete prat. Kade couldn't wait to see the idiot behind bars.

"That he is," he replied with a polite smile. "My lady, has Lord Kinloch retired for the evening?"

"He went to his study to write a letter," she said in an abstracted tone, her attention once more on her cards. "He'll return for tea."

"Then I beg you to excuse me as well," Kade said. "I'll also return for the tea table."

Morgan glanced up, his gaze suddenly wary.

"Going to the music room to work, old boy?" he asked in a deceptively casual voice. "You're quite the slave to your art."

"Yes, I might squeeze in a bit of work, but first I would like some fresh air. I thought to stroll about the gardens— down to the pond, perhaps."

Morgan's lips pressed flat before he mustered a smile. "And perhaps have a bit of a look for the brooch while you're at it, I'll wager. You're a sly one, Kendrick."

Lady Kinloch exhaled an exasperated sigh. "Please do not mention that infernal brooch. I am entirely sick of it."

"That's understandable, my lady," Kade said in a sympathetic tone. "But I'm sure the brooch will be found soon enough."

"Not much for nature walks myself, but have at it," Morgan

said. "Be careful down by the pond, though. Some of the rocks are quite slippery."

Kade raised his eyebrows. "I'm surprised you noticed, given your aversion to nature walks."

Something ugly flashed in Morgan's eyes. "I noticed it the other day when I was coming back from the stables."

"That's odd," replied Kade. "The path from the stables goes nowhere near the pond."

Now Morgan scowled at him. "You can't expect a fellow to remember every walk he takes. I did notice the rocks at some point."

Lady Kinloch eyed the man with disapproval before smiling graciously at Kade. "Enjoy your stroll, Mr. Kendrick, but be careful, because Sir Leslie is correct. The rocks around the pond can be slippery with lichen at this time of year, so it's best to avoid them. I would hate for you to have a fall."

"Yes, we don't need any more accidents," Morgan said with a sneer. "What with the Kinloch Fiddler still lurking about. Who knows what could happen?"

Melissa gave a startled squeak. "Don't even suggest such a thing! Perhaps you shouldn't go outside after all, Mr. Kendrick. If you were to have an accident, there would be no one to hear you cry for help."

He smiled at her. "Thank you, but I shall be perfectly fine."

"But—"

Lady Kinloch tapped the card table. "Melissa, I have the most *dreadful* hand. I cannot do a thing with these cards."

Properly distracted, Melissa looked to her mother. "Oh, dear. Give them to me, and I'll see what I can do."

"I say, that's cheating," Colin said in a humorous tone. "Melissa, you're the very devil with cards. You'll slaughter poor Morgan and me."

As his remark set off a good-natured round of jesting, Kade took the opportunity to slip out of the room. He was fairly convinced that it wouldn't take long for Morgan to find an excuse to leave the table and follow him.

Strolling down to the music room, he paused to scribble a few notes in his work journal. He'd finally cracked a small problem in the final movement, thanks to a casual observation Charlie had made earlier in the day. His sweet lass had both an excellent ear and a quicksilver mind. He looked forward to working with her on future compositions.

In fact, he looked forward to doing everything with Charlie—starting with a proper wedding night, which he hoped would come sooner rather than later.

He stowed his journal and went outside. The lights from the upstairs drawing room cast a gentle glow over the terrace, and the murmur of voices drifted through the open windows. He couldn't hear Morgan's voice, however, so he took the path straight to the gazebo. Given that Morgan was obviously rattled, he might make a quick exit from the card game.

The skies were clear tonight, and the moon, almost full, illuminated the path through the silent gardens. It was a beautiful night in the Highlands, the soft breeze scented with heather and pine and the pond up ahead shimmering with reflected starlight.

Kade paused on the steps of the gazebo to listen before going inside. He then began to circle the interior, lifting cushions, tapping panels, and generally making a show of it. Finally, he crouched down in front of the panel where Johnny had previously hidden the brooch, prying it off to retrieve a leather pouch.

As Kade straightened up, he heard a heavy footfall and a click he recognized all too well. He turned to find Morgan on the bottom step of the gazebo, holding a cocked pistol.

"I'll take that pouch, Kendrick," he drawled.

"This is a bit of a surprise, Morgan. I thought you were

out of the hunt. In any event, holding a weapon on me hardly seems like fair play."

Moonlight and shadow exaggerated the man's ugly sneer. "Don't play coy with me, old man. You know exactly what this is about."

"Actually, I'm at something of a loss. Why in God's name would you want to take the brooch from me at gunpoint? Do you really expect me to keep quiet about this when you hand it over to Lord Kinloch?"

"I'm not going to hand it over. You know that, so no more games." He waved the pistol. "Now, hand it over."

Kade nodded. "Now we come to it. Very well, but I have a few questions first."

"Why the bloody hell should I answer your questions?"

"Mind if I sit?" He didn't wait for a reply before settling onto the padded bench.

"What game are you playing, man?" Morgan blustered.

Kade extended a hand over the gazebo railing, dangling his precious cargo over the pond. Morgan sucked in a breath and started to move.

"One more step and I'll drop it," Kade sharply said. "Refuse to answer my questions, and I'll drop it. The brooch is quite heavy, so I imagine it'll sink to the bottom immediately."

Morgan hissed out a foul curse but remained on the top step. Fury permeated the air around him, almost visible in the moonlight.

"I suppose Johnny blabbed all," he spat out. "The little weasel."

"As young and naive as he is, Johnny is more a man than you'll ever be," Kade replied, his voice icy with contempt. "He stood up to you, despite your attempts to kill him."

"I never tried to kill him," Morgan retorted. "I was just trying to scare him into doing the right thing. Johnny owes me quite a lot of money, and he needed to know the consequences of reneging on his word. It's a matter of honor."

"You have a bizarre notion of honor, Morgan, one that apparently includes drugging unsuspecting victims with laudanum. You could have killed Johnny if you'd miscalculated the dose."

"I never miscalculate, and he was never in real danger. Now, if we're done with the questions, hand that bloody pouch over."

"Just one more. Why didn't you simply go to Lord Kinloch and ask him to settle Johnny's debts? I'm sure he would have paid you off."

Morgan snorted in derision. "Kinloch is an oaf and regrettably old-fashioned. Johnny made it clear that his father wouldn't pay me a farthing. That's why the brooch belongs to me. No one stiffs me and gets away with it, I assure you."

Kade gently swung the pouch by its cords. "So, what about me, then? What happens when I hand this over?"

"What do you think happens, you fool? I've got a pistol trained on you."

Kade almost laughed in disbelief. The man truly was an idiot.

"Now, there's an incentive to hand over the brooch," he replied. "And you do realize that half the household will be down here within minutes, once they hear the shot. Let's say you do somehow manage to escape from the gardens unseen. How will you explain your inconvenient absence right at the moment of my murder?"

Morgan gestured with his free hand. "I suppose one might conclude it was the original thief of the brooch, returning for more ill-gotten gains. You, sadly, stumbled across him and were killed in the process. Don't worry, Kendrick. You'll go down as a hero. I'll be sure of that."

"That's the most idiotic idea I've ever heard."

Morgan glared at him, and for a rather alarming moment Kade wondered if the bastard *was* actually going to shoot him.

"Then we'll go for a little stroll," Morgan finally ground out. "You'll slip on those rocks, bash your head, and take an unfortunate tumble into the pond. A terrible tragedy, but Lady Kinloch did warn you, as did I."

Kade shrugged. "Slightly better, but while you might fool the others, you won't fool Charlie or my grandfather—not to mention Johnny."

That gave Morgan a moment of pause, but then he forced out a laugh.

"As if anyone would believe them. Your grandfather is clearly deranged, and that hoyden of yours is not much better. As for Johnny, he knows better than to talk. After all, I still hold his vowels. He says one word and I go straight to his father. Kinloch will throw him out on his ear, and the boy knows that."

"Ah, but you no longer hold Johnny's vowels. I retrieved them this morning from their hiding place under the false bottom of your valise. They are now safely out of your reach, Morgan. If anything happens to me, Lord Kinloch will receive the vowels, along with the rest of the evidence we have against you."

Morgan froze for several moments, apparently bereft of speech.

"You bloody bastard," he finally spat out. "I've had enough of your interference in my affairs. Get up now and give me the bloody pouch, or I'll blow your brains out and take my chances."

Kade let out a dramatic sigh. "All right, you've convinced me."

He stood and untied the strings of the pouch, pretending to fumble a bit as he reached inside.

Morgan impatiently waved his weapon. "Come on, get on with it."

Kade smoothly withdrew a Deringer pistol and aimed it at his adversary. The small gun was cocked and ready to fire.

Morgan gaped at him for a moment before hissing out a string of curses.

"As you can see," Kade said, "I don't have the brooch on me. That is also safely stowed away. So unless we intend to engage in a shootout, I'd say it's over, Morgan. You have no more cards left to play."

"Why, you—"

A sudden rush of footsteps on the path interrupted him. Angus skidded to a halt in front of the gazebo, armed with what appeared to be an ancient pair of dueling pistols.

Kade mentally cursed. His grandfather was a terrible shot at the best of times, but in the dark, with an old set of pistols? Disaster loomed.

"Ye canna escape, Morgan," Angus said, puffing a bit. "Surrender now, or I'll shoot ye dead."

Morgan had already dodged inside the gazebo, positioning himself halfway between Kade and Angus, his pistol still trained on Kade.

"Do you really expect me to be intimidated by those?" Morgan said, his tone heavy with sarcasm. "I doubt they've been fired in decades."

Angus gave him a toothy grin. "Let's find out, shall we?"

"Grandda, I've got this under control," Kade sternly said. "You need to step away."

"Och, of course ye've got it handled. But ye shouldna have pulled the wool over my eyes," his grandfather replied. "Ye never ken when ye'll need backup, and that's what I'm here for."

One of the large rhododendrons beside the gazebo began

to rustle. Lord Kinloch, holding a shotgun, emerged from the shrubbery.

"I'm his blasted backup, MacDonald," Kinloch exclaimed, jabbing his weapon at Angus. "I've been here the whole bloody time."

Kade grimaced. His plan to trap Morgan was turning into a farce—albeit one with loaded weapons.

"And how in the name of all that's holy was I supposed to ken that, Kinloch?" Angus retorted. Then he glared at Kade. "Ye asked for his help and not mine? What the hell were ye thinkin', lad?"

"He was thinking that he could depend on a rational adult instead of a loony old man," Kinloch hotly replied.

Angus bristled with fury. "Loony, is it? I'll show ye—"

"That's enough," Kade interrupted. "Angus, please stop waving those old pistols about. One of them could misfire and kill someone."

"I'm sure nae one would mind if I shot Morgan," Angus replied, sounding aggrieved. "Even Kinloch couldna complain about that."

"Of course I could," Kinloch retorted. "I don't want that villain bleeding all over my gazebo. Elspeth just had it repainted and furnished."

Morgan lowered his pistol as he adopted his habitual expression of cynical amusement. Since he was now well outgunned, he would no doubt try to talk his way out of the trap he'd walked into.

"My dear Lord Kinloch," Morgan said. "This entire situation is simply a misunderstanding. If you give me the chance to explain, I'm sure we can sort everything out."

"Says the man who was just holding me at gunpoint," Kade dryly put in.

Morgan put his pistol down on the bench. "Dear chap, I

was simply responding to your aggressive behavior. One can't blame a fellow for defending himself."

"No respectable person needs to carry a pistol in my house," Kinloch sternly answered.

"Forgive me for stating the obvious," Morgan said with a casual shrug, "but everyone seems to be armed. Rather a dangerous state of affairs, if you ask me."

"Ho, Kinloch," Angus put in. "I'd still like to ken what ye were doin' lurkin' in the bushes like a bloody footpad."

His lordship bristled. "I should think it obvious. We were trying to trick Morgan into making a confession, which Kendrick was doing nicely until you waded into it."

Angus threw Kade a disgruntled look. "All right, but why didna ye tell me, lad? I could have helped."

"You were helping me by keeping Charlie out of the way," Kade replied. "She didn't need to be mixed up in this."

"In fact, I made it clear to Kendrick that I didn't want my daughter anywhere near this nonsense," Kinloch said. "Charlie likely would have shot Morgan between the eyes—not that one could blame her. I refuse to have my daughter hauled off to prison for murder, even a justifiable one."

"My lord, I fear you have this all backward," Morgan smoothly put in. "I am not the guilty party. That would be your son, I'm sorry to say. I've been trying to convince Johnny to return the brooch ever since he told me that he stole it. When he refused, I took it upon myself to search for it, intending to return it to Miss Charlotte. Kendrick took that amiss, obviously because *he* wanted to claim the prize. I, however, was simply trying to help poor Johnny."

Both Angus and Kinloch were now staring at Morgan with identical expressions of disbelief.

"Have you forgotten I was hiding in the blasted bushes?" Kinloch exclaimed. "I heard you threatening to kill Kendrick! And you keep my son out of it, you varlet. You've done enough harm to the poor lad. Why, for two shillings I'd shoot you myself."

Morgan heaved a dramatic sigh. "I have been nothing but a friend to Johnny. Sadly, though, your son is both a thief and a liar, which you surely comprehend by now. He's also a gambler who owes me a considerable sum of money. That's why he stole the brooch in the first place. He intended to pawn it to pay off his debts."

"Lord Kinloch knows exactly what Johnny has done, because I explained the situation to him," Kade said in a hard voice. "Again, the game is up, Morgan. You've no more cards left to play."

Morgan hesitated, clearly disconcerted. But then he recovered and managed an insouciant shrug.

"As a good friend, all I've done is try to help Johnny."

Angus glared at him. "Yer vermin is what ye are. Ye could have killed the lad, and we'll see ye locked up in the clink for that."

The vermin in question mustered a credible laugh. "Good luck with that, you old coot. You have no evidence beyond Johnny's wild stories, which no one will believe."

"They'll believe me," Kade said. "And Lord Kinloch."

Morgan actually had the nerve to smile. "Evidence, dear boy. You have none, which my lawyers will be happy to point out." Then he glanced at Kinloch. "In fact, the evidence that does exist clearly points to your son as the thief. It would be quite the scandal if reports became commonly known that your son and heir is a common thief, not to mention a wastrel and a gambler. It would be a truly sad reflection on your family honor."

"You dare to threaten me?" Kinloch thundered. "Why you—"

"For God's sake," snapped a feminine voice.

Charlie suddenly materialized out of the night. Like her father, she was armed with a shotgun.

Dammit to hell.

Kade held up his hand. "Sweetheart, we certainly don't need more guns at the moment."

She ignored him and brushed between her father and Angus. Stalking into the gazebo before Kade could stop her, she flipped up the butt end of her shotgun and clocked Morgan in the face. The man crumpled onto the bench without a sound. He would likely be out cold for some time.

"Well, that brings this discussion to an abrupt conclusion," Kade wryly said.

"As it should," Charlie retorted, "since it was both long-winded and absurd. As for you, Kade Kendrick, you owe me an explanation. So does my father. And I will not take no for an answer."

CHAPTER 23

When Angus had burst into Johnny's bedroom with the news that both Kade and Sir Leslie had disappeared into the night, Charlie's heart had leapt into her throat. By the time she secured her shotgun from the gunroom and pelted down to the gardens, her growing dread had conjured up images of mayhem and even bloodshed.

But what she actually found was yet another ridiculous scene. Kade was in complete control of the situation and seemed to be observing the lunatic discussion with nothing more than an attitude of polite disbelief. Charlie had felt so wobbly with relief that she'd stayed in the shadows for a few minutes to regain her equilibrium. Then as the fear dissipated, a massive surge of frustration had welled up in its place, along with an uncontrollable urge to silence Sir Leslie's obnoxious flow of words.

To the surprise of everyone, she'd done just that.

Now her dratted betrothed stood before her, a gently rueful smile on his face.

"I am happy to provide whatever explanations you wish," Kade said, "but it would be best if we get Morgan up to the house and under lock and key. Then we can sit and have a proper discussion."

"That's if yon lassie didn't knock the blighter's brains out," Angus put in. "What a nice, flush hit, Miss Charlie. Well done."

Kade bent over and checked on the man. "He's alive, although I suspect we'll have to carry him back to the house." He flashed her a quick grin. "I doubt Morgan even saw you coming, sweetheart."

"He can rot here for all I care," she retorted. "And don't you dare *sweetheart* me. You lied to me, and I'm most unhappy about that."

Kade winced. "I know, Charlie, and I am sorry about that. But if you give me a chance to explain—"

He broke off as Papa stomped into the gazebo. "I say, Kendrick, I don't like your manner with my daughter. I already have one scandal on my hands, so I don't need you playing fast and loose with the girl."

Angus barged up to Charlie's father. "Ho, Kinloch, I'll nae have ye besmirchin' my grandson's name. Yer actin' like a jinglebrains, ye ken."

"Grandda, that is *not* helpful," Kade said.

"Laddie, I'll nae have him besmirchin' yer honor."

"And I'll not have Kendrick besmirching my daughter's honor," barked Papa.

Angus jabbed one of his old—and presumably loaded—pistols at him. "Now, see here, ye stuck-up old—"

"Stop," Charlie yelled. "This is getting ridiculous—again."

Kade grimaced and tugged on an ear.

Angus, however, gave her an admiring glance. "We might make a bagpipe player out of ye after all, lassie. That's a fine set of lungs ye have."

"Indeed," Kade dryly said.

Papa snorted. "She always did, even as a child. Charlie used to sing so loudly in church that the vicar complained. Of course, the poor girl also used to sing off-key, so that was part of it."

For a moment, Charlie contemplated shoving the whole lot of them into the pond.

When Kade covered his mouth, she glared at him. "If you laugh, Kade Kendrick, I *will* shoot you."

He held up his hands, clearly trying mightily to suppress a laugh.

"Well, I don't like Kendrick's manner, but there's no need to threaten him," her father said. "After all, he rolled Morgan right up, confession and all."

"Yes, let's return to that discussion," she replied. "First, I would like to know why I was kept in the dark about this little scheme, Kade. Was it because you didn't think I could take care of myself?"

She hated even asking the question, but she had to know. If he thought she needed protecting or, worse, was somehow untrustworthy, Charlie was quite certain that her heart would break in two.

Kade placed his pistol on the bench and took her hand. "Of course not. I know how capable you are and how well you can defend both yourself and others. That was never in question."

His words were so obviously sincere that some of Charlie's tension started to bleed away.

"Then why did you keep me in the dark?" she gruffly asked, fighting a sudden, silly impulse to cry.

"Because I knew how furious you were with Morgan. So furious I feared you might shoot him on the spot."

She huffed. "Who could blame me if I did?"

"No one, quite likely. But you must admit it would have made the situation a great deal more complicated."

"Besides, I insisted that Kendrick keep you out of it," her

father added. "I'm your father, and it was my right and duty to keep you out of a volatile, dangerous situation."

Now, *that* was annoying. "Really, Papa? Since it's my brooch, not yours, I had to the right to at least know what you were planning."

Her father gaped at her. "Good God, Charlie, you were the one who stole the blasted thing in the first place."

"That's beside the point. I think it was very mean of you to keep me in the dark like this, Papa. You knew how worried I was."

Kade tugged on her hand. "He was trying to protect you, lass. You know that."

She blew out an exasperated sigh. "All right, but as much as I wanted to shoot Sir Leslie, I never would have gone through with it. I'm not an idiot, Kade."

"No, you're utterly brilliant," he said. "Forgive me. I was trying to protect you, too."

Angus nodded. "It's the Kendrick way, lassie. Our men always protect their ladies."

"And since when did my daughter become a Kendrick lady?" Papa said with a thunderous scowl. "This is most irregular, my girl, and very secretive of you. I do not approve."

"Ha. You've been keeping a few secrets yourself, Papa," she said, staring him down.

"Hang it," he finally muttered, clearly disgruntled by the whole situation.

She turned back to Kade. "Just when did you speak to Papa about this whole mess?" She paused for a moment. "And clearly you didn't tell him everything."

Meaning their relationship. Why hadn't Kade mentioned that to her father?

"I told him yesterday morning, when we went out for a ride," he replied.

She narrowed her gaze. "So you didn't just run into him

in the stables, then. Really, Kade, you simply must stop withholding important information from me. It's incredibly irritating."

"So says the Kinloch Fiddler," her father said in a sardonic tone.

In all fairness, Charlie had to admit Papa was right. She'd not been exactly forthcoming with Kade until he'd forced her hand.

Ignoring her father, Kade held up a hand, as if making a solemn vow. "From now on, I promise total honesty between us, Charlie. I'll hold nothing back."

While she fumed, trying to stay mad at him, Kade flashed her a charming, lopsided grin. Really, the man was incorrigible.

And wonderful.

"Well, see that you don't," she finally said.

"Now that we've sorted that out," Angus said, "why don't we lock up scabby Sir Leslie and then have a wee dram. Catchin' villains is thirsty work, ye ken."

"That is the first sensible suggestion you've made all evening, MacDonald," Papa said. "Possibly ever."

When Angus started to bristle, Charlie hastily stepped in to divert the discussion.

"You obviously know about Johnny and his troubles," she said to her father. "Please don't be too upset with him. Sir Leslie put such a fright into him that Johnny truly didn't know what to do. And he's very sorry. I'm sure he's learned his lesson."

"I'll admit I wasn't best pleased with either you or him," Papa replied. "But after discussing the situation with Kendrick, it's clear that Morgan was preying on the lad. Still, Johnny was exceedingly foolish to allow himself to get mixed up with such a scoundrel, and I will be giving him a good piece of my mind."

"But you won't do anything drastic, like cutting off his funds or disowning him?"

"Good God, Charlie," her father exclaimed. "How did you come up with such a ridiculous notion?"

Charlie declined to point out that he'd said exactly that only a few weeks ago, when falling into a massive snit about Johnny's spendthrift ways. She should have remembered, however, that Papa's bark was always worse than his bite, and that she was just as guilty of misreading the situation as Johnny was.

She gave him a hug. "Thank you, Papa. That's very understanding of you."

He hugged her back before letting her go. "I'm not done with you yet, missy. You have more than a few questions to answer when we get back to the house."

"I know, and I'm sorry about the brooch. It was very stupid of me to steal it."

He waved a dismissive hand. "Well, it was really your mamma and Melissa who were so upset. It's not as if *I* was pushing you to marry Richard, now was I?"

"What?" Angus exclaimed. "Ye were practically selling her off to booby Campbell, and ye know it."

Papa got huffy again. "That is a nonsensical—"

The sound of rapid footsteps interrupted him. A moment later, their butler came rushing up, closely followed by Tommy, one of the footmen.

"My lord," Simmons gasped, rather out of breath. "We've been searching for you everywhere."

"Well, you've found me. What's amiss?"

"Lady Kinloch was concerned that you and your guests had all gone missing. Mr. Johnny is in quite a state, and Miss Melissa . . ."

Simmons trailed off, his eyes suddenly popping wide at the sight of Sir Leslie, apparently lifeless.

"Is . . . is he . . . dead?" he asked in a horrified tone.

"Don't be so dramatic, Simmons," Papa brusquely replied. "Miss Charlotte simply knocked him out with the butt of her shotgun."

"Actually, I think he's already starting to rouse," Kade said.

A moan issued from Sir Leslie's mouth as he stirred.

Papa waved an impatient hand at Simmons and Tommy. "Don't just stand there, you two, haul the blighter up. We need to get him back to the house and locked away. Put him in his dressing room for now, I suppose. He shouldn't be able to cause any trouble in there."

"Yes, my lord," Simmons faintly replied.

"Here, I'll help you," Kade said.

Taking Sir Leslie by the collar, he hauled him to his feet, holding him steady while Simmons and Tommy came to relieve him.

"Kade, mind your shoulder," Charlie warned.

He smiled at her. "I'm fine, love."

"Ho, Kendrick," Papa barked. "You will cease flirting with my daughter this instant."

"I wouldn't dream of flirting with her, my lord," Kade replied.

"Then what the devil is going on between you two?"

"Kinloch, yer actin' mighty dense at the moment," Angus dryly put in.

Kade took his grandfather's arm and steered him out of the gazebo. "Enough, Grandda. Let's get back to the house."

"There's nae need to rush me," Angus protested. "I'm nae as young as I used to be."

"Charlotte, this is all *most* irregular," her father complained. "I do not approve."

"I know, Papa," she said, taking his arm. "I'll explain everything once we get back to the house."

She glanced back at Simmons and Tommy, who'd managed

to get their burden fairly steady on his feet. Sir Leslie was peering about him in some confusion, as if unsure of his whereabouts. That wasn't surprising, since she'd given him a rather stiff knock.

"Please put an armed footman outside the dressing room," she said to Simmons, handing him her shotgun. "My father will be up shortly to deal with Sir Leslie."

By now, their butler had recovered his countenance and simply gave her a dignified nod, as if locking up one's guests was an everyday occurrence. "Very good, Miss Charlotte."

"And have the housekeeper take a look at his head, will you? I gave him a rather good smash."

"Yes, miss."

"He can hang for all I care," her father grumbled. "Now, come along, Charlie."

They hurried along the path, catching up with Kade and Angus on the terrace.

"Everything all right, lass?" Kade asked with a wry smile.

She nodded, letting her father precede them into the house. "Papa is not in a good mood," she whispered. "I'm not sure how he'll react to—"

"Do not dawdle, Charlotte," her father said over his shoulder in a severe tone.

Sighing, she followed him upstairs to the drawing room. Kade and Angus brought up the rear.

"Good God," Mamma exclaimed, fluttering over when they filed in. "You look like a gang of Highland marauders. Why are you armed?"

"Because we were dealin' with a desperate villain," Angus said. "Scabby Sir Leslie was ready to bash our Kade over the head and throw him into the pond."

Melissa, who'd jumped to her feet when they entered the room, sank back onto the sofa with a little shriek. "Heavens, are you quite all right, Mr. Kendrick?"

Kade smiled at her. "Yes, I'm perfectly fine. We're all fine."

Colin took Melissa's hand. "See, darling? I told you everything would be all right. Your father and Mr. Kendrick had everything quite under control."

Kade glanced at Charlie, his eyes gleaming with amusement. "In point of fact, it was your sister who saved the day."

"And how exactly did she do that?" Mamma warily asked.

"She bashed the scoundrel in the face with her shotgun," Papa said as he stomped over to the drinks trolley.

Her mother simply sighed.

"Well done, old girl," Colin said to Charlie. "From what Johnny's been telling us, the man's a complete villain."

Melissa screwed up her face. "Very true. But I'm not sure if it's quite proper for Charlotte to go about smashing men in the face, even if they are villains."

"Och, lassie, yer sister's a heroine," Angus commented.

"That remains to be seen," Papa said.

He rested his shotgun against a nearby chair and he poured himself a double tot of whisky. When he bolted it down in one go, Charlie mentally winced. She was in for it now.

"Goodness, Henry, what's gotten into you?" Mamma exclaimed, scandalized.

"Ho, Kinloch, don't be hoggin' all the good stuff," Angus put in. "We could all use a wee dram."

"You can get it yourself," her father rudely replied.

He stomped back over and dropped heavily into the leather club chair near the fireplace—not, however, without first glaring at Charlie.

"I'll get you a glass, Grandda." Kade glanced at Charlie. "And for you as well, I think."

She nodded. "Yes, please."

"Where's Sir Leslie now?" Johnny asked in a wary tone.

"Simmons and Tommy are locking him in his dressing room, and Tommy will stand guard," Charlie said with a reassuring smile. "You've nothing to fear anymore, dearest. Sir Leslie told Kade everything, and Papa heard it all."

Johnny sank down on the other sofa, exhaling a shaky sigh. "Thank God, but what happens now?"

"We'll keep Morgan here overnight," their father replied. "Then I'll have the sheriff transport him to Edinburgh. As the local magistrate, I'll write up a report and send it along to the Edinburgh Constabulary. I'd prefer to let them deal with the blighter."

Johnny started to look anxious again. "But his family lives in Edinburgh, and they've quite a bit of influence. The constabulary might not believe me. And . . . and Sir Leslie's bound to say some terrible things about me. Some of which are quite true," he added on a miserable note.

"They'll bloody well believe me," Papa said. "I heard the whole deranged plan from start to finish. The magistrate in Edinburgh will hear it all, too, you can be sure."

"My family also has a great deal influence in Edinburgh," Kade said as he handed Charlie a glass of whisky. "They'll see to it that justice is done, Johnny. Never fear."

Papa bristled. "I'm perfectly capable of protecting my own son. I don't need Kendricks doing it for me."

"That goes without saying, my lord," Kade replied, gracious as ever.

"There's nae need to starch up, Kinloch," Angus said. "After all, it was our Kade who found the brooch *and* got Morgan to confess."

Papa snorted. "And Kendrick wouldn't have had to do so if Charlie hadn't stolen her own blasted brooch in the first place. This whole affair has been ridiculous from beginning to end."

Melissa frowned. "But I thought Johnny stole the brooch. That's what he was telling us before you came in."

"Yes, but I stole it first," Charlie explained. "And then Johnny stole it from me."

"Hang on," Colin said, looking confused. "Why would you steal your own brooch?"

Mamma let out an aggrieved sigh. "To put Richard Campbell off, obviously. Still, I would appreciate a clear explanation of the events, Charlotte."

"Of course, Mamma."

As succinctly as she could, Charlie outlined what had taken place over the last few weeks—an expurgated version that left out of the details of her intimate encounters with Kade.

"Mr. Kendrick, how *clever* of you," Melissa enthused after Charlie explained how Kade had deduced the initial whereabouts of the brooch. "I would never have guessed in a million years."

"No one would have had to guess if Charlotte had behaved in a rational manner," Mamma tartly noted.

Charlie crinkled her nose. "Sorry, Mamma. I didn't mean for it to turn into such a mess."

"Well, I certainly hope you've learned your lesson."

"I'm the one who's really to blame," Johnny gloomily said. "It's because of me that everything turned into such a mess. I caused all sorts of upset and almost got myself killed in the process. Charlie isn't the one who has to apologize, it's me."

Mamma reached over and took his hand. "My son, what you did was very wrong. But why didn't you come to us? Your father and I would have protected you from that awful man."

Charlie and Johnny both glanced at their father, who was now looking rather sheepish. The fact that neither she nor Johnny had felt they could trust him was obviously making the poor old dear rather uncomfortable.

"Never mind that now," Papa hastily said. "All's well that ends well, and whatnot."

Angus snorted. "No thanks to ye, Kinloch."

Kade, who was standing behind his grandfather's chair, gave Angus a little jab. "Grandda."

"I only speak the truth, lad."

"That is quite enough, Angus," Mamma said. "Henry is correct. That horrible man has been dealt with, and Johnny is safe." She smiled at Kade. "Thank you, Mr. Kendrick. Truly."

Kade bowed. "I was happy to help, my lady."

"Where is the brooch now?" Melissa asked.

"I've got it," Kade said.

He reached inside his coat and took out a small leather pouch. Opening it, he handed the brooch to Charlie.

"Back to its rightful owner," he said with a smile.

She cupped the glittering piece in both hands, relief flooding through her. The brooch was as beautiful as ever. In fact, the jewels shone so brightly that she could almost believe they'd been recently cleaned.

"Thank you," she said to Kade.

"It was my pleasure."

"I highly doubt that," she drolly replied.

His only response was a wink.

Melissa suddenly grabbed Colin by the arm.

"What is it, my love?" he asked with concern.

"Do you know what this means?" she said, bouncing a bit with excitement. "It means that Kade will now marry Charlotte. Not only did he find the brooch, he rescued Johnny and saved our family's honor. Just think of it—the great Kade Kendrick is going to be one of us!"

Mamma blinked. "In all the commotion, I'd quite forgotten about your father's vow. Yes, Mr. Kendrick did find the brooch, so Charlotte is obligated to marry him. There's nothing to be done for it, I suppose."

"You're very kind, my lady," Kade said. "But Miss

Charlotte—indeed none of you—is under any obligation to me, including one of marriage."

Startled, Charlie gaped at him. After all this, was he now saying that he *didn't* want to marry her?

Kade caught sight of her no-doubt astounded expression.

"Unless Miss Charlotte wants to marry me, of course," he hastily added.

And didn't that just sound horribly tepid?

Fighting the sensation that she'd just been dumped into an icy pond, Charlie forced herself to respond.

"Mamma, I have no intention of requiring Mr. Kendrick— or anyone else—to marry me over a silly vow that Papa made while in a temper."

"Hang on," Kade said, now looking slightly annoyed. "There isn't anyone else but me."

"And I was not in a temper," Papa huffed. "I made a solemn vow, and it's one that should be honored, for both your sake and that of our family. Even if Kendrick isn't the man I would have chosen for you."

"Are ye sayin' ye'd prefer the likes of booby Campbell to a Kendrick?" Angus indignantly asked. "Are ye a lunatic?"

"I would be a lunatic to desire our family to marry into your family," Papa retorted.

"Henry, in case you've forgotten," Mamma said, "Angus is a member of *my* family, which makes him a member of *your* family."

"Yes, but if Charlie marries Kendrick, we'll have to see MacDonald even more," Papa said. "Besides, Kendrick will take Charlie away from us, what with his touring about the Continent and whatnot. We'll never get to see her."

Angus rolled his eyes. "Yer not makin' any sense, Kinloch. Either ye see us, or ye don't."

Charlie glanced at Kade, whose irritation had now obviously been transformed into amusement. When she scowled at him, he simply widened his eyes, looking the picture of innocence.

"This is a stupendously foolish conversation," she said. "And beside the point."

"But Charlotte, it *is* a matter of honor," Melissa insisted. "Simply everyone knows about Papa's vow, including the servants."

"Thanks to your father's unfortunate announcement in front of them," Mamma said rather severely. "I understand from my maid that the entire village is gossiping about the matter."

Charlie felt her cheeks begin to flush. Her family was acting like a pack of ninnies, which was incredibly mortifying.

"I don't care who's gossiping, and I don't care about Papa's silly notions of honor, either," she replied. "No one is forcing Kade to do anything he doesn't want to do."

Kade held up a hand. "If I could just—"

Papa interrupted him. "I say, Charlie, that's a bit much. Honor is very important, you know."

"As much as I hate to agree with Kinloch," Angus put in, "he's right about that. Family honor is nae something to be trifled with."

Charlie gritted her teeth. "Let me make this perfectly clear—I am *not* forcing Kade to marry me."

"Just to clarify," Kade said, "you wouldn't have to force me."

She pointed a finger at him. "You, be quiet. I am still *quite* annoyed with you."

"Really, Charlotte," Mamma said. "Instead of snapping at the poor man, you should be forever grateful that he recovered the brooch. It would have been a dreadful blow to lose such a priceless heirloom."

"You do realize it was never really lost," Charlie replied. "Either Johnny or I knew where it was all the time."

Her mother leveled a stern gaze on her. "And what if that

dreadful Morgan person had found it first? Have you thought about that?"

Melissa visibly shuddered. "Perish the thought. Our family would have been cursed forever."

Kade again held up a hand. "As to that—"

"Hell and damnation, Kendrick," Papa snapped. "No one believed that curse nonsense but Melissa."

"I'm not referring to the curse, sir, but to the nature of the brooch itself," Kade replied. "You must forgive me for being the bearer of bad news, but the brooch is not, in fact, priceless. Just the opposite, I'm afraid."

Charlie's mind went blank. And from the sudden silence everyone else apparently suffered from the same affliction.

She forced herself to shake it off. "Kade, what can you possibly mean? Of course it's priceless. The gems alone are worth a fortune."

"I'm sure the original gems were invaluable." He reached over and tapped the large diamond in the center of the brooch. "This, however, is not."

Papa's forehead knit into a fierce scowl. "What the devil are you talking about, man?"

"Although the silver setting is obviously the original, the stones are not. They're made of paste. Excellent reproductions to be sure, but colored glass nonetheless. At some point in the last century, I imagine one of your noble ancestors removed the original stones and had them replaced with fakes."

"What?" Mamma shrieked.

Charlie grimaced, because her mother *never* shrieked. Not that she could blame the poor dear, under the circumstances.

"That's rather odd," said Colin, mildly puzzled. "Why would someone do such a barmy thing?"

Angus shook his head, looking disgusted. "For money, ye ken. It's an old trick. Sell off the precious stones and replace them with paste. If it's a good enough job, nae one will be the wiser."

"I refuse to believe it," Papa snapped. "You may be a world-renowned fiddler, Kendrick, but I hardly think you're an expert in fine jewels."

"You're correct, sir," Kade replied. "Nevertheless, the color in the diamonds seemed off to me, and the weight of the piece seemed too light. So I took it to the jeweler in Ballachulish. He is quite the expert, and he assured me without hesitation that the original stones were replaced with fakes. Naturally, he swore to keep that knowledge to himself."

Papa slumped in his chair. "Good God, what a disaster."

"If it's any consolation," Kade added, "the jeweler said the reproductions were excellent. They've obviously passed muster for quite some time, since none of you noticed."

"I'm sorry to say that is no consolation at all," Mamma responded in blighting tones. Then she glared at Papa. "Really, sir, how could you allow such a thing to happen? It's a shocking disgrace."

Papa's head reared up. "How in blazes is this my fault, Elspeth? The MacDonald Clan is responsible for the bloody thing, not the Stewarts." He snorted. "I don't know why I'm surprised, though, since the MacDonalds are utterly hopeless when it comes to managing their finances."

Angus sprang to his feet with remarkable alacrity. "I'll nae have ye defaming the MacDonalds, ye blasted Stewart ninny. One more word of insult and ye'll be looking down the barrel of my pistol."

Kade reached over and plucked the old dueling pistol from his grandfather's hand. "Angus, sit down and be quiet."

"But I'll nae have Kinloch—"

"I don't care," Kade bluntly replied.

"Angus, do stop," Mamma said. "As much as I deplore my

husband's attempt to cast aspersions on my relations, the truth cannot be denied. This is an utter disaster."

Melissa, who'd unearthed a vial of smelling salts and was holding them at the ready, cast Charlie a reproachful look. "Charlotte, how can you be so calm? It's *your* brooch, and it's been ruined. Who knows what disasters might befall us now?"

Charlie countered her sister with an encouraging smile. "I don't think you have to worry about any calamities befalling us, Mel. Clearly the stones were replaced years ago, and we've been bumping along all right so far."

Perhaps she had yet to recover from the shock, but the situation was beginning to strike her as more than slightly absurd. To think of all the tumult of the last few weeks, only to discover that the brooch was essentially worthless all along.

Laughter started to bubble up into her throat. No matter how hard she tried, she couldn't hold it back and was soon laughing so hard that she was hard-pressed not to double over.

"Charlotte Stewart, whatever can you be laughing about in this horrible situation?" her mother asked, clearly aghast.

"I'm . . . I'm just imagining the look on Sir Leslie's face," Charlie managed to gasp. "If he'd managed to pull it off only to find out the brooch was a fake."

Kade grinned. "It almost would have been worth it for that."

"I'm glad you can laugh," Papa gloomily said. "But now that we know the brooch is a fake, I suppose we've no choice but to release Kendrick from his obligation to marry Charlie. You can't force a fellow's hand over a false matter of honor."

Charlie struggled to catch her breath. "Papa, we were *never* going to force Mr. Kendrick's hand."

"Of course we were," he replied.

"If I may," Kade started.

Melissa waved her smelling salts. "No, he *must* still marry Charlie. Everyone else still thinks the brooch is real. So that *makes* it real, doesn't it?"

"It does not," Charlie replied, frowning at her sister. "I, for one, never took Papa's vow seriously."

Kade held up a hand. "Yes, but—"

"But a vow is a vow, Charlotte," Melissa insisted. "We'll all be completely disgraced if you don't marry Mr. Kendrick."

"Mel, that's ridiculous," Johnny said with a snort. "If it's a fake, it's a fake. Who cares if everyone finds out about it? It's not our fault that some nincompoop of an ancestor sold off the real gems."

Mamma grimaced. "I'm afraid Melissa is correct, Johnny. The debt of honor still stands, regardless, and Mr. Kendrick is obligated to marry Charlotte whether he wants to or not."

"If I could get a word in," Kade said, "I could—"

Melissa excitedly flapped her hands, cutting him off again. "Mamma's right, Mr. Kendrick. You simply *must* marry Charlotte for the sake of our family's honor. If you don't, the curse is sure to befall us all."

Now Papa jumped to his feet. "There is no blasted curse! And if you don't stop talking like an utter henwit, Melissa, I will send you to your room."

With unfortunate predictability, Melissa burst into tears and the room descended into chaos. Mamma rushed over to soothe Melissa, while Papa and Colin began to argue. Johnny entered the fray on their father's side, and Angus loudly and repeatedly announced to no one in particular that the entire family was barmy.

The only calm person was Kade, who wore a long-suffering expression.

He probably thinks we're all barmy, too.

What sane man could ever wish to marry into such a silly family? It was all so embarrassing.

Rampant frustration drove Charlie to her feet. "Enough!"

Kade, standing near her, winced. "Och, lass, my ears."

Charlie ignored him, glowering at her family. "You are *all* deranged. Each of you should go lock yourself in your room until you can behave like a rational human being instead of an escapee from Bedlam."

"Does that assessment include me?" Kade wryly asked.

She glared at him for a moment, and then started to stalk from the room. Kade reached for her but she dodged him and made a quick exit. By the time she hit the hallway she was practically running.

CHAPTER 24

Instinctively, Charlie headed for the music room, a haven of peace and quiet. She needed it to sort through her turbulent emotions. At the moment, she felt quite unsure of herself—and a wee bit unsure of Kade, too.

Once inside, she slammed the door and locked it. Someone would come looking for her sooner rather or later, but she hoped to gain at least a few minutes to herself. Decisions had to be made that could affect the course of her entire life.

She flopped down on the couch with a sigh, toeing off her shoes. For the last few days, she and Kade had rushed from one crisis to the next with no real opportunity to discuss their future together. Part of her was beginning to wonder if they *did* have a future together, and that was a truly hideous feeling.

Losing your nerve, are you?

Charlie grimaced, hating to think of herself as a coward. That she loved Kade beyond measure was not in doubt, and she felt certain that he loved her, too. But how solid were those feelings? Were they strong enough to overcome the challenges that still lay in their path? Kade had been curiously reluctant to discuss those things. He seemed to live entirely in the moment, content to address difficulties as they arose.

While that was eminently sensible in the middle of the crisis, the crisis had passed.

Tonight's adventures had introduced niggles of doubt about their future. Instead of trusting her with his plans, Kade had turned to her father for help. That decision, even with his reassurances, still stung. No matter how much she loved him, she couldn't play second fiddle to Kade. She couldn't remain one step behind, always trying to catch up.

Or, worse, become a hindrance to him.

She propped her chin in her hands and gloomily stared into the empty fireplace grate. Of course, after her family's idiotic performance, her questions might be entirely moot. Not that she'd acted much better, since she'd yelled at everyone, sounding more like a fishwife than a woman in love. If Kade had any sense he'd be packing to make his escape right now.

She heard a quick step in the hall, and then the doorknob rattled.

"Charlie, please let me in," Kade said.

"Go away," she shouted. "I need to think."

She immediately winced. She sounded *exactly* like a fishwife—or a Highland hooligan.

After a few moments, when Kade didn't answer, she blew out another sigh. She'd driven him away.

"You're a ninny," she muttered. "You don't even know what you want."

You want him.

The doorknob rattled once more. After a click, the door opened and Kade strolled into the room.

Charlie jumped up. "How did you do that?"

"I have my ways," he said as he slipped a small leather case into a coat pocket.

She huffed out a small snort. "Lockpicks, again."

He joined her. "You'd be surprised how useful they can

be. For instance, when one's betrothed locks herself into a room, refusing to talk to the poor fellow who loves her."

As she stared up into his handsome face, a surge of longing welled up, so strong it made her chest go tight. Kade patiently watched her, his gaze warm and infinitely kind.

"I would have talked to you eventually," she said. "I just . . ."

"Needed time to think," he replied. "I understand. That scene in the drawing room was rather gruesome."

She crinkled her nose. "I'm sorry I stormed out like that, but I was embarrassed. My family is *so* idiotic sometimes. And, sadly, so am I."

He took her hand and turned it over, raising it to press a kiss to her palm. The simple, gentle touch made her knees go wobbly but also soothed her soul.

"Nonsense," he said. "You're the most clearheaded person I know."

"My father—and the Kinloch Fiddler—might suggest otherwise."

He smiled. "I'm quite fond of the Kinloch Fiddler. While her methods are unconventional, they certainly achieved the desired result."

"I suppose that's true."

They gazed at each other while Charlie tried to sort out her muddled emotions. Mostly, she wanted to throw herself into Kade's arms and start kissing him, but that struck her as a bit risky at the moment.

As if reading her thoughts, he led her back to the sofa. "Let's sit down, sweetheart. Then you can tell me exactly what's bothering you."

After they sat, Kade stretched his arm across her shoulders, lightly holding her. Charlie resisted the impulse to snuggle closer, because she knew where that would lead, and it wouldn't be to talking.

"I was silly to run out, though," she said. "But it was getting rather too much."

"Trust me, I was grateful. It gave me the excuse to quit the room, too. By the time I followed you, Colin was on the verge of challenging your father to a duel, and Angus was offering to be his second."

Charlie practically gaped at him. "Good God, Colin? He's so mild-mannered. Melissa must have been hysterical at the prospect."

"The opposite, actually. She seemed impressed by Colin's bravery and leapt to his defense. Then she and Johnny got into it. By the time I left, Melissa was threatening to dump a vase of roses over your brother's head."

"Oh, dear," she replied, trying not to laugh. "Poor Mamma must have been beside herself."

"By then she'd also joined the fray and started brangling with Angus. It was full-on mayhem by the time I made my escape. I did, however, relieve my grandfather of his dueling pistols before leaving, just in case. We don't need another reprise of the Massacre of Glencoe."

Charlie burst into laughter, because, really, what else could one do?

As she struggled to control her hilarity, Kade handed over his handkerchief. Charlie wiped her streaming eyes and finally managed to regain control.

"I'm relieved to see you laughing," he said. "You were beginning to worry me, sweetheart. I was afraid you were going to throw me over."

"I rather thought you were going to do the same to me. Or at least wish you could. Of course, you're too honorable to do so, but I certainly wouldn't blame you. Not after everything that's . . ."

She faltered when a scowl descended on his brow.

"How could you possibly think I would wish to throw you

over?" Kade tipped up her chin with the edge of his hand. "I love you, lass, and don't you forget it."

Then he swooped down and pressed a swift, firm kiss to her lips, briefly plundering her mouth. Charlie dug her fingers into his coat, her senses swimming under the delicious assault.

Too soon, though, he pulled back, although his cobalt gaze still glittered with sensual intent.

"Are we clear now?" he asked, his voice husky and tinged with a brogue.

Charlie touched her mouth. "Uh, yes, I think so."

He snuggled her back under his arm. "Excellent. Now, perhaps you might tell me what's really bothering you. I certainly hope it's not your family, because they are definitely no more ridiculous than mine. Angus is proof of that, and I can recount any number of deranged Kendrick episodes that make your relatives seem dull in comparison."

"That's hard to believe."

"Believe it. Now, out with it, Charlie. What's bothering you? Is it that I didn't tell you about my plan to trick Morgan?"

She waggled a hand. "Yes and no. I understand why you did it, and I accept that. I was very angry with Sir Leslie, and I must confess the thought of shooting him crossed my mind."

"I think it was rather more than that," he dryly replied.

"Well, yes. Which I suppose makes me a horrible person."

"No, it makes you a person who believes in defending the innocent and protecting your family. Both admirable qualities."

Charlie hesitated for a moment, but then decided that she needed to be entirely honest. "Thank you. Well then, let me just say that I was hurt you didn't trust me enough to at least share your plans and let me decide how I wanted to respond.

I understand you were trying to protect me, as was Papa. But we need to trust each other completely, Kade, if our marriage is to have any chance of success."

He shifted a bit so he was facing her.

"I do trust you, Charlie. Completely," he quietly said. "I trust you with my life."

She blew out a wavering breath of relief. "I'm glad, and forgive me for being a pest, but I still don't quite understand why you felt the need to keep me in the dark."

He was quiet for a few moments, as if collecting his thoughts. "For a very long time when I was young, I was dependent on others. As much as I loved my family and was grateful for their care, I hated being so dependent, so weak. When I grew up and was no longer a frail boy, I suppose I went in the other direction, compensating for my frailty, as it were."

Charlie thought about that, and then nodded. "You decided to become completely independent, without the need to rely on anyone. I can certainly understand why."

In fact, she was much the same.

"I think that tendency became exaggerated when I took on missions for the Crown," he added. "By necessity, one learns to work independently."

"But you did enlist my father's help in this case."

"I felt I had to, given that he was unknowingly harboring a potential murderer under his roof. Besides, I needed some-one to hear Morgan's confession. Who better than the local magistrate?"

Charlie wrinkled her nose. "Drat. Your logic is impeccable."

"Still, I know I hurt you, and I'm deeply sorry for that," he contritely said. "As well as becoming lamentably inde-pendent, I'm also fairly single-minded. It's how I've always gotten things done, Charlie, especially when it comes to my work. It's become a habit, though I know it's not necessarily a comfortable one for others."

She pressed a hand to his chest as she searched his now solemn features. "Also understandable, but how will that habit affect us? I would never in a million years wish to hold you back, Kade, but I don't want to be *left* back, either. I want to be with you, not behind you."

Her heart now hammered in her chest. She'd finally been able to voice the all-important question. It was the one on which her entire future hung in the balance.

Kade wrapped his strong musician's hand around hers, the hand that brought such beauty into the world. "Charlie, you are already there. You are everywhere in my life—in my heart, in my music, in every particle of my being. And I wouldn't have it any other way. A life without you would be utterly dreary, my love, and I sincerely hope that is a prospect I won't have to face."

Charlie blinked back a rush of tears—joy mingled with gratitude for what still seemed to her an utter miracle.

"Thunderbolts," she gruffly said. "Here I am behaving like an absolute watering pot instead of the Highland hooligan I'm supposed to be. Whatever will you think of me?"

He dropped a quick kiss on the tip of her nose. "That you're the bonniest, most incredible woman I've ever met. And that I am the luckiest man in all of Scotland to have found you."

"Actually, I'm the one who found you all those years ago. And I think I've basically pestered you into falling in love with me."

He laughed. "Then feel free to continue pestering as much as you want, because I am looking forward to falling in love with you more each day."

She sniffed. "Kade you simply *must* stop trying to make me cry."

He suddenly slipped off the couch and went down on one knee before her.

"This looks rather serious," she said. "Are you going to propose to me?"

"I am, and I'm doing it properly. When I took your brooch to the jeweler, I happened to come across something else."

He reached into his vest pocket. "Give me your hand, love."

When she did, he slid a ring onto her finger.

She gasped. "It looks just like my brooch!"

The silver thistle ring was slender but sturdily made, with a brilliant amethyst as the center stone. The similarity in design to her brooch was uncanny.

Kade smiled. "Yes, I was quite struck by it. One might almost think I was destined to find it."

Charlie held up her hand, admiring the flash of silver and purple. "And it was because you set out to discover if my brooch was a fake. It's quite unbelievable, Kade."

"That's the Highlands for ye, lassie. Surprises around every corner."

She took his face in her hands—his dear, wonderful face— and kissed him, taking her time as she nuzzled his mouth. He gently cupped the back of her head, murmuring his regret when she drew back.

"Thank you," she said. "I couldn't ask for a more beautiful ring. Mamma will be thrilled, I know."

He got up and resumed his seat, pulling her into the shelter of his arms. "I hope your father will like it, too. He's definitely *not* thrilled with me, at the moment."

"I think he just needs to get used to the idea of us being together. It was rather unexpected, you must admit."

"I know."

She hesitated. "It . . . it might not always be easy, Kade. We've led very different lives, ye ken."

He tilted his head, so he could look her in the eye. "Can you guess why I picked a thistle ring?"

"You mean other than the similarity to my brooch?"

"Yes. I also picked it because of what the thistle represents. It's a symbol of resilience, along with courage and strength." He suddenly grinned. "And luck. We might need a little luck as we figure things out, but you have enough strength and courage for the both of us. Whatever challenges we encounter, we'll face them together and overcome. After all, we're Highlanders, Charlotte Stewart. Nothing can hold us back if we're together, ye ken."

Certainty rang in his voice, and her heart echoed it with equal clarity.

"Aye, that," she simply said.

"Then are you ready to leave the Highlands, my beautiful lass, at least for a little while?"

She patted his cheek. "As long as we come back for visits now and again."

"I don't think we'll have any other choice," he wryly replied. "Angus would hunt us down and drag us back if we didn't."

"As would my father." A sudden and rather hideous thought occurred to her. "Oh, Lord. Speaking of our families, I suppose we should go and separate the combatants before they trigger a clan feud."

Kade shook his head. "Not a chance, love."

Then he rose and strode to the door.

"What are you doing?" she asked.

He locked the door. "I'm ensuring that we have no interruptions."

Laughter bubbled up in her chest. "Mr. Kendrick, are you suggesting what I think you're suggesting?"

He returned to her and gathered her up in his arms. "Let's

find out, shall we? And I think we've had enough of our blasted families for one day. Right now, it's just you and me."

Charlie sank into his embrace, happiness flooding every part of her being. In Kade's arms, she knew she'd never be lonely again. And with him by her side, she could take on the world.

EPILOGUE

"Kade, tip your chin up," Nick said, frowning. "I'm not sure your neckcloth is sitting correctly."

His neckcloth was fine, but Kade knew that the Laird of Clan Kendrick was fussing to cover his emotions. It was a special day for all of them because Kade was about to be married to the woman he loved, with his entire family attending in all their chaotic glory.

Nick took a step back, inspecting him with a critical eye. "There, now you'll do. Even Lady Kinloch won't be able to find fault."

"It's not my future mother-in-law who's the problem," Kade replied. "It's Lord Kinloch. I'm not sure he truly approves of me."

"Only because you're taking his beloved daughter on a tour of England and then the Continent. I get the sense that Kinloch was hoping Charlotte would remain closer to home."

"The tour is bad timing in that respect, but I did promise we would return to Glencoe whenever we could. It's Charlie's home, and she loves it."

Thankfully, Charlie was now as excited for the tour as

Kade was. His new concerto, finally finished, was his best work to date—thanks to his fiancée. Her talent and her inspiration had been critical in bringing his ideas to fruition. It was a blessing beyond measure that they could be partners in all aspects of their new life.

"Her home is now with you, lad," his brother replied. "And yours with her."

Kade smiled. "True, that."

"Still, I certainly understand Lord Kinloch's feelings. We don't see you nearly as much as we'd like, either."

"Not to worry," he wryly replied. "Vicky practically made swear on the old family bible that Charlie and I would return to Scotland at least twice a year. If not, she'll send Angus after us, and I think we can all agree that is something to be avoided."

Nick laughed. "Yes, the notion of Grandda rampaging around the Continent in your wake is rather alarming."

"Especially to me."

With his usual uncanny timing, the old boy chose that moment to stomp into the vestry. "I'll have none of yer sass, laddie boy. Ye'll nae want me boxin' yer ears on yer weddin' day."

Kade snorted. "Well, at least I've graduated from you paddling my bum. I suppose that's a good thing."

"Och, yer too big now. But I've been thinkin' . . . it would nae be a bad thing if I went with ye on yer tour. Ye'll be wantin' to spend time with Charlie, and I can take care of all them little details ye hate fussin' about. Like talkin' to some nincompoop of an orchestra conductor and such. I could also look after yer health, just in case ye have any relapses."

"Grandda, I love you," Kade replied, "but taking care of me is now Charlie's job. I'll be just fine."

Angus shook his head. "Ye'll be wantin' to spend time with yer lady, not fiddlin' with fussy details. Besides, if ye get into any more spy business, ye'll be needin' me to watch yer back."

Kade glanced at Nick, silently pleading for help. His brother, however, was too busy stifling laughter.

"My spy days are over, Grandda," Kade firmly said. "From now on, I promise to stick to music only."

His grandfather looked doubtful. "Ye say that, but—"

Nick finally took pity on him. "I'm sorry, Angus, but I simply cannot spare you. Don't forget we've got another baby coming along. You know how much Vicky relies on you for help with the children."

Angus wavered for a few moments before capitulating. "Aye, she does need me to help with the bairns, especially the wee ones." He grimaced at Kade. "I'm sorry, lad. Ye'll just have to do without me."

"It's all right, Grandda. And I'll miss you, too."

Kade smiled at the two men who'd raised him. Their love had never failed through even the darkest of times. For too many years, Nick had carried punishing burdens on his broad shoulders, ones that would have crippled lesser men. Yet he'd never stopped fighting for all of his brothers, especially Kade, who knew that his big brother would have faced down every demon in hell to save him.

And then there was Grandda. Wizened and slight beside the brawny laird of the clan, he was still indomitable for all that. Angus had given up so much of his life for the Kendrick family. When his own beloved daughter had died giving birth to Kade, he'd put his grief aside and cherished and cared for him, steadfast through every crisis. Grandda, for all his hilarious ways, was the epitome of loyalty, and Kade's life had been infinitely enriched by his presence.

He was here today, happy and whole, in large part because of the two of them. He owed them more than he could ever express.

"I cannot tell you how proud I am to be your grandson and

your brother," Kade said, his voice gruff with emotion. "You are the best men I have ever known."

Nick cleared his throat and then pulled him in for a hug. "Och, you're the best of the Kendricks, lad. You've got more heart than all of us put together. I don't know what we would have done without you."

Kade hugged him back, while Angus extracted an enormous handkerchief from inside his coat and vigorously blew his nose. After stuffing it back in his pocket, he wagged a finger.

"None of yer sentimental blather, son. Ye'll be lookin' as queer as Dick's hatband on yer weddin' day. But know that we're all that proud of ye and as pleased as can be."

Kade pulled his grandfather in for a gentle embrace. "Thank you, Grandda. I'm fairly pleased myself."

Angus thumped him on the back before letting go. "As ye should be. Charlie's a grand lassie. She'll make a fine Kendrick—and she'll keep an eye on ye, too."

"The lad is in good hands, Grandda. No need to worry." Nick checked his watch. "It's almost gone eleven. Charlotte and her father should be arriving any moment."

Vicky popped her head into the vestry. "The bride's carriage just arrived, and all the guests are now seated. The vicar says we'll be starting in a few minutes."

Kade smiled at his sister-in-law. "Come in here and give us a hug before I go out and get myself leg-shackled."

Vicky bustled in, a slight frown marking her brow. "I don't think your neckcloth is quite straight, dear. Nicholas, please make sure that the hem of Kade's kilt is even in the back. We want him looking his best."

"My kilt is fine," Kade said. "As is my neckcloth."

Vicky ignored his comment as she made a few adjustments and then brushed imaginary lint from his shoulder. Over her head, Kade exchanged a smile with Nick.

"Och, he looks togged out to the nines, *Sassenach*," Angus said. "Nae need to fuss."

"Of course I need to fuss," she replied. "My wee lad is getting married."

"The wee lad could pick you up with one hand, my love," Nick wryly commented.

"I know. It's just—" She broke off and rubbed her nose.

Kade wrapped her in a hug. "Thank you for being the mother I never had, my dearest Vicky. I don't know what I would have done without you."

"You would have grown up to be an untutored Highlander, no doubt," she said, snuffling a bit.

Nick drew her away. "Now, love, you don't want to start crying before the wedding, do you? Lady Kinloch will be terribly shocked by so reckless a display of emotion."

Vicky let out a watery laugh as she carefully dried her tears with a gloved hand. "Shocked, with a daughter like Melissa? I think not. That young woman is a veritable watering pot."

"She's just bit overcome by all the excitement," Kade said. "They're happy tears, according to Charlie."

"I'll tell ye who else is happy aboot somethin'," Angus said. "Kinloch, because he managed to foist the weddin' on Nick instead of havin' to hold it at Laroch Manor. The cheap bugger."

"We're happy to host the wedding at Kinglas," Nick said. "After all, Kinloch had to fire off Melissa only a few months ago. It made perfect sense to move the festivities down here."

"And I've enjoyed every minute of it," Vicky said. "It's been wonderful having the entire family back together again."

Royal appeared in the vestry doorway. "It's time, lads and lady. The bride is now waiting in the vestibule, and our good vicar said to get your arses moving right now."

Vicky huffed. "As if Reverend Carrick would ever say any such thing."

"Actually, that was Ainsley," he replied. "She's at the back of the church with Charlie, and everyone is lined up and ready to go."

"Can't keep the bride waiting, old son," Nick said, clapping Kade on the back.

"I wouldn't dream of it."

Angus rubbed his hands together. "Aye, let's get this over with so I can pipe the bride and groom back to the castle."

When a slight spasm crossed Vicky's face, Kade bit back a laugh. It was a Scottish custom for a piper to lead the wedding party from the kirk back to the family home, and Angus had insisted on doing the honors. It would no doubt sound like a passel of screeching cats in a gunnysack, but Kade hadn't had the heart to refuse him.

As the others filed out of the vestry, Kade paused to grip Royal's hand. "Thank you, old man, for everything."

His brother smiled. "Och, it was nothing. Just be happy, lad. That's all we've ever wanted for you."

"I intend to be."

"Off with you, then. I'll see you after the ceremony."

Kade followed Nick and Angus out to the front of the church and joined them by the altar rail. They stood with him as groomsmen, as they'd stood with him at every important moment of his life.

The vicar waited in the center of the chancel, looking distinguished in his billowing white robes and also slightly annoyed.

"Are we ready, Mr. Kendrick?" he asked.

Kade gave him an apologetic smile. "More than ready, Reverend Carrick. Thank you."

The vicar nodded toward the west gallery of the chapel, and the small village choir launched into the opening verse of "Amazing Grace." Kade turned and took in the congregation, a gathering of family and clans from far and near. Aden St. George, Vicky's half brother and Kade's spymaster during his late and unlamented espionage career, had come from London with his wife, Vivien, and their children. Alec and Edie Gilbride, cousins on both sides of the Kendrick family, had also made the trip to Kinglas, as had other dear friends, like the Duke and Duchess of Leverton.

In the front pews sat Kade's brothers and their wives, headed by Logan and Donella and surrounded by all the Kendrick bairns, even the babies. There were beaming smiles but also a few tears—care of Graeme and Grant, the tough, brawny twins, who were both rubbing their eyes and looking rather sheepish about it.

Then there was Braden, who'd helped him all through his sickly childhood, watching over him like a mother hen. Braden had chosen the life of a physician because of Kade, making it his mission to restore his brother to health. He'd done that and so much more, and had finally found happiness with his splendid wife, Samantha, and their adorable little son.

Braden gave him a lopsided smile and a quick salute.

Angus tapped his arm. "Ready, lad? Here she comes."

Yes, there she was—his beautiful bride, coming toward him on her father's arm. Now Kade only had eyes for Charlie as the packed congregation faded into a colorful blur.

She was dressed in an astonishingly vibrant gown in the colors of her clan—red, dark green, yellow, and royal blue. No conventional pastel wedding dress for his lassie. Her hair was swept up in a crown of golden braids, interwoven with yellow and white roses that seemed to glow in the light that streamed through the kirk windows. Gleaming on her shoulder was the Clan Iain brooch, now fully restored with real diamonds and amethysts—the stones a wedding present from Clan Kendrick.

Charlie was the most beautiful thing Kade had ever seen.

When their gazes met, she unleashed a dazzling smile.

He had to blink back a few tears himself, ones of immense gratitude and overwhelming love.

A few moments later, she arrived at the altar rail with her father. Kinloch bent down and hugged his daughter.

"Thank you, Papa," Charlie said. "I love you."

Kinloch cleared his throat and then threw Kade a rather baleful look. "Take care of her, young man, or I will have something to say about it."

Angus started to huff, but Nick discreetly elbowed him into silence.

"I will, sir," Kade said as Kinloch placed Charlie's hand in his. "You have my promise."

"See that you do," her father replied before stalking off to join his wife in the pew.

Charlie wrinkled her nose. "Sorry about that."

"No worries, love," he murmured. "You look gorgeous, but I was rather expecting a kilt."

"I wanted to wear one, but Mamma pitched a fit and Melissa had the vapors."

When Kade laughed, the vicar leveled a scowl at them.

"Are we *finally* ready to begin, ladies and gentlemen?" he asked in an exasperated tone.

"Yes, Reverend Carrick," Charlie replied. "I believe we are."

She glanced up at Kade. Her velvet-brown eyes were alight with laughter, and her smile was one of unalloyed joy.

Kade smiled back, joy meeting joy. "Aye, that, lassie."

Aye, that.